D0823545

a note from the editor . . .

DON'T PUT THIS BOOK DOWN

. . . until you have read the introductions by Poul Anderson, Larry Niven and Jerry Pournelle. Seldom has a book received such high and unsolicited praise from masters of the genre. Never in my experience as an editor have I been surrounded by some of the people I respect most in the field and been told in no uncertain terms that it is my *duty* to bring a book before the public. Given my respect bordering on awe for the persons involved, I agreed. I didn't *really* think they would break both my arms if I refused.

Still, this was a first for me; generally I prefer to read a book before making such a commitment—and I did indeed read it as soon as possible. Within a few pages my duty had become my pleasure, then a sheer treat, then mind-boggled delight . . . followed at the end by a wistful sadness that never again would I come all-unawares on a book called *Silverlock*.

Now it's your turn. Lucky you.

Jim Baen

SILVERLOCK

JOHN MYERS MYERS

SF
ace books
A Division of Charter Communications Inc.
A GROSSET & DUNLAP COMPANY
360 Park Avenue South
New York, New York 10010

SILVERLOCK

Copyright © 1949 by John Myers Myers

An ACE Book

Cover art by Walter Velez

First Ace printing: May 1966
Second Ace printing: August 1979

2 4 6 8 0 9 7 5 3 1
Manufactured in the United States of America

TO MAC McCORRY MYERS

Who knows each point of call along the line
from misty islands clear to Riders' Shrine.

ᖇᕬ Contents ᖇᕬ

❧ A Word of Praise ❧

by

Poul Anderson

The first thing to say about *Silverlock* is that it's incomparable fun. There are few such glorious romps in all the world's literature, and surely none that surpass this one. A galloping narrative, endlessly inventive; people you must love or hate but can never be indifferent to; humor that ranges from the cat-subtle to the uproarious; discoveries, achievements, battles, feasts, drinking bouts, lovemaking, unabashed joy, celebration of life—what more do you want?

Well, as a matter of fact, you get a great deal more. Life is often stark and, in some sense, ultimately tragic. Good comedy recognizes this truth and draws strength from it. Myers' hero is neither heroic nor especially likeable when first we meet him. He has suffered shipwreck on the *Naglfar*, which name belongs to the craft made of dead men's nails that Loki will steer against the gods at the end of the world. In company with Golias, who makes the tale surge with energy from its beginning, he has experiences terrifying or heart-wrenching as well as pleasurable. Finally he must descend into Hell itself. Throughout, however, he grows; despite occasional backsliding, he becomes more and more a whole human being. That high seriousness is enhanced by the mirth, which culminates in Hell with a marvelous piece of flamboyancy.

In short, *Silverlock* is not just a story, it is an odyssey of the spirit. The odyssey happens in the Commonwealth, which is the Commonwealth of Letters; and I don't know of any other work so erudite yet so utterly unbookish. A lot of the fun lies in recognizing old friends in the new guises they wear here. It's a safe bet, though, that you won't identify everybody. Then, if you are like the rest of us *Silverlock* enthusiasts, you'll go out into the Commonwealth on your own quest, seeking for them, and have a lovely time.

I came upon the book by chance, when it was first published thirty years ago, and was instantly enchanted. Afterward I urged it on person after person, and thus may be partly responsible for the popularity it gained in a much too limited circle. What memories now cluster around it! Long bull sessions about the meaning of this or that passage; singing the songs, to excellent tunes which various folk have composed; a party which turned into a reading-aloud spree, including an enraptured Anthony Boucher (myself, I chose "Bowie Gizzardsbane"); perusing something else that was classic and suddenly realizing that here was a character I'd met before and not known at the time—Yes, *Silverlock* is among those books that become a part of people's lives.

John Myers Myers has written others, both fiction and nonfiction. They are very fine and I hope they too can be reissued and reach the audience they deserve. Meanwhile, here in your hand is the stuff of wonder.

❧ Silverlock's Progress? ❧

by

Larry Niven

I heard about *Silverlock* long before I saw it. It was a rare book. At the Westercon of 1964 a copy had gone for $30 at auction, to Hank Stine. I heard about that at a meeting of the Los Angeles Science Fantasy Society.

It roused my curiosity. Fans generally didn't have much money. I asked, "Huh?" And they told me about the book.

They sang me the songs. Fans have set many of the songs in *Silverlock* to music. They're great drinking songs. Especially Friar John's interrupted song—which has been completed.

Silverlock has thousands of references. I learned of the fine old game of reference hunting. It didn't sound exciting. But people who had read *Silverlock* acted excited.

That was it for a while. Not a collector, I wasn't going to spring for $30 for a book; and anyway, there weren't any. Nobody was selling their *Silverlock*s. But when the Ace paperback appeared, I grabbed a copy fast.

I've still got it. I just checked. Remarkable. You'd think I'd have forced it on somebody by now: my brother, for instance. Could it have been returned? Every time?

There's no date for this edition; but it's old. It's thick, 347 pages, and it sold for 75 cents. I've read it twice. I've got the plot memorized, I think. We'll see, because I'm about to read it again.

And what did it feel like, the first time through?

This John Myers Myers must be in love with words (as I am). He must roll them around in his mouth (as I do) to get the taste. He seems to love incongruities . . . as when Silverlock sends Don Quixote off to steal the blue ox Babe from Paul Bunyan. (So do I.) His picture of the universe is lifelike, but bigger than life . . . and I went through it like a tourist in Paradise.

Did Myers *teach* me to love these things? Damn, I'll never figure it out now.

I played the reference-hunting game. So will you. You can't help it. I recognized about a third of the terrain and the characters, and took the rest for granted. Afterward I went hunting for others. You could make a full time hobby out of that. From Irish and Norse and Greek and Sumerian myths, from Homer, and Tom Jones, and Dante, and Doctor Faustus, and Russian novels, and ancient and modern history they come: from everywhere in the Commonwealth of Letters.

Why do so many writers try to imitate PIL-GRIM'S PROGRESS? It's outdated and kind of dull, as I remember from high school . . . but the subject, the progress of a human soul through life's learning experience, is endlessly fascinating. I've been tempted myself. I succumbed.

Dante's DIVINE COMEDY was that kind of tale
. . . and so is the sequel that Jerry Pournelle and I
wrote. [Inferno, *From Pocket Books. Ed.*]

And Silverlock is a mundane (with a BA in
Business Administration!) discovering how to
read, and why.

So here it comes again: an allegory. Go ahead
and flinch; but you're going to have fun. You'll get
drunk on *Silverlock*. When you finish reading, it
will feel like you got monumentally drunk with
your oldest friends; you sang songs and told truth
and lies all night or all weekend; and you'll sit
there grinning at nothing and wondering why
there isn't any hangover.

🕮 In Appreciation 🕮
of the Commonwealth

by

Jerry Pournelle

Credit this book to me. Not that I had any hand in writing it, nor could I have written any part of it; nor would a masterpiece like this forever have stayed out of print; but you would not hold it now had life not dealt me a mean trick, and though I seldom ask any credit for others' work, in this case I need the compensation. Explanations follow.

More years ago than I care to remember, in those heady days that followed *sputnik* I visited my friends the Andersons; and found Karen marching around the room with pensive look, working madly to match music with as strange and delightful a song as ever I had heard. She would not be interrupted with questions, a curious thing indeed, for Karen is generally as polite and delightful a hostess as the chronic chaos of her household will permit. Finally she paused, more from exhaustion than anything else, and I could ask.

"It's Gordy's tune," she said, as if that explained anything.

"Tune, schume! The words! The poetry! Whose?"

And a look of joy came across her face, for she had assumed that I knew *Silverlock*, and now she could have the fun of introducing me to this strange book of marvels. I read the Andersons' copy, and set on a quest to find a copy of my own though, alas, the book was out of print and finding one took time. I have treasured it ever since, for *Silverlock* is not the sort of book one reads and puts away forever. You will return to it again and again, and mine is nearly worn out.

So what is this book? It is, as Poul observes, a passport to the Commonwealth—the Commonwealth of letters. Yet that sounds dull, and by God's teeth *Silverlock* is the furthest thing from dull that I can imagine. It is the sort of book that can take an engineer obsessed with putting man into space and send him to the reference library searching for *Manon,* or make him remember fondly books that he first read only because his university required students of the sciences to take courses in literature—I know, because it did this for me.

Enough. I will leave the poetic praise to those better equipped to write it. Suffice it to say that though I have three deadlines, one long past, I am not only writing this appreciation of *Silverlock*, I am hard pressed to keep from opening my tattered copy and reading it again this moment.

It was not always so. Though I loved it, in one way *Silverlock* annoyed me on first reading. All those obscure references! The smug looks of those who knew, my anguish at admitting that I did not!

But for reward there was the story itself. One need not know the originals to like them as they appear here. And more than that, one meets them here and there, and remembers meeting them earlier and in a more friendly guise . . .

Confusing? Aye, if you've no read the book. But imagine yourself, or anyone you know, set loose in the world of the Commonwealth, knowing nothing of its people; living the world of letters and not knowing that; seeing miracles abound. That is *Silverlock*, and you must read it to know more.

But I was telling my own story.

The 1978 World Science Fiction Convention was held in Phoenix, and when I arrived I was asked if I would care to meet John Myers Myers. There could be but one answer to that. I have long admired not only *Silverlock*, but *The Wild Yazoo* and a good half-dozen others of Myers' work. Alas, I was scheduled to autograph books at the time of the reception for Myers, and by the time I could get away Mr. Myers had left the hotel. I never did meet him; but good came of that, for I lamented this cruelty of fate to the Andersons in the hearing of Jim Baen. We fell to discussion of *Silverlock*. Baen allowed that he had not read it and asked who was the publisher.

"Why, ACE Books. But it's long out of print. We don't understand why ACE hasn't brought it out again," said Poul, Karen, Larry Niven and I with one accord.

"I think we can do something about that," said Mr. Baen; and thus my opening statement; and thus you can now have the pleasure of *Silverlock* for the first time. I envy you.

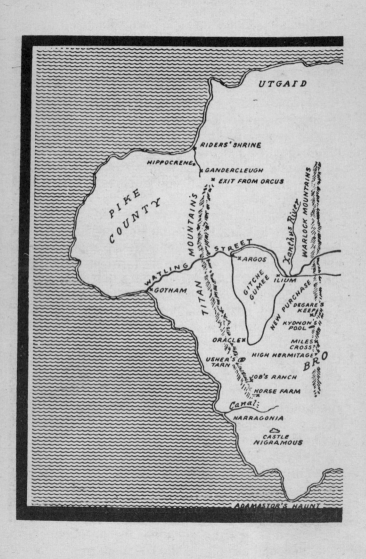

Map of Commonwealth

WAY ONE

Sea Roads, The Forests, and a Rendezvous

I

~ The Right Waters ~

IF I HAD cared to live, I would have died.

A storm had come up. While not sick, I found my bunk the most comfortable place, leaving it only to take my meals. Dozing after supper, I learned of disaster when a wave bashed in the door of my deck cabin. The backwash sluiced me out of it and stranded me by a stowage locker.

While I was still trying to figure out what was going on I caught a glimpse of men trying to lower boats. The ship was low in the water, although through oversight or indifference nobody had given me warning—any more than I would have bothered to take the trouble for them. At that I was first over the side; for before I could get purchase anywhere a following wave put me there.

As I swirled to leeward, I saw one lifeboat smashed. The next chance I had to look, the ship was going down by the nose. I was then far enough off to be free of the suction. It is my belief

3

that all other hands, feet, heads, and connecting torsos were dragged bottomwards along with every bolt of the craft.

Whether the *Naglfar* smashed on a reef, broke its back in the waves, hit a stray mine, or suffered loss of atomic union is something I never knew. Where it foundered is anybody's guess. There had been a fog for three days, so no bearings for a similar period. The radio failed to function, and a skipper trained to lean on such a gadget was small shakes at dead reckoning. On the fourth day the fog cleared; but the sky did not, and the wind came up. It blew the *Naglfar* no good, and somewhere, nine days out of Baltimore, down she went.

Once again: if I had cared to live, I would have died. I would have used myself up fleeing what could not be fled. Panic at being in a sea without a visible shore would have bound my muscles and broken the rhythm of my breathing. Not far from where the ship had vanished, I too would have filled with water that stopped my fires.

As it was, I floundered for just the first minute or so. Then I did what I could, aware that it would not be enough. The seas were high, but negotiable for anyone willing to go the way the waves did. These roughed me as they came up behind; but I could rest when they got their grip and carried me along. It was simpler to keep going than to stop and drown, though that was bound to happen at the end of a mile or so. I was a fair swimmer only.

I recall thinking that I was stroking toward either the end of all life or the beginning of a new one. Neither possibility stirred me. Every man knows he will die; and nobody believes it. On that paradox stand not only a host of religions but the entity of sane being. I wasn't able to credit my own non-existence any better than the next man; what I had lost was a healthy abhorrence of the state. It had not dropped from me because of any particular shock or misfortune. It had moulted from me year by year, for all of my thirty-five, to leave me naked in apathy.

When I first saw the chunk of mast I thought it was a shark. The next time I rode high I saw better what it was, and that broke me down. I had been resigned to no hope. More than that, I had achieved indifference to the lack. But seeing something which could help me was more than my loneliness could bear. I nearly scuttled myself, tightening up and beating the water instead of stroking cleanly.

It was three combers ahead when I first saw it, then only two. Next I topped three waves without finding it, shipping water on the third as I became sure that I had only seen a fish after all. I was in the act of fighting to regain resignation, when I found myself sliding down a trough directly toward the thing.

There was a man clinging to it, but my mind had no time for him. That piece of wood, my hope and my haven, was rising up again, and I felt that I could not survive the tussle with another wave. With almost the last motion of which I was capable, I reached out and threw my arm over it.

It might soon have been wrenched away from me, spent as I was, had there been no one to help. While I feebly clung to the slippery wood, the man I had noticed was busy. Certain ropes trailed from the spar, and he looped one of these under my shoulders. When he had made the free end fast, I could ride in the sling so formed, with no immediate problem except to keep from being battered by the mast as the water tossed it and me about.

I had managed a grunt of relief, which he could take for thanks if he wanted to, but the fellow said nothing until he had reestablished himself on the other side of our buoy. "You must be as fond of swimming as the Great Silkie himself."

Without knowing what he was talking about, I could grasp that he spoke banteringly. Unfit to answer in kind, I peered at him through a veil of spindrift. His hair, long for a man, lay on his head and clung around his lean face like tawny sea-weed. When the spray thinned, I observed that the big features were jauntily at odds with one another. The eyes were either gray or blue. It was hard to tell that late in the day under a cloudy sky.

I tried to say something less obvious, but my brain was geared only for facts. "The ship I was on sank, so I had to swim."

He nodded. "The one I was on ran afoul of the Maelstrom, but I dove for this spar and didn't get sucked down with the rest: It's a cylinder, you see."

Again I did not follow him. With a shrug I gazed skyward, trying to calculate how much daylight remained. As well as I could judge, it was just before or just after the late sunset of that season. Then I put the inevitable question.

"Do you know whether or not we're drifting toward shore; or if there is any shore near enough to count?"

"Somewhere off the Commonwealth is the best I can tell you. This is my second day as flotsam, and I've yet to see any landmarks." He lifted a hand from the mast in a deprecatory gesture. "I speak figuratively."

It made no difference to me how he spoke, or what he called the country I would probably never live to put my feet on. Having recovered from the panic brought on by my efforts to reach the spar, I could view things reasonably. The chances were that all I had achieved was to prolong my misery. Rescue could not be hoped for in the sense that it could be expected. If we did not die of exposure or shark bite, we would perish of hunger and thirst.

"Even if we're heading in the proper direction now," I reminded him, "we can't count on the wind to stick by us. Land had better be close to do us any good."

"I was beginning to think it wouldn't be close enough," he admitted. "But now that you've come along I feel it in my bones that we're getting somewhere. It ties things together in right Delian fashion."

Half wishing I had been left to drown in my own fashion, I wondered at his heartiness. Whatever was right, I was not. It had been a long while since I had taken pleasure in my own being, and I didn't expect anybody else to be glad of my company, even under favorable circumstances. I stared at him.

"You're pretty chipper for a man that's been in the soup for a couple of days. Doesn't it bother you?"

"Oh, I've felt better," he said, "but you get used to this sort of thing after just so many times. By the way, what's your name?"

It seemed ridiculous to be concerned with

amenities then. Moreover, it always irritated me to have to report my first and second names, even though I hid the worse one behind an initial.

"Shandon, A. Clarence Shandon," I growled. "Or at least I'll go by that for the next day or two. After that just call me fish food."

"Three names," he commented. "Very fancy." He was silent for a moment, evidently waiting for me to ask how he was called. When I didn't, he spoke. "I've got my share of names, too, though I don't commonly assemble them. If I did, I'd be O. Widsith Amergin Demodocus. . . . And let's see; there are others, of course, but to cut it short I'll wind up with Boyan Taliesin Golias."

He looked at me as if he expected to be known. "Not too well informed," he murmured to himself when he drew a blank. Then he spoke louder. "Where are you from?"

"Chicago." I hadn't liked his crack about my ignorance. "It's in the United States," I added by way of being nasty.

"Probably a good place for it," he conceded. "A seaport, I take it."

Unreasonably, I was annoyed because he had never heard of my home town, or possibly even of my native country. I couldn't be sure. "I found a railroad conductor who knew his way to a seaport," I informed him. Abruptly I snickered. "I took one of these tramp steamer cruises to get away from it all, Mr. Golias. By jiminy, I succeeded, too!"

"All what?" he enquired. I looked to see if he was pulling my leg, but he really seemed interested. "Someone hunting you?"

"No," I repudiated the notion. "Just nerves, I

guess." Yet a far worse thing than an attack of nerves had come upon me. I had reached the point where trouble was less of an affliction than the burden of common living. Only the healthy of hope can abide tranquillity.

A wave broke over our heads, but it did not cause him to lose the trend of our conversation. "Nerves," he mused when he had snorted the water out of his nose. "Dull stuff. You won't have much time for those sham battles in the Commonwealth."

"A place I never heard of," I pointed out, glad to be able to match him for his ignorance about my own country.

"Then that's what's the matter with you."

Considering what was the matter with me not his concern, I was nettled. "My, my, what local pride! There are no other places of real importance."

He fended off my sarcasm with a smile. "There are, now that you mention it. Nonetheless, we had a saying at the Academy that after you had been to the Commonwealth it was unimportant where you went, whereas before you visited it, it was useless to go anywhere."

It was not often that I found it worthwhile to flaunt the old college colors; but in view of his know-it-all attitude I decided not only to bring them out but to stuff them down his throat. "Typical prep-school hogwash," I sneered. "The kids in every academy are taught their school has a site indicated by the finger of God. Forget that stuff. If you'd gone on to the university, you'd have picked up an outlook with more than one peephole."

Instead of being crushed, he looked astonished.

"Are you a university man?"

"Oh, yes," I said, changing my tone from the pointed to the casual. "Somewhere under the old hats, dry flies, and dead tennis balls on the top shelf of a certain closet in Chicago you'll find a sheepskin swearing that the U. of Wisconsin gave me a degree in Business Administration."

From the way he looked I might as well have poked him in the solar plexus. Next he worked his mouth over the words "business administration" several times.

"Are you serious?" he finally demanded.

"Of course!" I tried to glare at him but some water got in my eyes. "As a matter of fact I was one of the top—"

It could have been only the cry of a sea bird, yet it was enough like a human voice to stop me in mid-sentence. Then it was unmistakable.

"The whale, the whale! Up helm, up helm!"

Climbing a comber, I kept my eyes fixed in the direction of that shriek, telling at once of wild actions and tiger terror. Reaching the crest, I saw a ship a short ways off, also riding high in the ocean. A stubby sailing vessel it was, black and ungainly against the darkening horizon. Under the circumstances we might never have been able to see it at all; but a rift in the pall let the afterglow through to pick the ship out of the dusk. For an instant we could see the sails flapping as men tugged on ropes, then we glided down into a watery hollow.

That shaft of light had faded but still limned the ship when we made the next ascent. The vessel was changing its course, and as the bow swung out of the way I could see what the shout had portended. A monstrous whale was charging the craft, a froth of water, like the slaver of a mad dog, trailing from its partly open mouth. It must have been the wan light which created the illusion, but the beast looked white.

Down and up again. Only a minute separated me from the knowledge of whether the ship had avoided the assault, but it was a hundred times too long. The light was still dimmer, yet I saw. The hunted vessel had been too slow. Just as my eyes focused on what they sought, the monster struck the starboard bow head on and stove in the planking.

Neither whale nor sail was in sight when we next mounted a wave. I thought, however, I could see an arm stretching toward the skies in entreaty or defiance. Then, even as I gazed, the light ceased to be.

The impact of the tableau had so stunned my feelings that I had no prompt reaction. I had forgotten Golias, but he had evidently been watching as intently as I. After a second I heard him give a long whistle.

"Consummate," he remarked. "Well, that settles it."

"It couldn't be any more settled," I muttered. "Do you think any of those poor devils are still living to float around like us?"

"Maybe one," he replied. "It's the usual number. But that isn't what I was talking about. We haven't been washed out of our course. We're in the right waters."

I had forgotten that I had been on the verge of quarreling with him. Now that I had time to absorb it, the vision of the disaster I had just witnessed haunted me. In combination with the deepening darkness it magnified the loneliness of our hopeless drifting. Never having looked upon the face of perdition before, I had the unbearable sense of falling and found myself hugging the mast tightly.

At the same time I knew the men who went down right away to be the lucky ones. They would not have to look forward, as I did, to exposure, privation, and madness. In a moment of prescience I could see myself, witless and poisoned from drinking salt water, raving while sea gulls pecked out my eyes. I wished that I had the courage to start swimming again to meet death on better terms, but that renunciation was beyond me. I clung to my refuge, knowing that it was none at all, and scorned myself for accepting the cheat.

For my companion's optimism I had only pity mixed with wonder that anyone could so fool himself. "And what," I asked, "would happen if we were swept out of our so-called course?"

"I don't know what would happen to you," he confessed. "After we had drowned, that is. I'd have to start from scratch again somewhere. But we're all right."

"You're easily pleased," I said, although keeping the derision which belonged to the words out of my tone. By then I was sure that my companion was either out of his head or had a mind with loose parts to begin with. Because of this conviction I smothered his attempts at further discussion.

It seemed to me the crowning absurdity of a pointless life that I should spend my last hours tied, to all intents and purposes, to a delirious crackpot. I was pleased when it shortly became so dark that his face lost its features. About then he gave up trying to be sociable, leaving me to brood on my desolation.

Even before I became chilled through, it was thoroughgoing. Utter darkness crowded to within a few yards of me. There was no sky above the opaque water. In this bleak fold in the elements I had my being all that night. Misery stayed with me, but consecutive thinking was unable to hold up. Finally I began to drowse, waking only when my head fell forward to hit the mast, or lolled back so that I scooped up a noseful. I can't say how long I was in that purgatory, but at length I emerged from sleep enough to regain control of myself. By then the sky was beginning to lighten.

Golias must have been going through a similar torture, and for the second night. Yet his eyes still had vitality in them, in contrast to the rest of his face, which looked as if all the blood had been washed out of his veins.

"We're not far from land," he said hoarsely.

"Not more than a mile, though that's just a guess." I found that my voice didn't work well either. "I haven't taken soundings."

"No. Land to walk on," he insisted. "When that breeze hit us a moment ago—maybe you haven't noticed, but what's left of the wind has swung around—I could smell earth."

The thought that this quarter-wit was trying to push straws at me stirred me to peevishness. "Did it smell like the Commonwealth?"

He grinned, making his face more ghastly than ever. "You're not going to let anybody talk you out of dying, are you?"

I disdained to answer, but he had already done his worst. As each wave picked us up and pushed us forward, I found myself staring ahead. Visibility increased, but a stretch of skyline directly in our course did not clear. Glancing at Golias, I found that he was studying the phenomenon also. Behind us the clearing sky reddened, but the mysterious lump on the horizon did not go away.

My companion drew a huge sigh and turned to me. "I was sure," he said, "but it helps a lot to see it. You're not going to be fish food after all, A. Clarence Shandon."

"Just Shandon will do," I snapped. My mind had reached a puerile state when it hated to be proved wrong, no matter on what score. "We aren't there yet," I pointed out. "We'll probably be swept past it or dashed against the rocks."

"There are sometimes rocks," he admitted, "and I'm in no shape to do much swimming. Well, let's see if we can find out what we're up against."

After saying that, and as promptly as if it had something to do with the case, he startled me by beginning to chant a sort of mad plain song:

I invoke the Commonwealth!
I know what was in Othroerir;
Othroerir was in it,
In it, it was hoarded,
Hoarded, it was stolen,
Stolen, it was spilled,
Spilled, I caught it;
Caught, it was given away,
Given away, it stays my own,
My own is the Commonwealth.
I invoke it!
The land may not be hidden from its lover.

As if some cosmic hand was taking off the lid, a bank of mist then lifted to show a bank of greenery. It was not very far off, and we were being impelled directly toward it.

"We're in the Archipelago," Golias said when we had washed a little nearer.

By then I had made the adjustment to take the fact of solid earth for granted. Yet I was so exhausted that the realization hardly dented my emotions. I stared at the land, which looked pleasant enough, although uninhabited.

"You need more than one island for that," I objected.

"There are at least two right in the offing." He pointed, and I realized that a bank of mist adjacent to what he insisted was an island had stayed put. "There's one or more tucked away in that fog, which is probably of the natural sort."

"Sure," I said, not thinking it worth while to challenge the observation. "Got any idea which one this island in front of us is?"

"I could better tell you which ones it is not." His head was turned away from me, but I could see him shake it. "From the way things are shaping up this could be P'eng Lai, Emne, or—oh, any one of a dozen others."

"Well, if you don't recognize it," I protested, "how the devil are you so sure it's an island at all? It might just as well be a cape."

"For one thing, it doesn't look like we're going to have any trouble landing," he told me. "There's usually somebody waiting to take a swing at you when you hit the mainland. Or if it isn't that, it's something else. Once when I thought I had it made, the ship cracked up just where a river ploughed through the ocean as if it had the right of way. Of course, I was in better condition then or I never could have stemmed it."

We were close enough to see that there was indeed no obstacle to landing. Between us and a dense woods was a gently shelving beach. Barring an undertow, we had it cinched, and I freed myself from the rope which bound me to the spar.

We landed as deliberately as driftwood. My legs, as I found when I tried to put them down, would not support me, so I had to stay with the mast after all. Moderate breakers rolled us back and forth in the shallows until we reached a point where we could crawl. Then every time the water flowed seaward we gained a foot or two. Even on all fours I could hardly hold myself up. The effort made me dizzy, so that I could not see where I was going; but in time I felt dry sand.

"We've got to get out of the reach of high tide," Golias gasped, when I let myself fall on my face. "Out of the sun, too."

My physical strength was gone, and I had no other to call upon. It seemed to me that I had made a reasonable effort. More than that was not worth while. If quitting cost me my life, it would not be costing me much that I valued.

"Go ahead," I mumbled. "I'm comfortable right here."

It angered me to be tugged at, but I was too weak to struggle with him. How he managed it is a mystery. I knew him to be worn out. Yet somehow he dragged me a few yards, while I helplessly cursed him. When he finally let me alone, I slept.

II

⚮ The Animal Fancier ⚮

THE SUN was well down when, after several brief awakenings, hunger and thirst fully roused me. Golias was still asleep, which was not surprising. He had had two nights in the water to my one.

As he wore only a loincloth I could see that, although not a big man, he was well muscled. He lay prone, just inside the shade to which he had dragged me, his right arm stretched into the sunlight. It had turned red, but I did not bother to move it for him. A sunburn on him would cause me no discomfort at all.

Rising, I found myself stiff but otherwise undamaged. What had to be done was as obvious as it was unpleasant. Exploring a strange wilderness in my circumstances did not appeal to me, but it was self-service or none. I hitched up my only garment, a pair of shorts starched with salt, and hobbled into the woods.

The trees were low-slung and wide-spreading,

cluttered with moss and vines. Save for occasional palmetto clumps there wasn't much underbrush. The fact, coupled with the absence of rocks, made the footing good. The air was woven of sweet odors; but the sweetest to me was the smell of fresh water. Before I had gone fifty yards I found a spring welling up between the mossy roots of a tree. Taking it slowly, I drank until I could all but feel the drying blood in my veins thin enough to flow freely again.

Next, feeling confident that I wouldn't lose my bearings as long as I could hear the ocean, I started searching for fruit or berries. I found none, but in the course of my rambling I ran across a little mound and climbed it for a lookout. Golias had been right. Beyond the trees, a short distance in every direction, lay the sea. My view was broken only to the north, where rain or a thick mist still hid the neighboring island. As a last resort I squinted into the low-lying sun. Rising black against it was a column of smoke.

I eyed it irresolutely. Whoever had lighted that fire in this desolate spot might not be friendly to strangers. On the other hand it might be wiser to look him or them over before they discovered my presence. In the end the position of the sun decided me. The temperature had been pleasant, but the night air might not be so gentle to a bare hide. If there was shelter, or at least warmth, handy, it would be foolish to shiver all night because I was afraid to try my luck.

Walking about had unknotted my muscles, and, except for being light-headed from hunger, I did not feel bad. My unshod feet considered, I made fair progress, though I was careful to watch ahead at all times. I was prepared for anything from a tribal village to a farm house; but not for what I eventually saw. The trees abruptly gave way to make room for a clearing with a villa in it. The sun was right behind it, but as nearly as I could make out the building was of polished marble.

This was more than reassuring. Without pausing to reconnoiter farther, I strolled into the clearing. I was halfway to the house before I saw how the sun had betrayed me. Walking with my head down to shield my eyes from the rays, I felt an animal rub against me. Set to give an ingratiating pat to the watch dog of the premises, I found myself caressing a lion. He was not a solitary lion, for there were quite a few in the herd of animals frisking toward me.

Mingled with them were leopards, wolves, and creatures I took to be hyenas, though it had been years since I had visited a zoo. Besides thinking it wiser to stand my ground, I was trembling so that I couldn't proceed. Not that they threatened; they were even less hostile than I found pleasant, what with licking my hands and other familiarities. They failed to win me with their fawning, yet in the end they gave me new assurance. It was senseless to fear where no harm threatened, and I pushed gingerly through them.

While engaged with the menagerie, I had been more or less aware of a woman singing inside the villa, but nobody showed him or herself until I banged on a bronze door. It opened then, and I beheld a person I took to be the singer.

Her sleeveless dress, if it was a dress, seemed to be her only garment. Taking swift inventory, I raised my eyes to see if her face was also attractive. Her features were framed in red hair, which she wore bound up with a fillet. They were lovely and in cool contrast to her tresses.

Although her lids drooped demurely, she had an eye for a man. Complacently I stood her inspection. I was six foot-two and stripped well. If I was unshaven, I had a long face that, I was confident, looked good in the tan I had picked up aboard the *Naglfar*. As more than one woman had noticed, my dark hair had been, since late adolescence, cut in two by a streak of pure white. Some women had professed to think this made me look distinguished, and, in the days when I still cared enough to give it a thought, I had been inclined to agree with them. My blue eyes had long, dark lashes, though this particular girl hadn't had a chance to find that out yet.

To give her an opportunity of making this discovery I stepped nearer and bowed. "Pardon the intrusion and the lack of clothes, but I'm a shipwrecked mariner."

To my satisfaction she responded in my own language. "You poor man," she said with a luscious throatiness. "Were you the only one tossed ashore here?"

Hungry as I was, there was the future to think of. So far no husband or what have you had put in his appearance, and I certainly wasn't going to introduce a third party. Golias would have to do his own foraging.

"The only one I know of," I said sorrowfully. She didn't look frightened, but I thought it well to give the gentlemanly touch. "I hope I haven't alarmed you, breaking in on you this way."

"On the contrary," she said. "When one lives all alone, as I do, a visit is a kindness. You're starved, aren't you? Come in and let me fix you something."

It was as simple as that. There was no fake hesitation, no pretence of wondering whether it would be the correct thing to do. She didn't even bother to introduce herself. Well, if she wanted things on an informal basis, that exactly fitted in with my plans. I swaggered a bit as I stepped inside.

The room into which she led me was foreign-looking but spacious. Its chief articles of furniture were chairs, a number of chaise longues, and a large dining-room table. All in all it did not suggest a solitary spinster, and I wanted to be sure.

"So you live all by yourself," I murmured. "Don't you get lonesome?"

"Oh, people drop in from time to time." She hesitated a moment. "And then I have my animals."

"An unusual collection." I seated myself on the chair to which she waved me. "Did you train them yourself?"

For the first time she smiled a little. "Yes. Why don't you lean back and be comfortable? I won't be long."

My jaws ached with the knowledge that food was at hand, but it felt good to rest. Stretched out, I no longer felt light-headed, and I began to figure the possibilities more exactly. As far as I was concerned, I had found a home until the next ship called at the island. With this lion tamer to entertain me it would be all right, if the steamer wasn't too long in coming. Of course, Golias would probably show up in the morning, but by then I expected to be master *pro tem* of the household.

Unless or until I happened to get tired of the redhead there would be no room under the roof for any other man. If Golias ran short of companionship, he could try the hyenas.

While the woman worked at her cooking, she had started to sing again, which I took for a good sign. The song was an odd one, though not especially so for an animal trainer.

> Some go and hunt their prey,
> Some let it come their way—
> That's for the spider.
> Some snag with bait and hook,
> Some hold with but a look—
> That's for the adder.

The habits of adders were not too clear to me, but I found amusement in the part about spiders. As she would soon learn, I was not bad at spinning a web myself.

> Some can both stalk and wait,
> Transfix on trap with bait—
> That's for my—

She broke off, "It's all ready," she called out. A second later she appeared, carrying a loaded tray. "I do hope you like it."

The fragrance of the food was almost more than my hunger could stand. "Let's find out," I said, taking the place she had set for me. She had forgotten the fork, but I didn't bother to remind her. Grabbing a spoon and knife, I went at it.

The food was not only good but made me feel exceptionally fine and ready to take up new business. After the meal we both reclined on chaise longues, not side by side, but not far apart either, drinking wine. Or rather I sipped and talked while she watched me and listened.

Nothing in her conduct made her seem approachable except the fact that she would never quite meet my eyes. It had been my experience that timidity was apt to be as much a help as a hindrance. Your bold girl is inclined to pick whom she wants, and it may well not be you, while your bashful one waits for some one who will take trouble. My hostess was either overawed in the presence of a man from one of the great cities of the world, or she was inexperienced. In due time I would determine which was the case and campaign accordingly.

I could summon that much detachment because no friendliness marred the purity of my motives. Having found it unnecessary to like women—a discovery I had made early enough to save me from ever having proposed marriage—I never traded my emotions for what I wanted of them. As to what they might think of me, I cared not at all. Some, to be sure, would have none of me on my terms, but there were enough who would. Here, in spite of the absence of overt encouragement, I felt I had knocked at the right door.

In this case I had a double stake, for I wanted bed and board as well as body. So while letting her see from the way I looked at her that I was willing to work for my living, I put myself out to be agreeable much more than I usually did. Incidentally I managed to tell her what an important fellow she was entertaining, stretching a point here and there after I learned she had never been to Chicago.

She made a good listener, another fact that encouraged me. While I chatted, slipping in pertinent biographical data when convenient, she lay still, watching me from beneath lowered lids and hardly saying a word. After a while she commenced toying with an object which looked not unlike a large golden knitting needle.

Her purpose, I reasoned, was to show off her hands, which were as sightly as the rest of her; but I also saw that the thing was unusual enough to make a suitable opening. When the right time came, that is to say when my supper felt comfortably digested, I rose.

"That's a fascinating-looking gizmo," I remarked, walking lazily over to her. "I'd like to see just what it is."

She held it to her bosom in her first sign of archness, but just the same she shifted her legs to make room for me to sit down. "Are you sure you want to?"

This was working out as planned. "Oh, very sure," I nodded, making my eyes big and looking very solemn. Already my hands were aware of how her body would feel beneath that filmy dress, but I was willing to play the game a little longer. I leaned toward her. "Please, darling."

"Very well," she said, and her voice was suddenly hard. With the words she at last let me look into her eyes. Far from being those of a woman inviting seduction, they were so brightly fierce that I blinked. Confused, I drew back—but not far enough.

"You wanted to know. Find out!" she cried. Without changing her position, she reached out and tapped me with the little golden stick.

Experiencing something between an electric

shock and a convulsion, I fainted. When I came to, I rose to my feet, only to find that the movement left my hands on the floor. I tried to look at them but found it difficult, because my eyes did not seem to be in the right location. While I was trying to get them to focus, I heard my hostess' voice, shrill with disgust.

"Outside, you nasty pig; shoo!"

As she spoke, a broomstick or something like it poked me in the ribs. Trying to turn on her, I found myself skidding on all fours on the marble floor.

"Get out!" she shrieked, poking me again.

In my wrath and dismay I stumbled, panting. I meant to tell her that as soon as I could pull myself together I would give her saddle sores, but my voice was on strike. While I was scrambling to get my balance, she walloped me. Catching me over the backbone, the blow hurt like the devil, and articulation returned to me in a rush.

"Oink!" I protested, trotting forward.

Utterly routed then, I made no further efforts to resist. I only wanted to get out of her way and skidded along at my best speed, as she hazed me out through the kitchen. Once on the ground outside I found the going easier, but I still couldn't outfoot her. Rapping me first on one side, then on the other, she steered me well away from the villa until, what with the night and my confusion, I butted into a wooden fence. There she poked me once more—with the golden thingamajig, I believe, for it was too sharp to be the end of a broomstick—and over the fence I went.

I landed up to my knees and elbows in ooze. It was dark, but there was no question as to where I

was. Once encountered, and I had lived in
Chicago most of my life, the smell of live pork is
never forgotten.

For a long while I stood as I had fallen, trembling, straddle-legged in the stinking slime. Accepting facts was a habit of mine on which I had
always prided myself, and I tried to bring what
had happened to me into comprehension. Reason
was stumped, though, until a slice of moon
cleared the trees around the clearing. Turning my
head to look at it, I was aware of a long-snouted
shadow moving, too. I tried to lose that shadow
but could not. First I walked, then I trotted, then I
plunged madly through the slop, but it came with
me. Reaching the other side of the pen, I threw
myself at it with a cry of despair. The squeal of a
terrified pig broke the night's silence.

Madness is a distrust of reason. The bitter faith
that I had in mine kept my brain from cracking.
Yet it also shut out comfort. A madman can ease
his griefs by outlawing facts. There was in my
case no use in telling myself that such a thing
could not happen to a man, because I knew it had
happened to me.

Nevertheless, comfort of a sort was at hand. My
squeals awakened other inmates of the sty to come
snuffling and grunting around me. At first I
scorned their overtures, but when I had worn myself out trying to avoid them, they gathered about
me again. Having worked myself into a sweat, I
was cold when I gave up. Their bodies pressed
against mine felt good. We spent the night heaped
together, hog-fashion, and by morning I had made
terms with my new life. What was to be gained by
arguing with reality? I still had fits of melan-
cholia, but the business of being a pig was absorb-

ing most of my time. All my associates were swine, too, so it didn't seem so bad.

Just the same my philosophy failed me when I heard human voices. Ashamed, I slunk into a far corner of the pen; warily, too, for I recognized the tones of my hostess of the night before. She was accompanied by Golias, whom she was apparently taking on a tour of the premises.

"And these are my swine," she was saying. "Wait; I'll bring them nearer."

With his help she dumped a huge basket of acorns into the sty, and I heard myself giving a grunt of satisfaction. Fear, hatred, and shame made me loth to get closer, but my stomach was master. In a jiffy I was shouldering my way through the dozen or so hogs which had quickly gathered.

The woman laughed delightedly. "Aren't they beauties?"

Keeping an eye on them as I champed, I saw that Golias' face was drawn. "Your animals are very interesting," he said, "but I'm looking for a man."

"H-m-m, so am I," she responded. She was not the quiet housebody she had been with me. Now she was playfully arch, canting her head as she laughed at him. "Have you seen one about?"

Trying to give a grunt of warning while I chewed, I choked on my acorns; but Golias inched away. "I've been on Aeaea before," he said huskily.

Instantly her face hardened, and her eyes blazed at him as they had so dreadfully at me. "What are you doing here, if you know better?"

Golias was nervous, but he stood his ground. "A fellow was cast ashore with me, Circe. I tracked him here."

I remembered how I had lied to cheat him out of her hospitality, and she did, too. "He didn't share your feeling of comradeship," she informed him. "He would have let you die."

"But I wouldn't let him die," Golias told her. "I took it upon me to save him in spite of himself, and now I'm bound to him. Where is he?"

"Not far away, if that's any comfort to you."

"One of these! Why?"

She met his look of horror with a cold smile. "I don't really change men very much, you know. All I do is bring about conformity between a state of being and the skin which holds it. Your friend cared only for food and fornication, so I did him a favor. As a swine he'll have no distracting influences."

"But he couldn't help desiring you," Golias smoothed his voice as he spoke. "It can be no news to you that you're lovely."

"Then I want to be loved in the way of my lions; or to meet with a lust I can take personally, in the way of my wolves. But he—" She bared white teeth and clicked them. "He looked at me as if I were an oyster he was about to slide past his palate. If I'd thought faster, I would have made him something lower."

"You weren't able to," he asserted.

Thinking about me, she had worked herself into a bad humor. His remark brought it to a boil.

"Oh, you think I wasn't? I tell you he got off easy, and as for you—"

"What?" He wasn't happy about the change of subject, yet he looked at her steadily. "I haven't touched your damned doped food."

"Maybe I can do nothing with you," she conceded; but the admission made her more furious than ever. "But I could have turned your friend into something a pig would look down on, and I still can."

"You're bragging," he insisted.

I listened anxiously, wishing Golias wouldn't aggravate her. About then, however, I lost track of the dispute. The acorns had been thinned out, and the competition was getting stiff. I nipped a hog that was trying to beat me to a small pile of them, but while I was gobbling the prize, he counter-attacked. Squealing with rage, I rushed him to the fence and pinned him there. I had just got my teeth set in his ear when I felt myself being hoisted by one of my own. Before I knew what was happening I was grabbed by a hind leg and dragged over the top rail of the pen.

"Come on!" Golias cried as he dumped me in free territory. "Start running!"

No doubt he meant well, but there was no sense to it that I could see. As long as I remained a hog the best place for me was the sty. Hearing the other pigs still grubbing acorns was more than I could stand, and I made a clumsy attempt to jump back over the fence. Once again Golias took my forelegs from the ground as he turned me to face the other way.

"Damn it, get moving!" he roared. "She's gone for her wand! She'll turn you into a bug or a dirt-eating worm!"

That reached me both as a man and a pig. As a man, the thought of further degradation was revolting. As a pig, the thought of lowering my eating standard was equally horrifying. I started to run, but he grabbed me by the tail.

"Not that way! Follow me!"

A lean boar, I was gratified to discover, can run fast. I had need of foot speed that day. When we reached the forest, I slowed down in spite of Golias' urgings. We seemed out of danger, and I wanted to keep my eye out for some food. I lost interest in foraging, though, when a conglomerate howling reached us.

"She's fired their natures against us," Golias gasped. "The whole menagerie will be on our trail."

The last words had to catch up with me. He didn't have to tell a pig what to do when wolves howled and lions gave the hunting roar. I scuttled along, never deviating for anything less than a palmetto. At first I distanced Golias, but I found myself a sprinter only. Soon the knowledge that the hunting cries were nearer was all that kept my hoofs working.

Golias took the lead, panting occasional words of encouragement. "We'll make it. Keep coming! It can't be much farther."

I didn't know what 'it' was, though I assumed he knew of a place to hide. Unable to see far ahead or to look over my shoulder, I doggedly worked my legs, kicking up leaves in a treadmill of terror.

Because of my short range of vision we were almost at the ocean before I was aware of it. Golias was already in the water, and I saw my doom. There was no refuge but the sea, which for me was no refuge at all. My strength exhausted with running, I knew I could not swim far enough to do any good.

Slowing, I looked up and down the beach. Finding nothing helpful, I peered behind me. Somewhere in the rear I could hear wolves, but in this short run the cats were having the best of it. The leading pair of leopards, one a pace behind the other, were not fifty yards away.

That was all I needed to see. A man might reason that the sea was a sure death trap, but a pig had to save his meat from the hunters while he could. Groaning, I gathered myself for a plunge into the water. I didn't move. Frantically I churned the sand with my feet, but I got no traction.

I could hear the soft thudding as the leopards bounded toward me. It seemed to me that I could hear their jaws snapping. My flesh winced in advance from the pain of their rending talons. Still I made no progress, and I knew myself lost. Throwing all the rest of my life into a cry of protest, I shut my eyes and squealed.

When I felt a grip on my ears I thought it was one of my pursuers until I felt fingers grip one of my legs. "Close," Golias panted as he waded into the sea with me. "I'd forgotten you couldn't leave under your own power while she had her spell on you."

If he added anything to that remark, I didn't catch it. For the second time in two days I blacked out.

III

⚬✦ A Map of the Commonwealth ✦⚬

WHEN I CAME out of it I was human again, but I wasn't glad of that or anything. After I had finished vomiting acorns, I was still sick. Yet physical malaise was but a small part of my grief. The complacence around which I had been moulded had been torn from me, leaving me propless.

My only philosophy, if you could call it that, had been a contempt for life backed by a pride in that contempt. Now even those cold allies had deserted me. It had not been contempt for life which had made me run so hard and which had squeezed that scream out of me when I thought my case hopeless. Every labored breath I had drawn through my snout had seemed precious to me, and I still shook from relief at my escape.

As for my pride, it bled from too many wounds to make any of them seem worth staunching. One alone was enough to be mortal. The cynic's vanity—the one which gives him license to be scornful where other men delight—is the assumption that he knows the inner workings of things. The fact was that I had reached a region where I didn't know the score at all.

"How do you feel?" Golias asked, when I finally pushed myself up to a sitting position.

I peered to get my bearings. We were obviously on the other island, a hilly one in contrast to flat Aeaea, which was again capped with mist. Then I glanced at my companion out of the corner of my eye. He was lying down, still breathing hard from the effort of towing me across the intervening channel. His right arm. the one I hadn't troubled to move in the shadow for him while he slept, must have pained him with every stroke he took. It was an angry red.

"Oh, all right for an ex-pig, I guess." I neither turned my face toward him nor offered a hook on which to hang further conversation. Instead I lay down, closing my eyes, and to my relief he let me alone.

Better yet, he soon murmured something about taking a look around and walked off along the shore. As soon as he was out of sight, I also left the spot, heading in the opposite direction. He had seen me exposed too completely as a skunk and a fool to make the idea of association tolerable.

The island turned out to be little else than a mountain jutting out of the ocean. Near the sea the slopes were free of timber here and there, but for the most part they were hidden by jungle. The chief visible inhabitants were goats, a variety of birds, and sundry sea creatures. Ready to serve were clams, crabs, and turtle eggs, though I would have preferred the last two cooked. Enough streams and runlets twisted down from the mountain to solve the problem of obtaining fresh water.

I learned that much the first day. It took me several more, picking my way along the rocky shore in my bare feet, to walk around the island. It would have been simpler to make a survey from the top of the mountain, but I was leery of entering the woods whose livestock was an unknown quantity. If I had learned nothing else on Aeaea, I had learned caution.

What I was seeking was human society—any society except that of Golias', that is—but when I did find a footprint in a patch of moist sand, it scared me. The print was a huge one, much too big to be made by the man I was sulkily dodging. If the foot had been shod, I would not have been alarmed; but it wasn't. Notwithstanding my own shoelessness, bare feet represented savagery. This was fitting to a jungle-covered mountain; and where there was one such man there might be hundreds. It was only mid-afternoon when I made the discovery. Nevertheless, I holed up at the next possible hiding place while I thought things over.

I spent a bad night, caused only in part by the footprint. For one thing my mind was fighting with my vanity. The issue was whether I should eat crow. My reason for considering the diet was that I could tell from the relative position of Aeaea that I had nearly circled the island. Meanwhile I had found no sign of civilized residents, nor any indication that ships called there. As things stood, my only possible companion, or ally in the event of trouble, was Golias—if he was still willing to put up with me.

Breakfasting moodily on raw turtle eggs, I suddenly saw that it was perhaps too late. A man who knew the ropes as well as Golias did might have found a way to get off the island. Alarmed, I set out in search of him. My feet had toughened somewhat, so it was no longer hard for me to make time.

He was not far from where we had landed, just emerging from a dip in the sea, when I came upon him. Making it easy for me, he greeted me as if he had seen me within the hour. Yet I couldn't take his fellowship again with nothing said. I scowled at him.

"By the way, thanks for helping me the other day. I wouldn't have done it for you."

He shrugged. "We'll see when the time comes."

This man whom I had once scorned as a pipe dreamer held the upper hand in every respect, but I wasn't going to let him think it mattered to me. "With one chance to double-cross you I batted a thousand," I reminded him. He made no comment, and I reluctantly asked a question to which I had to know the answer. "Of course, it's nice to be recognized, but how did you pick me out from that bunch of hogs?"

The skin crinkled around his eyes, though he didn't quite grin. "There was only one that was dark-haired with a patch of silver on his noggin. It had to be you."

I fingered the white streak in my hair. "Well, I'm glad it wasn't a special smell or something." Desperately as I hoped he wouldn't refuse, I meant to show him I wasn't tagging after anybody. "Look; I might not let you down again—or I might. Do we stick together?"

"Why do you think I came after you? The indications are plain that the Delian's given us to each other for a while, for whatever may come of it." Before I could comment, he was speaking again. "You walked all around the island?"

"Yes," I nodded. "And I didn't see anything good."

"Anything bad?"

He listened with interest while I told him about the footprint. "I thought it possible when I took a look from the peak; but it's been so long since I was in this part of the Archipelago I'd forgotten where this isle stood from Aeaea." He gazed up at the mountain thoughtfully. "I'm inclined to think that the footprint was left behind by a transient."

I gave a grunt of relief. "Then from what I've seen, we could have the place, if we wanted it."

"It's got us," he corrected me. "No matter what island you're on, the trick is to get off it, and it's never an easy trick."

While I watched in mild astonishment he removed his loin cloth. In one of its folds was a knife in a brine-cracked leather sheath. Drawing the blade, he cut the simple garment in two and handed me half.

"A man," he observed, "can carry almost everything he really needs in his mind except food and pants."

My shorts hadn't followed me through my transformations, a fact which had increased my sense of helplessness. A little of my self-confidence returned when I had rigged myself a sort of diaper.

"Speaking of food," I said, as I knotted it in place, "have you found anything to eat here except raw sea food?"

"Cooked sea food, for one thing." Unable to tuck his knife away again in his reduced loin cloth, Golias pointed with it to indicate a grove of palms not far back from the shore. "Come on over to my camp, and I'll show you."

We didn't get that far. Crossing an intervening stretch of meadow, we heard a snort. A young goat which had been taking it easy in the high grass jumped to its feet and returned my look of surprise. Possibly it had never seen a man before, and certainly it never saw one again. Golias' hand snapped back in a motion which shook the sheath from the blade. When his hand snapped forward again, the knife sped through the air to land in the kid's throat. The animal only made about thirty yards before dropping at the edge of the beach.

"Lunch," my companion remarked. "We ought to have something to go with it, though. How about going up hill and bringing in some grapes—I saw lots of them when I was reconnoitering—while I take this fellow out of his hide?"

"Shall I bring them to your camp?" That seemed an unnecessary question, but I wanted to stall a minute. I still thought it likely that things which would feed on me were as common in the jungle as anything I might consider edible.

"No use in going any farther, when we have everything to hand here." Golias nodded to where a runlet dribbled out of the meadow, then looked at me enquiringly.

Afraid he would guess why I hesitated, I started the ascent. I didn't walk very far into the jungle, but that wasn't necessary. Among the vines which swarmed among the trees I discovered wild grapes, just coming ripe. Delighted at making good so easily, I picked half a dozen huge bunches and hastened back to the edge of the meadow. There delight gave way to soberer feelings.

In that section of the mountain the jungle began well up the slope. Emerging from the trees higher up than my point of entry, I found myself on a ridge falling away to the ocean on both sides. My hope that we might be near a sea lane died as I looked. Around either shore swept an immensity of water, barren of ships. Moreover, the very notion that a ship could come from those empty horizons seemed untenable.

When I had been lost in the ocean, it had not daunted me; but I was daunted now. The shock of my recent experience was still with me. Having worn lesser garments, I could feel my humanity around me and knew its needs. Those needs could not be serviced in solitary confinement, which was the sentence I read on those otherwise blank waters. In an unguarded moment I opened my mind to the promised years. My reason raced down them and threatened not to come back.

As I fought with horror, I caught sight of Golias, still busy where I had left him on the beach. I stopped sweating, and my heart ceased to pound. At least my solitude was not complete. Unwontedly eager for companionship, I hurried downhill.

The kid was gutted and skinned. Golias had gathered driftwood also, and was in the act of laying a fire when I rejoined him. I had forgotten to ask him what he was going to do about the fire, but he had an answer. With a chip of flint he made sparks against the back of his knife. One of them caught in the tinder he had gathered, and careful breathing turned the glow into a flame. Salted with sea water, a haunch was soon roasting above it.

In the presence of such competence I was glad I had something to offer. The grapes were good, and we ate a quantity while waiting for the meat to be cooked. It was cozy enough lounging in the shade of the boulder. Nevertheless, I still felt subdued.

"Just how do you figure the chances of getting away from here?" I asked, after reflecting on what I had seen on the ridge.

Golias spit a grape seed at a crab six feet away, scoring a hit. "Not good," he said, helping himself to another cluster.

Coming from someone I regarded as a fourflusher who always filled his hand, this pessimism startled me. On the verge of expostulating, I shut my mouth. He was right.

"I didn't get a four-way view. Barring the one we came from, are there any islands fairly near?"

"One or two, but as I told you, and even if we could reach them, they're all tough to get away from. Unless caught in a squeeze the way we were on Aeaea, it's better to take the dice as they fall. We might run into one of these jobs where you're held in dalliance for anywhere from seven years to couple of parrot's lifetimes." He gave the wooden spit a quarter turn. "Dalliance is good fun in easy doses, but I've got other things to do."

"Like cooking goats?"

"Like finding a way to get off the island." He grinned at me. "The chances aren't good, figured as odds, but that doesn't mean it can't be done."

Such vague reassurance failed to comfort me. In

the course of two brief conversations we had explored the dimensions of our life. On the one hand was the problem of escape. On the other was food, representing the problem of how to live until we could leave. The larder now being full, I concentrated on ways of making a getaway. Golias was doubtless busy with similar thoughts, for he, too, was silent until the goat roast—the meat was somewhat flat and stringy but far superior to raw crab meat—was done and eaten.

"Did you put a marker where you found that footprint?" he enquired when we were through.

"Not necessary," I told him. "It's just beyond a promontory a couple of miles back. I'll recognize the spot."

"We'd better look the vicinity over," he decided, "to see if there are any signs of a regular landing place."

"Could we build a raft?" I asked, when we had walked in silence for a while. "Burn the logs instead of chopping them, say, and bind 'em with vines."

He shook his head. "Probably the most marvelous craft that ever floated was a raft, but it cruised a river. In the ocean there'd be no steerage way."

"We could paddle. No, we couldn't either," I agreed, when he gave me a satirical look. "But a sail, then." I was silent, following this new lead. "Maybe we could get enough goat skins to make one."

"The sail's a possibility," he assented. "Now all we need is something to put it on. A wind strong enough to push a raft would kick up sea enough to flip it over."

I could see that, but I had another idea. "That

mast drifted to the other island with us, because the wind sent the waves that way. Why wouldn't the raft drift to the mainland when the wind was right? What's the direction from here?"

"West," he said. "Everything always comes from the east and goes west."

"All right," I said. "Suppose, for the sake of argument, we shoved off with a steady east wind at our tail. We ought to make two or three miles an hour, I should think. How far is it anyhow?"

"I could say a hundred miles, but it might be twice that—doubled again the way we'd travel. Forget that idea. I'm not leaving here on any craft I can't move or guide."

He was being practical, but I felt stubborn about giving up the only means of escape I could imagine. "Before we forget it," I persisted, "let's calculate the odds. Or if you don't want to bother, give me a chance to." The promontory we were seeking was just ahead, but we had come to one of the rare stretches of sand along the rocky shore. "How about making me a map, so I can visualize just what we're up against?"

"All right, though, even allowing for the medium, drawing isn't what I get paid for." He picked up a stick. "These dots are the Archipelago. You'll have to make your own guess as to which one we're on, but in any case the nearest point of the mainland is this long peninsula, more or less due west. If we could disregard ocean currents and drift and could count on the wind to take us where we wanted to go, we might do all right. But it's damned hard to hit a target when you can't see it and haven't got any sights. If we slide past the peninsula either to the north or south, it doubles both the time for the trip and the chance of running into storms. Or we could be becalmed for weeks and die that way."

He looked up to see if I was convinced. I was, but I thought it as good an opportunity as any to learn something about a country I was perforce so anxious to visit.

"Finish your map," I suggested.

"Deryabar at the tip of Ever After Peninsula," he said, as he began to extend the lines he had made, "is not only the nearest place to us but the most easterly point of the entire coast. Laterally, then, the Commonwealth extends from there to—" he stretched as far as he could "—the western bulge of Pike County. North of the peninsula, after a sweep around the Boss of Arden here, the shoreline runs jaggedly to Utgard. South it is somewhat less irregular but ends with a jolt at Adamastor's Haunt.

"And so north again." He completed the line to indicate that the country was entirely sea-bound. "To locate some of the cities, here are Ilium, Carlion, Thebes, Valentia, Parouart, Argos, Troynovaunt, and Gotham. There are any number of others, though it often happens that a single building like the Red Branch, Swallow Barn, or Headlong Hall will overshadow the towns of a district."

I pondered that information. "What do they do for a living there?"

"They do better than that, Shandon; they live." Following that pronouncement he commenced drawing again. "Watling Street, running west from Deryabar, is the only highway which cuts completely across the country in either direction. The most extensive natural feature it pierces is

Broceliande Forest, which floods all unsettled areas from the Boss of Arden to the Warlock Mountains on the other side of Long River, which more or less, as you see, bisects the land north and south. Between the Warlocks and this generally parellel range to the west, the Titans, is an inland sea known as the Midwater or Gitche Gumee. It—"

He stopped, because we heard voices, half shouting, half singing. The sounds died away, then came again, as Golias and I looked at each other.

"They're on the other side of the point," I whispered. "Right where I saw the footprint."

"We'd better look 'em over," he decided. "If they look friendly, good. If not, the only way to stay hidden is to stay where you can keep an eye on whatever you're hiding from."

Leaving the beach, he began slithering through the tall grass of the meadow. I wriggled along the swathe he left. It was hot, hard work. I was soon lapped in sweat, most of my muscles ached, my knees and elbows were rubbed raw; and there were insects whose bite was an agonizing itch.

The racket made by the people we were stalking was a help, for it covered the sounds of our progress as well as guiding us. Nevertheless, Golias signaled to me to halt when we reached a certain point. Glad to oblige, I watched him crawl ahead. Then he motioned me to come on.

When I was stretched out beside him I gently pushed a tuft of grass aside and peered down at the beach. A dozen or so savages, naked as ourselves, were prancing about in circular follow-the-leader. All were men, and though they lacked the costume which movies had taught me to expect of redskins, I took them to be Indians. As centerpiece for their activities, the hot sunlight notwithstanding, there was a large fire. A seated savage was furnishing the only music for the dancers, beating a makeshift drum with both hands. His efforts could only be heard, however, when the others stopped shouting. This wasn't often, though every now and then their voices would drop to a murmur. Then the fellows would reverse their field, hunching their bodies, showing plenty of knee action, waving clubs, and bellowing again.

None of them cracked a smile, and I didn't find it amusing myself. There is something frightening about solemnity where mirth belongs. The only thing pleasurable in the scene was the presence of two big wooden canoes drawn up on the sand. They suggested that these might be only temporary visitors.

I looked to see how Golias was taking it, but I didn't have to meet his eyes. The hand which gripped his knife was white about the knuckles. Shortly after I resumed watching, the dancing stopped. Several of the performers made for the canoes, and my tension eased. I thought they were getting ready to leave until I saw them remove another Indian from the nearest dugout.

He was tied hand and foot. I believe he was gagged, too, but it soon made no difference. One of his captors jerked his head back, and a second cut his throat with a stone knife. They held him up then, like a beheaded chicken, to let the blood drain out of him. Even then I didn't get what they were up to until they ripped him up the middle.

After that they weren't the only killers there, for I was one in my mind, balked only by my impotence. It was not just the murder, it was the use to which they were going to put their victim. Only a few days before I had learned what a miracle a man's body is. To think that all its mastery of skills should end as gobbets of chewed flesh was unendurable. I had not known the meaning of sacrilege and profanation. Here were both. There should have been something I could do about it. There was nothing. Hate fizzed up in me so that I had to chew my arm to keep from crying out.

When they had hacked the body apart and skewered it for roasting, Golias signaled for me to follow him away. "No use watching the end of it," he said, when we were out of hearing.

My head hanging, I didn't say anything. It was bad enough to have watched without talking about it.

"We've got a chance of getting away from here now," he went on. "If you're willing to risk it, that is."

Both the hope and the challenge brought my head up. "With the canoes? But how?"

"If they run true to form, they'll gorge on that redskin they're barbecuing, then sleep it off. It's not as simple as that," he cautioned me, as my face brightened. "They landed, being sea-wise, after the tide started to go out. The canoes are high and dry and won't be launched until the water reaches them again. That's our margin of time, but it's no use to us if they wake before the water gets to the dugouts. We could move them a little way—I hope—but not far without kicking up a fuss. Should we wake those lads—" He shrugged. "If we hit the same stomach, a horn of mead says I'll beat you to the pylorus."

He looked at me steadily as he said that, and I

made myself stare back at him. At the same time I didn't hurry my decision.

"We might not get another chance," I muttered.

"If we do, it's apt to be the same one. It seems probable that these fellows make regular stops here. The odds for us will be unchanged, though."

Still I looked from the island to myself, then at the empty waters. "Let's go back for the goat meat and cut ourselves a couple of clubs," I said finally.

Even though we took our time, we were too prompt. The sands about the feasters were scattered with freshly gnawed bones, but the meal was still in progress. Bleakly we watched them as they tore at the flesh. Their bellies were swollen, but they ate everything except the feet and the head. The latter, stuck on a pole, watched the gorging with drooping lids.

Well before the last bite was bolted, Golias showed himself a prophet. The heat and the over-eating brought on sleep. One by one, like bloated slugs, they sought the shade of rocks or shrubbery and commenced snoring. Only one man stayed on guard.

From then on there was nothing to do but watch the tide, which was already setting in. It did not inch up the beach. It would surge to a point, then let that mark stand for minutes before it pushed on again. Meanwhile one or more of the sleepers would grunt and shift position.

The water got to within a yard of the canoes, and I touched Golias' arm. He shook his head, and again when the distance was halved. By the time foam touched the nearest dugout a savage was sitting up, yawning and scratching his chest. I was convinced we had missed our time, but Golias still looked from the cannibals to the water and back like a cat watching two mouse holes.

Three men had rejoined the sentry near the remains of the fire by the time Golias rose to a crouching position. He looked in my eyes, and I knew he wanted to see what I hoped was there. At his nod I drew my knees up under me.

"Now!" he whispered.

We were halfway to the canoes before one of the Indians shouted the alarm. We had reached them before they had collected themselves enough to see what we were after. Simultaneously I was making a discovery of my own. Golias had known what he was talking about when he had waited for the water to get well up under the craft we were trying to launch. The big canoe was heavy and moved grudgingly.

"Try the other one!" Golias gasped. "It might sit lighter."

That proved so. We shoved it two feet. Then I almost fell on my face, for the vessel started to slide. We got no farther. I had dropped my club to push, but I caught up a paddle as the cannibals rushed us. Bending to do so saved my life, for a spear zinged past my ear.

As I sprang to join Golias, the lead savage fell away from his knife, trying to hold his guts in place. Four others were a jump behind, and I swung my paddle. Catching one on the jaw, it felled him. Of the remaining three, two ducked back. The third was tripped by the man I had downed. Unluckily for him he stumbled forward, and Golias slit his throat.

The second echelon of Indians was by then halfway to us. The two survivors of the first were waiting for them, so we had a respite a shaved second long.

"I'll hold 'em!" I yelled. "Shove! Jesus! What are you doing that for?"

He had vaulted into the unlaunched canoe, but I was too busy to watch him. Seeing me alone, the two lurking redskins closed in. A step behind the rest of the band came leaping.

Had they been ordinary foemen they might have snowed me under. I would have fought, but not as I did fight, knowing them to be man-eaters. A few days earlier my flesh had been coveted, and I had merely squealed. Now the case was different. All hate and anger powered the blow I swung at them.

Again I stove in a man's face, but this time they were too many to be stopped. The one who grazed me with a spear thrust got the butt end of the paddle in the mouth, but another ducked under my arms. I went down under a pile of them, of which the man who had tackled me wasn't one. He lay still under me after the treatment I gave his neck.

In the scramble they couldn't always be sure whom they were fighting, while I could never be in doubt. Nevertheless, I had a rough time before I broke a man's grip, his thumb along with it. It was when I was getting to my feet that I saw why I had been able to break away. Golias was pulling his knife out of an Indian's back.

"Come on!" he snapped.

Turning, I staggered toward the canoe, now afloat and drifting a few feet off shore. With a lunge I flopped over the gunwale, started to rise, then fell full length, as the dugout shot seaward.

"Grab a paddle!" Golias ordered, as he dove over the bow.

The five or six able-bodied Indians were shoving out the other canoe, which didn't take them as long as I wished it would. Yet when they hauled themselves aboard, they didn't start paddling. Instead they took to the water again and sloshed toward us. Two men weren't enough to maneuver the big dugout fast. Luckily the rollers were small in the shelter of the promontory. We made headway toward the smoother water beyond the shallows, and I saw we were gaining on the wading cannibals.

Seeing that, too, the one who led them started to swim. He went faster thus and actually got a grip—we were still backing away, half paddling and half shoving—on the bow of the craft. His comrades gave a shout of triumph which he drowned out in a cry of pain. Golias had reached forward, and the clutching fingers slid down inside the canoe.

That was their last effort. They were wading ashore, as we turned the dugout to head toward the open sea. It was not until we were well out that I took the rest I needed. Aside from the spear graze, I was bruised, shaken, scratched, nicked and scraped. My head ached, and my right eye was closing. Meanwhile the exhilaration of action had gone flat in me. The incident just concluded absorbed my attention, but as if it were something which had happened to someone else.

After mulling over the action I realized that a facet of it puzzled me. "Why didn't they use their canoe?" I enquired.

Golias looked tired, too, but he grinned over his shoulder. "For one thing, we've got their paddles," he said. "Do you think we ought to return them?"

IV

❦ Driving for the Mainland ❦

THE CANOE was seaworthy, but our position was not otherwise good. We had provided ourselves with goat's meat wrapped in pieces of hide tied around our respective waists. Golias still had his chunk, but I had lost mine in the scrimmage. Carrying water had been out of the question. We had had to chance it that the savages, who had presumably carried some sort of supplies on their trip to the island, had left some water aboard. They had left very little.

From the moment I knew that my thirst began. "How far away do you think those fellows live?" I asked, dipping my paddle to keep us from swinging side on to the waves.

"Probably not too far," Golias answered. "The trouble is we don't want to go there. I've had my fill of cannibals and don't want them to have their fill of us. The only thing we can do is to head west and hope. Luckily the wind's with us."

When we were worn out with paddling, there was nothing for it but to let the waves and the wind take the craft as they would. In the light seas it floated like a cork and seldom shipped any water. We took on only a little water ourselves, being able to afford only a sip at a time.

It was near sundown when we started. Forty-eight hours later we had to face the fact that we had missed the peninsula and had a journey of indefinite length ahead of us. Our water used up, thirst took complete charge of our bodies as well as our minds the day following. The sun rose hot and screwed up the voltage by the minute. It bleached us like raisins. It starved us, too, for we were no longer able to swallow our meager rations.

It was well for us that our pelts had had a week of seasoning. It was the only thing which saved us from bad burning. Keeping wet helped some, though I grew nervous about scooping up water, wondering how long I could refrain from drinking it. We also put out one of the lines we had found in the canoe but had no luck. Golias explained that we might be able to eat raw fish, whose flesh would be moist.

That was about the last thing either of us said. Moving our dry lips split them. After a while I felt that my throat was closed. We paddled some, but not often now. Most of the time we looked out of eyes that were robbed of the needed moisture. We looked for land, and looked for a ship, we looked for clouds, or even a lone one that would hold off the heat for a little. We saw nothing but the sun and its glaring accomplice the sea.

It could not have been worse, but it did get

worse. The wind dropped, and the waves stopped, so that our craft lay on the water as if pinned there by the sun. We, too, had come to the end of our motion. Both on the same side, careening the canoe, we sprawled and stared.

The sea itself had curdled in the still heat. Out of it crawled the progeny of this festering to scuttle, many-legged, over the thickened, sour surface. It was vileness on a frolic, and all the life I had was to watch it.

I don't know how long it had been since I had looked at Golias. Probably I had thought him dead, for I had no sense of company in terror. He entered my consciousness again by making the first sound I had heard for hours.

"A sail!" he croaked.

To find the moisture to oil his voice he had bitten into a vein already short of blood. The arm which he pointed was still bleeding thinly. I watched his blackened lips crack as his mouth opened once more.

"A sail!" he repeated.

When his meaning had penetrated, I turned, slow motion. A vessel of a type new to me was drawing near. In spite of the fact that there was no wind, all sails on its three masts were set. Moreover, it is not enough to say it was moving. It was making airplane speed through the water. If there was an auxiliary engine, it gave off neither sound nor exhaust.

I wanted to hail it at Golias' price of sucking my own blood, but I found I could not lift my arm. Then I saw it wouldn't be necessary. We were almost in the ship's course, so those aboard couldn't miss seeing us. I had barely had time to reason that far, when it drew silently abreast.

A vessel that size could have been expected to have a wheel instead of a tiller. It didn't matter, for it wasn't manned. Or rather the helmsman hung over the tiller so that his hands touched the deck.

The only other person in sight stood at the rail midway between the high stem and stern. He was clutching a big seagull, I should say it was, dead as the man at the helm. Passing within a few yards, the fellow looked full at me, but I knew that he would do nothing for us. He could not. What I saw in his eyes I knew to be in my own. The life in him could not stir even to find an ending.

He was gone then. In a minute more the ship was hull down. Close to us as she had sped, she rocked us only a little, but to see the ocean stirred was much. It seemed to break the spell which bound the elements, for a breath of wind came. It blew stronger, bringing clouds. Then, unbelievably, it rained.

That rain was no drizzle. It was more like a waterfall, and we loved every drop of it. Where I had had no use of myself, it gave me back my faculties. To move deftly was to know delight and I shouted for the fun of hearing myself. It wasn't until the shower was over that I saw we had been reprieved, not rescued.

Even so I could not be downhearted, especially when eating for the first time that day. "What do you suppose powered that boat?" I asked between nibbles at my tiny portion of sun-dried meat.

"Some spirit, I reckon, but I wouldn't know which one." Golias scooped water from the bottom of the canoe and swallowed it. "The important thing is that that hooker is heading straight for the Commonwealth. What's more, the wind is taking us right after it."

"At a knot or two an hour," I pointed out. "Do you think you could find us one of those spirits?"

He grinned. "I've got several names, but none of them is Glendower. Never mind that, now that we've got water. If we don't run into a bad storm, we'll make it somehow. Are you ready to swing a paddle again?"

There was only one answer I could give. Now that I had my life back, I wanted to use it. Yet there was more to it than that. Since I had held my own in the fight with the cannibals, I had felt entitled to the good opinion I had forfeited on Aeaea. Once having his esteem, and with it my own, I was not content with less.

"Let's go," I said.

We were too weakened by hunger to be able to paddle long, however. Soon the best we could do was to take watch and watch, keeping the craft headed so it would run with the waves while, by turns, we slept. I had dreaded another blistering day, but needlessly. The sun was hot enough to warm the wind and no more. Better yet, a three-foot turtle bit on our line.

Then I saw something. Taking off the carapace, Golias wedged it in the bow of the dugout. Our goat's meat was gone, but a fold of the skin in which it had been wrapped still held the flint chip and some tinder. Whittling one of the extra paddles, he now made fire again, using the shell as a hearth. Then he roasted strips of turtle meat over the small blaze.

The rich meat, just a few minutes away from being alive, was fuel in the tank. The immediate effect was to make us more lethargic, but by the next day our strength had returned. My nicks and scratches had all but healed in the salt air. Sunburn had ceased to bother me. The stiffness brought on by paddling had gone out of my shoulders. My hands were developing protective calluses.

Altogether I felt fine. Moreover, my well-being either generated confidence or I had absorbed from my companion his faith that we would make a landfall.

"What will you do when we get ashore?" I wondered that afternoon.

Behind me I heard Golias, now paddling stern, whistle a few bars. "After we've found out whom we've got to lick to keep alive?" he asked at length. "There's no judging in advance. It depends on whether your course is plotted by chance, by choice, or by oracle, you see."

I didn't. "Well, you know the country," I said. "Where will you head for when you get there, for instance? You must have something in mind."

"Have you?" he countered.

"Of course," I snorted. "As soon as I can make my way to a port of any consequence, I'll look up the American consul and—" I fell silent. The phrase to complete my sentence was "tell him I want to go home." About to say it, I had stopped for the realization that there was nothing to which I especially wished to return.

"No, maybe I won't," I said. "If I can get along all right where we're going, I had just as soon be there." I wasn't used to optimism, but I took a sip of it. "Perhaps I'll like it better."

"You will like it, and you will hate it," he assured me. "It doesn't matter, for it's living."

Turning to tell him that it did matter to me, I

peered beyond him. At college I had been a crew man. They were a long ways off, but I knew oars in rhythm when I saw them.

"There must have been another wreck," I said. "Somebody's rowing ashore."

"That's no life boat," Golias declared. "Too big. It's Argo, maybe, or Prydwen. No, not that either," he corrected himself. "There's another, and another over there."

One by one, in the handsome fashion of well-rowed boats, they legged it out of the distance. At the end of five minutes twenty odd were in sight. Golias had the right of it. They were bigger than anything I had ever seen moved with oars.

"One of them ought to be good for a ride," I said. "It looks like our troubles are over."

"Or swapped in for new ones," Golias suggested. "H-m-m, asks, if I know anything about shipping. Well, it may not take long, but it shouldn't be dull."

We couldn't have avoided their notice even if we had wanted to. The lead ship was headed right for us, with the others winged out to the right and left behind. For their size they didn't have much freeboard, though they curved high forward and aft. There was a mast in each vessel, but in spite of the fair wind they weren't using sails.

We both faced about, holding the canoe pretty much in place, while the first ship, light riding, approached. The bow ended in a carving of something that looked like a cross between a snake and an alligator. It swooped to within just so many yards, then the rowers rested on their oars. The timing was so good that the ship glided even with us and no farther.

I would have taken more interest in the boat if I hadn't been so busy examining those aboard it. Of most of them I could see no more than shaggy heads peering between a series of painted discs strung along the gunwale. A cluster of men stood in the stern, however, visible from the waist up. All were big boned, most of them with blond or reddish hair. Hatless, they wore short-sleeved leather tunics, snugged with belts from which hung long hunting knives. It was curious to see gold bracelets on such a hard-looking crew. Rings, too, were plentiful.

The tallest of the lot, who incidentally wore the most jewelry, spoke after looking us over. Unlike the rest he had black hair, twisted in braids so long that the ends were tucked under his belt.

"Whose men are you?" he demanded, getting a grip on his beard.

"Who asks?" Golias returned. He was polite about it, but he was clearly making a point of order.

The fellow sharpened his voice a little. "Brodir Hardsark, master of this fleet."

"Sir," Golias said, "as things stand, we haven't got a land, much less a lord."

"At least you have names, I hope."

From the way Golias smiled I knew he had deliberately left the opening. "Our only possessions, Brodir. Mine's Widsith, and my friend here is called Shandon—Shandon Silverlock."

"We're traveling in the same direction you are," I hinted as Brodir turned his eyes on me.

"You mean returning to shore?" He pointed west as he spoke.

I shook my head. "The only shore we've seen so far was in the other direction."

That made him look disappointed. "If you've come from the east, too, you can't tell me anything."

He was turning with the evident intention of giving orders to his rowers when Golias spoke up again. "I can tell you one thing." he offered. "When a man hides his sails from a good wind, he doesn't want to be seen. Do you attack—or run?"

Brodir laughed, but he threw up his head. "Attack," he said, "for a kingdom and a woman."

"Worth it," Golias agreed, and dived overboard. As he surfaced, he whisked his head toward me. "Hit the water, Shandon! Come on!"

He was crawling up the looms of two oars before I had decided that at all costs I didn't want to be alone. The oarsmen let me follow him over the side, but they didn't answer my words of appreciation. Plumbing the cold curiosity in their eyes, I was aware that I might have forced myself upon enemies. It all depended on what Brodir might say. Golias was already standing before him, awaiting judgment. Gingerly I trod the catwalk between the port and starboard rowers until I had reached the platform astern. Brodir was angry, but hadn't quite made up his mind.

"In my ship," he pointed out, "I say who comes aboard. Are you spies or only fools?"

"We're just shipwrecked men," I explained. "All we want is to get ashore."

"If you can't keep your ship, drown," he advised. "You'll wish you did before you cluttered my deck."

Golias was not as impressed as I. "Since when," he asked, "have ring givers like Brodir Hardsark turned away skalds?"

"Oh, you're *that* Widsith—or you say you are. I'll find out." Because he was partially softened toward Golias, Brodir had that much more rage to spare for me. "How about you, Silverlock, or whatever your name is? Talk while you can."

"I've seen him kill," Golias volunteered. He touched the streak of hair by which he had nicknamed me. "He has the mark of Odin; and look at him. Where you're going you'll need men like that."

"I've seen big chunks of men no better in a fight than so much dog meat," Brodir commented. While speaking he put his hand on me like a man sizing up stock.

At that my annoyance conquered both nervousness and discretion. "Look here, Mr. Hardsark," I told him. "I'm not asking for anything. I can work my passage. Put me at an oar, and I'll show you."

Golias gave me a look in which relief was diluted with warning. "Are you good?"

"I may not be good at much," I said, extending my irritation to him for the moment, "But I can row. I was bow at Wisconsin for three years, and we ate 'em up at Poughkeepsie the last two."

"At Poughkeepsie!" Golias echoed, although it's probably that he had never heard of the place if he hadn't heard of Chicago. "You've got a hand, Brodir."

The latter was mollified but not yet ready to show it. He turned to one of those grouped around us.

"Have him row where I can watch him," he directed.

There were a pair of rowers at each oar. At a word the outside man made way for me at number two. As I took my place I glanced at the some thirty oars which would take their beat from mine. After that I didn't look around again. My eyes were on the outside man at stroke, a blond husky with a scar on his shoulder. A fellow standing beside Brodir yelled, and we all bent forward.

The ship was not a shell, and the sweep I was helping to man was no featherweight. On the other hand we weren't called on either to sprint or change the beat. Once I had got used to the absence of a sliding seat, I knew I could handle the assignment. After about ten minutes I sneaked a glance at Brodir and saw that he was no longer paying any attention to me. I was a member of the crew.

By that time I was enjoying myself. Of all sports rowing offers the least to outward seeming. It is hard work unleavened by variety. Worse, a man attending to business can't see where he's going. The pleasure compensating for this madness is at once simple and subtle. A need of men, generally denied them, is to feel a part of something which works smoothly and well. In a mated crew the ideal is reached, the feeling of perfection passing back and forth from the individual to the team like an electric current. Until exhaustion breaks the spell, there is no more to be desired.

In time I was so sure of myself that I could listen to the conversation of those loitering in the stern. I hoped to learn more of where we were going; but I heard nothing of interest until a man cried:

"Ships to starboard, Brodir! Way yonder."

A pause allowed time for Brodir to look them over. "That will be Sigtrygg," he said finally. "He's on time, but the fool's still got his sails up." He was silent for a time, apparently still watching. "Ah, there they go. Now where's that fellow who claims he's a skald?"

There had been a crap game going on for some time, and Golias must have staked his knife to get in it. More than once I heard him praying to the dice. Now, glancing up as I heard him called, I saw that his zeal had been blessed. He wore a leather tunic and carried a feathered helmet, as he reported to Brodir.

"Sir?" he said with military crispness.

"The man who owns those ships," the other told him, "is a king. I'm not yet; but I aim to be, and I want to practice. So I'm not going to follow him ashore, I'm going to lead him. That's not just show, either, for the first ashore gets the best spot to bivouac."

"So?" Golias prompted him.

"In a couple of hours we'll raise land against the sunset, but we'll be still outside their sight. We'll wait till full dark, then go in and thread the harbor. We're going to be first, and I want a song that'll make the men lift the boat out of the water. Start thinking of one."

"Have you a harp aboard?" Golias asked.

Brodir grinned, not too nicely. "The skald we started out with kept singing about women and other things apt to make the men homesick. I threw his harp after him. I thought maybe he could use it as a raft."

"You'll have your song," Golias promised; and

a few minutes later I heard him back at the dice game.

I was ready to rest when the word came to trail oars. As I sat twisting my shoulders to work out the soreness, I felt a slap between them.

"Here," a voice said. "Water's all we get, but it's damp."

Turning, I saw my oarmate holding out a leather bag with a nozzle on it. The water was warm and foul, but I needed it.

"That really wasn't the first time you had your hands on an oar," the fellow observed. He was a young, reckless-looking guy with light brown hair and a scar running out of one corner of his mouth.

Wiping my chin with my forearm, I grinned appreciation. "Never in such fast company," I said. In point of fact my pace hadn't been tried yet, but I was feeling good. I had worked well with these men, and they with me. I found myself wanting them to like me. "Are they going to feed us before we push this tub any farther? By the way, the name's—"

"Shandon Silverlock," he took me up. "I heard you talking to Brodir. How'd you get wrecked?"

Several others listened in, while I told as much as I wanted to of what had happened to me. Meanwhile salt fish and hard bread were distributed to be wolfed while we talked. Then, by order, the group broke up. We would have to start rowing again shortly, and Brodir wanted us to shake out the kinks before we returned to the benches. Working my way to the bow, I found Golias there, staring at the land.

I looked, too, though there wasn't anything to

be seen but a blur against the afterglow. "Is that the Commonwealth?"

"Yes, but I don't know what part except that we're probably somewhere north of Ever After Peninsula. Maybe I should know Brodir, but I can't place him." Abruptly he stopped frowning and chuckled. "I won us some armor and weapons. Brodir would have given us some, but I wanted to be sure we had the best, not somebody's castoffs."

It took me a moment to see just what he meant. "Look here," I then said, "we're not in this, whatever it is. I'm willing to work my way, but I'm going to jump ship as soon as we hit port. Why should I fight for Brodir? I don't even like the son of a bitch."

I had the discretion to speak low, and Golias' retort was no more than a murmur. "We'll take our chances fighting, because we won't have a chance at all, if we don't. If they saw us trying to get away, they'd be sure we were spies." He gripped my arm to be sure he was impressing me. "I don't know Brodir, but I do, too. He wasn't fooling when he threatened us. Where he can't get men to do his will, he'll murder."

It didn't take much thought for me to see that Golias knew what he was talking about. "I guess we're in it," I agreed, "though I may not last very long." I wasn't happy and didn't try to look it. "Our boys haven't got guns. Will there be guns against us?"

"No."

"Well, that's something. But what do I do? I don't know anything."

"It's an axe for you, then," he decided. "Luckily

you've got the build for it. I won us two swords, but I'll see if I can swap one of them for an axe."

He left me brooding until Brodir roared at us, ordering us back to the benches. Shuffling along the catwalk, I saw the rowers slipping on tunics and pullovers of linked metal. They were more talkative than they had been and betrayed their excitement by kidding each other and laughing a lot. The scene reminded me of a veteran crew in a locker room just before a race they felt sure of winning. It made me feel better, and I was able to put a smile on my face when one of the men I had had chow with hailed me. "Plant your butt, Silverlock. I thought maybe you'd run out on us."

"Didn't anybody give you a byrnie?" my oar-mate, Skeggie, demanded. "Or are you one of those goofy berserkers?"

I didn't know whether I was or not, but Golias joined us in time to answer for me. He plumped an armful of cloth, leather, and metal down between us.

"Here's his gear, but it's new to him. Different from the armor he's used to, you know. Show him how to put it on while I go for his axe, will you?"

My ignorance caused amusement, but I felt more at ease with steel rings between my torso and anyone who might want to poke a sword at it. Ready to take my seat, I cast one more look at the Commonwealth, now no more than a black streak against the fading ruddiness of the sky. Inescapably, knowing there were hostile forces awaiting us, I felt angered as I looked. Men were there who wanted to throw me and my new fellows back into the sea; and I felt that I had had enough of the water. Unconsciously I spoke my mind.

"If they shove us around, they're going to have to try hard."

"Man talk," a voice barked in my ear. I turned to find myself looking at Brodir. He was smiling approbation, wearing a likeable look which took me by surprise. "How's that byrnie?" he asked, slapping my metal pullover. "Is it too tight?"

"No," I assured him.

"And that axe now?" he went on. "If it's too light or heavy, we'll get you another one."

Golias had told the others that the clothes were new to me, but I didn't have to admit I didn't know anything about the weapons. I hefted the axe knowingly.

"It feels just about right."

"It's in good hands," Brodir said, and turned away. While he strolled between the benches, quizzing others, my mind followed him warmly. He wasn't a bad fellow after all. He knew a good man when he saw one, and he was counting on me.

"Seems like a pretty good guy," I remarked to Skeggi.

He nodded carelessly. "The old man's a fine one to follow, if you don't care where you're going."

The evening star hung over where the sun had disappeared when Brodir finished his check-up. "You there, Widsith," he called as he climbed to the half deck astern. "Got that song ready?"

"Any time you want it."

Golias stepped forward, and Brodir flung an arm around his shoulders. "None of those blasted kennings that nobody but the maker or a half-wit can understand," he cautioned.

"It's honest," Golias promised. "Start 'em row-ing."

The stroke oarsmen leaned forward, and I was one with them. We took it slow and short until the ship was sliding through the water, then we reached farther. It was then that Golias started to sing.

East of Agamemnon was a city he had sacked,
West of him his heart went home to Greece.
Good and ill wear each mask which never can be cracked;
He raced from what he thought was war to what he thought was peace.
He was cuckold by his cousin, and he'd find his death blow,
But he made them burn the thole pins, and still he called them slow—
He made them brace and bend their backs and row, ho, ho!

East of Ingcel One-eye were his kin without their lives,
Westward was a chance to square the loss.
Men will win and men will lose, and only Wyrd survives;
He aimed his fleet for Eriu and flitted it across.
He would conquer mighty Conaire, but that he couldn't know,
He only knew that he must strike and he must not be slow—
He made them brace and bend their backs and row, ho, ho!

It was too dark to see Golias' face when my head

came up for the pull. The disembodied voice
came out of the night and took charge of us. Stroke
oar lifted the beat, and we followed suit heartily.
Golias knew what was what; and I put care from
me. To man, never absent from danger, disaster
was where it was found. Meanwhile I, who had no
purpose except escaping the sea, had a positive
course. It was no bad thing.

> East of O. van Kortlandt all the world was traced
> and known,
> West of him the land leapt off the map.
> Luck or loss, the dice won't speak till after they
> are thrown;
> He stowed his gear and stepped aboard and
> dared Ginnunga Gap.
> He would come back to Communipaw, but that
> just happened so;
> He turned from men to mystery and did not
> travel slow—
> He made them brace and bend their backs and
> row, ho, ho!

I liked van Kortlandt's style. That was the thing
to do. Take a chance and see what you come up
with. Granted, some pressure had been needed to
steer me right, but that's what I was doing now. I
wondered just how much of a kingdom Brodir
was scheming to snatch. Maybe it would be
worthwhile to stay with him, especially as I was
lucky enough to be in his ship. I had seen enough
of politics to know that the best place to be is in
the boss's eye. He had already noticed me, and I
might do all right.

Golias sang the above stanzas, together with

some others, over and over until our beat was fixed at the fastest we could maintain. By then we couldn't change it of our own volition. We could only slow when exhausted, like worn machinery. I was beginning to think that was bound to happen, when the ship jarred on bottom.

"Pull!" Brodir shouted. "Once more, and peak oars!"

We had landed on the Commonwealth.

V

❧ A Day and A Night ❧

WE WENT OVER the side under arms, but wading ashore turned out to be a peaceful business. In place of anchoring, we dragged the ships up the beach out of reach of the tide. Forming ranks then, we marched to our bivouac on high ground. Brodir or some guide he had detailed had been there before and knew exactly where to go. As we had beaten both Sigtrygg and another ally called Sigurd there, we had the choice of place.

Brodir was pleased with himself and with us. To show his appreciation he served a grog called mead, double portions to oarsmen. It was a brew to take your head off, drinking for the fun of it, but after hours of hard rowing it was balm. Relaxed, I prepared to bed down, which wasn't complicated. We had sleeveless cloaks to serve as blankets; shields if we wanted pillows. I for one slept well, if not long enough. They roused us while the roosters were still clearing their throats.

It was damp dawn with mist rising all around us. Nobody had much to say, but the word was that the enemy was expected. Chilled, sleepy, stiff, and hungry as I was, this seemed the least of many evils.

"If those bastards are coming," I grumbled, "why the devil couldn't they have come along and killed me before I waked up?"

Skeggi slapped a horned helmet on his head and let it sit crooked. "Come on," he croaked. "We've got to find where they're dishing out breakfast. If I don't get my share, I'll start the killing myself."

Food restored us to purpose. It was still too early in the day to laugh, but we stopped bellyaching. Between mouthfuls we speculated on how soon action would begin, whether we would attack or defend the hill we were on, what the relative strength of the armies would be, and more of the same. Nobody bragged, but we were husky men taking strength from one another. Nobody was apprehensive, even I who should have been.

After the meal we formed by boat crews to receive instructions. Thereafter time slowed down while we waited for the mist to lift so we could see what we were up against. It was only then that I had leisure to wonder what I was going to do with the three-foot axe I held in my hand. Resembling a symbol for civics without the rods around it, it was sharp and well balanced. It was a dangerous weapon in the hands of a skilled man; and there would be practiced men, presumably, swinging just such tools at me. I gave much attention to my shield yet came to no conclusions. Made of hide and wood studded with rivets, it was strong. But was it strong enough to withstand an axe with, say, two hundred pounds behind it?

While I was fidgeting over that important problem, Golias joined me. Once I had thought him strange, but now he was my only landmark.

"How are things going, pardner?" I yawned to show how nonchalant I felt. "When's this thing going to start anyhow?"

He wasn't fooled. "Look, Shandon, I won't be able to be with you; Brodir wants me out front. You're new to this, but you're strong and quick. If you strike first, you're apt to miss and lay yourself open. Give your attention to guarding, and hold your axe for the counter stroke. When a man has struck—always providing he doesn't nail you—is when he's most ready for dissection."

"How about these shields?" I put my question to him. "Are they strong enough?"

"No defense is ever strong enough," he said, "but they'll shed most blows and break the force of others. It'll cover you well enough, if you keep your place in line. Hold shield lock at all costs."

"Thanks," I nodded. "You take care of yourself, too."

He had been speaking in a low voice, but now he barely murmured. "If we lose, don't wait around to surrender. Clear out, move fast, and keep going."

This was the first time anybody had hinted at the possibility of defeat. I was startled.

"You don't think we're coming out on top?"

"I don't know," he answered, "but it's always one of two chances. If we win, that's one thing. If we don't, it's every man for himself."

Men started shouting orders, and Golias talked

faster. "If things go sour here, I'll meet you at Heorot—H - E - O - R - O - T—in two weeks. I know where we are now, for I remember passing through here on my way to the Second Battle of Moytura. Heorot's southeast, on a bight the other side of the Boss of Arden. Don't follow the shore line, though; it's too dangerous. If you get there first, wait around, and I'll do the same."

"It's a deal," I said. I wanted to ask more specific directions, but Skeggi was roaring my name. Hurriedly I took my place beside him.

A moment later the mist left us. The ground we stood on rose above the estuary where we had landed. It was not such a hill as I had imagined it to be, though there were hills not far away. Between them and our lines there was a plain of sorts. Mostly it was well-cropped grazing land, but there were patches of woods, outliers to the forest beyond. An excited murmur ran along our ranks, though not in appreciation of the scenery. Men were drawn up before a great grove not a half-mile away.

They had been waiting as quietly as ourselves, but they waited no longer. Neither did we. The instinct was to rush, but under Brodir's eyes we kept the pace down.

"Walk and hold your line!" he shouted. "I'll kill the first man who breaks shield lock."

I knew that I wasn't going to be that man, and not just out of fear of him. Knowing that someone stood on either side of me, helping to guard me, gave me a confidence I would not otherwise have had.

Of the three allied groups Brodir's formed the left wing. Our crew was directly behind him and a picked vanguard, of which Golias was one. As we lined up by rowing benches, the two stroke oarsmen were on my right. One of them locked shields with me on that side, while Skeggi did so on my left. There was one supporting rank and a reserve group following at a distance.

At every step we took I felt better. Who was to stop us or break us? Thinking they knew, the enemy suddenly came on the double. I had been wondering how I would act, but when the time came I had no leisure to wonder. There was then but one thing to do, and that was to destroy to keep from being destroyed. Shortening my grip, I crouched behind my shield, holding my axe hand cocked and trying to remember what Golias had told me.

First they broke against Brodir and the van. Splitting on that rock, they whirled into us. There was lots going on, but my eyes picked out a rangy, red devil. He wasn't headed for me; but a fatal instinct told me he would veer, and he did. He didn't have armor, just a shield, and a sword longer than his gorilla arm. As he leaped in, he caught my eye and laughed, knowing we were for each other as surely as I did. Then his sword came down out of the air. It took a corner off my shield, but the blade was deflected. The hand which held it was exposed, and I took it off above the wrist.

I don't know what happened to the fellow beyond Skeggi, but after a while there was a different one there, stepped up from the rear rank. Then we were moving forward, as they backed away to reorganize. To cover their retreat they threw spears. One of them went through the thigh of the man on my right, causing him to drop out.

In spite of heavy casualties, I thought we had them. So did Brodir. He let us break shield lock, so we could follow faster, and was himself the first to smash through their disintegrating ranks. It surely looked like we had the battle in the bag. Wrecking this wing, we would be able to outflank the center.

Undoubtedly we could have done so except for one thing. Fresh enemy troops, as many again as those we were in the act of defeating, rushed out of a patch of woods towards which we had been sucked.

I will say for Brodir that he was just about as tough as he thought he was. I happened to be close behind him in the pursuit, and he was killing with the easy precision of a stockyard slaughterer. He was probably the second best man in our part of the field. The trouble was that the best man was leading the counterattack.

Brodir went down when they met. His armor must have been good, for he bounced to his feet. He lost the second round, too, then I temporarily lost track of him.

We were too few to fight and too tired to run from fresh men. I owe my life to the fact that my foot slipped in some blood. The hostile line passed over me, leaving me no more than some bruises. When they had gone on, I saw Brodir getting to his feet once more. He made for some woods flanking the field to our left. I followed him, and so did a few dozen others who had survived the attack by luck or playing possum. The enemy was sweeping on to crush our reserve and let us go.

Skeggi had fallen, but Golias came through. We

didn't speak, though; nobody spoke for a while except to himself. We made it to the edge of the woods, then, finding we were not harried, stayed there. Hidden in the shadows, we watched haggardly to see if our allies could do what we had failed to do.

We saw nothing to give us hope. Our center was retreating. We couldn't see our right wing, but the very fact that it was hidden by the center showed it had been pushed back. A half-hour later the battle had broken down into group engagements, where detachments of our men were dying under the blows of ten times their number.

While the rest of us cursed, fidgeted, and licked our wounds, Brodir was still as a snake, never taking his eyes from what was going on. Now he sprang up.

"On your feet!"

The rest of us stared at him, seeing nothing to do. "The shieldburg yonder," he explained. "We can break through it."

I had noticed the guard in front of the grove where the enemy headquarters was apparently located. Although the battle never came near them, the men had stood shield to shield throughout. With victory a certainty, however, their commander must have given them "rest." They lounged in careless groups, watching the mopping up.

"Now's the time. Now!" Brodir insisted. "They've won, but we can't let them have everything. Am I going alone?"

"No, we can't let them have everything," Golias agreed. We all felt that way and got to our feet. We didn't expect to get out of that hostile district, and we wanted something in exchange for our lives. It was all there was left to matter.

The distance must have been around five hundred yards, but nobody intercepted us. A small, disciplined detachment, marching behind the battle lines, was assumed to be friendly. Some members of the guard glanced our way but turned again to watch what remained of the action. We got to within a hundred yards of them, then sixty, then forty.

"Jump 'em!" Brodir barked, and set us the example.

We were under full steam before they comprehended. They fell all over each other, trying to find their places and get set. They didn't have a chance. We burst through them, killing a few, and swept into the headquarters they had failed to defend.

My recollection of the moment is a mosaic of horrified men, their mouths open, scrambling for weapons and running to intercept us. The few who did were unlucky. My own axe split one of them.

A single man among them was not confused. He had been standing by himself and, alone of us all, remained still. My eyes, keyed to take their last look at things, saw the whole and placed its parts. This man did not move, because he was the focal point. Without ever changing his course, Brodir was driving toward him. All the men who futilely flung themselves in our path did so with him in mind.

He was an old man, who knew what he had accomplished, why he had done it, and what it had cost him. He knew his position in the action of the moment, too. A slight smile wrinkled his crow feet as he awaited us. For a moment I looked upon greatness, then Brodir slew it. At the last instant a youngster lunged near enough to throw an arm in the way of the sword. One blow took off that arm and the old man's head.

We had seen to it that they had a victory they wouldn't celebrate. Now we began to pay. First there were enough men to slow us, then we could hardly move at all. We fought our way into a thicket, but men had been running to cut us off. We could go no farther and locked shields.

That patch of high brush was a fortress, as those who followed us in found out. We killed so many that they let us alone, contenting themselves with seeing that we didn't escape. Shortly I heard the sound of wood being chopped, though it didn't make as much noise as voices telling newcomers of the disaster.

"Brian's dead!"

"My God! No!"

"But he couldn't be! We won!"

"We did, eh? All right, you put his head back on."

The man had said they won expressed the feeling of all of them. Something had happened which was so unbelievable that it was unfair. Listening, grimly, I wanted to rub salt into their wound, but I was too parched to yell.

I had known they weren't simply waiting around for us to die, of course. My first knowledge of just what they were up to came when a tree fell. It crashed down among us, pinning men down and breaking our shield wall. Within a few minutes several others fell upon us, and we were done for. Those of us who weren't killed or maimed were trapped in the snarl of branches, unable to flee or fight.

They came after us, pulling us out like flies out of a spider web. Crouched under a fallen trunk, I saw them get Brodir, not three feet away from me. He was the one they wanted. The lynch mob gathered. Interest in the rest of us was temporarily lost, and, leaving my axe where it was, I started crawling.

The next tree, a huge one, was hollow. The opening had not originally been big enough to admit a man, but the fall had enlarged it. It wasn't much of a hiding place, but there was no other. I squeezed inside and worked my way up as far as I could go. For the first half-hour I took it for granted that I would be found. When nothing happened, I relaxed. Next exhaustion put me to sleep.

There was no sound of men stirring about when I waked. After waiting long enough to feel sure that wasn't a temporary condition, I slithered cautiously out. The sun had gone down. Nobody was to be seen in the grove, through I could now hear disturbing noises from the direction of the battlefield. As quietly as possible I stole to a point whence I could look forth. All corpses had been removed to the open, and for a reason. The noises which had alarmed me came from scavengers, much too well fed to bother to scratch around in the woods for food. There were buzzards, and crows, croaking and screaming in their satisfaction, as they hopped from one cadaver to another. Wolves were snarling good-humoredly as they tore men apart, but that wasn't the hardest thing to look at. Old women were ranging the field, beating the carrion birds off with sticks, so that they could frisk the dead.

It was clear that I could leave when I was ready. Withdrawing to the opposite side of the grove, I fumbled for my field rations. Before we went into battle we had each been given two heavy slices of rye bread with a hunk of cheese in between. In the pocket of my leather tunic this sandwich had suffered overheating and compression. The cheese had lost its identity in the pores of the bread, but, in spite of my thirst, I managed to down the crumbly mass.

Meanwhile I was deciding what to do when darkness offered me concealment. I knew the lay of the land in only one direction; but I certainly wasn't going to recross that battlefield and risk seeing buzzards battening on Skeggi or Golias. Thinking of the latter caused me to remember the last conversation we had had. His instructions had called for heading south and east, which I could do without again seeing the scene of our defeat.

With the aid of the pole star I kept my course until I found a dirt road. To my right were the lights of a town, doubtless the one where my enemies were billeted. I turned left. It wasn't exactly my chosen direction, but I decided to worry about that later. My object was to escape trouble by getting out of range of patrols on the lookout for foreigners who couldn't explain their presence. I had kept my knife, but without my axe, shield, helmet, and byrnie I didn't look any more militant than I now felt.

The road was unpeopled and soon entered the

forest. After a while I felt secure enough about the present to think of the past and the future.

Gradually desolation came upon me. They were good, ready fellows that I had rowed and fought with. I had got on well with them; even Brodir I had come to like. Now they were dead, and I did not know that I was happy about outliving them. A man had to make the effort, or he couldn't help making it, given the chance; but I wished I hadn't found that hollow tree. In the shield wall I had felt an interchange of trust such as I had never known. Grieving, I felt I had deserted Skeggi and the rest where they had been faithful to me.

As for Golias, he had apparently been confident he would survive. I didn't believe he had, yet as soon as I got reasonably clear of the district I would act as if I did. It is not enough for a man to leave one place; he must head for another. My tryst with Golias at Heorot, wherever and whatever that was, formed my only future. It was a dismal one. When and if I found Heorot, I would wait around for a man I didn't expect to see. When he didn't show up—well, what then? There was a vacuum on the other side which cowed my mind as well as my spirit.

A wayside spring had relieved my thirst, but I made no other stop until the weight of my thoughts confused my will. Once I had surrendered motion, despond fixed me. After a while I slid off the rock I was perched on, lay down, and rolled over on my face. In time feeling was so narrowed that even hopelessness was squeezed out. I all but was not.

A man is not dead until he ceases to be curious.

Something happened that my mind took note of.
A bird began to sing. With that change I changed,
though sluggisly at first.

The song was no ordinary cheeping. The bird
had technique. It used forty different kinds of
notes and tied them together in logical order. The
third time it went through its repertoire I raised
my head to make sure it was still night. As it was,
the next move was to make sure that what I was
hearing was indeed a bird. At the fifth rendition I
rose and stepped softly into the woods. When I
had gone a few yards, a note was broken in two,
and I heard the flutter of wings.

It might not have affected me so strongly at
another time. Yet even when the mind stands
plumb, it is stunned to find a new fact in a pigeon
hole reserved for something marked "understood." Here, contrary to all my experience, was a
bird singing at night. It generated wonder, which
can't cohabit with despair.

From another perch the bird sang again, more
sweetly for being a little farther off. There was just
enough light under the trees so that, although
things could be seen, nothing quite took form.
Amidst the freshness welling from the ground
there were the scents of wood flowers. An inter-
mittent breeze wafted the heavier scents of a forest
in midsummer. My thoughts were as touch-me-
not as the odors I couldn't name, but I felt that was
no partition between the heart and the joy for
which it searches.

Twice more the bird sang before it flew out of
hearing. It left me quiet in spirit till I made a
disturbing discovery. Walking toward where I

thought the road was, I covered the necessary
distance, then twice that. I was no longer forlorn,
but I was lost.

I was only briefly upset, for I hadn't known
where I was going while on the road either. Still,
in a different mood I might have waited for daylight to help me find the highway. As things
stood, a dreamy fatalism urged me to amble
through Broceliande.

Dawn, I found, was not far off. Soon the trees
had identity but not life. The leaves drooped like
newly hung wash. I kept on, but I could feel the
quiet in the pit of my stomach. As soon as it grew
warm enough to render it pleasant, I meant to lie
down and sleep.

Though not given to nerves, I was so in the grip
of the silence that I jumped when I heard a little
shriek. A girl was running toward me through the
half light. She had mistaken me for somebody
else, for when almost to me she stopped.

"Oh!" she said in a tone expressing both embarrassment and disappointment. "I thought you
were Aucando."

Her hair was around her head like mist around
moonlight; and her figure was a proper stalk for
such a blossom. She was, in fact, just such a girl as
the bird song of the night before had made it seem
possible to meet. I gawked at her before I recovered myself.

"I'm not Aucando," I admitted, "though it must
be fun." As I spoke, I smiled in a way to blunt the
edge of my impudence. It was not only that some
of my brashness toward women had been left behind on Aeaea. There was a quality to this girl
which restrained me from looking wolfish.

She was frightened, though she needn't have been. Even when lechery was in my mind I couldn't be bothered with anyone disinclined to reciprocate. Yet I didn't want her to go away before she had answered some questions.

"Don't worry," I reassured her. "I never make passes before breakfast. By the way, do you know where I could get any?"

Anything that her eyes could tell her she was learning about me. I waited while she made up her mind.

"Are you a pilgrim?" she finally asked.

"I'm not only a pilgrim but a lost one." Naturally I meant to keep my mouth shut about my part in the thwarted invasion. "I strayed off the road in the dark last night, you see, and now I'm just drifting."

"There's no place anywhere near that I know of," she said hesitantly, "but if you're hungry—"

"Very hungry," I interrupted.

"Well, I can give you a little something to eat, if you'll wait a minute. I want to borrow some honey from the bees before they wake up."

The bee tree was not far away. The black hole which betrayed its hollowness looked ominous to me, but I held my ground while she thrust an arm inside. When she withdrew it, she held a sizeable section of honey-comb. There were drowsy bees on it which she lightly brushed off. Then she skipped away—a pace, I confess, behind me.

"That was a neat job," I remarked.

She was pleased at the praise. "They work so hard for it," she laughed, "but they have more than they need, and anyhow honey's much too nice for bugs." She placed the comb in a leaf-lined basket and licked her fingers. "I'm Rosalette."

Everybody else in the Commonwealth seemed to get along with only one name. With relief I shucked the "A. Clarence" I had so long hated.

"Shandon," I said, touching my hair. "Sometimes called Silverlock."

She led me to a lean-to made of boughs and prettily woven with flowers. It stood, I noted, at the junction of seven little-used forest roads.

"Here we are," she stated. "Wait till I milk the goat—which may not belong to me but does—and then I'll be hospitable."

Nobody joined us at our berries, milk, bread, and honey. I considered that fact, the bivouac, and the location.

"Doesn't your husband like breakfast?"

She blushed, but as if I had said something that pleased her. "Do you mean Aucando? He's not my husband yet."

Several questions wanted to be asked, but I picked the most urgent. "You mean to say you actually live out here in the woods alone? But why?"

She took a drink of milk. "They were going to kill me, so I escaped and hid out here."

I could only stare, but she went on of her own accord. "Aucando's father doesn't want me to marry him."

She couldn't have been twenty. Moreover, if I knew anything at all, she was as nice as she looked. The very notion of planned violence to her was preposterous. I was in a passion by the time I found my voice.

"Why that ba—that buzzard! He wants to— well, what's your family doing about it? Or what's little Aucando got to say?"

"He's nearly as big as you are!" she cried. "And stronger—lots stronger." Then she cooled off. "He can't do anything, because his father's the ruler hereabouts."

I brightened. "Never mind how I know, but if his name is Brian, your troubles are over."

"No, that's not the one."

"Is that right?" From the way she talked I was out of Brian's territory—or rather the one his aggrieved subjects might be scouring for strays—which was a relief. "Where's your fiancé now? Can't he get away to join you?"

"Of course. He's in the forest somewhere looking for me this minute."

The whole business of her being there by herself worried me. It seemed to me that there was as good a chance of her being found by those who wanted to kill her as by her sweetheart.

"How many minutes has it been all told?" I persisted.

"Well—three days." Not as confident of being found as she liked to think, she didn't look at me when she said that.

"But suppose," I suggested, "he doesn't happen to pass by this particular spot?"

At that she raised her eyes, and I saw she had already faced that challenge from destiny. "If he doesn't come today," she said, "I'll go looking for him."

VI

⊱ Random Faring ⊰

UNTIL I SAT DOWN TO EAT, I hadn't realized how tired I was. Food started me blinking with drowsiness, and Rosalette was quick to notice.

"Why don't you lie down for a while?" she asked, pointing inside to a balsam-sprig bunk. "You won't be in the way."

In spite of that assurance, I meant to stretch out for just a few minutes. She had treated me right, and I had no intention of usurping her tiny quarters. Looking up at the flowers dotting the roof of the lean-to, I thought of the girl who had put them there. There was the same sure blending of appearance with identity.

Outside I could hear her humming. Finally she put words to the tune.

Seven roads could bring you here;
Seven have betrayed me, dear.
Seven could, and none have done,

Rank imposters every one,
Liars caught in lies, my sweet—
There's no road without your feet.
Where you're not there is no land,
There's no touch without your hand;
Here, I know, is not a place,
For it does not hold your face;
But there's one that I must find
Where you wander, though I'm blind
          Without your eyes.

The voice was sweet, like everything else about her. It soothed me, and I slept.

The forty winks I had intended to take stretched into hours of solid slumber. It was noon before I sat up. The first thing I observed was that the girl's little bundle of belongings was gone. It took me a couple of minutes more to see that a piece of birch bark beside me had letters scratched on it.

"Aucando didn't come, so I'm leaving," the message ran. "The little hut is yours, if you want it. There's bread and honey rolled in the other piece of bark."

The lean-to suddenly felt like a room where someone had died. As I got out of it, I noted that the flowers were already withered. Munching my saccharine sandwich, I looked around.

The seven roads which Rosalette had accused of letting her down still ran inscrutably to no place I could imagine. I kicked myself for not having asked if any of them went in the general direction of Heorot. It hadn't occured to me that I would sleep so late or that she would leave so early.

If the sun hadn't been at zenith, I might have

been able to set a course. As it was, the best I could
decide was that three of the roads probably ran in
a more or less southerly direction. I tried the feel
of all three, without being able to work up a
hunch. On my second round however, I noticed a
blurred footprint which I took to be Rosalette's.
The road might not lead me toward Heorot, but at
least I had some reason for following it. Perhaps I
could catch up with her and give her a hand, if the
going got rough. Or—or just perhaps. Anyhow the
road was better for knowing she was on it.

As I took stock of the wilderness by daylight, I
was all the more impressed by what she had done.
With no observable equipment she had come into
the woods and made herself at home like a sour-
dough. Then she had deliberately set out to sift
big timber for her man.

The road led uphill. The forest through which it
wound was, I should judge, a virgin stand. Mostly
it was hardwoods that threw branches towards
each other at levels of never less than sixty or
seventy feet. Except for birds, squirrels, and a few
deer, I saw nothing but these trees and the trifling
shrubbery in the cool spaces between them, until
the road forked again.

Following Rosalette had been largely a whim
whose strength had petered out. I wasn't a good
enough tracker to find footprints in the leaf-
covered road; but it might have made no difference if I had seen any. One of the roads sloped
downward, suggesting a descent into some valley—the natural locus for a town. That was for
me. My objective was to find a place where I could
somehow get housed, fed, and oriented.

I had gone possibly a quarter of a mile when a

deer sprang across the road just in front of me. Simultaneously I heard an unmistakable buzzing, followed by the sound of a shot. The deer stumbled, and I whirled to vent my wrath on whoever had startled me.

A man with a long, smoking rifle was approaching through the woods. "What's the idea?" I snarled, striding to meet him. "Don't you know enough not to shoot when somebody's near your target? Any fathead who doesn't know any more about handling firearms than that shouldn't be let loose with a popgun."

He was a tall, stringy fellow with a face weathered to match his leather clothes. He had been smiling when I first turned to yell at him, but at my words he stopped. Planting the butt of his piece and draping a fringed buckskin sleeve over the muzzle, he looked at me thoughtfully.

"When a man has trailed a buck for an hour, it's opposing nature to pass up the only shot at it he's likely to get. I'm sorry I scared you, friend."

"Friend, my eye!" I snorted. "You might've hit me."

"But I didn't want to," he said simply.

As my indignation hadn't caused any sparks, my temper was improving, though I wasn't yet ready to admit it. "That's not the point," I told him. "Nobody can be that sure of where he's shooting."

At that it was his turn to look annoyed. "Friend," he retorted, "all I can say is to repeat that it was your good fortune that I didn't have any sights on you. As long as I didn't, you had no cause to worry, even if you'd been only an inch away from being in line with that buck instead of better than a yard. People that know me say I have the gift."

Seeing that I still looked skeptical, he removed his arm from the muzzle. The gun, I was astonished to find, was a flintlock, but he had it loaded and primed in jig time. Then he glanced around.

"Do you see that hawk?" he enquired.

I did see it, a big specimen fifty or more yards away down a forest aisle. Having just swooped on a red squirrel, which it had caught on the ground, the bird was bearing it swiftly aloft. The tail of the little animal waved feebly.

"The squirrel is past saving and won't need his brush," my companion observed as he threw up his gun. In another moment the small tail was falling to the ground while the hawk soared on, unharmed. "I do have the gift," the fellow commented, "and it would be opposing truth for me to say otherwise."

"It sure would," I agreed. "I've seen some pretty good shooting from time to time, but nothing to touch that. What are you, a guide?"

"They call me Pathfinder, friend."

"They call me Silverlock," I matched him. "Pathfinder, eh? Do you happen to know the way to a place called Heorot?"

"He-or-ot." He paused in the act of running a patch through his gun. "It's no name from the Lenape tongue, or that of the Mingoes, either."

"It's supposed to be along the coast."

His face lost its look of concentration. "I was sure it was no name for any of these parts. Never having been to the big sea, I can't help you, friend." Slipping the ramrod into its place be-

neath the barrel, he gripped his weapon at the
balance. "I'd be proud to have you share meat
with me, if you're minded to eat."

Having found honey and berries thin fare for
marching, I welcomed the offer. The road, as it
happened, was between us and the dead deer.
Instead of promptly crossing it, the woodsman
paused to give it a searching glance.

"Nobody's trod it today but you," he said
matter-of-factly.

To my own eyes the way was trackless, and I
couldn't help wondering if he was justified in
being so positive. I continued to wonder about
that while he rapidly skinned the deer, and I
gathered firewood.

"Did you happen to cross the other fork of the
road?" I asked, snapping a fallen branch over my
knee.

Busy skewering the roast he had cut for us, he
didn't look up. "Only one man been along that,
too."

"One *man!*" I thought I had caught him bluf-
fing; though, as he was the fellow with the food, I
didn't put much of a jeer in my voice. "I happen to
know that a woman took one of these two forks."

Ceasing operations, he deliberated. "It could
have been a woman's track," he mused aloud. "I
never thought of that, small though it was, because she was all alone."

He looked at me reproachfully, as he made that
remark. "I didn't have anything to do with the fact
that she's traveling alone," I pointed out. "As a
matter of fact," I went on, giving myself a little
more credit than I deserved, "I'd been following
her, so I could look after her."

His face cleared. "It's the thing for a man to do, and I honor you for it, friend. Now I'll tell you what we'll do. As long as you've already lost time going down the wrong road here, we'll put this chunk of meat aside. I'll wait and eat later, and meanwhile I'll give you a piece of liver, which will broil in a jiffy."

Without confessing myself a heel to a man who took decency for granted, there was no way out of the corner into which I had painted myself. I acknowledged his admiring look with a sickly grin.

"Why—er—thanks," I said. The liver wasn't bad, but I was still thinking glumly of that fine-looking roast, as I backtracked to where the roads joined. In my dismay at what had happened I had neglected to ask Pathfinder where the other fork would take me, so I was walking as blindly as before. Nevertheless, I was walking as fast as I could, for now I was pursuing Rosalette in earnest. Having sacrificed the venison in order to be able to catch up with her, I felt I owed it to myself to do so.

If the brain directs action, action channels the brain. Because it was what I was working at, finding the girl became an absorbing matter. Convinced that I could cover two yards to her one, I began looking for her around every bend in the road. From that state of mind it was a small jump to feeling that the business was a matter of personal importance to me.

Even when she did not soon materialize, I wasn't discouraged. It was drawing toward sundown. Whether she arrived at some habitation or was forced to bivouac, as she had done back at the seven corners, she must shortly halt for the night. What I would say when I joined her was something I hadn't bothered to figure out, though it didn't occur to me that she might resent being followed. Acceptance of my protection on her part was something else I was taking for granted.

I had stopped to drink at a brook when the shrieks and shouting started. There was a terror-stricken woman and at least one man, horrified and infuriated both. Mixed with their cries was a muffled snarling and the sound of crashing underbrush.

As I jumped to my feet, coughing out water that had gone down the wrong way, a living nightmare was drawing near the road. The shrieking went with him, as he sped between the trees, and a glimpse of bright cloth trailing from his mouth told me why. In sick disbelief I rechecked my first impression. There the animal was, and inspection didn't improve it. In running position it was about the length and height of a station wagon. It was also about the same color. I was sloshing through the brook toward it, as I took in the tusks, the scaly tail, and the porthole of an eye. At the same time I added my shout of outraged helplessness to the din.

Why I took the scene so to heart is one of the simplicities of consciousness. I knew but one girl in Broceliande; therefore a girl seen in Broceliande must be the one I knew. Sure Rosalette was the victim, I couldn't be passive. It is now not possible to imagine what I would have done. Luckily I wasn't needed.

Unbalanced as the monster was with the weight of a grown woman in its jaws, it was running

heavily. The man tailing it was gaining in spite of
the fact that he wore overall metal protection. By
the time I was across the stream the beast had
reached the road. At about the same time it decided that it wasn't going to outsprint the pursuer.
It dropped the girl like a dog dropping a stolen
lamb chop.

This jettison was almost too late to do the animal any good. It could not escape and had just
time to turn and defend itself before the man
caught up. Sword against claws the length of railroad spikes, they mixed it while I looked around
for a rock small enough to throw and big enough
to bruise the meat under the scaly hide.

In spite of the disparity in size, it was the man
who took the offensive. Reared back on its hind
legs, the beast was a good twelve feet tall; but
without pausing to look for an opening, the man
threw up his shield and bored in. Howling and
slavering, the monster folded down on top of him
with tusk and talon.

Having found what I wanted, I was lugging it
warily into range, when it was all over. Against
my expectations, the man had more to offer than
the beast was willing to take. Frantically tearing
free, it managed to jump clear over the fellow's
head and bolted back whence it had come. I had
the satisfaction of bouncing my rock off its head,
but didn't even slow it down. Roaring and trailing
an evil stench, it vanished.

About to run to the injured girl, I saw that she
was already being cared for. A second man had
issued from the woods and was giving her attention that was manifestly not impersonal. Discovering, through a glimpse of her dark hair, that the

woman was not Rosalette after all, I came closer. Instead I looked at the man who had done the work.

He had pushed up a shutter in his helmet and was leaning against a tree. By the way he grinned, I saw he wasn't hurt. While I waited for him to get his wind back, I sat down on a deadfall, only then realizing how scared I had been. He was the first to speak. "Many thanks for your timely aid."

That was nice of him, but I wasn't having any. "You had him cold. I was just throwing pop bottles from the bleachers." Just the same I had tried, and I was glad that he had noticed. "That was a nice piece of in-fighting you did."

He smiled. "Oh, those things aren't as dangerous as they look, once you've had a little experience with them."

I thought that statement over. "Are there many more like that in this neck of the woods?"

Busy wiping his sword with some leaves, he nodded. "There have always been monsters in the forest, though not all like that. Some are bigger."

"The devil, you say!" Yet it wasn't solely on my own account that his statement made me nervous. "You haven't met a girl—another girl, I mean—along this road, have you?"

His look this time was one of commiserative understanding. "No, but I've been faring across country, not along the road. Has your lady been abducted?"

"Nothing like that, and she isn't my lady." He was giving me more sympathy than I wanted. "I'm just sort of a friend of hers," I explained, growing more embarrassed as I did so, "and well—well, the woods is no place for her."

"I know." He clicked his tongue. "But it's been my experience that you can't keep them out of it." Giving his sword a final polishing, he sheathed the weapon. "Shall we go over and see how this poor maiden is getting along?"

"Which way are you heading from here?" I asked, as I fell into step beside him.

I had been hoping that his direction would be my own, but he pointed into the forest. "As soon as I get back to my horse, I'm riding on that beast's track." He spoke matter-of-factly and had a look to match. "Those things shouldn't be allowed to live, you know."

He was so right that any direct comment seemed out of the question. I let it ride for a few paces.

"It seems to me you've already done your part where this one's concerned," I then ventured.

"Put a part on a pedestal, and it's still nothing more than a part," he smiled. We had reached the other two, and he changed his tone.

"This lady isn't seriously harmed, I hope?"

The man addressed, a youngster, raised a wretched face. "She hasn't come to," he said.

"She still breathes, and her pulse is good," my companion declared after a brief examination. "If you can—"

"Here come a couple of people," I interrupted him. "One of them's a woman, too."

"She'll give you the help you need. The shelter also, for undoubtedly they live near here." My new acquaintance and I both had the feeling of being relieved of a responsibility that would interfere with our own projects. "I'll be on my way then."

While not as anxious as he to venture on alone, I had determined to do so. "Do you happen to know where this road goes? By the way, I'm Shandon."

"The name is Calidore." He shook his head, as he removed his steel glove to take my hand. "I know nothing of that road, but it will soon bring you to some castle, I should think."

He was starting toward his horse, but I had one more question. "Will there be any place to spend the night?"

He looked puzzled, then decided I was in earnest. "At the castle," he called back. "You'll get the best of hospitality, and you may well find the lady you seek there."

As I proceeded, the forest was not the pleasant, green place it had been. Having seen one of the resident monsters, I heard another every time a branch snapped. They watched me from the deepening shadows. Their snarls came down the wind which sprang up.

At first my sustaining purpose was the hope of joining and convoying Rosalette. When dusk drew near, however, I had to conclude that if I did see her that night, it would be only after she had already found comfort and protection in some household along the way. No doubt, indeed, she was eating a fine meal while I still struggled, worn and empty, through a dark, beast-haunted wood.

Thus my sympathies shifted from her to myself. There had to be a new goal in keeping with my new conception of the state of affairs. A choice of two was offered. Deliverance from evil would come either when I stepped clear of the forest or when I saw the castle Calidore had mentioned. I chose the second as the most probable. In time my

mind became so engaged with it that I was sure of
the castle's existence. Calidore hadn't exactly
guaranteed it was there, but he knew the ropes. In
his expert opinion it should be no more than a few
miles off.

Unwilling to halt, I was tired out by twilight.
But no matter how hard I pushed myself the castle
failed to materialize. This did't make me despondent. As I had it in my mind that the building
was bound to be somewhere near, I was exasperated instead.

I was, in fact, in a bad humor generally. It annoyed me to be jittery. Failing to find Rosalette
was a disappointment. Then my feet hurt, my
muscles ached, and I was gone in the stomach.

"Hold it!" a voice ordered. "Grip your tracks!"
A man had sprung out from behind a great sugar
maple just ahead of me; a man who laughed when
he saw me jump. That was all that was necessary.
At last my anger had a concrete object of a size to
cope with.

"Are you talking to me or do you just like to
yell?" While I was speaking, I moved forward to
show my unconcern.

He stopped laughing. "You'd better do what
you're told," he said.

He was a well set-up fellow dressed in a green
jacket and tights. Incongruously for such a rugged
customer, he wore a little hat with a feather in it.
I couldn't see his face too clearly, but clearly
enough to measure the distance to his chin. He
carried a long stick but had made the mistake of
letting me inside its range.

"Look, mister;" I said to him, "this road has
room for two-way traffic; but if you can't see it that
way, get off and let me by."

"I may let you go on," he retorted with a calmness which further infuriated me, "but not until I find out a few things."

"Such as what?"

"Oh, where you're headed and whether you've got anything I could use."

Without lifting my feet, I inched nearer. "I guess I've got at least one thing you could use," I muttered.

At this suggestion of compliance he took one hand from the stick and thrust it out, snapping the fingers. "We'll see. Turn around and—"

He didn't finish, because I grabbed his hand with my left and uppercut him as I jerked him nearer. He was still falling when my own feet were pulled out from under me.

Rolling when I hit the ground, I crouched. Nobody attacked me, though a pair of legs straddled the earth not a foot away. Looking up and up, I found the top. The man could not have been less than seven feet tall, and he was built like the Cardiff Giant. What I could see of his face looked hard, but his voice was not ill-humored.

"Would you rather talk it over?"

There were six or eight men surrounding me in addition to him—all of him. No one interfering, I rose and dusted myself off.

"All right," I sulked, "but I haven't got anything but an appetite."

"You ain't the only one," he informed me.

VII

❧ Under the Leaves ❧

INSTEAD OF SEARCHING ME on the spot, they led me off the road. Above us branches from trees fifty feet apart interlocked. The gloom could only be told from night because colors were still more or less distinguishable. We weren't on a path, but we hustled along as if late for the office.

Most of my captors seemed to be in a genial mood. They were talking and joking among themselves, and there was a certain amount of horseplay. It made me feel better, even if I couldn't share their high spirits. That doesn't mean I was glad to go with them; but I didn't try to make a break for it, either. For one thing, aside from the fact I was too tired, that seven-footer had a grip on my arm.

After a while he imitated the whippoorwill. He was answered from somewhere ahead, and soon I could hear human voices from the same direction. About the same time I caught a glimpse of light.

In a minute more we had reached our destination—and it was no place at all. In place of the building or buildings I had expected, there was merely a space. Ringing the spot were trees, and high up the leaves met. Though it was now dark, that much could be seen, because several fires were burning. Of these the large one in the center was evidently for illumination. The lesser ones were cooking fires.

Lounging in the glow of these blazes were a hundred-odd men wearing the same uniform as my captors. Some jumped up with a cheer, as we came near enough to be identified.

"They've bagged somebody!" a man crowed. "We eat!"

"Sit down until Robin's had a look at him," another advised.

" 'Tain't no good, if he decides to throw him back in the pond."

In spite of the first fellow's remark, I didn't suspect cannibalism here. To begin with, there wasn't enough of me to go around; and there was enough cooked meat warming by the fires to feed a small army. As much puzzled as worried, I passed to the other side of the great wood fire. At that point those who had been leading me stood aside to let me see and be seen.

A fellow was sitting on a log, tying feathers on an arrow. He was dressed like the others, but I saw from their attitude that this was the man I had to talk to. His teeth were helping his hands tie a knot, so it was a moment before he looked up. His eyes passed over me, then went to my captor.

"What you got, John?"

"This is all we could find," the big fellow said

defensively, "but it's getting late, you know."

"Yes, and I know the men are sharp set; but a vow is a vow. Is there anything unusual about him?"

After a moment of thought the man beside me chuckled. "He was unusual enough to put Scarlok to sleep when he was first stopped."

Everybody within hearing seemed to think this a great joke. Even the man I had hit gave a sheepish grin.

"Aw, he caught me with my guard down. Besides, I wasn't out."

His chief, who had laughed as heartily as anybody, still had merriment in his eyes when he pointed his reddish beard my way. "Have you any money?"

"We were going to frisk him," John said hastily, "but it was getting dark, and I—"

"Let the man answer, John."

"I haven't even got a slug for a slot machine," I said, happy to spite them.

"You'll be glad, if you're telling the truth," he told me. "Find out, John."

Of course, they didn't find anything, though they were thorough. "He ain't got a thing but this knife, Robin."

There was a pathetic desperation in the report which pierced my own grim misery. This skyscraper was hungry. Everybody else was very grave about it, but Robin's eyes met mine. In answer to my grin his mouth twitched.

"Maybe," he said to John, "we can find something else about him that will make him qualify." He looked at me again. "A man is only in the woods because he's lost, because he's running away, because he's going to meet a man, or because he's looking for a woman."

"I'm doing all four," I informed him. "More than that, I'm looking for dinner."

As I said this, I could feel that everyone else was holding his breath. Then, as their chief rose lithely, that breath was loosed in a sigh.

"You've come to the right place," Robin said. "We're just about to eat."

That was a swell barbecue. There was plenty of well-cooked venison and plenty of ale to wash it down with. The fire tempered the evening chill without robbing the air of its freshness. Sandwiched between light and dark, I could see both sides of the world at once. The food, the earth, the woodsmoke, the ale, and the forest provided an incomparable salad of smells. Below me the forest floor was yielding. Above, the night wind riffled the leaves.

The company was all right, too. Society may take a different view, but to the individual the man who does not steal from him is no thief at all. As far as I was concerned, they were my pleasant benefactors, and I took to Robin. He and I ate together, talking as we worked at the meat with knife and fingers.

"We don't have many holy days in the woods here," he said. "Lady's Day is about the only one we keep, but to make up for it we keep it several times a year."

"Uh-huh." I didn't know what he was getting at, so I let him talk.

He chewed hurriedly and cleared his throat with ale. "On that day we hold dinner until our Lady sends us a guest."

I chuckled comfortably. "Preferably one with money?"

"We like it better that way," he admitted, "but on Lady's Day that's not the main point. If he has too much cash, we'll ease him of his load, of course; but on the other hand, if he's broke, we'll help him out. In either case dinner is on us, and we try to make it a good one."

"As long as I don't have to pay the shot, it seems like a great idea." I savored a chunk of venison while I considered. "And I'm the only stooge you could find today?"

"You don't appreciate the compliment. Just anybody won't do. The woods are full of chicken thieves and kids who can't get along with their families. We picked one of those up this afternoon. No, to qualify as our Lady's Day guest a man has to be out of the ordinary."

"Who isn't?" I asked, blowing the foam off a fresh horn of ale. After drinking, I shoved the sharp end in the ground, as I had seen the others do. "Incidentally, what was my selling point?"

"A hunch of mine, prompted by that white hank of hair. Just a minute. There's the only other fellow we collared today. Hey, Nicolind; come here."

A slender youngster approached and, by invitation, sat down. Black hair straggled out of a tam o' shanter to frame handsome, tanned features.

"He's come to the woods because he says town got too hot for him," Robin explained, winking at me with the eye the other couldn't see. "Nicolind, this is Shandon Silverlock."

The hand the youth gave me was firm, but it had never done much work. My mind, meanwhile, was occupied. If those woods-running gangsters had been watching the road, why hadn't they seen Rosalette? Or had they seen her?

"Tell me something," I said. "Do you ever catch yourselves any ladies on Lady's Day?"

"Nope." That was finality speaking. "Any of the boys who want to bother women can go elsewhere. It is not to be done on my stamping ground." For the first time his face showed the toughness that enabled him to hold and direct this crew of roughnecks. "Ask any of them what happens, if they forget that."

His stand on that point made me feel less concerned about Rosalette. "Did your men happen to see a girl on that road, do you know? I'm not chasing her," I added hasitly. "But she was all alone, and I'm worried about her."

"That's right; you said you were looking for a woman. What about it, Nicolind? You were with the crew that picked you up, until it was relieved and brought you in. Did you see any maids or madames?"

The youth reflected. "I saw one, come to think of it, when I stepped off the road to drink from a spring."

"That must have been she," I declared. "Did you talk to her?"

"No. She didn't seem to feel like it, and even without knowing how Robin here felt about it, I never was one for running after girls."

"They probably don't know you're anything to run from yet," Robin suggested. "Wait till you get a few whiskers on your chin." He winked at me again. "Nicolind says he wants to join up and be an outlaw. How about you?"

When I hesitated, he smiled. "I'm pledged to help anybody I pick up on Lady's Day who's in trouble. I won't find that girl for you and couldn't make her love you, if I did; but if you're looking for a home, we might try each other out for a few days."

If Rosalette hadn't passed Robin's patrols, she was straying in the forest somewhere, probably not too far away. Even if I didn't find her, I would feel better if I spared some time for the effort. And if I stayed in the woods, I had to have some source of nourishment.

"Suppose we leave it at that," I said. "And thanks."

"Think it over. Anybody who can knock Scarlok down is wasting his time leading a peaceful life." Jabbing his knife in the earth to clean it, he rose. "I've got to take a look around to see that everyone gets all he can eat and a little less than that to drink. See you later."

When he had gone, I reappraised the scene from a new angle. It might not be too bad a life for a while, although I realized I was now looking at the butter side of it. Some were still eating, though most, like myself, were just enjoying being at peace with their stomachs. The cooking fires were dying out, but the camp fire still blazed. As men finished their meal, they tended to draw nearer to it. After a while Nicolind suggested that we do so, too.

I had been feeling rather than thinking, but now my mind turned on again. "Just what did that girl look like—the one you saw back there at the spring?" I asked.

"Oh, I don't know." He smiled and shrugged. "I didn't pay as much attention as I sometimes do."

Nevertheless, the point-by-point description I exacted convinced me he had seen Rosalette. "How far was it from the spring to where you were picked up by this crowd?" I next enquired.

"A mile, maybe. You would certainly think she would have showed up before you did; but then she may have turned around and started back."

"But I would have met her," I pointed out. "Besides, there'd be no sense in her doing that. Not if she's the one I have in mind."

Nicolind looked at me curiously. "Are you really following that girl all this way?"

"No, I'm not, but I tried to."

"Why?"

Only a youngster could have been guilty of such baldfaced impertinence. "Why does any man follow a woman?" Then I laughed, mostly at myself. "But that's not the reason I was trying to catch up with her."

"Then you're not in love with her, as Robin said you were?"

"You don't have to be in love with a girl to follow her," I rasped. "Sometimes you only want to know her recipe for bread pudding."

Having had his nose chopped off for putting it where it didn't belong, he looked at me as if it was all my fault. "I know about men and women, too; but Robin said—"

"Robin implied I was in love," I interrupted, "and suspected I was doing some cold-blooded skirt trailing. As a matter of fact, he's got it all wrong."

"Really?"

The knowing way he pursed his lips when he said that annoyed me enough to make me want to clarify my position. "She's just a sort of friend of mine, or even less than that. But she has no business traipsing around these woods by herself, and I'd like to make sure she's all right."

"Oh." He paused, staring at the fire. "That's nice."

As long as we were dealing in personal curiosity, I thought it was my turn. "What makes an educated kid like you want to throw in with these thugs?"

"Robin's educated."

I flicked that quibble away with my hand. "Robin has his own reasons. I'm asking yours."

"Well, I told them I want to be one of them, because I'm going to be in the woods; and it's safer that way. With people like these you're either an ally or an enemy."

That showed more philosophy than I looked for in such youth. "Sure. If you can't lick 'em, join 'em," I conceded. "But what really brought you into the woods in the first place?"

"Nothing so romantic as your motive. I'm looking for a man."

"Does he owe you money, or do you want to take a swing at him?"

Nicolind smiled, but as if half thinking of something else. "Neither," he said after a moment. "Our relations are quite satisfactory."

"A pal, eh?" As I spoke, however, my attention had shifted. The man with the ale was coming our way, and I was anxious to catch his eye. At length I did so. "Fill her up, chum. Easy. Save some of that foam for the others."

The fire was not blazing so high now. The hardwood logs had settled down to a steady burning, and there was a blue core to the flame. The men sitting across from us did not have whole faces. Of most of them all I could see were brows, noses, and cheekbones shining against the night. But if many mouths were invisible, a lot of them were making plenty of noise. There was some wrangling but more laughing. A small group was shooting dice, but talk was the order of the moment. The men to our right were arguing as to how long wood should be seasoned before it became right for bow making. Those nearest my left ear were trading their Sunday lies and making the saints go bail for them.

"There was something like that happened to me," one of them said after hearing a companion out. "The month before I took to the woods—no, it must have been two months before—the prettiest little brown-eyed buttercup you ever set eyes on came to visit the folks next door." For lack of adequate words he whistled. "She was really stacked! Well, sir, she fell for me like a ton of bricks through greased air. When I played dumb, she started makin' passes at me, but I'd made up my mind I wasn't goin' to touch her. She was just a kid, and she'd spent all her life in a convent, see?"

One of his hearers had apparently had to fight off similar attentions from beautiful innocence. "Yeah," he said. "I know how that is. You just don't feel right about it."

"That's it. Well, for a week or so it went along that way, until one night—"

I never did learn how his nobility was undermined, as I have no doubt it was, for just then there was an uproar from somewhere on our side of the fire. It ceased instantly, however, when a horn blew.

"What's going on?" Robin's voice demanded.

"We want Little John," a chorus shouted.

"Aw, hell!" I heard the big man say. "Let somebody else sing. I'm drinking."

Robin laughed. "Take his ale away from him and throw him into the ring," he advised.

It took some doing. Six or seven men were knocked flat in the process, but eventually John was thrust inside the circle. At that point he stopped opposing the general will. It was clear from his expression that he was pleased at the demand and that he would try to give satisfaction.

"Wait till I get my breath back," he said. "And remember. The guy who drinks my ale better get ready to swallow the horn, too."

My first thought was that his singing and his size teamed to make a popular joke. I changed my mind when he started. He had the volume of a moose on the make, but there was quality also.

> They said they caught me in the act,
> > Green leaves,
> The sheriff rode, the bloodhounds tracked,
> > Green leaves;
> There was the law, there was not any doubt of
> > it,
> There was the law, so I hustled right out of it;
> Having but one life, I thought I'd refuse it
> To those who were seeking but never would
> > use it,
> > So I hit for cover in green leaves.

> They meant me for a gallow's nut,
> > Green leaves,
> A rope to hold my gullet shut,
> > Green leaves;

That was their plan, there is not any doubt of
    it,
That was their plan, I was shrewd to get out
    of it;
Some of my guts I'd give up without thinking
But never my gullet, I need it for drinking,
    So I took it with me to green leaves.

My woman sleeps alone tonight,
    Green leaves,
Or cuddles with some other wight,
    Green leaves;
This is my grief, there is not any doubt of it,
This is my grief, I can make no good out of it;
Hunting and stealing, I'm pleased to
    discover,
Are simpler than working, but I had a lover
    I couldn't take with me to green leaves.
But, oh, the stalking of the stag,
    Green leaves,
The ale cask found amongst the swag,
    Green leaves;
Here is what's good, there is not any doubt of
    it,
Here is what's good, and I take my pay out of
    it;
Robbing the rich man to help the poor devil—
Myself—and rewarding myself with a revel,
    It's not a bad life under green leaves.

John sang one or two others, then started leading songs. They were all ready for it, as each had
had enough ale to be carried away by the feeling of
the words and the music. They weren't alone in
that. There probably wasn't as much melody as I

remember—I had had some ale, too—but I experienced a pervasive sense of blending with life at its most dramatic.

"Is this bellowing going to make a recruit out of you?"

The spell snapped, as I looked into Robin's lively eyes. "If you'd caught me just as I was reaching soulfully for one of those deep notes, I'd have signed up," I confessed. "What's happened to the ale?"

"It's turned off, so it won't be long before the harmony is." The outlaw smiled at Nicolind. "What about you, youngblood? You haven't changed your mind?"

Nicolind hadn't been singing, though I had heard him humming several of the tunes. "Not a chance of that. I know it will be fun."

"You do, eh? Well, if you still feel that way after the sheriff's men start shooting arrows at you, we'll talk business." He looked at me. "Shandon, you're my Lady's Day guest. Remember. If you need any money or help, you're entitled to it."

No doubt they all behaved while right under Robin's eye; but even if I could persuade him that my intentions were of the best, I didn't want Rosalette hunted for by his women-starved men. "Thanks," I said. "So far I've got along all right without cash. In case I decided to pull out, though, could you show me where a place called Heorot is?"

"Never heard of it, but I'll try to find out." Robin stood up. "Come along, and I'll give you some pelts to bed down with before somebody else takes them all."

By the time he had supplied us with some skins

to wrap around us, the singing had begun to die down. Robin promptly left us. Saying good night to Nicolind, I was facing the dark, waiting for my eyes to get used to it, when he touched me on the arm.

"Where are you going to sleep?"

The only thing to do was to find a spot far enough from the fire so that late comers wouldn't step on you. "You'll find me in the bridal suite," I grunted.

He tried to laugh but didn't make it. "Do you mind if I go where you do?"

Later I might pick a partner, but I didn't expect to choose a youngster whose voice hadn't yet finished changing. The fact that we had been thrown together our first night with the gang was not a bond I recognized. I was about to tell him to look after himself when I realized that since speaking he had held his breath. He was afraid either of being by himself or of being with the outlaws at night.

"All right," I said, "Let's go. But don't blame me if we land on an ant hill."

By that time I was able to see fairly well and led the way through the trees. When I figured that we had reached a zone which would be free of disturbance, I dropped my bedding. Then, telling Nicolind to wait there, so I wouldn't lose it, I went scouting. Some of the most comfortable places to bivouac in the woods are the worst spots when it rains, and I had been on enough hunting trips to know that. Eventually I found what I was looking for, a well-drained, level place, near enough to the trunk of a big tree to offer our heads shelter from the wind.

"Nicolind!" I called. "Come on; and don't forget my bedding." Apparently I had strayed quite a ways, because I had to call again before he answered.

"Those skins are heavy," he panted, when he had picked his way toward me.

"You'll be glad of it by morning," I told him. "Look; I've staked my claim right where I am now. There's room for you next door, if you're not one of those rambling sleepers; but don't crowd me."

"No man has had the right to complain that I've done so yet," he retorted.

At this sign of boyish hauteur I grinned. "O.K. Then you've got a record to uphold. Ah, this feels good!"

The boughs overhead were just visible, not as branch and leaf, but as gently swaying masses. The same wind that whispered through them brought me all the richness of the forest. I didn't drop off to sleep; the descent was a gentle slope.

"Silverlock," a voice called when I had just about reached the bottom.

That brought me back to the top, and I would have to start all over again. "What?" I demanded.

"I'm not crowding you, am I?"

"Oh, for God's sake! No, you're giving me plenty of room."

My annoyance must have been plain to him, but he still made one more remark. "I just like to be considerate. Good night."

VIII

❦ Two Big Cats ❦

A NIGHT IN THE WOODS is seldom a matter of steady slumber. I waked and dozed off a dozen or more times before it was light enough under the leaves to see clearly. Nicolind wasn't in his bedding, and after a couple of more catnaps the fact alarmed me. Fearing that I might be missing breakfast, I sat up.

The trees looked as if they didn't have their eyes open yet. There was no wind, and I could hear nothing else stirring either. Puzzled, I blinked at where Nicolind had been lying, to make sure he wasn't in the crumple of skins. Next I reached over and held something close enough for examination. It was a couple of feet long, and one end of it curled softly about my fingers. Undoubtedly I was holding a strand of dark, feminine hair.

"I'll be damned!" I said. Then I thought of some of our conversation of the night before. "Why the little devil!"

When some minutes more passed, I was convinced that Nicolind, or whatever her name really was, had left camp at daybreak. By then I had defined my attitude toward the matter. Her disguise was her own business. Moreover, it was something I didn't want to go on record as knowing anything about. My wanderings the night before had taken me pretty far from the center of camp; and there was still no sign that anybody else was alert. I took Nicolind's bedding a hundred or so feet away, then returned to my own to wait until I heard breakfast preparations.

I was almost through eating before the question was raised. "Where's young Nicolind?" Robin asked, sitting down beside me.

My mouth busy with the drumstick of a wild goose I shook my head. "Somewhere around," I said when I could talk.

"Not around at all," he corrected me. "John takes the muster every morning, and he's had a look."

Turning the bone over, I discovered another morsel of meat. "Maybe he's a heavy sleeper," I suggested.

"Maybe, but I tell you John searched. In these open woods there's no chance of anyone getting mislaid."

"Not now," I mumbled, wishing I could share his pun with him. Tossing the drumstick into the fire, I wiped my hands on some leaves. "That's funny," I commented aloud.

"You were with him last night," Robin pointed out.

I had been waiting for him to bring that up. "Yes, until it was time to cork in," I nodded. If somebody had seen me moving that bedding, I would be in trouble, but I took a chance. "I don't know where he spent the night."

His face told me that I was in the clear. "I can't decide whether to be amused or worried," he confessed. "When a whelp his age doesn't wait around for breakfast, you can bet your last bowstring there's a reason for it. Either he's decided that being an outlaw wasn't his calling and has run home to mommy, or he's one of the sheriff's spies."

I thought about that. If Nicolind was a spy, I owed it to Robin to tell what I knew, even though it might not help much. Yet if I told him Nicolind was disguised, he might put some of his strong-arm men on her trail. In the end, I didn't tell him. Having given thought to the things that could happen to Rosalette alone in the forest, my sympathy was extended to other women in the same boat.

"Are you going to have him followed?" I asked.

"No, he's probably just a punk kid," he relieved me by saying, "but I'll move camp south just for luck."

Previously I hadn't made up my mind whether I would stay with the outlaws or not, but now I had no choice. If I tried to hurry away, they would suspect me, too. Robin didn't tell me why he was jittery about being spied on. That I got from Scarlock, with whom I grew pretty friendly. One night when we had our noses in the ale he told me that Robin had recently rescued a friend of his from the law. In the course of the fracas the sheriff died, and so did quite a few of the posse.

I spent over a week slowly drifting south with

that bunch. They fitted me out with one of their green uniforms, which, with the exception of the dinky feathered hat, I was glad to get. The outfit which Golias had won for me had got hard usage in the battle where Brian was killed. My beard was pretty well grown, so all in all I couldn't be told from the others, until I tried to shoot the bow I carried. Still I was making progress when Robin took me aside one morning.

"Shandon," he said, "we've got to clear out of this part of the timber, but you're not going along."

Well, if they didn't want me, they didn't want me. I looked at him.

"We're in big trouble," he explained. "The king himself is after us."

So the heat was on for killing that sheriff. "I don't mind," I offered.

"No," he said. "There's no sense in you being hunted for something you weren't in on."

That was so, and I didn't make myself absurd by pretending an anxiety for martyrdom. "Good luck," I said.

He gave me a hard smile. "I expect to have it, but I expect to work for it, too."

Some of the men were out on assignment and had to be called in with the horn. While they were waiting around I hung my hat on a bush and left them, my bindle slung on my bow stave. I had long given up the thought of seeing Rosalette again, so Heorot, for luck or disappointment, was the only goal I could have. There was no path, and the day was sunless, but Scarlok indicated the southeast for me.

It was with a mixture of feelings that I found

myself on my own again. On the one hand I knew enough about Broceliande to be wary of what I might encounter. On the other, the nine or ten days I had lived in it had given me a feeling I was a competent of the environment. If this confidence was hardly justified by my limited woodcraft, it stood for my changed attitude toward the Commonwealth in general. Having made my way so far, I saw no reason why I shouldn't continue to get along.

This feeling was strengthened when, after walking for an hour or so, I found a creek. By following it I would inevitably reach a river, some part of whose valley was bound to be inhabited. Once I arrived at a town of any size I would consult an atlas at the public library and get myself positively located.

About noon the character of Broceliande changed. The ground, which had been sloping down, leveled off. The undergrowth grew rank. The trees were now strung with vines, and the footing was spongy. The stream was different also. Where it had moved swiftly over a rocky bed, it now glided slowly between mud banks.

Soon it entered a swamp, which was more than I was prepared to do. The trees looked like hired mourners, and their roots hunched up as if they were trying to avoid touching the bog holes. A snake swam lazily across the nearest opaque pool.

While I was trying to decide in which direction to detour, I heard what sounded like the war screech of a giant tomcat. I let my bindle slip to the ground and began rigging my bow. About the time I had an arrow nocked, I heard a sound like a horse running on a sloppy track. Whether this animal was the one that was doing the screeching I couldn't tell, but it was coming nearer. Hoping I wouldn't be noticed, I hid behind a tree.

The screaming grew more ferocious and the running more furious. My ears had been right on both counts. First I saw the horse and rider, then, following as snugly as a dinghy trailing a yacht, a gigantic panther. As they burst from the swamp, the rider stabbed his mount with an instrument of some sort. He must have severed the spinal cord, for the horse promptly collapsed.

Jumping clear, the man started sprinting. Undoubtedly he had killed his mount for a decoy, but horse flesh wasn't what the big cat wanted. After giving the carcass the once over with his nose, the beast began yowling in pursuit of the man once more.

I had to try. My arrow scored a perfect hit on that dead horse. The panther didn't even know it had been shot at. Fumbling in my hurry, I drew another arrow from my quiver. Before I could get it nocked, the catamount had leaped.

From where I stood it looked as if the man hit it on the jaw. The next instant he crumpled to the ground. With a final howl, the animal did the same.

I contemplated the prostrate bodies for some minutes before I gingerly drew near. My bow was drawn, as I stopped short of them for a final appraisal. Dropping my weapon, I then sprang forward to examine the man.

His eyes opened when I bent over him. "Has it gone away?" he whispered.

As he asked this, he turned his head and saw for himself that the beast was still there. After a little he sat up and touched it with one finger. Next he pried open the jaws, which had been clenched in death on one of his jacket pockets.

"Valerian!" he breathed. "Good God! Valerian. And to think it never occurred to me."

As he seemed to have pulled himself together, I thought it time to appease my curiosity. "What," I demanded, "did you hit him with?"

He turned a weathered, high cheek-boned face to me. His hazel eyes smiled.

"I didn't hit him. I administered cyanide by pitching it down his throat."

"Oh," I sat down on the catamount to discuss that. "It was forethoughted of you to have it handy."

"There are compensations even for being a swamp doctor. For instance," and his smile spread to his mouth, "I always carry a restorative for nerves. My own are sagging bad. "

"So are mine," I admitted when he reached into his hip pocket. "No, you first. You must really need it, er—"

"M. Tensas, M.D." He breathed deeply, as he gave me my turn at the bottle. "It's an unsettling experience at that, Mr.—"

"Shandon." It was good liquor. "Do you hunt that way often?"

"It was just an experiment." He gave me a cigar, my first smoke since I was aboard the *Naglfar*. "And," he went on after lighting up, "I don't think I'll repeat it." He held his cigar to mine. "Getting the right timing is too difficult."

"It would be hard on your stable, too," I suggested.

"That's right. Lucky he was a borrowed steed, wasn't it?"

This man had nothing but the best in whiskey and tobacco. I beamed upon him.

"It's better that way. Then you don't get all choked up, when the time comes to give him the works. By the way, what did you do that job with?"

"A scalpel." He stared at his fallen mount, then he studied me. "Was it a personal grudge, or do you just dislike horses?"

I, too, peered at the arrow sticking out of the animal's belly. "He didn't get away from me, did he?" I said complacently. "Of course, I might have hit him a little farther forward, but I forgot to lead him."

We had another drink before he put the flask back in his pocket. "No use in leaving the saddle on. Besides, it aggravates the buzzards." He was a tall, loose-jointed fellow. I wondered where he had bought the Currier and Ives clothes; but I thought that as long as he didn't ask about my green tights I could afford to be silent. "As so often happens," he continued, while he loosened the girth, "this poor creature owes disaster to another's personal vanity. In this case my own. Nothing in my past experience justifies me in supposing that a panther would covet my stringy carcass, but I was convinced of it."

"Well, what the deuce did he want? He passed the nag up."

For an answer he reached into the pocket torn by the catamount's teeth and showed me a hand-

ful of dried roots. "In the backwoods here a doctor's got to be his own pharmacist, so I always
carry a stock of herbs along with me; but I forgot
that all felines have a mania for valerian." He
picked up his saddle and saddlebags. "Which
way are you traveling?"

Having retrieved my bindle, I slung it on my
bow stave again. "That's hard to say. Where I'm
going and where I want to go may be two different
things. Does the name Heorot register with you?"

He shook his head.

"Then what I'm trying to do is to bust out of the
woods and get to some town."

"I'm on my way to a patient or I'd show you
how. Let's see; there's a short cut through the
swamp." Dr. Tensas nodded in the direction from
which he had come. "I wouldn't advise it without
a horse, but you're welcome to mine."

"Not without the saddle, thanks. How about the
long cut?"

"Cross on that fallen tree; it's not as rotten as it
looks," he said, pointing to a windfall athwart the
stream. "Keep on skirting the swamp. You'll get
tired of that, but eventually it'll peter out. Peel
your eyes for a blazed trail, and turn right on it.
Can I shoot you in the other foot?"

He could. When he had corked his flask again, I
shouldered my bow, jammed my cigar in my
teeth, and ambled happily toward the fallen tree.
The Boss of Arden seemed to be full of good
people.

Camping on the trail that night, I felt confident
of reaching the town Tensas had mentioned during the afternoon of the next day. My lunch had
hardly settled, however, when I lost the blazes

where a hurricane, by the look of things, had ploughed a swathe through the woods. I failed to pick them up on the other side. Finally I gave up looking and bulled ahead the best I could with the aid of the sun.

The worst of it was that there was no way of telling how I was doing, and therefore no sense of progress. By mid-afternoon this situation had depressed me; and I sat dunking my feet in a small brook, while I tried to think of a better course of action. Absorbed, I didn't pay much attention to the sounds of splashing downstream. Vaguely I had assigned them to some animal, until I heard a sneeze. My bow ready, I stole along the bank to investigate.

Around a bend from where I had been resting, the stream widened into a little pool. Beside it knelt a man with his head in a bucket. Unwilling to disturb him at this curious but peaceful pursuit, I sat down and waited for him to finish.

By the time I had made myself comfortable I had decided that he was doing nothing more strange or interesting than washing his hair. I had hardly made this diagnosis, when he started to lift his head, wringing blond locks as he withdrew it. They were a half a foot long, then a foot, and still the end hadn't been reached. My eye went from them to the costume, which I now found familiar. Light was dawning, but it still had some fog to burn away.

The clothes belonged to Nicolind and so, to judge from the general size of it, did the body in them. But Nicolind had had black hair, while this was golden enough to belong to—

"Rosalette!" I cried, jumping to my feet.

With a shriek she sprang up also, pushing her

hair away from her face. She had been about to run but relaxed when she recognized me.

"Oh, it's you, Silverlock. I can't remember your other name."

"I can remember both of yours," I informed her.

She laughed, offering both her hands. "I felt awful about that when you were nice enough to worry about me; but at night with all those men around, and everybody drinking, I was pretty frightened."

She was genuinely glad to see me, which pleased me more than I would have expected. "I don't blame you," I told her. "A stag party is no place for a careful doe to bleat. Did you ever meet up with your boy friend?"

"Yes." She laughed delightedly. "I see him every day, and he doesn't recognize me any more than you did."

"What's the sport in that?"

"Oh, we have lots of fun talking about me and how much he loves me. As you know, I'd dyed my face and hair as part of my disguise, and it takes a week to get looking right again. I certainly wasn't going to let him know who I was before I was looking my best."

"Don't overdo it," I cautioned her. "You're leading the league right now."

She made a kissing motion with her lips. "You're sweet, Silverlock." I tried to think when any girl had said such a thing to me before; then I tried to remember whether I'd ever given any girl much reason to. "Anyhow," she went on, "he won't have to pine for me after tonight. I was just rinsing after the final hair washing when you came along."

"And then what? Wedding bells?"

"Tomorrow!" In her enthusiasm she let go of her hair and gave me her hands again. "Isn't it wonderful?"

I wasn't so sure. It was not that I was in love with her, or even had designs upon her. To me she was like honeysuckle, that I could admire on the vine without wanting to pick. Still it might be better if the option could be kept open.

"What's your boy going to do for a living, now that he's left home?" I demanded.

"Well, father says he—"

"Is you dad here, too?"

"He's been in the forest ever since he lost his dukedom, but he'll get it back, I expect." She shrugged and beamed. "But if he doesn't, why we'll just live here."

I let it go. "Where have you been living meanwhile? Did you make yourself another one of those flower-lined shanties?"

"No, I bought a shepherd's cabin." She took a last look in the pool and smiled at herself. "I've got to go there now, so I can get my hair dry. Can you stop by? I'd love to talk with you."

Dumping the bucket, I took it by the bail. "About Aucando?"

She chuckled. "Maybe other things, too, though there probably won't be time."

Her cabin was a cozy-looking shack, but I stared beyond it. Only a fringe of trees separated the clearing it was in from a meadow.

"Is that just a break in the woods," I asked, "or are we really at timber edge?"

"That's the beginning of open country," she affirmed. She seated herself on a patch of grass, her back to the sun, and began spreading out her hair. After a moment I stretched out beside her.

"And people live there?"

"Shepherds. There's farming land beyond, of course."

"And towns?" I persisted.

"Oh, there are always towns."

"But which ones are they, and how far?"

"I never asked," she closed the subject. "Silverlock, you're not going away, are you? I couldn't bear to be alone now."

Well, at least I was out of the woods, and from then on I would have some way of keeping my bearings. "I'll stick around until it's time for your date," I assured her, "but I expect to get supper out of it."

A fine meal it was, when she got around to making it. Afterwards I mooned around outside, while she bathed and dressed. She was going to have a good night for necking, mild but not sultry. And while she and her fiancé were cooing at each other, I would be bunking in rugged solitude.

"How do I look?" she asked, when she at last stepped through the doorway.

It was such a pleasure to find out that I temporarily forgot to be sorry for myself. Her dress was one of those long, simple jobs, which neither concealed nor exhibited her. She wore no ornaments, but to slur the effect of low decolletage a lock of hair, wrapped around her throat, pinch-hit for a necklace.

"Honey," I said, "get out of my sight before you break my heart."

"I've half a mind to try, just to test the effect I'll have on Aucando.

"He doesn't seem to be in a hurry," I was mean enough to point out.

She made a face at me. "He's not coming here.

As Nicolind, I promised that if he'd meet me by the wishing well at moonrise, I was magician enough to produce Rosalette for him. He doesn't really believe it, but he's so much in love—" Here she did a dance step and a pirouette "—that he'll try anything. Isn't he silly and magnificent?"

She was gone then, seeking the moment for which she was designed. I watched her leave with a dog-in-the-manger grudging. When she was no more than a simmer in the twilit woods, I turned and grumpily headed in the other direction.

In the morning I would strike out across fields, but the forest was the better place to bed down. When I had found a likely spot, however, it was still too early to think of sleep. Wishing that I had another of Dr. Tensas' cigars, I sat leaning against a tree, waiting to feel drowsy.

The hallucinations that go with moonlight under the leaves diverted me somewhat from my moodiness. Several times I was convinced I saw something move. Finally there was no doubt about it. Shadows blacked parts of it out like the missing pieces of a jig-saw puzzle, but there were enough left to make it easy to identify a male lion.

Although not happy about it, I stayed where I was. The wind was blowing toward me, and I knew that whatever keeps still is apt to be safe from the eyes of animals. That knowledge didn't offer as much comfort as I could have used. Its course would take it within a dozen feet of me.

At that point it entered a pool of moonlight and became an entity. Its belly sagged, and it rolled in its ponderous stride. Noting these things, I lost much of my fear. Here was just a fat, happy king of the beasts making port after a good feed.

It didn't neglect all security measures, however. Just after passing me, it stopped, its head lifted, one foot up in the air. It did not hold this classic pose long. It had hardly got set, when an animal stole upon its moonlit rear. No, it was human, or something very like it. Out of the shadows he skipped, to swagger forward in a manner so suggestive of the lion's weighty dignity that I grinned. Three such strides brought him as far as the beast's gently waving tail. With an ineffable gesture he pushed it to one side with his hand. At the same time his left hand jerked forward. I couldn't see what was in it, but anyone who has ever had the youthful pleasure of applying a pin to the bulge in a hammock would recognize the motion.

No occupant of a hammock ever reacted as satisfactorily as that lion, though. In almost the same breath it yelped, snarled, and roared. In almost the same action it jumped, whirled, and struck. His tormentor had to be fast to live to enjoy his joke, and he was. By the time the lion had turned around he was stretched behind a clump of fern, near enough for me to kick if I had wanted to move. I had no such inclination, while that beast was having a tantrum. It pawed the air as if it hoped to manufacture an enemy to take vengeance on. Several times it sprang and spun around to make sure it wasn't again being taken from the rear. In the end it made itself nervous by this shadow boxing. Giving a sudden screech, it bounded out of sight.

Now that the lion was gone, the fellow who had jabbed it proceeded to have a good time. He rolled over on his back, kicking his feet and nearly strangling on his mirth. My own shoulders shook, too. In part I was amused by what had happened, but what really tickled me was a glimpse of the mind that would buy a moment of slapstick comedy with a mortal risk.

Feeling that the lion was out of earshot, I finally laughed outright. "That's nice for a hobby, bub," I complimented him, "but it couldn't be steady enough work for a living."

It was his turn to be startled. He shot up from the gound, stayed aloft in a manner best known to himself, and backed away a little. Almost instantly, however, he alighted.

"I had him talking to himself, didn't I?" he chuckled. "That's what's known as letting something get under your skin."

In shadow as we were, I couldn't make him out too clearly. He was very short, with his head and shoulders large out of all proportion to his underpinnings. To judge from the outline of his noggin, his hair was thick and tousled. Nevertheless, his ears, or something that grew where ears belonged, were long enough to stand free of it.

"What did you jab him with?" I enquired.

"A fine, three-inch black thorn; and I sheathed it to the hilt. He's got a hasty temper, eh?"

I thought of the furious speed with which the lion had wheeled and struck. "He was hasty," I agreed. "How do they figure your life expectancy hereabouts?"

He snickered. "Oh, better than a lot of people's, I reckon. That is, if you go by past performance."

"They must die early in these sticks."

"Not necessarily." He seated himself and hugged his knees. "I've started counting by centuries instead of years, but then I'm the oldest."

"It must be rough to be an orphan," I sympathized. Still if you cut a good lie in two, you might find that the small end of it had an alloy of fact. "If you really are the oldest inhabitant," I went on, "perhaps you can tell me how to get where I want to go. Nobody else that I've met has even heard of the place, though."

"It doesn't exist if I couldn't tell you," he said. "I know the country and what's in it like our lion's rump knows that thorn. Never mind asking the big things. I know what Geri and Freki feed on and what Jack Wilton did at the house of Pontius Pilate. I know what the Dagda said to call his harp and the stakes Setna played for. I know who Kuwarbis got tight with and why Ilmarinen didn't have much fun with his second wife. What's your question?"

"Well, I have a date to meet a friend—if he's still alive, that is—at a place called Heorot. Do you know it?"

"Know it!" he snorted. "You might as well ask what the suppliant maidens wanted. Not what you'd think at all. Why if you want to go to Heorot—" I didn't hear anything, but he jumped to his feet. "Oops! There's my signal. I've got to skedaddle."

"Hey, nix! Not yet!" The thought of losing a knowledgeable guide just as I was on the verge of learning what I wished to know was too much. I made a determined grab for him, but he was on his way.

IX

A Guide and No Guides

AFTER MY ANNOYANCE had abated I lay down, but sleep wouldn't come. Everything, indeed, conspired to keep it away. The soft air felt like a woman's breath on my cheek. A nearby stream sounded like girls talking and chuckling. The leaves stirred by the night breeze rustled like silk skirts. Catching the moonlight, the ferns looked damnably like golden hair. A glowing stone had the curve and texture of a bare shoulder. Disgusted I sat up again.

For one little spot in the woods that was a busy place. In a little while I heard leaves crackling and twigs snapping as accompaniment to footfalls. Voices showed more than one person was coming, but I couldn't make out what they were saying until they were almost opposite me.

"Wait up!" the man's voice begged. "Please, sweetheart. Oh, damn it all, why won't you listen to me?"

The girl, who was a pace in front, increased her

lead by a little flouncing run. "I have better things to do, thank goodness."

Feeling sure that she must be Rosalette, I had risen; but when I heard her voice I sat down to mind my own affairs. "But what has changed you?" the man demanded, as he partially caught up. "What have you got against me?"

"Your existence," she told him.

They disappeared, still quarreling. Hopefully I waited for something else to happen or for my lion-baiting acquaintance to return. Both soon took place.

First there were sounds indicating a single person was approaching on the run. Sobbing, she probably couldn't see where she was going. She had hardly entered my range of vision, when she tripped and fell.

"Oh, Aucando!" she wailed. "How could you do this to me?"

"Rosalette! What happened?" I demanded, as I scrambled to my feet.

She was crying so wildly that she didn't know or care who was speaking to her. "He—just—left me," she wailed, rising to her knees, "And—I can't find him!"

"Well, hell—that's too bad, honey." I didn't have much experience comforting people, but I started toward her. Halfway there I raised my voice. "You be careful what you do, or I'll atomize you!"

That trickster was back, flying not walking this time. Zooming up behind Rosalette, he paused an instant. I leaped to catch him, but he backed away like a humming bird leaving a blossom, turned with a laugh, and was gone.

Rosalette didn't shriek or jump, so all was probably well, but I knelt beside her. "Did he do anything to you?"

"Who?" She had stopped sobbing. Now she raised her head and smiled. "Oh, Silverlock, I'm so glad you're here."

The way she said it was something new between us. My pulse did a double shuffle, but my mind knew that she talked so because she was glad to see anybody.

"What's this about your boy friend," I asked, "and why did the louse run out on you?"

"Who?" she asked again, giving me her hands to help her up.

"Who! Why Aucando." I was puzzled, but I couldn't sound exasperated while holding her hands. She made no move to draw them away, so I hung on just for luck. "You told me just a few hours ago that you were going to marry him tomorrow."

"Oh, a few hours ago. But that wasn't I. I've just been born now—this minute—when I opened my eyes and saw you."

It was not so much the words that I took seriously. I had once passed too much counterfeit myself to expect a dollar to have silver in it. It was her voice which persuaded me. Using those tones, she could have said: "There is no joy in Mudville"; and I would have known she was talking to the man she loved.

There could be no mistake about it. And I wanted it to be so. It had to be so. There could be no future but agony unless it was true. Yet its suddenness dared me to believe it.

"Rosalette," I said shakily. "Oh, my—" I didn't

finish the phrase, because I was kissing her. It was not so much conscious desire that drew us together as the knowledge we belonged with one another. Apart, each would lack entity. There was no match in life for one kiss but another.

For the tenth or the hundredth time—I've no idea—I was closing my eyes the better to distill this sweetness when something brushed my face. Rosalette must have felt it, too, for she jerked away from me. Turning in anger to slap at the bug or moth which had disturbed us, I was just in time to see a familiar figure disappearing.

Rosalette was walking away, and I sprang to catch up with her. "Rosalette!" I cried, taking her arms. "Did he hurt you?"

"Oh, hello, Silverlock." Her voice had a nice friendliness. "You're always worrying about me, aren't you? No, nobody's hurt me."

Chilled, I let go of her arm. "What's the trouble, then?"

"Nothing much," she said. "Aucando went off—I forget just why, though it doesn't matter—but he'll be back directly. What are you doing here?"

Then I knew. Somehow it had something to do with that practical joker. He had sold my heart down the river for a laugh. It was all over, and there was no use in being reproachful to a girl who didn't remember. I was afraid my voice wouldn't work, but it did.

"I'm not doing anything. This is where I bunk, you see, but I couldn't sleep and—"

She didn't hear me out. Someone was coming, and she dashed to meet him. It was Aucando, but I was spared the introduction. They went off together in a rush of endearments to find privacy.

Left stunned and gasping, I had a bad time of it.
I felt as if I had been cut in half without an
anaesthetic, nor could I catch sight of any future
betterment. To stay still under this affliction was
more than I could manage, so I caught up my
belongings. With no bearings at all I started striding through the forest.

Previously I had not known that passion can be
a sweetness in the mind as well as a rage in the
body. Nor had I known that the loss of its object
can leave a gap too big for reason to jump. It must
work its way around, and at that finds the going
hard. I could tell myself that what had touched me
so briefly could not have burned deep. I could tell
myself that marrying, under my present circumstances, was an impracticality. It did no good
for the time being.

If only that little heel with the over-developed
sense of humor hadn't come back! My mind had
used that track so many times that it had a hot box.
Yet I was driving it along there again, when the
cause of my grief caught up with me.

Having learned how fast he was, I didn't try to
hit him. "What the hell do you want?" I growled.

As usual he laughed, but this time in a deprecatory manner. "I'm sorry you got caught in the
works, but I was only trying to follow orders. You
see," he went on, when I simply glowered at him,
"a mess of lovers' quarrels were disturbing the
peace hereabouts, and I was detailed to straighten
things out. Rest your legs, won't you. I'm kind of
tired."

Now that I had stopped moving, I was aware of
weariness, too. "I miscued the first time around,"

he continued when we had seated ourselves on a handy rock, "and I screwed up the assignment. As far as you are concerned, it was your tough luck to be around while I was pairing people off. There you were looking foolish, and there she was bawling. The set-up was a dead ringer for a lovers' quarrel, so I patched it up."

"Why didn't you leave us alone after that?" I muttered. "We were doing all right."

"Couldn't," he said. The boss found out that I'd goofed off and made me unscramble things and get the arrows in the hearts where they belonged. That meant you were out in the cold. Not so good?"

"I'll live."

"You will," he agreed, "and you'll forget this and you won't, and be glad on both scores. But anyways I felt I owed you something for getting you into it, which is why I took the trouble to hunt you up. Now, you wanted to go to Heorot."

I made myself realize that I couldn't wander around, brooding on the might-have-been indefinitely. "Yeah, I guess so. But if you can even get me out of Broceliande, it'll help. I've been walking around so long without knowing where I'm going that I feel like I'm slipping my chain."

"You're as good as out now," he assured me, as he hopped to the ground. "There's your path right under your feet."

I could feel it and follow it for a brief distance with my eyes, but I didn't have much confidence in it. There had been other forest byways which I had followed, only to have them slip out from under foot.

"Which way do I go?"

"That way." He pointed left. "This trail will take you to a road. Turn right on it and then take the first left-hand turn. Heorot will be the largest building in the first town you come to."

"How far is it?"

"The way you're going? H-m-m, let's see. Watling Street couldn't be more than twenty-five miles, and the turn off is about a mile this side."

His mention of Watling Street, of which Golias had told me, gave me the feeling of being on familiar ground. At last I began to believe in my guide.

"You say Heorot is just a building and not a town? I'd been afraid I'd have to start ringing door bells to find my side-kick, but that simplifies things."

"It should be simple enough if you're used to walking. Are you hungry?"

Having thought about something besides my bereavement for a moment, I was feeling a little better. "Hollow as Finnegan's legs."

"Well, there's a night and day joint just before you come to the road. There won't be any other place along the way, so you'd better stoke up well. So long."

I came in sight of the eating place he had mentioned within half an hour. Day had by then just commenced to break, so I could make the building out with some exactness. It was cottage-type, with an extra long chimney at each end of the roof. There was no light in it, but, as promised, service was continuous. A table was set up outdoors, and I heard the rattle of china before I drew near enough to see who was eating.

The table, a huge one, was laid for several dozen, but the only customers were a threesome at the far end. I peered at them, then decided to see if I was right the first time. There was no doubt about it. One of them was dressed in his grandfather's duds, complete with stovepipe hat, skyscraper collar, and wallpaper tie. Of the others, one was in the costume of a rabbit and the second in that of a mouse. The latter had passed out.

Many of the places showed signs of earlier occupancy, but I found one which didn't at their end of the table. "You boys must have had quite a night of it," I remarked.

The man in the hat took exception to this statement. "We haven't had any night at all; in fact we're still waiting for it." He held out a watch whose face it was too dim for me to see. "Look; it's just six o'clock."

It must have been closer to three-thirty, but I knew better than to argue with a drunk's timepiece. "So it is," I said. No waiter had appeared, so I helped myself to bread, butter, marmalade, cold cuts, and deviled eggs. Meanwhile it occurred to me that it might be well to check on the directions I had been given, to make sure my recent guide wasn't indulging his sense of humor again.

"Do you fellows live around here?" I asked.

The hat man seemed to be struck with my question. "I always live here," he said at length. "Don't you?"

"Nope," I said, pouring myself some tea, which was the only potable in sight. "I live in Chicago."

"How odd," he commented. "It find it so much easier to live where I am."

"All right," I groaned. "You win. I live here."

"It's too late," the rabbit said. "You had your chance. People keep on getting into these difficulties," he confided to his companion. "And it's all just a product of sloppy thinking."

Being out of sorts, I wasn't going to let that pass. "See here, mister," I warned him. "I know you're carrying a load, and I don't care what you think, sane or sober; but keep it to yourself."

Instead of answering, he began arguing with the other about that six o'clock watch and whether they'd done the right thing greasing it with butter that might have had bread crumbs mixed up in it. It was such a typical barroom discussion that my aggravation gave way to amusement.

"What I started out to ask," I interrupted them, sure they had forgotten my bad humor, "is simply: can you tell me where this road runs to?"

The man in the old-fashioned get-up dunked a piece of cake and took a bite. "That road doesn't run," he mumbled. "It's scarcely been known to creep."

We were back at that again, but I tried to overlook it. "O.K. O.K. But where does it go?"

"It's a home-loving road," he informed me. "There's no record of it straying."

"I'm serious," I said, trying to get through to them with the force of my urgency. "I really need to be straightened out, because I'm not sure where I'm heading."

"How do you think a road can lead you there, then? You expect far too much of a road." After reproving me, the rabbit fellow spoke in a stage whisper to his companion. "There's nothing sillier than unbridled optimism."

I had determined not to lose my temper again,

but I was having a hard time. "Let's take a look from the other side," I persisted. "Could I follow it to Heorot?"

The man in the hat brooded before responding. "I should certainly think so, assuming that it got there first."

"You can both go to Hell!" I roared at them. They appeared undisturbed, but the mouse gink waked up.

"Why," he asked, leaning toward me, "is an angleworm like a parallelogram?"

As I had no quarrel with him so far, I decided to answer. "I don't know, Mr. Bones," I said, reaching for the cake. "Suppose you tell me."

He considered, while I made away with two pieces. "Well, I don't know as they are alike," he decided, "but if you don't think about it, it won't worry you." Having pronounced this dictum, he forthwith went to sleep again.

No representative of the management had showed up, and there was still no light in the house. I was just as glad, having remembered halfway through the meal I had no money. Still I was unwilling to be a deadbeat. My bow could be of no value to me in town, even if I had learned how to use it. Here at the forest's edge, however, it should be considered as worth far more than the food I had consumed. I left it and the quiver by my place, nodded curtly to the others, and strode off toward the road.

Hearing a plate overturned, I looked back. The one disguised as a mouse was still asleep. The one with the old-fashioned clothes was placing a deviled egg on his head. The one masqueraded as a rabbit was in the act of stringing my bow. Thinking it better not to be a witness, I hastened away.

By and large the encounter did me good. Reviewing it, I laughed; and the laughter helped me to realize that I would not forever be a tortured spirit. Moreover, the mouse lad had something there. I wouldn't forget Rosalette; but if I didn't think about what had happened, it wouldn't worry me. I began instead to figure out courses of procedure if Golias didn't turn up at Heorot.

Counting the few hours I devoted to needed sleep, it took me most of the day to reach the turn-off my guide had mentioned. Or I supposed it to be the one and anxiously scanned the signpost to be certain. By following this road, I could, it told me, reach Sandhills and Wayland's Forge. But it was not this information that made me exclaim with satisfaction. On the topmost of the three wooden arrows was the legend: "HEOROT ½ Mile."

From the moment I faced down that road I smelled the sea. Soon I caught sight of it beyond a cluster of buildings. The fact that the principal one of these and not the town itself had been designated ceased to puzzle me. Heorot was what took your eye when you approached. The visual function of the burg's other structures was to give a measuring rod for grandeur.

Impressed though I was, my physical reaction was to cross my fingers. It was a long way to come for a meeting that might not take place.

Suppertime had swept the streets clear. It was not until I stood before Heorot that I noted much in the way of signs of life. The doors of the great edifice stood open, but it was something above the doorway that drew my eyes. Pinned there with daggers was a monstrous trophy. If it was like anything I had seen before, it was like an arm. Yet

it was big as the hind leg of a dinosaur; the hair on
it grew out from between scales, like weeds pushing out from cracks in the sidewalk; and the hand
or paw ended in talons. It had been wrenched off,
not cut; very recently, too. Blood still oozed from
the raw joint, each drop landing with a hiss in the
iron pot placed to receive it.

Meanwhile I was conscious of the jovial riot
which seemed to be taking place inside. When I
had gazed my fill at the thing above the doors, I
glanced at the two men who stood guard on either
side of the entrance. They were dressed, and in
general looked, much like Brodir's men. Although on duty, they were feeling informal about
it, and one of them grinned as our eyes met.

"Pretty big game you get around here," I ventured.

His grin broadened. "That there's pretty big
even for these parts."

Having found him friendly, I got down to business. "I'm supposed to be meeting a pal here. All
right to go in?"

"Today. Even for people in funny clothes." I
was then near enough to discover that he hadn't
gone sober to his post. "We're keepin' open
house."

Thus passed by the sentry, I crossed the
threshold. A grand jamboree was in progress.
Hundreds of men were seated at long tables piled
with food. Each of them had a mug in his hand,
and dozens of waiters were rushing around keeping them filled. It was futile to search for Golias
under the conditions, but it all looked good to me
just the same. Except for a sandwich I had made to
carry away from the breakfast table, I had had
nothing to eat since before sun up.

While I was wondering whether it would be safe to muscle in somewhere, a man whom I took to be a member of the banquet committee approached. There was so much yelling and laughing that we didn't try to exchange words. He merely beckoned and smiled—everybody there was in a wonderful humor—and in a minute I was wedged in between a couple of long haired gorillas who good-naturedly made room for me.

I was so busy catching up that I didn't have a mouth to spare for conversation for a while. Then, wiping my fingers on a piece of bread and flipping it to a dog, as I had observed to be the custom, I sat up to take notice. Evidently some of the wives were out to see that the men had a good time. A sweet-faced woman wearing a gold tiara was coming down the line, asking how everyone was doing. She must have been popular, for there was comparative quiet as men waited to exchange words with her.

"You must be a foreigner," she said when she came to me. "I hope you're enjoying yourself."

"I am, thanks. It looks like it's going to be a tall evening."

She smiled. "We'll all be very happy tonight. It's the first time we've been able to enjoy this place in twelve years."

When she had passed on, I took a solid slug of mead. With its encouragement I was swiftly getting in the spirit of things. Not bothering about introductions, I started out to make a place for myself in the conversation.

"What was wrong with this joint," I asked the man on my right, "that you weren't able to use it for twelve years?"

Busy swapping dirty jokes with men across the board, he previously had paid no attention to me. Now he turned his broken nose and green eyes in my direction. After considering me, they lighted up.

"You mean that, don't you? I bet there ain't anybody else in a hundred miles that don't know the answer, and to think I got you all to myself. Shall I lie a little?"

"Dealer's choice."

"It won't be necessary," he decided. "It's a good enough story pared down to hard facts. Well, there ain't been nothin' wrong with the premises that a good murder wouldn't cure, but nobody was man enough to attend to it. I figure to be as tough as some; but I listened carefully, and I didn't hear myself volunteering." He gulped swiftly as if afraid of losing my attention. "You saw that arm above the door, didn't you?"

"I sure did."

"Well, the rest of the fiend was made to match. It used to come every night, grab up a few guys, and stuff 'em in his mouth. It didn't make any difference to his belly whether you fought or went peaceably. We stood it just so long, then moved out."

I had a fleeting vision of what it would be like, waiting for that man-eater to drop in out of the dark. "God damn! I should think you would."

"We did, all right. And for twelve years nobody said anythin' about movin' back until—You see that fellow holding out his cup for a refill? Wait till he turns around."

At one side of the banquet hall was a table, raised above the rest in the usual fashion, for guests of honor. It was toward this that my neighbor pointed. The king—I had learned that much about the set-up—could be easily identified by his special chair. At his right was a broad-shouldered man in the act of facing around to us. Just by the way he swung his body you could see the perfect control he had of it. Even though his face was flushed with mead, it was the face of competence.

"Nice looking joe," I commented.

"More than that." The broken nose twitched earnestly. "If there was only one man you could have to help you, pick that one. Look; he doesn't even belong here. Our troubles were no skin off his butt, but he came—uninvited, mind you—and volunteered to take the field on. Let's drink to him."

We did. I saw that he meant to fetch bottom and imitated him.

"What did he do the job with," I asked professionally, "an axe?"

"You saw." My companion wiped the suds off his moustache with his forearm. "He used nothin'. Nothin'! He just naturally got his grip, braced himself, and yanked the fiend's arm out of its socket."

"The devil he did!" I looked over at the raised table with renewed respect. The king was just getting to his feet. As he did so, several horns sounded, and the hall quieted.

X

⧼ At Heorot ⧽

THE PURPOSE of the king was to praise the man of the occasion, and there was enough to say. It turned out that the fellow—Beowulf, he named him—had killed not only one fiend but two, thereby wiping out the whole local nest. In the second encounter it had been necessary to follow his dreadful antagonist under water and finish it off there.

Next Beowulf made his acknowledgment. I thought he hit just the right note. He had done a great thing and knew he had. Instead of bragging, either directly or by a show of false modesty, he merely said, in effect, he was glad to own the ability which made his service possible. It was a pleasure to cheer him, especially as it was good fun to yell anyhow. Not to mention drinking the toasts that were called for.

I was enjoying the party and a thing besides: I was enjoying my own high spirits in contrast to the glumness I had felt the night before. There's no cure for thwarted yearning like a rousing stag evening. Yearning had given me a bad time of it, and now it was my inning. I dunked him in mead, then drew him out to crawl away like a half-drowned fly. I crushed him with my fist, as I beat time to a jolly song of which everyone knew the words except me. Lastly I rolled him up in ribald jokes and blew him away with my laughter.

About half an hour after the speeches was when it started. A bunch of men at the table behind me began stamping their feet and yelling. Then the men seated with me took it up. They were shouting so loudly that it was a minute before I caught what they were saying.

"We want Widsith! We want Widsith! We want Widsith!"

I had temporarily forgotten why I had come to Heorot, but now I sat up excitedly. Of course, Widsith could be a common local name, but the coincidence made me hopeful. I had a right to be. Locating him by the cheers which followed his progress, I saw Golias making his way toward the table where Beowulf sat. Vaulting up on the platform, he bowed to the king, then turned toward the rest of us.

Wherever an old friend is, home is. I gazed at him with satisfaction, anticipating the moment of reunion. He, like myself, wore a different outfit from the one he had on when I had last seen him. He was dressed like a jonquil, in a yellow coat that would knock your eye out and form-fitting green breeches. These were covered in their lower reaches by short boots. He had also shortened his hair; but the changes were not changes in the man. His body had the same alert bearing, his face the same look of being interested in whatever he was doing, that I remembered.

"What would you like tonight?" he asked smilingly.

I hadn't been able to see what was slung over his shoulder before, but as he swung it into view I saw that it was a small harp. Unconcernedly he turned it while the debate his question had started went on.

"Give us 'Walter's Stand.' "

" 'Sigmund Siggeirsbane.' "

"No, 'Burnt Finnsburg.' "

"Aw, we had that last night."

"How about 'Helgi Hundingsbane?' "

"Something new! Something new!"

Golias held up his hand. "Would you all settle for something new?" he asked when they had quieted.

"Yes!" they roared; and I with them, because I had been left out of the shouting long enough.

"All right, fill all cups, so you'll have something to shove in your mouths when your tongues itch." Golias grinned at us, and we grinned back. "From now on, I'm making all the noise for a while. Understood?"

"Understood!" we chorused.

"Good, then!" After waiting for all to be served, he beat a couple of chords out of his harp to gain our attention. "I'm giving you," he announced, " 'The Death of Bowie Gizzardsbane.' "

Harsh that hearing for Houston the Raven:
Fools had enfeebled the fortress at Bexar,
Leaving it lacking and looted the while
Hordes were sweeping swift on his land,

Hell-bent to crush him. The cunning old
    prince
Did not, though, despair at danger's
    onrushing;
Hardy with peril, he held it, perused it,
Reading each rune of it. Reaching the facts,
    he
Thumbed through his thanes and thought of
    the one
Whose guts and gray matter were grafted
    most neatly.
"Riders!" he rasped, "to race after Bowie!"
"Bowie," he barked when that bearcat of
    heroes
Bowed to his loved prince, "Bexar must be
    ours
Or no one must have it. So hightail, burn
    leather!
Hold me that fortress or fire it and raze it.
Do what you can or else do what you must."

Fame has its fosterlings, free of the limits
Boxing all others, and Bowie was one of
    them.
Who has not heard of the holmgang at
    Natchez?
Fifty were warriors, but he fought the best,
Wielding a long knife, a nonesuch of daggers
Worthy of Wayland. That weapon had
    chewed
The entrails of dozens. In diverse pitched
    battles
That thane had been leader; by land and by
    sea
Winning such treasure that trolls, it is said,

Closed hills out of fear he'd frisk them of
    silver.
Racing now westward, he rode into Bexar,
Gathered the garrison, gave them his orders:
"Houston the Raven is raising a host;
Time's what he asks while he tempers an
    army.
Never give up this gate to our land.
Hold this door fast, though death comes
    against us."

We cheered Bowie's decision and drank to him,
too. Golias allowed for such activity, refreshing
himself also, then he went on.

The flood of the foemen flowed up to
    Bexar,
Beat on the dam braced there to contain it.
But Wyrd has no fosterlings, favors no
    clients;
Bowie, the war-wise winner of battles,
Laid out by fever, lost his first combat,
Melting with death. Yet the might of his spirit
Kept a tight grip on the trust he'd been given.
"Buy time, my bucks," he told his
    companions.
"Be proud of the price; our prince is the
    gainer."
Bold thanes were with him, thirsty for honor,
Schooled well in battle and skilled in all
    weapons;
Avid for slaughter there, each against thirty,
They stood to the walls and struck for their
    chieftains,
Houston and Bowie, the bearcat of heroes.

Twelve days they ravaged the ranks of the
    foemen.
Tens, though can't harrow the hundreds
    forever;
That tide had to turn. Tiredly the thanes
Blocked two wild stormings and bled them to
    death.
The third had the drive of Thor's mighty
    hammer,
Roared at the walls and rose to spill over,
Winning the fort. But the foemen must pay.
Heroes were waiting them, hardy at killing,
Shaken no whit, though sure they were lost.
Ten lives for one was the tariff for entry;
And no man got credit. Crushed and split
    skulls,
Blasted off limbs and lathers of blood
Were the money they soughted and minted
    themselves—
Worth every ounce of the weregild they
    asked.

They liked that, and Golias had known they
would. He waved in answer to their shouts, his
gesture on the down sweep finding its way to his
cup.

Of every eleven, though, one was a hero
Turned to a corpse there. Cornered and
    hopeless,
They strove while they yet stood, stabbing
    and throttling,
Meeting the bear's death, dying while
    fighting.
Chieftains of prowess, not chary of slaying,

Led and fell with them. Alone by the wall,
Travis, the red-maned, the truest of warriors,
Pierced through the pate and pouring out
 blood,
Kept death marking time, defied it until
His sword again sank, sucking blood from a
 foeman.
Content, then, he ended. So also died
 Crockett,
Who shaved with a star and stamped to make
 earthquakes,
Kimball, the leader of loyal riders,
Bonham whose vow was valor's own hall
 mark.

Crazed by their losses, the conquerors offered
No truce to cadavers; the corpses were
 stabbed
In hopes that life's spark would be spared to
 afford them
Seconds on killing. Then some, taking count,
Bawled out that Bowie was balking them
 still;
Like weasels in warrens they wound through
 the fort,
Hunting the hero they hated the most.
Least of the lucky, at last some found him,
Fettered to bed by the fever and dying,
Burnt up and shrunken, a shred of himself.
Gladly they rushed him, but glee became
 panic.
Up from the gripe of the grave, gripping
 weapons,
Gizzardsbane rose to wreak his last slaughter,
Killing, though killed. Conquered, he won.

In brief is the death lay of Bowie, the leader
Who laid down his life for his lord and ring
    giver,
Holding the doorway for Houston the Raven,
Pearl among princes, who paid in the sequel:
Never was vassal avenged with more
    slayings!

It meant as much to me as to everyone else there
that Bowie had accomplished his purpose and
gone down fighting. Like everybody else, too, I
was highly pleased with the vengeance taken for
him. We cheered Gizzardsbane, the Raven, and
Golias, and drank to them all with indiscriminate
enthusiasm.

For me a special source of satisfaction was pride
in my friend's successful performance. I resisted
bragging that I knew him, but I was feeling too
expansive to keep all of my emotion to myself. I
jogged the elbow of my neighbor, whose name I
had now learned.

"He sure can put it across, can't he, Hoc?"

"Who, Widsith?" It took Hoc a moment to re-
focus his eyes as he turned to look at me. "Listen;
I'll lie to you about Widsith, but only a little. I
don't know so much about words, except that I
always like them out of his mouth, but he's got a
voice like a call to dinner. He can make a dog leave
a bone and fleas leave a dog to hear him. Got the
know-how from a mermaid he laid in the
Skaggerack. That part's just hearsay, so don't
claim you got it from me; but he sure picked up
pointers somewhere, that he can make the rest of
the scops sound like crows. Let's drink to him."

Golias went back to his place, but there was no

sense in trying to locate him in that jam of people. Therefore, and feeling better than ever now that I knew he was around, I carried on where I was. It was a lively evening, and, unlike Robin, the king didn't see fit to put the cork back.

The competition got too stiff for me. These fellows were in earnest, and they had been practicing. Some of the younger ones had passed out, but most of them were still going strong, when I decided that if I was going to be any good the next day I had better take a walk. As I had taken care to keep eating while I drank, I wasn't in bad shape. I was proud of how straight I could walk, though my shadow wasn't doing so well. Eventually the exercise cured even this defect, and after a couple of hours spent strolling along the harbor I returned, hungry and wanting a night cap.

Heorot was not as I had left it. It resembled rather a battle where a whole army had died game. Men lay on the tables and under the tables; on the benches with their heads on the tables, and on the floor with their feet on the benches. And over their motionless forms, loud as an onrushing subway train, sighed the wind of their snoring.

The torches which furnished the only light had burned so low that I first thought that was all there was to it. Then one flared up enough to show me what had been the king's table. Mead had been victorious there also, but a pitiful garrison of two still held out. They were recognizable, when I had picked my way nearer, as Beowulf and Golias.

The latter saw me and jumped to his feet. "Hey! Shandon," he called, hurrying to the meeting. "Good man! I was getting worried about you."

The friendliness in his voice doubled the pleasure I felt. Not content with shaking hands, I slapped him on the shoulder.

"I didn't expect to find you at all," I said. "I was sure you'd lined some wolf's belly back there with the rest of Brodir's men."

"And yet you came anyway." He was looking me over keenly. "That's great."

He was, I felt, giving me more credit for constancy than I rated. "Well, I didn't know where the hell else to go, and anyhow once or twice I'd have let you down if things had turned out different."

"It was a matter of chance, understood." He was still examining me. "Did you have yourself a time?"

Unprepared for the question, I thought back. Who would willingly forfeit any experience that is not shameful or crippling?

"Well," I said, "I'm glad I took the hike, I guess. What sort of a trip did you have?"

"Oh, a fine one! First off I played possum while they dragged me out to be food for the ravens. I looked bloody enough to be a corpse at that, but they didn't stop to find out that most of the blood wasn't mind. When I saw fit to revive, there was a line of retreat open to the west, so west I went and—But come on over and join us at the mead. As you can see," he waved a hand to include the noisy sleepers, "You've missed the best of the party."

I was explaining that this wasn't my first appearance that evening, when we reached the table. There I paused to acknowledge the introduction to Beowulf. Golias found me a cup, I found myself some bread and a big slab of cheese, and we sat down to it.

"You don't mind if we swap experiences, do you, Wulf?" Golias filled all three mugs, to the surface tension point without spilling so much as a nodule of foam. "This is the fellow I came here to meet, and we have some catching up to do."

"Go right ahead." Beowulf had an easy way about him that I liked. "Everybody, including me, has been talking about what I've done for the last three days. I'll be glad of a change of subject."

"You'll have it," Golias promised. "Let's see; where was I?"

That momentary lapse of memory was almost the only sign he had shown of the terrific bout of which he and Beowulf were the only honest finalists. Awed, I wagged my head at them both.

"You were heading west," I reminded him.

"Oh, yes. I made westing—more than I wanted, because a bunch of Brian's men spotted me and chased me clear out of the Boss of Arden. Well, when I'd shaken them and rested up, I cut south and east, got mixed up in the Calydonian Boar hunt, got lost by following the wrong dogs and ended up dining with Bricriu. He's a bastard, but the rest of the company was good. Then I went to King Fisherman's, on a Sunday that was; bivouacked a couple of nights with Arjuna, Bhima and the rest; visited Pwyll—he wasn't there, as a matter of fact, but Arawn's a good fellow; and here's to it." We drank with him, and he went on. "So far I'd been able to keep a pretty straight course; but after leaving Pwyll's I ran into Orlando, absolutely off his rocker and out for blood—anybody's. Hell, I've known Orlando for years, but I didn't stop for any 'remember whens' after I saw the way he was tearing up the forest and bashing rocks to pieces. I had to make another westward detour and didn't try to make southing again until I came to the Terne Wathelyne." He drank once more.

"Well, Graelent—did I tell you I met Graelent near there?—had a beautiful friend who had a beautiful friend who didn't have any friend just then until I came along." He blew a kiss with the fingers that weren't gripping his cup. "That was charming, but I had to meet you: besides she was trying to pin me down to a long-term contract. So I did a night march, figuring to get clear of Broceliande, and cut across the Troyan prairie, which was a good enough idea only I damned near got myself killed with Igor. Well, Igor got captured, so I demobilized myself and made it to Watling Street." He started filling cups again, but I held mine out of reach. "Due to that business with Orlando I didn't make my point by a long shot. It was just short of Tilbury town where I hit the street, so I cut back east, dined the next night but one at Woodlands, where Johnny Quae Genus slipped me this outfit, and pulled in here yesterday. How's Robin?"

I hadn't mentioned Robin, but apparently the green uniform was known to him. Leaving out such things as I saw fit, I sketched my own experiences since Brian's slaying. I chose not to let him see my eyes, but even so his own watchful ones caught something. Although I had flattered myself that I had been sufficiently casual whenever it was necessary to mention Rosalette, he had but one comment when I was through.

"A lovely girl, eh?"

I felt my face flushing, but I tried to carry it off. "Pretty enough," I yawned. "Just a kid, of course."

"A youngster, and no doubt a gentle one," he conceded, "but just the same she had a bite of your heart."

Beowulf was looking as if he hadn't caught a word of what was being said. Anger started out behind my embarrassment, but it was catching up fast. Golias saw that and laughed.

"Don't take it hard. Your heart will heal up, if it hasn't already, and will be all the stronger for having had a work out. Here, clink 'em."

"What's the program?" I asked by way of changing the subject. "Got any ideas?"

He grew serious. "I know what I'm going to do, and I'd like for you to come with me. But I warn you it may mean long traveling on rough roads."

"I'm used to that," I shrugged. Mentioning Rosalette had brought on a relapse into melancholy; and I was beginning to feel generally let down. "What's on your books?"

He poured all around, and this time I let him fill my mug. "I'll have to ask you to excuse us again, Wulf," Golias said. "But listen in; we may want your advice."

"No apologies needed," Beowulf assured him. "If an undertaking's worth tackling, it's worth talking about first."

"Check." Golias turned to me again. "The day before I ran into young Quae Genus I was fed and lodged through the hospitality of a stranger. His name is Lucius G. Jones; the middle name is spelled G-I-L, and just for the record rhymes with eel not ill. There was no reason for him to foot my bills except that I was broke, and he's a fine fellow.

"Not being clam-mouthed like you," he went on when I merely nodded, "he opened up over the third or fourth bottle we split and told me what was eating him. I always give the courtesy of my ear to the man who's buying the drinks, but this time I was really interested. So I didn't listen noncommittally, like you're doing."

"I'm just tired," I told him. And that was an understatement. The long day and night of walking and drinking had finally caught up with me, straining all the fire from the mead and leaving me only the heaviness. Every cell in my body felt the dead hour of the morning. I wanted to go to bed, provided I could find one, but I wasn't sure it would be worth the effort.

"We all ought to knock off soon," he observed. "Well, this Jones told me what he's up against, which is plenty. He can't marry his girl, he has no place to live, he has no occupation, only a little money left, and no source of income."

Instead of feeling sorry for Jones, I felt sorry for myself. It struck me that he wasn't the only one who couldn't marry the girl he wanted. And if I couldn't do anything about that problem on my own account, it certainly seemed nonsensical to try to do it for someone I had never met.

"He wants the world with a pink ribbon around it, and he hasn't found a job," I commented. "Let him get the occupation and quit beefing."

He raised his brows at my tone. "That's one of his aims, but in some ways it will be the hardest to achieve."

"But how can we help him?" I protested. "We're both broke; and I don't even know what I can find to do here myself."

"I'm offering you something to do," he insisted. "I don't think you've seen all around this prob-

lem, Shandon. It's big. In essence this fellow is
looking for all there is of life. The great questions
for a man are what to do about his time and his
passion, and where to find friends and the money
to live with them. When he's found the right
answers, he's got all the four legs a man needs to
walk on. Could anything be more interesting or
important?"

"Not to him, I expect."

"To us!" he snorted. "To hold the city, to battle
the beast, and to gaze, after biting, on the half-
worm of evil—these are more to do in many ways,
and yet they only solve the great questions if a
man dies doing them. This is a mighty undertaking, too, though you wouldn't think so to hear
some Delian damned fools talk."

I had gone stale on drinking, but nevertheless I
sipped. "What would we have to do?" I asked.

"Everything from living to dying. I warned you
it might be rough; but he treated me like a brother,
when he was almost broke himself. Are you with
me?"

My body was almost asleep, but my mind had
the disillusioned clarity which sometimes comes
as a sort of second wind of late drinking. What did
it matter to me that this fellow had been Golias'
benefactor? Certainly the prospect of putting my
neck on the line for such a reason didn't invite me.
Besides, it seemed to me that I had had enough
excitement and more than enough of foreign
parts.

Golias noticed my hesitation. "No hard feelings
if you don't want to," he said, albeit with a slight
change in his voice. "I never tried to get out of the
Commonwealth myself—my problem has always

been to get in and keep something of a whole skin in the process—but if you shop around, no doubt you can find a way to get back where you came from."

As he said this, I had an overwhelming vision of lying in bed in my snappy little Chicago apartment, waiting for the radio to lull me to sleep. I would hate to say good-bye to Golias, of course; but if he wanted to go chasing somebody else's business all over the country, that was his affair. But as I opened my mouth to tell him as much I noticed that Beowulf was looking at me, waiting to hear my decision.

Suddenly I could not say what I had intended. Remembering what he had done to help out strangers, I simply could not let him hear me say that I would back out on a friend who was asking my help. I wished then that I had never hesitated at all, and belatedly I manufactured a cough.

"Had a tickle in my throat and couldn't talk for a minute," I explained. "Sure. Count me in."

WAY TWO

Highways, A City, The River, and Beyond It

XI

❧ The Undertaking ❧

WHEN HE HAD drained the cup he was drinking, Golias looked at Beowulf. "Think it's time to make our beds?"

The other finished his own drink, looked inside the cup thoughtfully, then placed it on the table upside down. "Yes," he decided. "Will you take the heads or the feet?"

I had risen to accompany them wherever they were going, but I promptly saw that that wasn't far. Among those at our table who had preceded us into slumber a half dozen were wholly or partially supported by the long bench on which we had been sitting. Methodically my two companions picked these up one by one and stretched them out on the floor.

"Just room enough for three of us tandem," Golias observed when they had finished. "Good night, Shandon; good night, Wulf. Ah!"

That was where I lay down instead of between the white sheets I had nostalgically recalled, but I must say my hard bunk didn't keep me awake. It was noon when we breakfasted. Golias and Beowulf, I was amazed to find, didn't have bad hangovers, though all of us were quiet. Late as we had risen, we turned in early that night; and the next morning we were fit for the road.

Brisk and sunny, it was a day for moving. I felt good, especially after having felt not good the day before. Physical well-being was only part of the reason for my fine spirits, however. I was pleased with myself. I hadn't let Golias down. I had chosen to do instead of not to do. My manhood felt the hair on its chest. My mind smouldered with the pleasant fire of curiosity.

We made short work of our farewells, and twenty-five minutes later we reached Watling Street. Eastward signs invited us to Deryabar, at the end of the peninsula, but we turned westward with the breadth of the Commonwealth before us.

The road itself was excellent for walking. It had a firm dirt surface, neither dusty, muddy, nor deeply rutted. Moreover, it had none of the three vices to which many superficially good roads are given. It did not run in a straight line, denying expectation. It did not run on the level, banishing horizons. And certainly it did not offer a sameness of sights and scenery.

It was fortunate that I had worked the kinks out of my legs in Broceliande, for Golias set a stiff pace. But the very speed with which we walked allowed us, he explained, leeway for self-indulgence without keeping us from covering the distance to our rendezvous in the two days he had allotted us. We felt free, therefore, to take our time over beer at some wayside bar, to refresh ourselves with a swim or so, and to stop for a look whenever we found it worth while.

This happened with some frequency, but only one occasion made a genuine place for itself in my memory. Passing through a town, we encountered the local ruler out for an airing with a small bodyguard of troops. Taking a hint from their commander's thumb, we moved to give them plenty of clearance. Then we jumped—but not on their account. Our spryness was the only thing which saved us from being run down by a young girl. In a flowing sequence of actions she pulled her horse back on its hind legs, flung herself off, fell on her knees before the king, and threw back her veil. She had the kind of hot beauty which you wouldn't like if her mind was against you.

We halted to see what was going to happen. His majesty had already stopped, as who wouldn't have?

"Doña Ximena is always welcome to our presence," he announced, not looking as if he meant it.

Her voice went with her face. As she had turned no hostile fire on me, I liked it.

"Doña Ximena hopes your highness will still feel that way, when he hears what she has to say."

He cleared his throat. "Can there be any doubt of it?"

"Sire," she said, without any more sparring, "you know Ruy Diaz de Bivar killed my father."

"Somebody did say something about that." The king wore the look of a man whose painful expectations are being fulfilled. "It is regrettable, but these things will happen when there is bad blood between men."

He looked as if he were going to add that, but she didn't give him time. "As a subject seeking what her sovereign owes her, I demand justice."

She looked to me like an eye-for-an-eye girl. Shifting my glance to the king, I saw he was sure she was.

"It was in fair fight, they tell me. Er—what do you wish me to do?"

"Give him to me!" she cried. "Or rather give me to him in marriage. Ruy Diaz took from me the only man I had; in fact nobody else on earth could have. I ask—and a just king will not deny me—a man for a man."

The relief that showed on his majesty's face was matched only by my astonishment. "Now I've seen everything," I said as we walked on.

"Don't say that until you've been on Watling Street a little longer," Golias cautioned me.

The incident had taken place during the morning of the second day. It was late afternoon when we reached our destination. This was a small hotel called the Reine Pedauque in a town named Hypata. It was built with the second and third stories extending beyond the first and hanging out over the narrow street.

Not that I much cared what the place looked like. I was empty, and my tongue was hanging out. As we approached, my appetites were brought to the boiling point by the rattling of dishes and the clink of glassware. I hadn't quite made up my mind about food, but there was no question about what I wanted to drink. For the past half-hour I had been imagining the delights of sluicing my drought with cold beer. In the faith of this mission I was eagerly crossing the street, my eyes fixed on the open door of the tap room, when Golias gave me a shove. It was timely, for a man descending from the upper story window just missed me.

Until that instant the street had been quiet. That changed. A woman partly hidden from public view by a sheet leaned out of a casement and screamed for the law. A man appeared at the next window cursing and yelling. The pistol he held concerned me more, however. It had a barrel like a sawed-off shotgun. Luckily the bullet only skinned my knuckles, and the weapon wasn't a repeater. A second woman stuck her head out and asked what kind of a house did the fugitive think she kept anyhow. A young girl gave something of an answer by shrieking that he was a two-timing tomcat who had better stay away from her bed in the future. Inside there were shoutings, the slamming of doors, and the pounding of feet on stairs.

The man who was the object of all this attention made no rebuttal. Not having a parachute, he had landed solidly, though evidently without breaks or sprains. It took him an instant to throw off the shock of his jump, but when he did he scrambled to his feet. Without waiting to dust himself off, he dashed away.

I was dazedly sucking my knuckles, when Golias grabbed me by the arm. "Come on!" he cried. "Don't lose him!"

With the words he took after the fugitive, and I grumpily trailed them. Leaving the hotel when I all but had refreshment in my mouth peeved me. Having to run, tired and stiff as I was, further soured my disposition. I didn't exert myself until I heard people yelling behind us. Then it occurred to me that I would probably be taken for an accomplice, so I made better time.

Fortunately our pursuers weren't athletes.

Once we had ducked down a side street and through an alley to another, we had lost them. Calling this information to the others, I walked my bad disposition to where they waited.

Golias didn't share my irritation. On the contrary, he grinned at the stranger and myself as if a comfortable bond had already been established between us.

"Shandon," he panted, "Meet Lucius G. Jones."

Unabashed by the circumstances of the introduction, the latter gave me his hand. He was a handsome young fellow, well set up, clean-cut, and sandy-haired. Yet it wasn't his looks but the winning good nature of his expression that got around me. In spite of the stitch in my side and my smarting hand, I found myself responding to his smile.

"Are you that popular everywhere you go?" I asked him.

He chuckled. "There really wasn't as much to it as seemed probable from all the noise they made."

"There's the Saracen's Head across the street," Golias suggested.

"After you had left to meet Shandon here," Jones said to him, when we had given our orders, "there wasn't much to do while waiting for your return, and—was there a girl, did you notice, joining to castigate me?"

"If you mean was there a girl telling the world you were a son of a bitch, there was," I informed him.

"One of the maids," he explained. "A curious misnomer, and not by my original fault, I assure you." The beer was brought. We drank and put the mugs down, sighing. "Now in spite of what you may have gathered from her attitude," he went on, "our relations were of the friendliest; and if she had any cause for complaint, she made none. I on my part was true to her every minute I was with her, but that, due to the rigors of her duties, could only be during the night. There remained the days.

"As it happened, a woman checked into the room next to mine the day before yesterday. She was too chary of her reputation to risk having visitors at night; but she was, she told me, under her physician's orders to take a nap every afternoon. Not much later she let me know that she was not one of these timorous ladies who locks herself in. In fact she was so informative that I wonder why she didn't tell me she was expecting her husband this evening—which perhaps she wasn't."

Jones chased a fly from his beer. "At any rate he arrived just before you did and was shown to his wife's room by the landlady, three lads carrying his traveling bag, and a maid—the one who considered herself entitled to the local rights on my person—bearing refreshment. Being, luckily, less incautious than the lady—who began to yell 'rape!' as soon as she heard her husband's voice—I had locked the door. The time it took them to smash it in synchronized with the time it took me to dress. It was by then apparent to me that nobody liked me, and, rather than participate in a scene, I left as they entered."

"Next time you draw fire," I proposed, "catch the bullets yourself."

For the first time he looked serious. "I'm sorry about that, Shandon. I know how aggravated you must feel. If a man gets shot he should at least have the satisfaction of having earned it."

"He's probably deserved shooting somewhere along the line," Golias remarked. "I can think of few men who didn't, and I can't remember liking any of them. What are you planning to do about your luggage?"

Jones looked blank. "Do you know," he said after a minute, "that that's something I overlooked in my well executed retreat?"

"One of us will get it," Golias said. "Is your bill paid, by any chance?"

"Up until yesterday at noon. But I'm afraid I can't pay what's still owing and buy us all a supper tonight."

"Do that now." Golias took up the offer as matter-of-factly as it had been made. Fumbling in his pockets, he drew forth a couple of huge gold bracelets. "Hrothgar—the king at Heorot, you know, Shandon—gave me these for my singing. Eighteen-karat stuff. I'll swap 'em in for cash tomorrow, and we'll be flush again."

After supper we engaged rooms for the night. Jones ordered a bottle of wine—port jacked up with brandy, to judge from the taste—and we made ourselves comfortable in a corner of the hotel tap room. Seeing others smoking, I learned that, although no cigarettes or cigars were available, the house supplied pipes and tobacco. The others weren't interested, but I enjoyed several pipefuls, while we held our council of war.

"Suppose you tell Shandon what you told me the other day," Golias proposed by way of opening the discussion. "I've given him only the general idea of what you're up against, thinking it better that he should learn the details from you at first hand."

Up to that moment Jones had seemed remarkably assured. Now he showed how young he was by blushing.

"A man shouldn't blurt out the things I've got to say, but—well, I need help, and you two are kind enough to offer it. The fact is, though, that I'm not at all sure that anything can be done."

"Shoot the story, if you don't mind," I suggested.

"I probably don't mind as much as I should. As Golias already knows, I'm one of these damnable people who find it soothing to talk about their personal affairs." He grimaced deprecatingly. "It's easy to blow to strangers about being reared in luxury. It so happens, and I won't bore you with elaboration, that I was. One consequence of this was that it did not occur to me that I had enemies. Another was that I was trained for nothing except to look after the land."

"You mean be a farmer?" I asked.

He smiled. "You can call it that, though we say 'baron.' Seeing that the land keeps productive is one of the most important parts of the job, but there's a great deal more to it. There are hundreds of people living on the land who have to be kept healthy, kept at work, kept out of jail, educated, rewarded, punished, helped in the pinches, and so forth. Others might not like it; but I consider it the best work in the world, and it's all I know."

My acquaintance with him so far hadn't prepared me for a strain of idealism. I decided, however, to reserve that for future consideration. Taking my pipe out of my mouth, I pointed the stem at him.

"But you're not doing that now."

"I'm not, damn it, nor other things I'd like to be doing. Some of it's my own fault, though, as I hinted, I have other enemies. No, wait a minute; I'll speak of them a little later. To take things up in order, it was always believed that I'd fall heir to my grandfather's title. My father, naturally, had been next in line, but he disappeared."

"And you never could locate him?"

"My grandfather—I was an infant at the time— never could find out what happened, or who was at the bottom of it. It is only recently that I've had reason to suspect that his enemy was Don Rodrigo Monks Ravan, a cousin of mine—if I'm legitimate, that is."

After a quick double take, I passed over this latter point. "What makes you think he's the weasel in the henyard?"

He made a roundabout answer to this question. "The fellow had shown me no enmity I was clever enough to detect, until I seemed likely to succeed in making what the world would consider a very good match, and I would view as the greatest happiness life could offer." Jones showed his teeth. "In spite of the lady's refusal, Don Rodrigo wanted her, or at least the property she is to inherit. He therefore produced evidence purporting to show that I was born out of wedlock."

"So what?" I demanded.

Golias cocked an amused eye at me, and Jones looked startled. "Well, my grandfather—and he's a dear old gentleman—probably wouldn't care if I was his son's bastard, but the accusation ran that I was my dead mother's, aided by some third party. The property goes with the blood, and he now believes that I haven't got it."

"And this Ravan has, you say?"

Jones laughed harshly. "Would you believe it? I never gave the matter any thought even when a closer cousin was shot by a highwayman not long ago; but with both of us out of the way, my Lord Ravan is the heir."

This Don Rodrigo was undoubtedly something you wouldn't want to get on your shoes, but I couldn't help shaking my head in admiration of this methods. "So in one move, without taking his feet off the desk, he pays you off for being your dad's son, keeps you from marrying his girl, and deals himself a fortune. What did he have against your old man?"

"My father, assuming that I know who he is?" Jones shook his head. "If I knew that, I might have some idea of where to begin an investigation."

"Never mind what you don't know," Golias cut in. "Tell Shandon just why you set out from home."

"Aside from the fact I was no longer too welcome, you mean." Jones had spilled a little wine in the course of his recital. Now he dipped his finger in it and began doodling on the table. "Well, when you can't stay, you go, and hope for the best, but I'm trying to do more than that. That land is where I want to be, the only place I'll ever want to stay, and I believe it to be mine. The key to retrieving it is the establishment of my legitimacy. I was starting out to try to do so, when I ran into Golias back there at the Reine Pedauque."

There was still a matter he hadn't dealt with.

"What about your girl? Does she care whether you have a birth certificate or not?"

"She probably cares to eat," Golias said.

"She does not!" Jones protested. "Well, naturally, she does, but she doesn't care about money and title as such." Jumping to his feet, he raised his glass. "Gentlemen, I give you the Lady Hermione Steingerd ap Hawthorn."

"I can't place her, unless she's some kin of old Penkawr's," Golias murmured thoughtfully. "A mean old coot."

"I repeat," Jones said, overriding this interruption, "I give you the lovely Hermione Steingerd ap Hawthorn, a lady who would go anywhere and live under any conditions with a man—" Here he drank with a flourish, then let his glass hang from a limp hand to spill its last few drops on the floor "—if only she loved him," he whispered.

This reversal of form took me aback. "I thought you said she did."

"Exactly." Reseating himself, he filled his glass moodily. "I used the past tense, and correctly. Two things happened. A witch—and one of the things I wish to find out is whether or not she is in Don Rodrigo's employ—put a curse upon us."

"Of what nature?" Golias asked sharply before I could comment.

"It's design was to bar our union," Jones answered, "and so far it has operated to make all our meetings since then break off in bitterness. That's just one of the things," he went on, holding up his hand as Golias looked ready to speak again. "The other, which may or may not be related, is that Ravan or someone, used some youthful peccadillos of mine to poison Hermione's mind against me."

Having just lost Rosalette myself, I could almost have echoed the sigh which trailed his statement, until I remembered something. "And is that," I enquired, "the thing that was worrying you, when you baled out of that window?"

Jones stopped looking soulful to glance at me sidewise. Finally he gave a shamefaced snicker.

"I'd have a hard time proving it, wouldn't I? But I know better than my conduct witnesses. At present my soul—which my charmer can't reject—is living on one level, while my person, which she has banished, exists on another. Only with her benediction can they join company in the heights to which they both aspire."

Once having been stirred, my native skepticism still had its fur up. "Is that on the level, or are you just hitching words together for the fun of it?"

He put his hand on his heart. "I swear to you, Shandon, that if my Hermione had not exiled me from her favor, I would never again look twice at another woman."

"Well, we'll see what can be done about squaring things for you." Golias signaled the waiter. "If not, we'll find somebody equally lovely somewhere in the course of our expedition."

Jones stiffened. "There *is* nobody equally lovely."

"I haven't had the honor of meeting the lady in question," Golias said, "though I have no doubt she is above praise. Nevertheless, I don't like this business about the curse put on you—it's a tough thing to get around—and a reasonably wide acquaintance in the Commonwealth convinces me that there are others—"

"Not for me!" Jones insisted. He leaned forward earnestly. "This isn't just a fancy, gentlemen. Years ago a soothsayer told me that I would wed Hawthorn's daughter or die wifeless."

To my astonishment Golias took this as seriously as he had taken the curse. "Oh, that's different," he asserted. "All right, we pledge ourselves to do what we can to help win her for you."

While Jones was thanking him, the new bottle was brought, and there was silence until it was opened. Now that we had apparently seen the dimensions of his trouble, it seemed to me high time to find out what I, as his volunteer ally, had let myself in for.

"You said a while back," I remarked, when the waiter had gone, "that you thought the first thing to do was to get yourself in line for your inheritance again."

"It's an essential of success in all directions," Jones said. "I certainly would never ask my darling to marry a pauper."

"And old Hawthorn would no doubt see you and her damned before he'd let her," Golias put in. "Now when I first met you, you told me that you intended to begin by locating Ravan with a view to trying to squeeze the truth out of him. Are you still of that mind?"

"Yes. I said 'locate,' because I've temporarily lost track of him. As Don Rodrigo is the king's favorite, he is apt to be in court when not in these parts, although it's possible that he may be at another one of his numerous estates. It is also possible that the king himself is rusticating rather than holding formal court; but that's one of the things we have to find out." Jones looked from one to the other of us. "With your approval we'll go to the City, then."

"The logical course," Golias assented.

"Which city?" I demanded.

"When you speak of 'the City' here," Golias explained, "you mean Ilium. Although the Commonwealth is rich in famous towns, none is of comparable importance. Inasmuch as the arch king holds court there, it can also be considered the capital."

As I had yet to see one of the country's major cities, that part of the idea suited me well enough. My attention was fixed, however, on a different aspect of the trip.

"You say this bird whose tail we're trying to salt is the king's favorite," I said. "Won't that make him hard to squeeze?"

"It will," Jones agreed. He ran a hand through his hair. "That's why I need help. It is also perhaps a reason why I shouldn't ask it. It will be such a dangerous undertaking that we'll be lucky to come out with our lives."

"Oh, Shandon doesn't mind," Golias announced, while I was somberly reviewing Jones' statement. "Here, let me fill around."

XII

⟡ Down Watling Street ⟡

RIGHT AFTER breakfast the next day Golias hocked his gold and paid Jones' hotel bill, thereby releasing his luggage. For a man on the road he had quite a wardrobe, but with coaching he whittled it down to what he could carry in a small knapsack. Due to limited means, walking was to remain our way of traveling.

My own costume and that of Golias I have already described, except for the two sword canes the latter insisted on purchasing for us. Jones was dressed like neither one of us. Above tawny stockings were azure knee pants, while above them was a red jacket frilled with gold braid. A sword hung at his belt.

The thought of actually being on his way to do something about his destiny put him in high spirits, and I felt good myself. There is a special feeling attendant upon traveling a region's greatest road toward its greatest city. Moreover, I was acquiring the comfortable sensation of belonging wherever I was that is the property of a seasoned traveler. In proportion as the Commonwealth ceased to confound me with its strangeness, my interest in it grew.

I don't mean to imply that the element of novelty disappeared from my experiences. About two in the afternoon of the third day out of Hypata, the road ran through a grove of oaks. We had hardly reached it, when we heard a commotion around the bend just ahead of us. We kept on our way, though slowing down, until a woman's scream was mixed with other noises of a struggle. I was still willing to investigate with caution, but Jones started to hurry forward. Grabbing for him, I hauled him back.

"Take it easy, Lucius," I advised.

"But that's a woman calling!" he cried, tugging away from me and trying to draw his sword.

"Look, son," I said, "all women aren't hurt when they yell, and some that are hurt ought to be. Let's find out before you start carving people."

There was another screech, and Jones grew wild-eyed. "Let me go, damn it!" He tore away from me to dash down the road, waving his sword and shouting for persons unknown to quit whatever they were doing on pain of death.

It made me nervous, and I looked at Golias. "We can't let him go alone," he said. Well, we couldn't, so we began running, too.

When we reached the turn of the road, Jones had slowed down for understandable reasons. There were women in trouble, but not women who could be helped. The commotion we had heard had plainly been the thrashing of a body as it dangled from a branch. The first shriek had been the last cry before the hanged woman's breath was shut inside of her. The second had been a wail of discovery on the part of a mourner.

Left to myself, I would have detoured, not out of fear of the dead but out of distrust of the living. Being found by a corpse in a country where I was unable to produce credentials was not to my liking. Nor, as we could do nothing useful, was there anything to exchange for the risk. Golias didn't like it either and yelled to Jones to hold off, but it was too late. Lucius had slowed, but he hadn't stopped.

"We've got to find out who did this," he called back.

Exchanging resigned glances, we joined him. By then he had squatted down by the live woman, who had thrown herself on the ground, and was trying to comfort her. We on our part first gave our attention to the dead one. I can't remember ever having seen an uglier hag. She had a face like one of the shriveled cocoanut masks which bar owners are unaccountably given to importing from the tropics. Her complexion was nearly as hairy as a cocoanut, and only a shade or two lighter. The body below was shapeless, as though it had been stuffed piecemeal into the dirty garments, which were those of a gypsy. The fact that her clothes were gaudy contributed to make them look horrible.

The other person, we found when we turned to look at her, was but a girl, a jump from puberty one side or the other. She, too, was a gypsy, to judge from her clothes and what we could see of her face. Jones had it pressed against his shoulder and was patting her on the back.

"Tell us who did it," he alarmed me by volunteering, "and we'll go and see that they get what's coming to them."

Much as I wanted to get away from there, I had to admit that the child was in need of comfort. I felt even worse about her when she finally checked her sobs enough to be able to talk.

"No—nobody d-done it. She—scragged herself."

That knowledge must have made the discovery doubly awful for her, though I was relieved that we wouldn't have to undertake vengeance for the hanging in addition to the business we already had on our hands. Aside from the fact that I couldn't see that it was any of our concern, I felt that anybody who had killed that crone would have been guilty of no more than a misdemeanor, at the worst.

Still the fact that I wouldn't be called on to do anything released more sympathy for the girl. Lucius was gawking, not knowing how to comment on the suicide, so I took over.

"Is she a relative of yours, kid?"

"My grannam."

"Your granny, eh? Are you sure she hanged herself?"

"I know she done it. She was disapp'inted."

She was talking more steadily. Thinking that anything would be better for her than speechless grief, I pursued the subject.

"She was disappointed, eh?" Knowing that the lack of security is the bogey-man of the aged, I made a stab in the dark. "Did she lose out on some money she was expecting to get?"

The girl still wouldn't raise her head from Jones' shoulder, but she freed one eye. "The poor people don't need money," she said enigmatically. Then she suddenly burst into tears again. "But he didn't die!"

Lucius and I blinked at each other. "Who didn't die?" he asked.

"My gr-grannam's enemy."

I hadn't noticed what Golias was doing, but, hearing him cough, I glanced at him. He was leaning against the bole of the fatal tree, surveying us with sardonic interest. His voice, however, was winning when he spoke.

"If a woman doesn't love, she must hate," he remarked.

The girl sat up to stare at him. "My grannam had no one to love except me. She left her people."

Golias' voice was now that of a cross-examiner who knows the facts. "Because of this enemy?"

"Yes."

"What had he done?"

"He—she hated him, because her people liked him."

"That happens," he agreed. "Listen; we are not the law and couldn't hurt your grandmother if we were. What could an old woman do to a man?"

For a while the little gypsy hesitated, then she looked up from under her straggling hair with a half grin. "I don't think my grannam could've done anything to that man—a big strong one, tall as this rye with the run of silver in his hair—but somebody give him some milk." She brightened at the recollection. "It made him sick. We saw him, and he thought he was going to die." Then her face fell, and her voice dropped with it. "But he got well."

"And your grandmother was very old." Golias' voice had become warmly sympathetic.

"It was what she had to live for," the girl whispered, "and she knew she'd never have another chance."

It had taken Jones a moment to absorb the fact that the girl he had been comforting was mourning for a thwarted poisoner. He sat back, then rose to edge sheepishly away from her. Remembering how I had warned him, I was mean enough to be gratified. I grinned at his embarrassment, though I liked him for having been so eager to help.

"Ready to go on now?" I enquired.

"In a minute," Golias answered for him. "We can't leave her hanging for the child to look at, Shandon."

"Right," I admitted.

The girl bounced to her feet. "You won't take her away?"

"Not I, sister." I thought of making off with that hideous corpse and shook my head again. "Your grandma will be right here for the coroner."

Apparently she was convinced. "You cut her from tree, and I go for friends," she said, and darted away through the trees.

When she had gone, I hitched up my belt and walked over to take hold of the old woman's foot. This was bravado, because I wasn't happy about the task ahead.

"She's a hefty cadaver," I announced, after giving the body a shake.

"Oh, I wish I'd done that!"

Hearing a strange voice at such a time made me start. During our preoccupation a man had approached to within a few yards of us unheard. In cut his clothes resembled those of Golias, although they were at once more subdued and more dandified. The fellow himself was small and chubby. Where his cheeks weren't hidden by a moustache like black porcupine quills, they were round and pink. From above this bundle of whiskers he was staring at us from mild blue eyes.

Irritated, because I was jittery, I snapped at him. "Done what?"

He started to point with his hand and then, as if that made him nervous, he indicated the corpse with his riding crop. "That," he said respectfully. "If I could only get up the resolution to hang somebody—not to mention the extra points I'd make if it was a defenseless old woman—I could live in peace for the rest of my life."

Finding I still had hold of the hag's foot, I let it go. It swung with the body, as if kicking at me, and I jumped again.

"Let's get this straight," I said. "Are you accusing us of lynching this old dame?"

Taking out a glorified snoose box, he dipped into it. Guides and lumber jacks, the only people I had ever seen use snuff, mouth it; but he stuffed some up his nose. As he might have known, he sneezed. His dog bone of a moustache came off, more to my surprise than his. Matter-of-factly he replaced it.

"I wasn't accusing you," he pointed out. "I was envying you." His tone became professional. "Where did you catch her?"

He had annoyed me so much that I couldn't put my mind together about him. While I was trying to decide whether he was crazy or just a smart aleck, Jones spoke up.

"I assure you, sir, that you're under a misapprehension. This is a case of suicide, of which we were unlucky enough to be early witnesses."

The newcomer looked astonished. "Then she's not a witch?"

"I wouldn't go bail for the fact that she's not a witch," Golias said. "If I had to bet, I'd chance it that she was; but we had nothing to do with her death."

"Nothing at all!" Lucius said.

Sucking at the silver tip of his riding crop, the fellow stared at the dead woman, as if waiting for her to testify against us. "Then she didn't curse you?" he said finally.

I wanted to tell him to scat, but I feared he might get suspicious and put the finger on us before we could get out of the neighborhood. "No," I told him, as mildly as I could manage, "of course not."

"You were luckier than Rupert," he remarked.

I was about to speak again, and with less restraint, when Golias put his hand on my arm. "Who's Rupert?" he asked.

"The first baronet," the man answered. "Oh, I didn't introduce myself, did I? I'm Sir Despard Murgatroyd—the twenty-second baronet, you know." He made a sweeping gesture with his crop. "Own all this."

That didn't make me feel good, and I was even more uncomfortable when Jones whispered to me: "That means he's a justice of the peace." Then he addressed the baronet. "If you wish to know why you found us here with the body, there'll be a member of the old woman's family along in a minute."

"I'll take your word for it. I always do." Sir Despard took some more snuff, sneezed, shook his moustache loose from its mooring again, and put it back. "I never prosecute anyone, because I know nobody's a sinner compared with us Murgatroyds."

His face assumed a gloomy pride, as he said this, but he quickly lost that expression. "Except for me," he added. "I just naturally can't make myself live up to the curse."

"But why should it bother you?" Jones asked. "I thought you said it was the first baronet whom the witch cursed."

"Runs in the family," the other explained. "We have to do an evil deed every day, but I only sort of fake it. Makes the older baronets furious, and they come from their graves and devil me. Gives me insomnia."

He seemed well disposed toward us, but under the circumstances and as long as he was a justice of the peace, I thought it best to show him our hearts were kind. "That's bad," I said, clicking my tongue and shaking my head.

"What I want to know," Golias siad, "is how you avoid fatal consequences, if you're not fulfilling the terms?"

Murgatroyed looked embarrassed. "Oh, I promise to do better, and that's a lie, you know, and helps some. Then I *do* do some things, like abducting innocent girls. Of course, I see that they're home before it's late, and I always let their parents know where they are, so they won't be wor—Ah, there's my carriage now, I think. I asked my man to pick me up here."

With the words he trotted over to the side of the road and gazed toward the bend around which we had come. I, too, could hear horses approaching, and in a moment four of them appeared, drawing a gaily painted vehicle. They were traveling fast, but the driver brought them to an abrupt halt. A man jumped from the seat beside him and gave the baronet a salute.

"She's been run off with, your honor."

"Good, good," Sir Despard stroked his phony moustache. "Er—did she scream?"

The man looked concerned. "I had to pay extra to have her scream. She done a pretty good job, though."

"Worth it, then," the baronet decided. "Take me home, and then you'd best go back after her. We wouldn't want to make her late for tea."

"Rather not!" the other agreed. He opened the door of the coach and gave Murgatroyd a boost in. The latter waved to us as he seated himself. The former sprang back to the seat beside the driver. The driver cracked a twenty-foot whip. The horses sprang forward.

To my surprise I found myself wishing that the baronet had stayed a little longer. "At times," I chuckled, "there's not better company than an earnest nut. Just the same, I'm glad he took those other two away before they saw the old hag."

"I was worrying about that myself," Jones said. "But I'm sure they didn't, as she was well back in the shade."

"Keeping right still and not making a sound," Golias added. "Well, we better get her down before somebody else comes along."

Glancing at the crone with distaste, I decided to stall a moment longer. "What do you figure was really the matter with that screwball?"

"Why you heard him," Lucius protested. "The

poor devil's under a curse! Having the same affliction, I can tell you it's no fun."

"A curse often livens things up," Golias asserted, "but one ought to be tried on for size before a man walks off with it." He seemed pleased with his thoughts. "That's the trouble with hand-me-downs. Speaking of which, will you hand her down to me, or shall I hand her down to you?"

"I'll flip you," I said, unwilling to make a choice in such a business. "Heads, I climb; tails you do."

Tails came up, and as I had foreseen, I immediately felt as though he had the best of the bargain. Glumly I watched while he ascended. This in itself was not difficult. A low crotch and a series of small branches explained how it had been possible for the old woman to reach the big limb from which she was suspended. More quickly than I wanted him to, Golias was straddling it directly above her. Then he drew the knife I remembered.

"Ready?"

"Ready as I'll ever be." I stretched my arms up along side of her, thought I wasn't going to grab hold of her until it was aboslutely necessary.

Probably I looked as disturbed as I felt, for Golias was grinning at me. "There are women you're luckier to have in your arms dead than alive, and this is one of them." Placing his knife between his teeth, he shifted position, let go with his hands, and swung by his knees. Getting a grip on the woman's hair, so she wouldn't fall sideways, he started sawing at the harness strap which had choked her.

It was a good thing he did have a steadying hold

on her. I couldn't reach high enough to get her above the center of balance. She was even heavier than I had thought, and I nearly dropped her when the strap snapped and Golias let go. For a horrible moment, staggering to keep my footing, I wrestled with that dead crone, my face pressed into her greasy, rank garments.

Before I could get the situation under control, a stranger's voice cried: "Unhand that damsel, recreant! And don't think to escape the consequences of your vicious lust even when you do. Unhand her, I say!"

I was in no mood for jokes, as I meant to point out to this new kibitzer. Whoever it was, his voice came from the direction of the road, but I was too busy to look at him. Disengaging my face from the hag's blouse, I began to lower her to the ground.

"What, a rape before my very eyes, you lascivious scoundrel!" If the fellow wasn't really angy, he was a good actor. "Never fear, princess, help is at hand. I will blast this rascal as Mudarra blasted Velasquez. Now, minion, make what pitiful attempt to guard yourself that you can."

Intent on getting what I had to do over with, I still ignored him. Gritting my teeth, I composed the corpse's arms and legs as decently as I could.

"Shandon! Watch out!" Jones shouted.

Before he spoke I had heard a scuffling noise. Glancing up, I saw a startling sight. Rapt in my task, I either hadn't heard the horse coming around the bend or the sound hadn't made any impression on me. But there was a horse there, all right, and a donkey, too. Both had riders, but the man on the horse held my eyes, because he was spurring in my direction. There were peculiar things about this fellow, but I concentrated on the fact that he had a long, pointed stick in his hand. As the horse picked up speed, he swung this weapon so that it was aimed right at me.

Dropping the hag's right arm, I took off from a squatting position in a dive designed to take me out of my assailant's path. It was only mostly successful. I avoided being speared, but I didn't entirely clear the horse. One of his hoofs caught me in the fanny while I was in midair. The effect, not counting a bruise, was to spin me around so that I landed sitting down, in a position to watch the further activities of my attacker. They were not without interest.

In the first place, I had been right about his intentions. He had meant to stick me like a park attendant collecting trash. In my absence the point of the pole struck the ground and stayed fixed. The horse, the rider, and the rest of the weapon the latter was holding continued to move. The thing didn't give, and the rider would not or could not let go. I had never seen a man pole vault from horseback before, but he made it. With a rattle and a clank he swung from out of the saddle and hit the identical limb from which Golias had just lowered the old woman. He had lost interest in his stick by then. It fell, but he just managed not to. It was a tough scramble, but he held on and perched there fifteen feet above the ground.

As Golias had descended, he had the branch all to himself; but he needed no foil to make him an arresting figure. He was dressed in rusty boiler plate. The parts didn't match, all looking either too big or too small for him. His helmet, which

was of bronze instead of iron, sat on top of his
head, giving his face no protection. I could therefore see that this fellow who had tried so hard to
kill me was a cadaverous old man. For an extra
touch he was straddling the branch at the spot
where the hag had jumped off. Her suicide strap,
dangling between his legs, looked like a tail as
stringy as his whiskers.

"Enchantment," he muttered. "Overcome by
enchantment."

His grief wasn't mine. That bruise hurt, and I
had been shaken up. My nerves had received even
worse treatment. Furiously I rose and stooped for
his pole.

"Come on down and let's talk this over," I
snarled.

With intent to prod him toward the trunk, I was
raising the point of the stick toward him when
something hit me in the knees. They buckled, but
the impact wasn't enough to sink me. Looking
down, I saw that my new assailant was a fat, little
man, the one who had been riding the donkey. He
clung to my legs until I poked him with the blunt
end of the pole, then he rose and started for me
once more. Again using the pole, I held him off
without difficulty, seeing that he kept his eyes
tightly shut. For a full two minutes he aimed blind
haymakers at me. During that period, though he
was naturally heating himself up, I was cooling
down. I was almost ready to smile when he found
he had run out of juice and simply leaned against
the pole.

"Are you through," I asked, "or are you just
resting between rounds?"

I could see he had been expecting a counterattack. When nothing happened to him, he opened one eye.

"Do you give up?"

"No," I said, "I'm afraid I'm still in the ring."

With a magnificent shrug he turned his back on me. "Master," he reported to the man in the tree, "he says he won't surrender."

The old fellow didn't answer, as his attention was elsewhere. I hadn't had time to find out what Golias and Jones were doing while I was having my troubles. Now I saw that the former had climbed back up the tree, while the latter had caught the horse—a skinny nag—and was leading it back. My forearm was looking from one to the other to see what they were up to.

It was Golias who gave the first clue as to what they had in mind. "Bring the charger right below us, Lucius," he called. Then he addressed the iron-plated scarecrow. "Most worthy paladin, I have come to help you descend from a place and position so unfitting to one of your high birth, noble accomplishments, and dignified bearing."

Like myself, my enemy was in a less hostile frame of mind. "You speak graciously, and I will meet your courtesy with suitable frankness. I would most gladly leave this uncomfortable perch if the redoubtable enchanter," here he waved a rusty glove at me, "will release me from his spell."

"We," Golias astonished me by saying, "are servants of the mighty wizard, and he has sent us, out of his magnanimity, to aid you. No, a little more to the right, Lucius. Just there." He had by then reached the old boy and took him by the arm. "Do you think if I lower you, you can stand in the saddle and alight safely?"

"Naturally," the fellow said. "It goes without saying that the most renowned knight-errant of this or any age is exquisitely versed in equitation."

"I expect no less," Golias assured him, "but remember your saddle's been worn pretty smooth. All right now, swing your right leg over the branch. I've got you."

"Standing in the saddle," the other said as he complied, "is merely a matter of practice, amplifying, you will understand, a native aptitude. Observe how I do it."

We observed. While he had been talking, Golias had succeeded in lowering him, metal casing and all, from the perch which they shared. The old geezer had hardly ceased speaking when his feet touched the saddle. As this was as far as Golias could reach while still maintaining a firm position, he let go.

He might as well have shoved him, or whipped the horse. The man's feet had barely established contact with the saddle when they were on their way again. Fortunately they were both pointed in the same direction. With a sound like an iron testicle smashing scrap steel he sat down, bounced upward and forward, and would have hit the ground with another awful clank if Lucius hadn't been there to break his fall.

I was still wincing at the thought of his crash landing when he straightened himself with a series of creaking jerks and smiled. "That's the way it's done, gentlemen. The feather touch to the saddle, a deft vault into the arms of one's equerry, and here we are."

XIII

❦ Shenanigans at Upton ❦

WHILE HIS COMPANION had been engaged in the described maneuvers, the little fat chap had sidled up to inspect the dead hag. "Master," he announced, "she looks powerfully like just a dead old bitch to me."

"Of course, she's dead," I declared. "We found her hanging from that tree."

"Women aren't found on tress," the old codger corrected me. "They are engendered and born exactly like other people.

"It's a clear case of enchantment all around," he went on before I could think of anything to say. "Only the most diabolical of magicians could give that beautiful damsel, whose name, if I mistake not, is Princess Erminia of Colchis, such an odious appearance. It is wonderful, too, how the trance she is in apes death. A man less experienced in such matters than I would be completely fooled."

He glanced at Jones, who, polite as usual, was trying to look respectfully interested, then at Golias, who did, in fact, seem absorbed. "To close more loopholes for doubt, I refer once more to the statement she was plucked from a tree. My first hasty conclusion was to doubt this, but I can now see that I was wrong. The fact that she was dangling from a bough is of a piece with the rest of the evil spell of which she is the victim. Lastly, it is obvious that I, the supreme paladin of paladins, could never have been overcome—as I am forced to confess that I was—except through means of the most potent incantations." With this statement he turned to his chubby partner. "Is it all clear to you now, my son?"

The other scratched his head. "Your being on that branch is the clincher for me. Nobody couldn't have put you up there, loaded down with junk the way you are, without he knew a barrel full of magic."

"Let me," Golias put in, "present to you the mighty magician, Shandon Silverlock, whose wiles have rendered powerless your else all-conquering arms. Shandon, this is the noble, puissant, and chivalrous Don Quixote de la Mancha, conquerer of High Utopia and Low Cockaigne, savior of Lubberland, shield of Dun Coba, protector of Saffron-Walden, prince of paladins, squire of dames, and dean of knights errant."

The old fellow worked up a squeaky bow. "I yield not to your prowess, but to the overwhelming force of your magic. I trust, as you have been magnanimous enough to release me from the tree, that you will not demand my sword?"

"No," I said. I didn't ask him what he thought I

would do with the chunk of rust he referred to, nor
did I smile.

He managed another bow. "That's very gracious of you. Indeed, you conduct yourself so well
that I grieve to have to remain your enemy."
Somehow he succeeded in folding his arms.
"Well, then, what disposition will you make of
me as your prisoner?"

Instinctively I looked at Golias. All I gained was
the knowledge that he was interested in finding
out what I would do. What he saw in my eyes
changed his, and he nodded, as if confirming an
opinion.

I think it was then that I really comprehended
what had been happening to me ever since
the *Naglfar* let me down into the waters off Aeaea.
It was nothing less than a searching change in my
conception of my own character. Everybody has
an idea of himself which augments, aggravates, or
modifies the actuality. In my own case the idea
had been clear enough. I had taken not a melancholy but an unjoyous pride in thinking of myself
as a cold-eyed factualist who saw no reason for
acting otherwise than selfishly. Recognizing myself for such a person, I had for years worked, like
other men, to contain myself in the bounds allotted by my individuality.

Now, since reaching the Commonwealth, there
had been alterations. My thinking and my emotions had got so they paid no attention to my
fences. I had acquired the faculties of wonder and
credulity. Most different of all, my actions tended
to be sparked by what I read in other people as
well as by my own undiluted impulses.

This old gazook had tried to kill me, and I still

felt the bruise I had collected in escaping him. He belonged in the nut hatch. By all the canons of reasons and civic welfare, he shouldn't be allowed to go on riding around poking poles at people who had done him no harm. If nothing else was considered, somebody ought to take that hardware away from him before he got himself killed. But it wasn't going to be I. Crazy or not, there was something sweet about the old crackpot; and I liked the thoroughness with which he carried the thing off.

I hesitated a while before I spoke, though. Pretense, at least for anybody's benefit except my own, was new to me.

"What will you do if I release you from my spell?" I finally began.

"Attack you and rescue the beautiful princess you have so wrongfully abducted and misformed."

"Well, I can't afford to let that happen. You can understand that. Let's see—" I was having a hard time, stumbling through unfamiliar territory. "Suppose we make a bargain; will you keep it?"

He inclined his head. "If it's an honorable one, on the word of a knight."

"So will I, on the word of a magician. Well, it's this way, Mr. de la Mancha: way down south of here in Aphasia—" I glanced at Golias to see how I was doing.

"Basse or Haute Aphasia?" he enquired.

"Oh, Basse," I said, though not having any notion as to what he meant. "In Basse Aphasia—and not Haute, mind you—there's a giant named Paul Bunyan. He's so tough my magic just bounces off him, but I imagine you could lick him—conquer him, that is to say."

"Undoubtedly," de la Mancha said, "always provided he's not a wizard or a sorcerer."

"No, he's nothing like that. He's just big and strong and a hell of a fighter."

"The greater my glory when I defeat him," the old boy pointed out.

"Exactly. Now this giant has a blue ox, which can do more work than a fleet of tractors."

"Or ten thousand mules," Golias suggested.

"Yes, that's more like it," I agreed. "You see, he promised me that ox in exchange for helping him make the Big Rock Candy Mountains, but when pay day came around, he just laughed at me."

De la Mancha had been following my remarks with care. "It need hardly be said that I can win the remarkable creature for you," he told me, when I had finished telling of my helplessness in the face of Bunyan's perfidy, "but first let me hear your side of the bargain."

For answer I pointed at the hag. "I'll guarantee to see that she will be in her own proper shape and appearance, not in the least changed from the moment I first saw her."

He looked at me searchingly. "Will you hand her over to her friends and kindred?"

Not knowing what else to do to emphasize my good faith, I crossed my heart. "Before this day is over. You see, I trust you. I won't wait until I see the blue ox. I'll take your word for it that you'll bring it to me."

I had overlooked the necessity of a trysting place, but Golias thought of it. "Suppose you have him bring it here, Shandon."

"I'll do it!" the old fellow cried. He grabbed my hand in both of his iron mitts and pumped it. "It'll take some time to get to Basse Aphasia and back, but shall we say a year and a day from now?"

"At 3:30 P.M.," I nodded.

"Done! Sancho, my son," he called to his companion, "we have, in effect, rescued the Princess Erminia of Colchis, and now we're off on a new adventure. Mount, mount, as you love God, my lady, and me!"

The little fat man didn't share the other's happiness. "Something was left out of that there bargain," he declared. "The magician here gets a nice ox, and the princess gets to be alive and look pretty again, but what do we get out of it?"

"The honor of having served such a sweet lady, toad."

"Well, but don't you think she'd feel better about it if we'd let her give us a duchy or so to show her appreciation?"

De la Mancha snorted. "It's enough for me that she will know to whose good sword she owes her renewed happiness. Mount, I say. No, hold my steed first."

Even with the assistance of Jones it was quite a business getting him back up on his scrawny crow bait. When he had finally managed it, and Sancho had handed him that pole again, he made a jerky salute with his free hand before he dropped it to the reins.

"A year and a day from today," he smiled. Sancho scrambled up on his donkey, and they trotted down Watling Street.

Jones had effaced himself during our discussion of terms. "A fine old gentleman," he said when de la Mancha was out of hearing. Then he slapped me on the back. "That was well done. I wouldn't have known how to be as nice to him as you were."

"You knew how to get us, or rather me, in the way of that damned pointed stick," I reminded him. For the time being I had used up my novel stock of humanitarianism; and I remembered how I had been scared, hurt, and nearly killed, because Lucius hadn't minded his own affairs. I took a few steps, limping more than was necessary. "I told you not to butt in here."

If he had intended to answer, he was stopped by the return of the little girl, accompanied by a gypsy man and woman. Ignoring us, they loaded the hag into the one-horse farm wagon in which they came and drove off.

Thus released from responsibility, we got moving again. Twice, however, before we rounded the next turn, I looked back at the place where we had held that impromptu wake. By then I had almost forgotten my injury and entirely forgotten my irritation with Jones. In spite of the way I had responded to his praise, I was pleased with my part in the encounter with de la Mancha. There was something else about it, in addition to the fact that I had been kind to a likeable old lunatic, that sitrred my wonder at myself. For a man whose imagination had never had much practice that wasn't a bad story I had concocted out of vague recollections of things related to me by sundry guides. I told it over to myself several times and liked it on every repetition, although there were a couple of touches I belatedly wished I had thought to insert.

Golias, I believe, had a pretty good idea of what was driving my wheels. Once when I caught him smiling at me, I realized that I had been staring into vacancy and silently moving my lips. I smiled back uneasily.

"How far is it to the next town? I'm getting thirsty."

"I think you are," he commented.

The important physical result of Jones' impetuosity was that we were an hour or so behind schedule. In consequence we didn't reach Thebes, the city where we had expected to spend the night, but halted a few miles short of it at a crossroads village named Upton.

The inn, as they insisted on calling it, was a clean jerkwater hostelry, boasting good refreshments. I had been worried as to whether such a small town would have a bar, but my fears were groundless.

"One thing I must say for the Commonwealth," I remarked after licking the suds off my lips, "is that I haven't run across any damned prohibition."

"It isn't allowed," Golias assured me, "except in Tantalus' precinct. There the measure is punitive, and in my opinion justified. He had a rotten sense of humor."

"In the worst possible taste," Lucius agreed.

"As to the rest of the country," Golias continued, after pausing to drink and sigh contentedly, "there was a famous test case made some years ago when one of the Ynglings, Fjolne, I think it was, got tight and fell into a vat of mead one night when nobody was around to pull him out. Because of his royal status, his death caused quite a stir, and certain wingless harpies managed to take enough advantage of the situation to have a trial: *Grundy* vs. *Dionysus, Gambrinus,* and *Barleycorn.* The demand was for a sentence of banishment."

We joined him as he paused to gulp his ale. "I've forgotten who the Drys' attorney was, though it might have been Heep, but in any case Panurge was defense counsel. Old Toby Belch was the presiding magistrate, and—notwithstanding the fact that Tom Norman was there —Seithenyn ap Seithin was foreman of the jury. Incidentally there were so many challenges on both sides that they had quite a time impaneling a jury for him to be foreman of. When the dust finally settled, it could be seen that Panurge hadn't done too badly. Sitting in judgment at the behest of their fellow citizens were Friars John and Tuck, Sut Lovingood, Colas Brugnon, Elinor Rummin, Eumolpus, Rex Cole, Celm Hawley— oh, I see."

Jones had not been giving his usual courteous attention. Now I, too, felt free to turn and find out what he was staring at. Without surprise I found it was a woman.

She was alighting from the coach I had heard draw up a moment or two before. The young squirt who was helping her down did so as if he was handling a thin-skinned egg. When he had got her safely to earth, he attended to collecting their baggage, skipping back to her every now and then to make sure she was still well and happy. He looked so much like a combination of a frisking puppy and a cow with a calf that I watched with interest as she removed her gloves in order to touch up her hair-do. Sure enough there was no wedding ring, and I grinned to myself. Whatever the experience of the woman, the young rooster she was with was out with his first hen.

Meanwhile I hadn't had a full view of her features. She had been standing half faced away from me while she waited for her escort. Now, however, he had turned their luggage over to a bell-hop, and he was free to steer her inside. She was even younger than the boy, with a beauty in which vivacity and sensuousness struggled for halves. Her voluminous clothes made it difficult to be sure, but the signs indicated that there was a dainty figure to match the facial charm.

A moment later the pair entered with Will Boniface, our landlord, in unctuous attendance. "I must ask your ladyship and your honor to wait just a minute," he was saying. "Our best apartment—and I wouldn't think of offering you anything but our best, you may be sure—has just been vacated. It will take a few minutes—no more than that, you may be sure—to freshen it up. Can I show you to a private parlor while you wait?"

"Yes, please," the boy said. "Doesn't that suit you, Manon?"

While Boniface had been giving his sales talk, the girl had been casing the room. I don't know whether she observed the furnishings, but she assayed all the men. My pulse acknowledged it when it was my turn to meet her sultry appraisal. Jones' turn was next. She took a little longer with him, and I noticed that when she was through with the rest, her eyes came back for a second visit.

It was about this time that her escort had agreed

to accept the advantages of a private waiting room. He offered her his arm, but she refused it.

"We don't need a private room. We can wait right here."

The boy didn't like that. "It will be much pleasanter in a private parlor."

"But it was so hot and dusty in that nasty old coach," she said. "I'll simply perish if I don't have a glass of wine."

"We'll have it served there," the youngster declared. "Landlord, a bottle of your best Chablis—and right away."

He tried to tug at her, but she freed herself. "Manon's tired and can't go a step farther. Can't you understand?"

There was only a trace of petulance in her voice, but it had him crawling. "Oh, dearest, I didn't think. Landlord, the lady's tired and must have a table right here right away."

Thinking back, it seemed to me that she had entered briskly enough, but she was almost tottering when she accepted the boy's help across the room. She did not, however, like the first table to which they were shown, indicating a preference for one nearer ours. There she let the youngster enthrone her in the chair that faced us. After fussing around to assure himself that she wasn't going to die on the spot, he sat down in the opposite seat.

In her exhaustion, as it happened, she had so slumped in her chair that her skirts were not completely arranged. Only one ankle and a short stretch above it were showing, but cheesecake is a state of mind. Hearing Jones breathe heavily, I saw that his gaze was fixed on the brief but pleasant view afforded him. Golias and I exchanged

glances and shrugged. This could end in unpleas-
antness, although on the whole I didn't believe
anything would happen. It was a cinch that Manon's companion would stick to her like a postage
stamp, and Lucius was at once too good natured
and too good mannered to try to cut in on them.

Or I thought he was. He kept giving her the
eye—and got it back past her unconscious escort's
shoulder. I was relieved when the wine revived
her sufficiently to allow her to make it up to the
bedroom.

The fact that she was a tart made her no less
pleasing to the eye. I joined every man there in
watching her as she left and therefore saw her
hand open as she passed close to our table. The
white thing which fell from her fingers was only
in sight for an instant when Jones snatched it out
of the air. The poor monkey, walking on the other
side of the girl, remained oblivious; and he helped
to hide the byplay from everybody else in the
room except Golias and myself.

Still it was a bootless triumph, and I couldn't
see why Lucius—except that he was young—got
such a kick out of it. All through supper he was
bursting with good humor, laughing at almost
any remark. With the food we had switched to
wine, and he began emptying his glass with great
regularity. Not long after the meal was over, he
was mildly spiflicated and suggested a round of
songs.

"It's too early for that in a place like this,"
Golias said. "Maybe after the next bottle, if the
crowd thins out."

"Well, if I can't sing," Jones announced, "I'll
give you a toast."

Lifting his glass with a flourish, he rose. I

steeled myself for some noble, sentimental, or bawdy aphorism, but instead of delivering he abruptly sat down.

"Ah," he said with satisfaction.

Turning to see what he noted, I observed Manon's escort hustling into the room. "Where's the landlord?" he cried. "Oh, there you are. Landlord, is there a perfumer's shop in town?"

"No, your honor." Boniface succeeded in looking miserable as he made this admission. "I'm very sorry, you may be sure, but you won't find one nearer than Thebes. That's four miles away, you know."

"The devil!" The boy frowned desperately. "Madam left her perfume in that confounded stage coach," he explained.

"And naturally she is heartbroken," the landlord sympathized. "I can find a man to send for some if you like."

The youngster hesitated. "No, she said she wanted me to pick it out myself." Pathetically, he looked proud for a moment. "She doesn't trust anybody's judgment but mine in such matters, you see. Can you get me a horse?"

"It'll be waiting by the time your honor gets his boots on, you may be sure."

Golias and I looked at each other again as the boy raced upstairs. Jones said nothing, and the only sign of impatience he gave was to drum on the table with fingers of one hand. He kept this up until the sounds of the galloping horse began to grow faint. Then he drained his cup and pushed back his chair.

"If you gentlemen will excuse me, I'll do the young lady the courtesy of returning her handkerchief."

We merely lifted a hand each in reserved benediction. He might be walking into a mess, but not so many will keep away from poison if it's sweet enough. And if I had had the inside track instead of him, I might not have paused for even that moral reflection.

"We'd better keep an ear waiting for that horse to come back," Golias said, when he was out of hearing.

"I don't know," I said. "A bull that comes when some other moose's cow calls had better handle that part of it, too, don't you think?"

"I do," he concurred, "but I'd hate to be thrown out of here in the middle of the night because of the ruckus that'll be started if that lad finds somebody else's mast stepped in his flagship. This is the only inn in town."

His reasoning impressed me. "You're right, we should stand guard," I conceded. "Oh—oh! There's a horse now."

"With wheels behind it." I had started to rise, but Golias pulled me down. "We won't have to be on the alert for a while yet."

The vehicle halted at the door, to judge from the sounds, and after an interval Boniface ushered in two more travelers. These were both women. The first was richly if simply dressed. Albeit gayer, the apparel of the other was not so stylish.

As they came in, the landlord was playing a record we had already heard once that evening. "My best apartment has just been vacated; but I'm having it cleaned, and it'll be ready for you in a few minutes, you may be sure."

"Oh, you needn't trouble." The first voice was low but clear. "Any room you have will do for us."

"I should think he would trouble, too," her

companion said loudly. "He shouldn't even consider not giving your ladyship the best in the
house."

"I'm not considering it, you may be sure,"
Boniface said. He turned from the maid to appeal
to her mistress. "Couldn't it be possible for you to
wait just a few minutes, my lady? Surely you're in
need of refreshment, traveling at this time of
night."

"Surely you're right," she agreed. Before he
could follow up his gambit by offering to rent her
a private parlor to wait in, however, she stepped
to the nearest vacant table and sat down. "Two
glasses of claret, please."

"Didn't you hear my lady?" the maid snapped.
"A glass of claret and a glass of brandy—and
hurry up with them!"

In spite of her officiousness she had already
taken the time to turn her sharp features to every
corner. Her mistress had not bothered to look
about her, but luckily she was so placed that we
could observe her from time to time without being
obvious. It was a pleasure of a different sort from
staring at Manon. A man not infatuated with the
latter could only look at her in one way, but he
washed his eyes when he glanced at the cool
loveliness now in the room with us. Although her
features were more mature, and although general
coloring was the sole actual point of resemblance,
she reminded me of Rosalette. I think it was because she had the same quality of imparting without ostentation the feeling that her character was
of a piece with her beauty.

All too soon, for my satisfaction, "the best
apartment in the house" was ready. The lady went
out, leaving a darker room.

"You know so many people in the Commonwealth," I said, when we had turned back to our
wine. "Any idea who she is?"

"No," Golias said. He had a faraway look in his
eyes and didn't have much to say for a while.

During the middle of the week in a tank town
like Upton, it wasn't surprising to find that the
local drinkers retired early. One by one our fellow
guests did likewise, until we eventually had the
tap room to ourselves.

"Now," Golias declared, "it is time to sing."

He sang a couple of times, and I came back
with one of my parlor tricks, a one-man demonstration of a glee club rendering of "The
Wreck of the Hesperus." I was fully in the spirit of
things, but I was yet aware, knowing more than I
once did, when he lugged out the song I had been
waiting for. There was a certain way he watched
me that made me sure it was newly minted.

> To me it's all one who she is, or if I meet her;
> Blanchefleur's smile was never mine, nor
>   Enid's slender hand,
> Yet merely the knowing they live makes
>   living sweeter:
>   Just to have scanned
> The face of each was a grace, and so I bless
>   them;
> And here was their match, or one fashioned
>   more lovely still;
> In passing alone they're seen, yet I gently
>   possess them
>   And always will.

I could tell from his expression that there
was more to the song, but he never got around to

finishing it. We had been so taken up with our vocalizing that we hadn't heard other sounds—notably those made by a hurrying horse. We had, indeed, forgotten all about Manon's anxious lover, when he flung the door open and made the stairs two at a time.

Exchanging lugubrious glances, we listened while he knocked. Next he started to pound on the door. The expected explosion didn't follow, however. We couldn't hear Manon's voice, but whatever she said sent the boy slowly down the steps. Preoccupied, he didn't notice that there was anyone in the tap room, so he therefore felt free to talk to the housemaid he met at the foot of the stairs.

"Is the landlord about? No, you'll do." Inexperienced as he was in other matters, he knew enough to show her some money. "Madame—my-er-wife, you know—is feeling ill, and it would upset her to share her bed tonight. Show me to another room, please."

I didn't know which awed me most, the girl's effrontery or the brazen way Jones was crowding his luck. "Lucius must have given satisfaction," I remarked. "Well, we won't have to worry about getting the bounce because of our disreputable pal."

Golias continued to look disturbed. "Lucius shouldn't have done that. It reminds me of what the Cu Roi MacDairi did to Cuchullain. It was all right for him to manhandle Cuchullain. He could whip anybody in the Commonwealth, except possibly Heracles. Unfortunately they never met for the championship."

Golias divided the last of the bottle with care.

"As I say, it was all right for MacDairi to kick Cuchullain around, because up to that point it was a fair fight—MacDairi against a few hundred odd—but when he got Setanta down, he rubbed dung in his hair. It's that sort of thing that breeds vengeance; if not from the injured party, from outraged Delian Law. I'm afriad Lucius will regret this business."

XIV

❧ Hot Water for Lucius ❧

I LEARNED that Golias' dark prophecy was fulfilled early the next morning. I had waked and was just turning over for another nap when Jones came in and threw himself upon the cot—a low-slung affair that wheeled under the double bed Golias and I shared—which he had not previously occupied. My first idea was that he was worn out, and no wonder, but he started writhing and beating the pillow with his clenched fists. Next, as if unable to remain still, he rose and commenced pacing the floor. As he did so, he groaned.

At length I waked up enough to be curious. "What's the matter?" I yawned. "Did that chippie find somebody with a stronger back?"

He came out of it slowly, as if it was hard for any but his own ideas to reach him. "Oh, hello, Shandon. I thought you were still asleep. What did you say?"

When I repeated my query, he winced as if I had shoved something under his finger nail. "That lecherous little bitch! I wish I had never heard of

214

her. No, I haven't got any right to curse her. It was all my fault. It wouldn't have happened if I hadn't met her halfway. I did what I did of my own volition, and it served me right."

I began to grow concerned. "Don't tell me you found out she's got something?"

He was so distracted he didn't even know what I was talking about. "She's not the one that's worrying me," he said, throwing himself into a chair and burying his face in his hand. "Oh, damn that witch and her curse!"

His exclamation roused Golias. As usual he had full possession of his faculties when he awoke.

"Let's hear what happened," he said, sitting up.

Jones closed his eyes, as if to protect them from another sight of the incident he was about to rehearse. "I don't have to tell you where and with whom I spent the night."

"No. We're quick that way."

"Well, for the girl's sake and in the interest of good taste, I determined to leave her room as soon as it was light enough to see. It did not occur to me that other people would be stirring that early." He opened his eyes once more. "Tell me; did you happen to see another beautiful young woman— but a lady, this time—last night?"

I grimaced, as I got an inkling of what had happened. "A most lovely one," Golias said, and from the sober tone of his voice I knew he had the same idea. "She arrived not long after you left us to return a certain handkerchief."

"Oh, God in Heaven!" Lucius cried. "If I hadn't—or if I hadn't been in such a hurry to be a damned fool. Why if I had waited to have another glass or two of wine, say—" He broke off, shaking his head. Then he said quietly, as though no expression of his voice could contain his despair: "Gentlemen, the lady you had the happiness of seeing, and the one I cheated myself of seeing in time to preserve any chance of enjoying happiness, was Hermione Steingerd ap Hawthorn. She and her waiting woman were passing by just as I was leaving Miss Lescaut's room."

"How could she tell you were off the reservation?" I demanded.

"Miss Lescaut left no doubt as to that." Lucious held out a hand which sported a ring I had often noticed, for it was set with a ruby about the size of a maraschino cherry. "It never crossed my mind that she had mercenary motives, but as I was leaving she tried to persuade me to give her this. It so happens that this was a gift from Lady Hermione in happier days. When I refused, the wench became argumentative; and at the critical moment when I opened the door, she was right behind me, scantily attired and complaining of my stinginess in rewarding specified services rendered."

He rose and sank into the chair again. "I couldn't speak, and my lady would not. As if I did not exist, she walked on."

Remembering the girl I had seen the night before, and the bedroom doll for whom he had put himself in bad with her, I could see why he felt as he did. It seemed to me that if he wanted a wife, he had better write Miss ap Hawthorn off the books, soothsayer or no soothsayer, and look for somebody else as soon as he caught his breath again.

"Is there anything I can do?" Jones burst out, when we were both silent.

"Well," I said, "you could cut your throat, but if you wait long enough, you probably won't want to. It's tough, boy, but lots of things are."

I felt genuinely sorry for Jones, yet there was no use in giving him false assurances. When he nodded, haggardly accepting my opinion of the situation, I none the less gave up the idea of going back to sleep. It would be barbarous to leave him at the complete mercy of his thought, and with a sigh I swung my legs out of bed.

"We'd better get breakfast," I muttered.

Golias hadn't yet made any comment. "Where is the Lady Hermione going?" he now spoke up.

"I hadn't had time to wonder about that." Lucius wrinkled his brow. "Was there anybody with her besides her servant when she arrived?"

"No. And in addition to being unescorted she was traveling by stage coach. Doesn't that suggest something unusual?"

"Perhaps. What difference does it make?" Jones asked. "If you could have seen the way she looked at me."

"She may expect to continue to look at you that way," Golias admitted. He swung his legs to the floor in turn. "But if she met something she liked worse, you mightn't seem so bad."

That didn't appear very comforting to me, but Lucius straightened up. "Do you think she's in any danger?"

"I have no reason to think anything. But she is following an abnormal course of procedure, and she must have strong reasons for doing so. Certainly if I was interested in the welfare of a young lady—"

"Interested! Welfare! Why I'd do anything! I

don't even care whether she ever speaks to me
again, if only she's all right.''

"In that case," Golias said, reaching for his
pants, "it would seem that our immediate mission
is to trace her route. We can do that, as well as
locate the general vicinity of her destination, by
enquiring at stage stops along the way. Luckily,
innkeepers as a class are both observant and gar-
rulous.''

Whether or not he believed there was any point
in the course he suggested, he had the medicine
for Lucius. The latter didn't cheer up, which
wasn't to be expected, but he saw a reason for
continuing to want to be. He ate well, too, which
he probably wouldn't have done otherwise. Every
grim mouthful, you could see, was so many vita-
mins stored for use against Miss ap Hawthorn's so
far hypothetical enemies.

We found that the stage she had caught was
bound for a town along the way to the City, so we
kept on down Watling Street when we set out. It
was drizzling and early, so Thebes looked almost
deserted when we passed through it. An inn a few
miles beyond that town was, as Boniface had told
us, the stage relay point. Stopping there for ale,
we found that Miss ap Hawthorn and her maid
had continued westward, so we did.

From there on a heavy fog made it dreary going.
We had walked out of it by noon, however, and
about the same time we came in sight of an
ecclesiastical-looking structure, where, Golias
said, we could count on getting a bite of lunch. As
we approached the establishment from one direction, though, a column of troops bore down toward it from the other, yelling and cheering. They
reached it first and didn't stand on ceremony

when they got there. We could see the vanguard
rushing forward with ladders. Meeting no opposi-
tion, men commenced swarming over the walls.

Jones and I halted. "We don't want to get mixed
up in this," I said. "Hadn't we better detour?"

"Yes," Golias assented, "but let's not side step
so far that we can't see what's going on. This
might be good."

It didn't sound good. As we drew abreast of the
place in our sweep around, we could hear screaming, howling, and pleas for mercy mixed with the
running and stamping of feet, the rattle of
weapons, and terrible crunching sounds.

I was feeling sick at my stomach. "Hurry up!" I
growled to Golias, who kept dragging behind,
staring.

So far, as it happened, there had been nothing to
watch. The walls hid from us the terrible doings of
the army, whose collective voice—as an under-
tone to the other alarming sounds we heard—was
the satisfied snarl of bulldogs that have got their
death grip. Now that changed. All sounds made
way for one mass shriek of fright.

"Wait!" Golias called to us.

He had hardly said the word when men started
coming back over the walls. Some in front were
pushed so frantically by those behind that they
literally popped over. Others were yanked back or
tripped and trampled on by colleagues unwilling
to wait their turn. Those who fell when they
cleared the wall served as cushions for oncoming
echelons. This was panic with no holds barred;
but I was too amazed to be really appalled. My
chief emotion was curiosity as to what could have
so frightened that large a body of armed men.

Most of them milled around when they got outside, evidently afraid to choose any direction for fear it would be the one taken by the pursuing force. One group of a few hundred, however, tore off down Watling Street.

"There's Friar John!" Golias cried excitedly. "Now watch."

Even then I didn't realize that the bald-headed man in the gunny sack wasn't making a getaway likewise. I didn't get the pitch until he caught up with the others and swung a club that he carried. It didn't look like much of a weapon—from where I stood it looked like nothing more than a sort of long handled tomahawk—but he knew how to use it. The first swing knocked a dozen or so soldiers up in the air. Three or four heads were soloing before they hit the ground; and most of the men who weren't decapitated didn't move again either.

"Lord God Almighty!" Lucius exclaimed.

"Deft," Golias commented. "Lots of power, too. I think it's the wrist snap and the timing."

He was pleased with the way things were turning out, and I became aware that I was also. The bunch had asked for trouble, and they were getting it. I watched while baldy mowed down every man on the road, then sprinted toward a brigade or thereabouts fleeing through the fields.

"Well, all I can say," I breathed, "is that he's a going son of a bitch. There, he's caught 'em. Look at him swing that thing!"

He hit them high, low, and in the middle. He hooked them up in the air and clipped them before they came down. He bashed in heads, sliced off legs, disemboweled, and salivated them. He reaped squads, smashed platoons, mangled companies, shattered batalions, and mopped up regiments. I suppose he could have played weasel in the hen yard until they were all dead, but when he had crushed them beyond any hope of being able to rally, he abruptly sat down.

"Bring me wine!" he yelled. "I'm thirsty."

"Let's see if we can get a drink, too," Golias said.

Having seen people I'd rather approach, I was grateful when Jones spoke up. "This isn't a good time for strangers to be bothering them, I should say."

"Oh, they can tell from our clothes that we're not from this part of the country," Golias said. "Come on."

As I had feared, he led the way directly to where that bald-headed fellow was resting. Not that he had a corner on baldness thereabouts. In answer to his bellow for wine, several inmates of the establishment had come forth, bearing demijohns of the refreshment in question. The tops of their heads were all bare and sunburned.

Having shown their appreciation of Friar John's prowess in the practical fashion demanded of them, these newcomers did not linger. Instead they lined up and marched off, singing a psalm. Their champion was therefore alone when we drew near, Golias a good six strides in the lead.

"Nice going, John," he said.

To my relief the fellow didn't reach for his weapon. Instead he glanced at the heaps of men he had slaughtered.

"I've always been a peace-loving man," he remarked, smacking his lips. "They made me angry."

"That's a mistake a lot of them won't repeat."
Not wanting to make him angry myself, I didn't
touch his club, though I examined it as well as I
could. It looked remarkably like a crucifix such as
is a prop for a church parade. I shook my head.
"Just what was the trouble?"

He downed a beer mug full of white wine and
filled it up again. "I'm a peacable servant of the
Lord," he insisted again, "so when the Lernists
invaded our country, contrary to all the laws of
Christiandom, the tenets of diplomacy, the coun-
sels of good taste, the pleasure of King Gran-
gousier, the desires of my fellow countrymen, the
welfare of their own sundry concerns, and the
advice of their wives, who will now be in fine
position to say 'I told you so' to the survivors, I
merely uttered a prayer for their souls. When they
started sacking and burning our towns, I gave
them a *pax vobiscum*. When they began ravishing
the women, I said no more than a few *aves*. When
they commenced killing our men, I replied with a
pater noster. When they swarmed into the sacred
precincts of our holy order, my only comment was
to tell, if I remember correctly, three beads. But
when I saw them stealing our grapes and cutting
down our vines, then *I* lost my temper." He
swigged down his drink, refilled the mug, and
held it out. "Have some, Golias?"

While not so heartily as he, we drank each in
turn. It was a good wine. Friar John watched us
benevolently.

"I think that where these poor sinners most
transgressed," he said, "was in trying to upset the
balance of nature as instituted by the one om-
nipotent and holy God when the universe sprang

from his brain—simply because it occurred to him, and it became a fact—somewhat in the manner of Athena popping out of Zeus' head, greatly to his relief."

A nearby victim stirred, but he didn't do it twice, because Friar John poked him with the small end of his club. "Unfortunately," he went on, "only deity can manage to get a woman off his mind so easily and completely; but that isn't what I started out to say. The universe as conceived and delivered is held together by a set of natural relationships. My turn, my friend." He took the mug from me and sloshed it full again. "What, for instance, holds clam shells together?"

"Well," I said, "I've never given much thought to the structure of clam shells."

"A clam holds clam shells together," he announced after drinking, "and by the same token the shell holds the clam in place and keeps it from wandering, an activity for which it is fitted neither by physical prowess nor spiritual elan. You see how things are designed to balance? Marvelous. Similarly we note the close natural kinship between wine and friars. As far as I have been able to observe, and I have made a close study of the matter, one is unthinkable without the other. The friar is the destined container of the wine—which else would be imperfectly kept and utilized; and the friar would come unstuck and fall apart if he didn't have the vinous mucilage which omniscience has provided to knit his seams. Have you lunched?"

"No," Golias said. "We hope to eat here if your menage hasn't been too upset by what happened today."

"Come on inside. I'll see that you get something." Friar John picked up the only jug which still had something in it. "As the burden of killing all these misguided sinners fell upon me, the business of blessing and burying them—which is not, in this case, unlike jerking the lid of hell from underneath them after wishing them *bon voyage*—I'll leave to my brothers of the order. Ah, it's time we left. Here comes the prayer and shovel brigade now."

We lunched on cold ham, venison, capon, beef, salami, bologna, liverwurst, partridge, half a dozen lively cheeses, and that wine, which seemed to go with everything singularly well. Even Jones, I was gratified to see, enjoyed the meal. All that morning he had been glum as a zombie, but under the influence of good cheer and Friar John's conversation he began to feel better. After a while he stopped insisting that we cut it short and get going again.

As for me, I had never had much to do with any fathers of the church, and I found I had been missing something. Of course, as our host himself pointed out, he was not strictly representative of his kind in all respects. For example, there was a song he taught us. It took our fancy, and we were singing it as we stepped out down Watling Street once more.

At times the mind works on two levels at once, and it was so with mine on this occasion. Half of it was giving itself gleefully to the moment, while the other half was revolving a new idea. What had impressed me was that this friar was well-informed and had a lot of fun out of that fact alone. In the past, if I had wanted to find out anything, it was always for a practical reason. Now I glimpsed

the concept that to know a thing for itself could be
a source of joy. Take the song we were bellowing.
It was easy to appreciate, but I would have had
more chuckles out of it if I had known, as the
others did, about the personages involved. From
then on I intended to begin picking up data from
Golias or any other handy source.

But, as I say, this resolution, made with the
solemn half of my mind, didn't interfere with the
attention the other half was giving to making as
much noise as possible.

> Old man Zeus he   kept a heifer in his yard;
> Hera smelled a   rat and took the matter hard.
> She swore she would   watch the varmint
>   anyhow,
> Damned if she'd play   second fiddle to a
>   cow!
>   Here's to Zeus and his hot pants!   He
>   learned to pay his debts.
>   The more he started to explain,
>   The more she jawed him with disdain.
>   She wouldn't hear; it was in vain
>   He vowed he just liked pets.

Once afood with the song, we made pleasing
discoveries. The break in the lines of the verse was
admirable. In it there was room for a hiccough or a
belch before, with a lurch and a stamp, we hit the
accented first syllable of the second half.

> Young Adonis   was a handsome lad, I hear,
> But some parts were   missing from him, as I
>   fear;
> Aphrodite   swung her hips and rolled her
>   eyes,
> But for once she   couldn't even get a rise.

Here's to young Adonis, who is dead and
 ought to be!
He chased a pig, he shot and missed,
So he got killed instead of kissed.
I wish that what slipped through his fist
Had only come to me!

Once a centaur loved a Lapithaean dame,
So he thought he'd work to try to snatch
 the same;
But that cutie didn't thank him for his pass,
For she said she knew he was a horse's—

"Hold on!" Jones interrupted. "Keep it. There's
a woman."

Trust him to see her, though only her head was
visible. Then the rest of her emerged, as she
crawled out of a ditch beside the road. Disheveled
and with her face smeared with dirt, she was
anything but an attractive figure. She seemed
dazed, too, and not sure of where she was as she
peered first westward and then east toward us.
When she did so, Golias gave a startled exclamation.

"It's the woman who was with Lady Hermione
last night!"

An instant later she herself spoke. "Master
Lucius!" she croaked. "Oh, Master Lucius."

We were all sober by then, knowing there was
bad trouble, and Jones was naturally in a panic.
"What happened?" he cried, as he sprang toward
her. "Tell me where she is!" He reached the
woman, then stood helplessly holding her up.
"Oh, my god! She fainted."

She didn't come out of it, although we worked

over her, until Golias made a suggestion. "They
say," he remarked, "that when everything else
fails, the best remedy is to take a rock and bang
some sense back into the patient's noggin. Hand
me that stone, Shandon. Not the small one; the big
jagged one."

"She's coming to!" Lucius cried.

Sure enough the eyelids fluttered, then stayed
open. "Tell me where she is, my Hermione!"
Jones urged.

She twitched the shoulders he was supporting.
"Nobody cares what happened to me. I'm the one
who got hurt."

"Of course, we care," Jones made haste to say,
"but we want to know why you're not with her."

"Folks that swoon—really swoon," she added,
looking indignantly at Golias, "don't remember
much."

From inside his coat Golias drew his sheath
knife. "We'd better blood her to clear her brain,"
he suggested.

I had already concluded that he was not being
as callous as he had at first seemed. "Modern
medicine," I remarked, "holds that the patient is
bled most successfully through the jugular. Tilt
her head back, Lucius."

With a squeal she sat up. "I suppose you think
it's funny to be tied up and thrown out of a coach
and have to lie in a dirty ditch for hours. And with
my best dress on."

"Of course, you're upset. We didn't understand," Golias soothed her. "Let me add that I
think it was mighty clever of you to get yourself
untied."

" 'Twas, 'twasn't it? And I didn't call for help

neither." She smiled at him, then gave of her
sunshine to the rest of us. All she wanted was to be
appreciated, and it had dawned on her that the
role of heroine could be just as dramatic as that of
a sufferer. "Did I tell you they had a gag on me,
too?"

All this talk aside from the purpose was more
than Lucius could bear. "You haven't got a gag on
now, Mrs. Jenkins. For God's sake tell us what
happened!"

"You mean after we saw you and your friend
this morning?" That was a sneak punch, and it left
poor Jones gasping. Having punished him for his
impatience, she smiled again and went on. "Well,
the stage was early and would have waited for us,
but my lady wouldn't eat breakfast under the
same roof where you was, and I can't say I blame
her, though I did blame her, being famished. So
we left right away, and there's nothing worse than
joggling a stomach lonesome for victuals in a
coach with a bad wheel, I can tell you. It wasn't
until we reached the relay point way this side of
Thebes that we ate, and I was most ready to swoon
before—"

Lucius clenched his fists in agony. "Please," he
mumbled.

She rode over that feeble interruption. "Well, I
must say it was a good breakfast when we got
there, for I can't remember three nicer mutton
chops, and I'd be glad to eat 'em again any time.
Thanks be to gracious that it wasn't on an empty
stomach those men stopped the stage, threatening
everybody with pistols, and took us out and put us
in a coach of their own. I'd've swooned for sure."

Evidently unable to trust his voice, Jones

looked at us appealingly. "How far from the relay point?" I asked.

"It must have been about an hour, because those mutton chops was just beginning to ride easy."

"That would be about the middle of that foggy stretch," Golias calculated, "where the road bores through the fen near Hereward's old hangout. How many men were there, Mrs. Jenkins?"

"There was four, and one of them had the strongest arms when they went around a body to pick her up. He tasted sort of good when I bit him, too, but that other one that had holt of me to put the gag on was nasty."

"Not all men rank with mutton chops as provender," Golias averred, "and it's probably just as well. I take it that the other two you mentioned were binding and gagging your mistress."

"Yes, when they dumped me in the coach my lady was already there, which is to be expected, I suppose. Servants must wait their turn."

"If they took the trouble to put you in the coach, why didn't they keep you there?" I wanted to know.

"Instead of my lady? Well, there ain't any accounting for tastes, and then she didn't kick one of them on the backside just as he was leaning out the door to talk to the driver. It turned out the door wasn't fast shut, and—"

"I thought you said you were all tied up."

"Well, I was." She tried to wipe some mud from her cheek and only succeeded in smearing it. "Now when your legs—excuse me, limbs—is hitched together, you can't boot a man in the bum with only one foot, but there ain't anything to keep you from doing it with two, if so be you can reach him. He stepped on my toes when he got up to lean out the window, which made me mad; and being rolled over by the back wheel after I kicked him made him mad, so he started hauling me out even before he got his wind back enough to swear with it. Down I go into the ditch and off goes the coach."

"Did you recognize any of the men?" Golias asked.

She got to her feet, and we rose with her. "I don't keep that kind of company. Not that I keep any company just now—steady, you know—though I've had plenty of offers."

"But," Lucius burst out, "didn't you hear them say anything? Haven't you any idea who they were or why they perpetrated this outrage?"

"I was waiting to see if any of you was going to ask that." She beamed with self-satisfaction. "If my Lord Ravan didn't want to be known as the villain who had his men misuse me and my lady—though her not so much—he shouldn't have given one of them a letter sealed with his ring, which I've seen many a time when he paid me, and always very handsomely, too, I must say, for carrying love notes from him to you-know-who. Anyhow the fellow I kicked must have lost it on the road along with those two teeth, and thinking just of me, you see, he didn't notice it. Neither did I, until the wind blew it into the ditch with me, and even then I didn't open it until I got my hands loose."

XV

A Change of Route

THE NOTE which Mrs. Jenkins then produced didn't say much and nothing explicit. Addressed to Elias Hoseason, it contained only the words: "Keep watching what you were told to watch. I am detained. Bring anything of value to where I would be if I could, and wait there." There was no signature, but there was a design pressed in wax. Examining it, Jones also identified it as Don Rodrigo's seal.

Dropping the piece of paper, he grabbed Mrs. Jenkins by the shoulder. "Where was the coach going? Was it to the City, or some estate of his, or where? Speak up, damn it!"

For once too overawed to gab, she began to whimper. "Don't, Master Lucius! I ain't the one that done it."

"Easy, fellow," I said. "She can't talk if you scare her to death."

"Can't you see he's got her—that swine has got her? I have to find them and kill him!"

"They're not together." Golias, who had picked up the note, thrust it before Jones' eyes. "That's why he had to send this. Now you will be quiet and help us figure things out?"

As he reread the missive, some of the wildness left Lucius' face. "He does say he's detained, doesn't he?"

"Yes," I assured him. "Hang on to that idea while we try to find out something. Did they say anything at all worth repeating, Mrs. Jenkins?"

She had recovered her self-possession. "Well, one of 'em said she's a beauty, though whether he was talking about me or my lady I don't know, and it ain't for me to guess."

I tried not to look pained. "Did they say anything that gave you an idea where they were going?"

"No," she looked frustrated at being pinned down to a monosyllable. "That is—no."

"Your witness," I said to Golias.

"Let's go back before the kidnapping," the latter suggested. "It's clear from the text of Ravan's note that he had ordered this Hoseason to watch for a chance to abduct Lady Hermione. Finding that she was traveling Watling Street, he apparently got ahead of her and waited for her where the heavy fen mists made the hold-up relatively simple. But how did she happen to give him such an excellent opportunity? Why did you take to the road in the first place?"

"That's it!" Lucius came to life. "I meant to ask that myself."

"Well, you should've done it instead of scaring a body out of her wits," Mrs. Jenkins observed. "Well, I left home because she did, as old Haw-

thorn couldn't use a lady's maid, at least not for
honest purposes—and he needn't think it
would've done him any good for him to come
high stepping and clucking around me, the rascal.
As for my lady, she packed up, and without telling old Hawthorn, who won't like such goings
on, especially for the sake of a penniless bastard.
Anyhow she packed up, because she thought
Master Lucius here was going to the City."

"What!" Jones cried. "Why when I left home
she wouldn't even speak to me."

"Well, she said she'd found out that my Lord
Ravan had lied to blacken your character, and she
was following to tell you she was sorry for believ-
ing him."

"Oh!" The word came out as if it were knocked
out of him.

"Well, back there at Upton," she went on, "my
lady found out that my Lord Ravan maybe wasn't
lying; but she didn't want to go back home until
old Hawthorn had cooled off about her running
away, so she decided to visit friends in the City,
which I was just as glad for, never having been
there. Weeping and wailing all the way, she was,
and—"

"That's enough," Golias said.

She blinked and looked indignant. "You asked
me to tell you."

"Now I'm asking you to stop," he pointed out,
"and if you don't, we'll find that gag and replace
it." He turned to Jones. "Pull yourself together,
Lucius. What could be so important that it would
keep Don Rodrigo from joining a lady after having
taken the trouble to have her abducted?"

Jones made an obvious effort to get his mind

moving in spite of the misery which was clogging it. "He would only stay away," he said talking to himself but aloud to help himself concentrate, "for the king. Of course!" He didn't exactly brighten, but keenness replaced his look of hopeless suffering. "He must have had to go to court either because the king wants him for something or to mend his fences and keep his place as the royal favorite."

"Good," Golias said. "But that doesn't tell us where Lady Hermione is."

"No," Lucius agreed; but instead of relapsing into despond, he hardened his jaw. "He has a dozen or so castles and manors and might use any of them. The only way to find out her whereabouts is to get him to tell. And I think we can locate him shortly."

"If he isn't at court, we should at least be able to get on his trail there," Golias nodded. "Let's get started."

At the next inn, a few miles down the road, we made arrangements for Mrs. Jenkins to take the coach back east. We then pushed on to Carlion, partly to lose her and partly to help pass the time before the west-bound stage—which we had decided to take, the expense notwithstanding—was due.

Carlion was an interesting-looking place, but I didn't get to see much of it. Soon after we had arrived at the inn from which the stages left, Golias made it a point, as he usually did, to look up the landlord and pump him for information. In a few minutes he came hustling back to our table.

"We've got to eat in a hurry," he told us.

"What's the rush?" I asked. "Have they changed the schedule?"

"We're not going to Ilium, or down Watling Street at all," he said. "The word is that the king isn't in the City, but is holding court at a summer palace of his, not far from Parouart. That's north and west along a branch road."

Fortunately the meal we bolted, abetting our potations and day of exercise, made us sleepy. Anybody who seeks rest in a stagecoach needs all the soporifics available. However, I hadn't yet discovered that when I climbed in, pleased to find but one other passenger.

"See you in the morning," I said, snuggling into a corner and closing my eyes.

"Right," Golias yawned. "These crack lines make the miles get out of the way, so we'll be there by breakfast time."

It didn't take a hundred yards to jolt me out of my visions of coziness. In the end I was never so glad to leave a vehicle or less capable of doing so. I felt like a network of charley-horses, as I dismounted and peered through the dirt in my eyes at Parouart.

In a general way the place reminded me of the old part of New Orleans. The buildings had the same secretive air. If anything, the streets were narrower, though, and certainly they were busier and noisier. For the time being my sightseeing went no farther. I wanted a wash and food.

"What do you plan to do first?" Golias asked Jones, when breakfast and the ale with which we chased it made us more ready for action.

Lucius lifted his head from his hands. "Find a cutler's where I can have my sword sharpened," he said. "Then, while they're working on it, I'll go to the Hell Fire Club. I'm not a member, but several who are were classmates at the university.

Being up to snuff on court doings is an article of
faith with them, so they'll know if Don Rodrigo's
with the king. There may also be some gossip
about his recent activities."

Golias nodded. "We'll meet you back here at the
Fir Cone, then. Shandon and I have to get new
outfits, so we can look presentable at Xanadu."

That was to my liking. The clothes I had got
from the outlaws were only three weeks old, but
we needed a rest from each other. Although the
shirts we ordered were too frilly for my taste, I
rather fancied myself in an outfit on the style of
that worn by Jones. It was drabber than Golias'
gold jacket with lipstick-red trimmings, but a ma-
roon coat riding over lime-colored pants was still
louder than anything I could have worn with
comfort in Chicago.

"The only trouble," Golias remarked after we
had been fitted for shoes, "is that they'll probably
want cash—and plenty of it, too, in view of the
rush alterations we're demanding—when they
deliver our stuff this afternoon." He flipped a
small coin. "We'll be lucky to have this left."

"Gosh, what'll we do? Do you think you could
make some money singing for the arch king, like
you did for what's his name—Hrothgar?"

"Not unless you tied him up first. Jamshyd no
longer sees eye to eye with me on enter-
tainment—if anything does still entertain him,
that is. We'll have to try something else."

"How about hocking Lucius' ring?"

"No. He values it, and it shouldn't be necessary."

Presumably resolved into a ways and means
committee, he was silent as we walked back to the

inn. Not having any other ideas to contribute, my own attention had the freedom of the city. It was therefore I who saw the young woman seated in an open carriage halted before a store, just ahead of us and across the street. Either the careless breeze or her own careful hand had pushed her skirt up above her knee.

I closed my eyes and looked again to make sure. Golias didn't appear in the mood to indulge idle curiosity, but I remembered my resolution to enquire about people in the Commonwealth who seemed noteworthy.

"Who's the babe in the carriage?" I asked. "If that shank she's exhibiting doesn't look like gold, I never saw any."

"What? Oh, that's the Kilmansegg." Golias took another step, stopped, then led the way on an altered course. Jaywalking, we passed that glittering leg on a line that would bring us to the opposite sidewalk barely past the team hitched to the carriage.

Gawking at the girl, who seemed to be pleased that the value of her underpinning was recognized, I was startled when the near horse suddenly squealed and bucked. I had just time to see Golias slip his knife into his pocket with one hand, as he leaped to grab the head reins with the other. He had a struggle, for the horse he had stuck wanted to get away from there and communicated its urge to its mate. The girl didn't help. She screeched at the top of her voice, making the beasts still more panicky.

"Shandon!" Golias yelped. "Come and hold them."

I thought he needed my help and was dismayed

to find myself in complete charge of two horses who were trying their best to stand on their hind legs. "Never mind that girl now," I shouted, for Golias had darted toward her. "Get that damned driver!"

The racket she was making, which increased instead of diminishing after Golias approached her, had luckily attracted the driver's attention. Dashing from the store, he jumped to his seat and caught up the reins.

"Let go! Right now!" Golias roared to me.

I didn't know whether I really should let go until the driver had had time to get the team under control; but in addition to being glad to do so, I figured Golias knew best. Releasing the reins, I sprang clear, none too swiftly. The horses, finding the lines still slack, lunged forward. It didn't look like a runaway, but the driver would have his hands full for a block or so. I didn't blame him for cursing me, though I couldn't see why the girl, having all she could do to hang on, kept shrieking hysterically back at us.

Unless, of course, she had seen Golias dig that nag. I looked around to swear at him for playing such a fool trick and to tell him we ought to get out of there before the police came around to investigate; but he was way ahead of me. Or rather he had reversed his field, and was about to charge down an alley.

"Shandon, come on!" he barked. When he turned to yell this, I caught a glimpse of something. Then I really gave my best speed to catch up with him. Eventually I did so, even though he did have three legs to my two.

Golias was delighted with himself, but I didn't like the business. Consideration for the decencies may not always have been my longest suit, but stealing an artificial leg seemed downright mean. I jabbed a thumb at the thing with its dangling fragments of straps, newly severed.

"What in hell did you do that for?"

He chuckled. "Even though it's hollow—and a good thing, too, or I wouldn't have been able to snatch it—it can be pawned for a nice sum. This isn't plate or alloy, my boy; it's as much the real thing as if Midas had touched it."

"Who's Midas? No, never mind that now. I know we need money and all that, but did you have to pick on a cripple?"

He refused to be abashed. "She'll get another shank—maybe diamond-studded next time—and if she wasn't one-legged, she'd think of another piece of swank. Quit worrying about her. Besides, rank ostentation is punishable under Delian Law."

"She was sure putting it on display," I admitted. I felt better now that I had been told the girl was wealthy enough to buy another gold gam. I grinned a little. "How did you get her peg off so quickly? Didn't she give you any argument at all?"

"As a matter of fact, no. The horses were bucking, but the carriage was staying so comparatively still that she thought she could afford to swoon when she saw me coming, as she imagined, to the rescue. Come on. Let's cash in on this at Barabas' before a member of the watch catches us with it."

When we came in sight of the Fir Cone again, Jones was there, pacing up and down in front of it. "What did you find out?" I asked, as we filed into the taproom.

He jerked back a chair and plumped himself

into it. "Ravan's at court, apparently so busy that he never has time to come to town."

"Not good," Golias said. "I'd much rather have our interview with him out of earshot of the king, not to mention the royal guards." He pulled thoughtfully at his nose. "It might be well to wait until he's less engaged with his arch majesty; but you want to go out there right away, I suppose."

"I am going out there," Lucius declared. "Why if I wait until Don Rodrigo's at leisure—"

"I can see that point," Golias conceded. "Well, let's get our beards off. Then we'll have a snack—I'd hate to be killed on an empty stomach—and by that time our new duds should be here. How far is it to Xanadu, would you say, Lucius?"

"About seven miles."

"That jibes with my own recollection." Golias clinked his full purse. "Now that we're in funds, we'll hire a coach to take us as far as the gardens."

"Why not to the palace itself?" I asked.

"We're not exactly invited, and by driving up in style we'd attract more attention than I care to."

"I wish we had some plan of campaign," I said, when we were on our way a couple of hours later.

Golias stopped whistling to smile. "We're not being as foolish as you might think," he observed. "It's only good sense to go looking for trouble, because then at least you have your eyes open; while if you stay still, trouble will sneak up on you and pot you like a sitting bird. As for a plan to use against it, there's no such thing. When your tail's in a crack, you improvise if you're good enough. Otherwise you give your pelt to the trapper."

I wasn't much comforted by his philosophy, and I didn't feel better when I saw Xanadu. It was a town boxed in by walls like those of a state prison. There were gates with soldiers at them, and if those gates closed, you stayed inside.

The sight of the palace itself on the other hand cheered me somewhat. It was built for fun and comfort, so obviously so that the thought of violence seemed incongruous. Even pleasanter to the eye was the park around it, a mass of fountains, greenery, and blossoms, seamed with winding walks. Dismounting, we began making our way along one of them.

Most of the other people we saw were sauntering rather than going anywhere. Allowing for the fact that all the men were armed, it was rather like Lincoln Park on a Sunday afternoon, minus the pigeons and children. We drew some notice by our brisk advance along walks dedicated to idleness and flirtation, a fact that gave me concern. Golias evidently felt the same way.

"We'd do better not to be conspicuous, Lucius."

"Don't accompany me, if it worries you," Jones told him. Instantly he was sorry. "No, I didn't mean that! But I can't go slow."

"Take your pace then," I growled, "and watch where you're walking. You don't have to run over other people just because you're in a hurry."

I made this remark, because Jones, while apologizing to Golias, wasn't giving clearance to a pair of men riding a twist in the path just ahead of us. Lucius looked up, but instead of yielding space he stepped directly in their way.

"Rodrigo!" he exclaimed; and the name was a threat and a curse as well as recognition.

I would have stood on my guard if a man had spoken to me like that, but the fellow Jones was glaring at halted as if he was slightly puzzled about something. "Watch it, Lucius!" I cried, but in place of the pistol I had expected, he pulled a lorgnette out of his pocket. Through this instrument of superciliousness he peered at the fuming man who confronted him.

"If it's not my pseudo-kinsman, Mr. Jones," he said to his companion, "it's somebody just as silly-looking."

I think Lucius was already too deep in fury to be bothered by insults; but the fact that Ravan was amused rather than on the defensive did get under his skin. He reached out and bunched the other's blouse in his big left fist.

"Damn you! Where is she?"

"Careful, you fool, that's the king's favorite!" Ravan's companion made the mistake of tugging at the offending arm, as he gave that warning.

I wouldn't have believed that so much anger could have lived in the same carcass with so much good nature. Jones was wild with it beyond all the drags of discretion.

"What the hell do I care if the king doesn't know any better?" he shouted. While so doing he gave the man a push which tripped him over his own sword and sat him on his can in a rain pool just big enough to accommodate it. Then Lucius tugged at Don Rodrigo's blouse. "Where is she, I asked you."

In my experience two handsomer men never confronted each other. But leaving out of account the fact that they were about the same height, their looks had little in common. Lucius was sandy-haired, rugged, and healthy. Ravan was twenty years old, dark, and of a wirier build. He appeared athletic enough, but his complexion had ripened indoors, and the mice, small ones as yet, had crept under his eyes to stay. The eyes themselves had the gift of concealing emotion.

Now they looked mild, as he gazed back at Jones. "Whom do you refer to? And, by the way, you're crinkling my newest tunic."

Seeing that he had got him to talk, Lucius let go. "I mean the Lady Hermione ap Hawthorn, kidnapped by some bastards of your hiring. Where is she?"

"Oh, you mean my fiancée?"

"Mine, blast you! Or she would still be if it wasn't for you."

"The king says otherwise," Don Rodrigo said. "I expressly asked him for his blessing on my marriage to the Lady Hermione."

"Blast the king!" Jones roared. "What's he got to do with it? She's not his ward."

Ravan's companion had arisen from his puddle. "You can't talk about his majesty that way!" he cried.

I myself was uneasy about the way Lucius was throwing the king's name around. "What about it?" I whispered to Golias. "Do you think we'd better call him off?"

"He wouldn't listen," Golias murmured. "We'll be lucky if he blows off steam with words only."

While we were muttering, Don Rodrigo was deciding where to slip his knfe in next. "I understand that the lady herself has raised an objection to the match, but if she didn't want the king to bestow her, she shouldn't have run away from her natural guardian. In other words, she had made her bed, and I shall lie in it."

Lucius let him have it then, a smash to the jaw that sent his enemy crashing into the shrubbery which lined the path. It was only one point of action among several. Golias jumped for Ravan's companion, but didn't get there in time. Before his hands closed on the fellow's throat the latter had bleated.

"Help! The guards! My Lord Ravan!"

Meanwhile, and though I could hear shouts and running feet, Jones had drawn his sword. "You were hit, weren't you," he yelled. "Draw, so I can kill you."

Ravan did know he had been hit. It took him a minute to pull himself together, but he was ready enough then. That blow had taken the enamel off him, and he wasn't posing when his sword came out. His face was that of a killer who thought he had found fresh meat.

As for me, I ended by drawing my cane sword, although not knowing how to use it or whom I was going to use it on, simply because I couldn't stand there and do nothing. Thus we were all three obvious enemies to the peace when the royal guards charged on the scene.

There were too many of them to resist, even if we had wanted to make our position worse by defying these direct representatives of the arch king's authority. Having seen to it that each of us was collared by no less than four of his men apiece, the officer in command saluted Ravan.

"The Chateau d'If, my lord?"

It was his lord's companion, his throat not yet recovered from the grip of Golias' fingers, who replied. "Yes, the Chateau d'If," he whispered, wheezing and coughing. "Put 'em deep down, and in irons."

The officer flipped open a note book. "And the charges, sir?"

"Attempted murder in his blessed majesty's own royal enclosure, and—"

"Wait a minute, Varney," Ravan intervened. "As the person murderously assaulted, I have something to say here."

"You have everything to say, my lord," Varney agreed. "I was only—"

"Talking out of turn," Ravan cut him off. "Now, captain, can I ask you to be patient a few minutes while I quiz one of your prisoners?"

"We can wait an hour—or three—if your lordship wishes."

Stepping past him, Don Rodrigo stepped in front of the glowering Jones. "Another man might be angry with you," he remarked, "but I can't find it in my heart to hold a grudge so near my nuptials."

The wildness had passed from Lucius' eyes to leave a look of despairing loathing. He said nothing.

"Now if you enter the Chateau d'If," the other went on reflectively, "you will leave it alive only in the event that the king, which Heaven forbid, dies before you."

He took off his hat when he asked Heaven to look after the king. Varney did likewise, and the captain snapped to attention, both saying: "Amen."

"The new monarch would probably honor custom by granting a general amnesty on his assumption of the throne," Ravan explained. "But I should point out that the present all-wise and gracious ruler is healthy, which is more than can be said for the Chateau d'If. Your chances of being out by my wedding day are slight."

If Jones had glanced my way, he must have seen a face as pale and sick as his own. I took it that his sentence would also be that of Golias and myself. And if I wasn't losing my sweetheart in the bargain, I was agonizingly conscious of the fact that this wasn't basically my affair at all.

"Now," Don Rodrigo went on when Lucius remained silent, "I should hate for anyone who was once considered my kinsman not to be present to wish joy to my lovely bride and myself when the marital bond makes us one in the spirit—and, of course, in the flesh." He had the screw way down now, and he was ready to crush the bone. "Out of my magnanimity, augmented by my strong family feeling, I will see to it that instead of rotting in prison you will be released—free to eat, drink, be merry, and to wed whomever will have a man of dubious ancestry and no patrimony—if only I have your sworn word that you will come to my wedding."

So great was my relief that I hardly appreciated the mind which could devise such careful cruelty. I could feel that the soldiers' grip on my arms had slackened, and I stopped sweating. I felt sorry for Jones meanwhile—but not half so sorry as I felt for myself a moment later.

"No!" Lucius was snarling again. "Fight me!"

"Why, to tell the truth," Ravan said, "you're a better swordsman than I would have thought, and I never fight anybody I'm not sure of beating.

Fight the walls of Chateau d'If. I'll leave you your
sword and will send every day to find out who's
winning. You can also try your blade on the bad
air, the dampness, the dark, the dog food, the
groans of your dying neighbors, the seconds, the
minutes, the hours, the days, the weeks, the
months and the years."

Everything in his catalogue scorched my imagination, as he let the items fall on it one by one. It
must have had a similar effect on Jones, for he had
to brace himself before he opened his mouth.

"Stop talking and do what you're going to do,"
he said.

I wanted to yell at him that he had us to think of,
too; but I couldn't quite bring myself to do it. It
took guts for Lucius to do what he was doing, and
it wasn't for me to bring added pressure to make
him knuckle down. Ravan, however, was not the
man to pass over this weapon.

"If you persist in being disobliging in so trivial
a matter, you are also dooming your associates,"
he pointed out.

It wasn't in my power to tell Lucius to go ahead
and never mind me, though I tried to keep my eyes
blank as he looked my way. He hadn't had time to
think of us, naturally, and I could see that he was
stunned by this new attack. He gave a little moan,
and Don Rodrigo smiled.

So engrossed had I been with my own feelings
and those of Jones that I hadn't given Golias a
thought. Now he spoke up.

"He's only asked you to go to *his* wedding,
Lucius. The request included no mention of
whom he was going to marry. Am I right, my
lord?"

Ravan looked more amused than ever. "I believe you are, and although I might amend my phrasing now that you've called the oversight to my attention, I'll allow the quibble."

It was the only thing that could help. In prison, for whatsoever noble reasons, Lucius couldn't rescue his girl. He might not be able to anyhow, but he would be free to try without breaking his word. It was not until then that I reflected that I had never once wondered why Lucius hadn't promised, just so he could get out from under. And I saw the answer, too, though it never would have occurred to me before I came to the Commonwealth. In a way it would have been a more crushing victory over him for Ravan—and certainly Don Rodrigo would have known and relished it—than the latter could win either by imprisoning him or stealing his fiancée.

But that was at the back of my mind. In its front was the desire to shout at him to take the opening Golias had found. Yet I couldn't mention the argument which would hold most weight with him, for fear Ravan might take back his offer. I added several strands of white hair to my lock while Lucius was working the problem over; and when he started to speak I felt like a man up for homicide waiting for the foreman of the jury to open his mouth.

"All right," he said. "When does your damned lordship propose to marry, and where will the ceremony take place?"

Don Rodrigo laughed. "Hard to get out, wasn't it? Let's see; the place will naturally be wherever the king is holding court, and the time will be as soon as I return from the confidential mission on which his benign majesty is sending me tonight. That will make it necessary to defer my wedding and honeymoon plans for some weeks, possibly even a couple of months." He then addressed the waiting officer again. "As this is more or less a family quarrel, complicated by a little boyish jealousy on the part of my backdoor cousin here, I'm going to ask you to forget that this incident took place. Possibly your promotion is overdue?"

The captain thought it was, but we didn't listen to the details. We were free and got out of there.

XVI

❦ A New Problem ❧

"WE DIDN'T gain much by a frontal attack," I said, when we were back at the Fir Cone, "but at least we found out that we have some time to spare."

"Not too much," Lucius said. He unbuckled his sword and picked up my sword cane. "I'm going to the Hell Fire Club again. There'll be a lot more around than were present this morning, so it's possible that I'll learn something useful."

"Will you wait here for him?" Golias asked when Jones had left us.

"There's nothing else to do," I said, and thankfully, for I was beginning to know that I hadn't had much rest the night before. "Why, what are you planning on?"

For answer he showed me a pair of dice, then closed his fist on them and made them cackle. "I'm going to finance this rescue expedition. I know from experience that such a business costs money. Guessing that leg wasn't mine in fee simple, Barabas screwed me way down on what he gave for it; and we'll need horses and maybe a gang of armed bravos before we're through."

If I hadn't recalled his success on Brodir's ship, I might had warned him about gambling with strangers. As it was, I only said: "Do they let you play with your own dice hereabouts?"

"Mine or theirs, it won't matter tonight," he said. "I feel lucky."

In view of his plans, we ate early. Golias left as soon as we had finished, and I settled myself to hold the fort. I would rather have gone to our room to hit the sack for a few hours, or maybe ten, but Lucius would be in need of company when he returned. So I dozed where I was, coming out of it every now and then to fiddle dopily with the pipe I had ordered. After about an hour of this, when I was beginning to come out of it a little, Lucius showed up. He was looking so excited that I was sure he had found out something.

"What did you hear?" I demanded.

His gloom returned for a moment. "Nothing at all."

"That's too bad," I sympathized, turning to look for a waiter. "Where's that soup caddy? You must be starved."

"No—er—I hope you didn't wait for me."

"Not a chance. Golias had a project, and we didn't know how late you'd be."

"That's fine, for I've already eaten. I wouldn't have, knowing there was a possibility you might be waiting; but I met somebody."

"Where is she now?"

He flushed, half shamefaced and half indignant. "It was a man, Shandon. You see, I was pretty despondent when I didn't learn anything on my second visit to the club, and as I didn't feel up to joining any of those roaring boys, I stopped at a tavern instead for a drink of brandy to keep me company on the way here. No doubt I looked as downhearted as I felt, for this officer—an awfully jolly, considerate fellow—asked me if he could buy me another drink in hopes of making me feel better. Then he was kind enough to enquire as to what was troubling me."

"I hope to the devil you didn't tell him."

"Oh, I didn't give him any particulars," Jones said, "but I told him in a general way."

"What for? You don't look potted, let alone true-confession drunk."

"I wasn't just looking for tavern sympathy," he repudiated the suggestion, "but he said he'd be able to help—or rather he knew somebody who would."

"Huh?" The waiter had come, and while Lucius was speaking I had been ordering a bottle. "Why should he want to help and how could he? Especially as he doesn't know, according to you, who's doing what to whom."

"No, he doesn't; but this friend of his will be able to find out for himself, if he's as good as Captain Face says he is. You see, he's an alchemist."

"Come again?"

"He's a—well, an alchemist. By his science he can change a substance into something else. He can also see into the future and advise you as to how to deal with what's going to happen."

"A fortune teller, eh?" I was still dubious about such things, but I no longer laughed at the idea. "Well, maybe it's what the doctor ordered. If he's on the level, that is."

"We can easily judge his honesty, Shandon, by whether he can find out who our enemy is, say. But I'm sure he's a legitimate practitioner. Captain Face says he is really a scholar who hates to have his studies interrupted even by an opportunity to make money by his vast knowledge. The captain thinks he can persuade him to take the case, though, out of friendship for him."

The fact that he was dealing with a military man was somewhat reassuring. An officer may be every other sort of a scoundrel, but the nature of his duties makes it difficult for him to be a con man or a shill.

"Where is this captain?" I asked.

"After supper, which I insisted that he have with me in view of his kindness, he went straight to the doctor—the alchemist, you know—in hopes of persuading him to see me tonight. I hurried here, so I could let you and Golias know what's going on. The captain will be along later."

I watched the waiter pour. "Did this joker ask you for money by any chance?"

"No. I tell you he wasn't that kind. He did say he thought it would be all right to make a gift to the doctor that would help him carry on his studies. But I was the one who brought the subject up."

"Uh-huh." There was no use in saying anything further until I had had a look at the man in question. I was tapping the dottle out of my pipe when the quiet which the taproom in general had shared with us after my noncommittal rejoinder was interrupted. There was an altercation at the door. Then the words were loud enough to reach us.

"I tell you I gotta see somebody here," a harsh voice said.

The next voice was that of Robin Turgis, our landlord. "If any of my customers saw you," he retorted, "they'd stop drinking, and I'd go bankrupt. Get along now."

"I tell you I come in."

"Sure, but not here. All right, lads."

They must have given the intruder the heave-ho, for I heard a scuffle, followed by the slamming of the door. A minute later there was a noise at one of the open tap room windows, which were of the casement type. Next a figure vaulted over the sill, and I saw what the landlord meant. It was a man, but it took a second look to make sure. It is no exaggeration to state that I've seen chimpanzees whose features appeared more human. The fellow walked as awkwardly as an ape, too, knock-kneed, stooped, and hump-backed, and with long arms hanging.

All of us there were startled, but the greatest shock was reserved for us. "I wanna see a man called Jones," the fellow growled.

I wished later that I had had the inspiration to ask Lucius if that was his friend, the captain, but at the time all I hoped was that he wouldn't admit his identity. Attracted by the voice, Turgis and two of his bouncers rushed the trespasser, but the latter held them at bay with an upraised chair.

"You make trouble, so do I," he warned. "I ain't gonna leave without seen' if Jones is here."

"Yes! I'm the one you're looking for," Lucius announced. "It's all right, landlord. If he has business with me, I want to hear about it." Rising, he drew back a chair. "Sit down, won't you?"

The hunchback approached, peering at Lucius from amidst the knot of wens framing his one good eye. "Lucius Gil Jones?" he asked.

"That's right. What do you wish with me?"

The fellow continued to examine him. "You know anybody called ap Hawthorn?"

"Yes! Lady Hermione Steingerd ap Hawthorn. Is she all right? Do you know where she. is?" Lucius was so overcome with excitement, pleasure, and anxiety that he couldn't stop for answers. "Tell me where she is! I really am Jones; Lucius Gil Jones, that is. Ask Mr. Shandon, here."

"Give the guy a chance to say something." I put my hand on Lucius' arms until he quit yammering. "That is the man you're looking for," I told the hunchback. "What do you know?"

"You got her name right anyhow." Lifting himself into the chair with his arms, he leaned toward Jones. "Ravan own me," he said, "but she kind to me like nobody else is. She smile at me, and sweet."

"The sweetest smile in the—" Lucius began.

"Shut up and let him talk," I ordered. "Go on, chum."

"Ravan put her in house here—"

"Here! Right in Parouart?" Jones nearly knocked over the table jumping to his feet.

"Was here," the other said. "Ravan move her."

"Oh." Lucius slumped back into his seat. "Do you know where they took her?"

"No."

I was beginning to wonder whether this unaccountable visit wasn't something Don Rodrigo had dreamed up by way of torturing Jones. "Where did they have her locked up?" I asked.

"Right across from Hell Fire Club." Sensing my suspicion, he stared at me. "Why you ask?"

"Because among other things, I want to know how she knew Jones was here at the Fir Cone."

"She see him this morning when he leave club, but too much racket from whores fighting. They outyell her."

"Oh, she was free to call out." I thought I had him then. "Not even guarded."

"I guard her part of time. She not supposed to yell, but I let her. She call to lots of people, you know." He shrugged. "Nobody listen to woman yelling in Parouart unless she ask him to lay her."

"I guess you've got something, there," I conceded, reflecting that I wouldn't have answered distress calls from strange windows in that town. "This burg looks to me like it might be the place where the badger game was invented."

"Especially near the Hell Fire Club," Lucius agreed. "My God! To think that she called to me, and I didn't hear."

"She watch all day for you and see you come again," the hunchback proceeded, "But too much racket from Hell Fire Club then. So she show you me as you go through club door." He put a finger to his usable eye. "What I see with this I don't forget."

"And you tailed him here when he came out," I nodded, all but convinced of his sincerity. "But if you left to do that, how do you know Lady Hermione's gone?"

"They take her away while I still at window, looking for Jones. I hear them say Ravan move her because somebody in Parouart looking for her, and Ravan don't got time to see her anyhow, like he hope to."

"Our one comfort," Jones said. "And you really don't have any idea where they were taking her?"

"I hear them say one place of his, but he got

lots." The fellow shrugged again. "Anyhow I follow you; but you talk to soldier, so I wait outside tavern."

"You showed good sense," I remarked. "From what we saw this afternoon Ravan's got the army eating out of his hand."

He paid no heed to my commendation. "Then I follow you again, but lose you on this corner and try inn across street first. Then I come here and have to ask because I know your back good but not your face. So I want you," he said, pointing a finger at Jones, "to turn around."

"What for?" Lucius was dazed with disappointment at learning that he had been on the right trail, only to lose it. "Oh, all right."

Standing up again, he faced away from the hunchback. The latter looked him over, then darted a hand into his shirt. My own hand grabbed the bottle but relinquished it when he produced a fold of paper instead of a weapon. He slipped the paper into Jones' hand and slid from the chair. In another moment he had vaulted out of the window again.

When I turned from watching his departure, Lucius was reading the message which the hunchback had brought. Upon finishing it, he buried his face in his hands.

"Oh, my Christ! She's wonderful, but what can I do?"

"Did she give you any clue as to where she's bein taken?" I enquired.

"No, she—Oh, you read it." He shoved the note across the table at me, then, disregarding the stares of the other patrons, he rose to pace the floor. Filling his glass again, in case he should feel the need of it, I scanned the letter.

To Lucius Gil Jones, wherever located:

You saw me last a girl while I was cold
With anger at an infidelity
Not half so great as I was guilty of
When I let treachery seduce my faith
From you, to whom it properly belongs.
But this is a woman speaking to a man
Out of the new maturity that's mine
By right of knowing evil. Now I know
What I owe you as well as what's my due,
And, given the chance to prove it, I will try.
I know another thing, and that is this:
There is no haven for my heart but yours.
There, it is said; I mend my loyalty
Whether you choose to do the same or not;
I'm half myself at that rate anyhow.
But whether or not you choose to make me
    whole,
I ask you by the words which we once said—
And you at least have never taken back—
To find and save me from the brothel
    marriage
Which Ravan, some for pleasure, more for
    wealth,
Will wreak upon me if you do not care.
My father, crippled by his wounds and blind,
Or half so, as you know, can give no help;
My friends will think I've made a lucky
    match;
The law, were Ravan not above the law,
Could but avenge me when it is too late.
I am beyond all other help but yours:
Will you not come and save

                              Hermione.

At the end I didn't look at Lucius right away. I could sense that the message made an unbearable attack on so many of his emotions that his mind was still racing from one point to another in stunned confusion. At length, because I had to make some comment, I cleared my throat.

"Quite a girl," I said.

Jones lifted his head haggardly. "She wonders if I still love her." He reached out a shaking hand for the letter. "She not only forgives me, she takes the blame for what—er, happened at Upton. How can she write that?"

"She's got some blame coming to her." I hesitated, as my mind dawdled along a path it had never used before. "Of course, it's not her fault that you got yourself mixed up with that floozie, but a man—and a woman, too, I guess—needs all the props he can get to keep him from falling into foolishness. In this particular instance she had taken away one of yours. Not too many girls would have seen that."

He waited for me to finish, but to all intents and purposes I had been talking to myself. Relief that he was square with his sweetheart was being by-passed in his attention by the bad facets of the case.

"If only I had been diplomatic instead of picking a—oh, there he is!" I just steadied the bottle in time, as he shook the table, jumping up again. "Here we are, Captain! Right here. Waiter—where's that waiter? Oh. You, there, bring a glass for the captain, and another bottle, please. Captain Face, this is my excellent friend, Mr. Shandon."

I looked the captain over, as we shook hands. To

outward appearances, a hearty soul dwelt within his blue and gold uniform and behind his beard.

"Your servant, Mr. Shandon." Next he saluted the bottle. "And your servant anytime." Dragging a chair back, he expertly kicked his sword out of the way with one booted foot and sat down.

"I certainly take this kindly of you," Lucius said. "Have you seen your friend, the learned doctor?"

The waiter arriving with the extra glass, the captain reached out to grip the bottle by the neck, snapped off the loose cork, with his thumb, and swept the wine toward him with a motion that ended in pouring. "First things come first," he laughed, lifting his drink toward the flask which the waiter was opening. "Here's to the newcomer. Ah!" Filling his glass anew, he twitched each spike of his moustache and beamed at Lucius. "I had a time talking him into it. I believe I told you how reserved and sunk in his studies he is; but I'm glad to report that he has consented to take time out to consider your problem."

"Oh, that's wonderful!" Jones gripped the soldier's hand. "Will he see me tonight?"

"We had quite a discussion about that, too," the captain chuckled. "At first he swore that he couldn't possibly spare you a moment in under a week, but—well, I suppose it's the attraction of opposites. I admire him for his great learning and interest him in turn as a man of action. At any rate, ever since we met—due to the fact that I was able to be of service to him in the matter of killing a couple of ruffians who were assaulting him— we've got on amazingly well. I honestly think I can do as much with him as any man in the world, and in this instance I wouldn't take no for an answer. He grumbled a lot; but he's a soft hearted old codger really, and when I told him how distressed you were, he yielded."

"You're a good fellow!" Lucius told him. "Shall we go now?"

Captain Face flicked an eye at the bottle we hadn't yet started on. "I wouldn't advise going for another half-hour. We mustn't impose on the old boy's good nature, you know, and he always sups late."

"I want to give him something—something to help him along with his studies, as you suggested. How much money do you think would be right?"

"Don't mention money to him; it'll hurt his feelings. Give him something he can use in his work." The captain sloshed his glass full. "I don't understand these things myself, but it seems that gold is as useful in alchemistry as it is hard for a scholar to come by. In your place I'd give him that ring, say."

He was pointing to the valuable piece of jewelry which Miss Lescaut had vainly coveted. "If he just wants the gold, there's no use bothering him with that chunk of ruby," I said. "You'd better cut it out, so you can have it reset, Lucius."

The suggestion embarrassed Jones. "Why, I can'd do that. I'll give him the whole thing."

"The whole hog or nothing," Captain Face approved. "However, I'll tell you what I'll do. I'll ask the doctor whether he has any use for the stone— if you didn't ask him, he'd never think of it, he's so absent-minded—and perhaps he'll insist on giving it back."

That wine was fortified like Gibraltar, but the

captain made away with almost the whole bottle
in something under thirty minutes. "I'd insist on
you gentlemen allowing me to return the courtesy," he said, as he swallowed the lees, "but I
appreciate the fact that Jones here is in a hurry."

Getting around Parouart at night is work for
moles. The buildings crowded out all benefit of
starlight, and the only artificial substitute was an
occasional glowing window. Captain Face knew
his way, however, and after we had stumbled in
his wake along a tangle of alleys, he banged on a
door.

"I always do the right thing by knocking," he
explained, "but nine times out of ten he never
hears me. Fortunately he seldom remembers to
lock up. Step in, gentlemen."

The hall was dark, but at some distance down
it there was a streak of light the width of a doorway. In a minute the captain thrust the door itself
open. I found myself blinking at the back of a man
perched on a high stool. He didn't turn when we
clumped into the room, and Face nudged me in
the ribs.

"A million leagues deep in some calculation,"
he chuckled. "He probably forgot to eat tonight."
The captain raised his voice. "Good evening, doctor."

The man on the stool turned as if he thought he
had heard something but wasn't quite sure. He
had a beard as long and white as that of Santa
Claus, and the hair which straggled out from beneath his skull cap matched it. What I could see of
his face was long and solemn. His body was
swathed in a voluminous dressing gown, incongruously gay with stars and moons of all phases.

After peering a while, he descended from his perch and approved.

"Well, well, a good evening to you, my valiant young friend. I'm glad to see you. Come on over and watch what I'm doing. You've been neglecting me lately."

"Why I was here not two hours ago," Face reminded him, "and I've brought the man you promised to see."

"What man?" The doctor looked annoyed. "I can't see anyone now, captain—anyone but you, of course. I'm just on the verge of consummating an important experiment. Tell him to go away."

In answer to Jones' look of concern, the captain tipped him a wink. Then he hooked his arm in that of the old man.

"Doctor, you're not going to treat a very special friend of mine like that. And besides, you promised."

"Did I really?" The doctor looked worried. "Well, I don't know that I can help him. We want to know so much, and we actually know so little. But I'll try."

"Thank you, sir," Lucius said. "I'm sure that my problem, although it seems insoluble to me, will be easy for your wisdom."

"It may be so," the doctor said. "Somebody taught you to have a good tongue. Let's look at your face. No, come over here by the candle, Yes, a good face and a lucky one, too, or I've spent a lifetime of study in vain. Now the hands. No, backs up first, so I can observe their structure."

He could thus observe the ring also, but I couldn't swear that he gave it any attention before he began to examine Jones' palms. While he was doing so, I took stock of the room we were in. It looked like a blend of chem lab, a photo dark-room, and a pawnbroker's attic. Outside of an antique shop I have never seen so many things I would rejoice not to own, but I wasn't scornful of the place at that. The doctor had impressed me in spite of myself, and I looked respectfully at the brew bubbling in a glass retort. It smelled bad enough to be an authentic experiment.

Meanwhile the old fellow had finished mumbling over Jones' hands. "Just as I thought. You're a man born to succeed," he declared. "I could tell you much more; but I wanted to establish that fact, so we'd see whether it was worthwhile to try to do anything further. Now just what is your dilemma, my son?"

"Well, a certain man—I'd rather not give his name—has abducted, or rather he's had his men abduct my fiancée; and—"

"Wait!" the doctor commanded. He slapped himself on the forehead. "You're *that* one. Now it comes back to me. Captain Face—am I right?—told me that you know who's responsible for the crime but not where your inamorata was taken."

"Yes, you have it. We did find out where she was, though, but only after she had been removed to one of my Lord—to one of my enemy's other strongholds."

"She was moved, to be sure." The doctor wagged his head. "That accounts for it. After the good captain left, I stole a few minutes from my labors to consult the heavens about your case; but when I rechecked the stars, as I am always careful to do, they told me she was further away than when they had originally reported."

"Do you know where she is, then?" Lucius asked.

"No, I am not that perfect in my knowledge. The most I can assure you is that she is still in this vicinity. And as long as that is so, it seems to me that a little preparation of mine, a minor achievement but still useful, would go far toward solving your problem. Come with me, my son."

Taking a candle, he led Lucius into an adjoining room. They were gone only a few minutes, but when they returned Jones was smiling for the first time since he found that Hermione had been kidnapped. He was holding a jar of something in his left fist, from which his ring was now missing.

"Once more let me thank you, sir," he said, shaking the old fellow's hand. "Believe me, If ever I come into a fortune, you will have all the materials you need."

I was about to prompt the captain, but he made good on his word. "Speaking of materials, doctor; you may not have noticed, but in that ring Jones becomingly gave you, there's a ruby? Do you have any use for such a thing?"

"A ruby?" The doctor took the ring out of his pocket and looked at it as if he had never seen it before. "By Trismegistus, you're right! Young sir," he said to Lucius, "for ten years I've longed for such a jewel, not out of any desire for personal ornamentation but because I've long suspected it was the missing ingredient in my so far abortive efforts to create the philosopher's stone. God bless you for your generosity to an old man!"

On that note of piety we left, to be guided back to the Fir Cone by the captain. He would not come in, however.

"I'd like to buy you that bottle I owe you," he stated, "but I'll have to defer the pleasure. A soldier can't afford to make a night of it when early morning duty is lying in wait for him."

Neither of us pressed him, Lucius because he wanted to gloat over his acquisition and I because I wanted my curiosity relieved. "What did he give you?" I demanded, when we were alone.

"The means of locating Hermione," Jones said, as we entered the tap room. "We know from the hunchback that she's in one of my Lord Ravan's castles, and we have learned from the doctor that her new prison isn't far away. That narrows things down to simplicity."

"Uh-huh."

Someone was at the table we had formerly used, so we selected one in another corner. "Even at that," Lucius continued, "we might be entirely stumped. We could stare at a castle and its high walls for years without being able to tell whether or not it held my darling. And when we take the risk—which'll be a big one, I promise you—of entering a castle, we want to be sure it's the one she's in."

"No use being shot for cracking the wrong safe," I agreed. "So what?"

"The great doctor," Lucius said, patting the jar, "has given me the means at once of disguising myself and of gaining access unseen in the night to any window. And windows are sure to be open at this season."

"The doc did that, eh? No, I don't want any more of that slugged wine. Bring us a couple of glasses of brandy."

"He did, indeed," Lucius said, when the waiter had gone. "In this jar, Shandon, is an ointment which will change me into an owl."

I started to laugh, then I didn't. The recollection of what had happened to me on Aeaea shut out complete skepticism. It also prompted my next words.

"How about changing back into a man? Did he tell you the way to do that?"

"Oh, surely. All that's necessary is to screech twenty-one times and fly nine times in a circle counter-clockwise." Lucius looked as apologetic as his excitement would permit. "Would you mind very much if I left you and went up to the room to try it now?"

"Go right ahead," I urged him. I was reasonably sure he had been played for a sucker, and I thought it would be less embarrassing for him if he found it out with no witnesses. "But when you get to be an owl, remember to be a housebroken one."

Sipping slowly, I was about halfway through my pony when Golias came in. "Did you have any luck?" I asked.

"My associates thought so." He made his pockets clink. "And that's not groats, obols, or picayunes, either. That's gold, my boy. Where's Lucius?"

I grinned as I nudged Jones' untasted brandy toward him. The more I thought of it, the more I thought I had something funny to tell.

"He's practicing to be an owl."

"What for?"

"Well, he wants to be able to fly around and look in windows at night."

"H-m. That could be very useful, if he can work it."

Golias was being too matter-of-fact to suit me.

"Damn it all, I know it can happen, but he's been shaken down by a couple of phonies. They took him for that ring of his. It's worth a small fortune, and the one who ran the medicine show pretended he only wanted the gold and that ruby for experiments in alchemistry, or some such thing."

"I see." Golias, I was pleased to observe, was looking more alert. "How'd you meet this alchemist?"

"A guy who calls himself Captain Face picked Lucius up at a bar and—"

"Face!" Golias took his brandy at a gulp and rose. "Come on. We'd better see how he's doing."

Leading the way, he took the steps two at a time, and hurried down the corridor toward our room. I heard a scuffling sound and a succession of queer grunts as we approached. Then we pushed through the door.

Jones' clothes, hastily shucked, were draped over various articles of furniture, but their owner wasn't in evidence. The only tenant of the room was a donkey. While we stared, it gurgled twenty-one times, a jackass unsuccessfully imitating an owl, and ran around and around. Then as I watched in growing horror, it repeated the act. At the end of the second performance it stood still, but nothing happened.

"He can't work the antidote," I groaned. "Good God, Golias! What do we do now?"

XVII

❧ Jones Meets Admirers ❧

HAVE YOU EVER SEEN a hysterical donkey? When it finally dawned upon Jones that he wasn't going to regain human form, he blew his long-eared top, prancing, wriggling, and jumping, as if in hopes of shaking off the loathsome shape. He ended by standing straddle-legged in the middle of the room and venting his anguish in a mournful bray.

The ear that wasn't listening to him was alerted for the approach of an indignant management. I didn't know what to do, but Golias took charge of the situation.

"Stop it, Lucius!" he commanded. "We'll get you straightened out, but you've got to give us a chance."

Jones tried to speak but only succeeded in giving a horse squeal. "Be quiet!" Golias snapped. "If you don't, we'll be arrested, you'll be confiscated, and you'll stay a donkey."

I heard doors opened, and two or three people called questions; but apparently nobody had located the site of the disturbance. Lucius, although he trembled violently, stopped making noise.

"That's it; just take it easy." Golias patted him. "This Captain Face, Shandon. He was a jolly-looking, bearded, dark-haired fellow?"

"That's the one."

"This is the sort of trick he and his partner would pull, peddling any old lotion they happened to get hold of, without knowing or caring just what it would do. Fortunately I have enough on both of them to twist their tails and make them snag an antidote from whomever they got it from. Lead me to them."

"I couldn't find the place in a million years. Could you?" I added to Jones. I spoke with some diffidence, not sure I would be understood; but the donkey shook his head. "You see," I explained, "it was dark, and Face must have led us down a dozen small change streets, but how about you, Golias? You seem to have known these lice before."

It was his turn to shake his head sadly. "Too many years ago for me to remember how to get to their hangout, which they've probably changed a half-dozen times since then anyhow. And with loot like Lucius' ring in hand they'll lie so low it'll be useless to try to hunt 'em in the streets. I'm afraid they've beat us."

If he was stumped, I saw no help at all. Lucius felt the same way, for his ears drooped, and he gave a sob. The very inhumanness of the sound went to my heart.

"Can't anything be done?" I whispered, so that Jones wouldn't hear if the answer was negative. "Can't we take him some place else, like you did with me that time on the island?"

Once more Golias shook his head. "You were under a personally applied spell, and all that was necessary was to get you outside the sphere of influence of the person casting it. This stuff Lucius rubbed on can be applied anywhere and consequently will stick with him anywhere."

"Maybe we can scare up another alchemist who'll give us the right answer," I suggested.

"That'd probably be a waste of time. Unless we stumbled on the one who made it, he wouldn't know what was in it, so he wouldn't have any idea how to go about making an antidote." Golias sighed. "There's only one thing—No, before we do that there's a letter to be sent to Lady Hermione's family, telling what's happened to her. I'll write it before we go to bed and send it off by early stage post. That might help her and give us more time to help Lucius."

"Do you think her people can beat Ravan's hand with the arch king in it?" I asked, recalling that Hermione herself had counted on no such thing.

"It's possible. As members of the old noblesse they have influential connections; and whereas they might not object to the match as such, they might very well object to having the lady held in durance unwed. They could perhaps raise such an outcry on a point of order that even Jamshyd himself would see fit to heed it."

"What do we do in the meantime? You said there was one thing."

"Consult the Oracle. We can find out what to do for Lucius there all right, but it'll take a while to make the trip. Don Rodrigo may be back from his own journey before we return."

I made a wry face. "That'll be a hard idea for Lucius to take with him, but he's got to risk it. Do you want to break it to him, or shall I?"

Neither liking the dirty job, we both tackled it. Once we had persuaded Jones that it was the only thing to do, we had to consider other problems which Lucius' transformation had raised for us. First in point of time if not of importance was where Lucius should be quartered.

"No management is going to let us keep a jackass in the room with us," I murmured. "And—how about food?"

"It's a delicate point, but you're right." Golias glanced to where Jones stood blinking at a mirror. It reflected a sleek donkey, uniformly dark brown except for a heart-shaped white patch on its left shoulder, where, in his human state, Lucius had a similarly shaped birth mark. "As a matter of fact we ought to try to smuggle him out to the stable tonight. If we bring him down by daylight, there's apt to be trouble."

I didn't say so, but I was pleased at the suggestion. It would have been impossible to sleep while Lucius sadly ambled about the room. Fortunately he agreed as to the propriety of going to the stable; the hitch came in executing his removal. He was unable to negotiate the stairs, and we had to half carry him down. The two late mainstays of the tap room looked as if they were accustomed to view donkeys or anything else at that hour, but the waiter was less sophisticated. To him, after greasing his credulity with silver, Golias slipped the explanation that some rowdy friends, whose sense of humor we deplored, had introduced the animal to our room.

Having left Lucius in the stable boy's charge, with admonitions that he should under no provocation be abused, we had the drink our shaken nerves needed. Then Golias wrote his letter to Hermione's family, and I went to bed. It had been a rough forty-odd hours since I had last slept, and in a way that was a good thing. Only an overwhelming weariness made it possible for me to get the rest I needed.

"How far away is the oracle, and how do we get there?" I asked, as we ate breakfast the next morning.

"It's a ways south and a cut west," Golias responded with his usual indifference to distances.

"Oh, yes; I remember asking the same thing and getting the same answer before I dropped off last night." I took a gulp of ale. "Does any road go there directly?"

"We'll cross Long River just below Erech, then follow the shore road to Troynovaunt. From there we'll head south and west. There'll be some roads, but you'll get your fill of cross-country work before we get there and back." Golias munched thoughtfully. "Do you reckon we ought to have Lucius shod before we leave?"

A snort made us turn toward the window by which our table was placed. "Good morning," I mumbled, still not used to passing the amenities to an animal. "It's a pet of ours," I said to the waiter, who was not the one we had bribed the night before. "Don't drive him away; he'll behave."

"Well, tell him to keep his goddam snoot away from the bread," the waiter growled. "It'll give the joint a bad name if it got around—Look at that, now!"

I did look. Lucius had transferred his attention

to my beefsteak and was wolfing the remains of it. As I gazed at the unwholesome sight, he returned to the bread. This time he snapped up a couple of slices. He had his muzzle in my ale before I found voice.

"Hey, quit that!" I commanded. "You're supposed to be a; that is you are a—See here; don't you know you're supposed to like hay instead of this stuff?"

"This is very interesting," Golias said, but I noticed he moved his own breakfast out of reach. "Apparently donkey appetites don't go with the hide."

"I'm going for the landlord," the waiter announced.

"Beat it before you get us in trouble!" I said to Jones, half beseechingly and half angrily. As yet I wasn't convinced, either by his demonstration or Golias' explanation. "You've already had a big wad of hay, haven't you?"

He shook his head, and with it the fragment of a halter he'd chewed through to escape.

"Well, I'll see that you get some as soon as I've ordered another breakfast. Now please scram before that damned waiter—and if he wants a tip, he'd better mint it himself—comes back with the proprietor."

In place of obliging, Jones ate three more pieces of bread and lapped up the rest of my ale. He was in the act of so doing when Turgis came hustling in. Golias commenced jingling the coins in his pocket, but it was an unnecessary gesture. The landlord saw what we had been too flustered to see. His other patrons, far from being outraged, were delighted with the novel spectacle. So instead of blasting us, he looked thoughtful.

"What do you want for him?"

"Some hay," I fenced. "I guess your stable boy neglected to feed him. He'll be all right when he has some hay."

Turgis refused to be put off. "I mean how much will you take for him?"

"He's not for sale," Golias said. "How about some more breakfast for my friend here?"

Anxious as I was for breakfast, I was becoming more anxious to get gone. I didn't like all the attention we were drawing.

"We'd better pay Jones' bill and explain that he's already left," I murmured.

"Right," Golias agreed. "Oh, here comes trouble. There's the waiter who was on deck last night."

It is not to be expected that a man who will take a bribe will be faithful to his hire. As we apprehensively watched, the newcomer approached the proprietor and whispered something in his ear. Turgis, who had withdrawn when his proposal was refused, now drew near again.

"I want to see a bill of sale for that jackass," he said.

"Take your shadow snipe hunting," Golias ordered. He spoke quietly, but he jabbed at the man's waistband with his knive.

The fellow jumped back. "That donkey was left in your room, so it's the property of the inn. You try to take him away, and I'll have you arrested."

There were two more bites on Golias' plate. He ate them while Turgis waited for a retort and I tried to think of a good one. Then Golias rose.

"Meet me outside, Shandon," he said casually. With the words he vaulted through the window from which Jones withdrew his head just in time. "Lucius, let's go!" he roared.

The maneuver divided their forces and attention. The landlord couldn't decide whether he was more anxious to follow the donkey or retain me as hostage. By the time he decided that he had better hold the prize in hand, I had grasped the situation and was on my feet.

"Stop him!" he yelled.

Well, a man has a right to say "stop him" when someone is taking a swing at him. It was an ineffective defense, though. I caught him on the cheek with a punch that made him stagger against a table behind him. A couple of waiters and a busybody patron were between me and the door, but there was a hundred and ninety-five pounds of me backed by momentum. I stiff-armed one, scraped a second off on the jamb, and took the other out into the hall. There we fell together, but as I was using him for a cushion, the wind was knocked out of him. He let go when we hit, and in an instant I was out in the street.

Everybody in the vicinity was running, yelling, and pointing. Probably most of them were entertained rather than outraged; but at the time I was convinced that everyone in sight was a volunteer deputy, and I really legged it. There was, indeed, some yelling for the watch, though nobody followed us for any distance except Mr. R. Turgis, now in a more conciliatory mood.

"The reckoning!" he kept shouting. "Never mind about the donkey; just pay the reckoning."

By the time I had caught up with my companions there was no longer any reason for running. "He wants his reckoning," Golias said to Lucius, as we waited for the pleading landlord. "Do you think you could supply it?"

"There—were—three—of you—remember?" the fellow puffed as he joined us. "I—don't—know where—the third—went, but—"

He was so out of breath that speech must have been painful. An anaesthetic was at hand. Golias and I had turned to face Turgis, but Jones had only looked around without moving. At the precise moment when the proprietor was neither too far away nor yet too near, Lucius gave a joyful bray and kicked him in the belly.

"We won't wait for a receipt," Golias said.

From the outrageous sounds Lucius was making, it was plain that he was as pleased as we with the manner in which the incident had ended. Indeed, for a few minutes he was as unmindful of his disaster as I was of the fact that he had eaten most of my breakfast.

When, in the course of a little more walking, my loss was brought home to me again, I checked our progress. "I've got to eat," I insisted, "and maybe brother Jones here could do with a little more also. But we must be careful."

"I don't think anybody will question our title to him from now on," Golias said, "though it's a fact someone might try to steal him. Meanwhile Robin Turgis has called it to our attention that we've got an asset we hadn't listed." He sprang in front of Lucius. "How about some hay?"

Jones let his ears droop.

"Well, how about some breast of guinea hen?"

The ears came up and a long tongue slid across the upper lip.

"That's better, eh?" Golias pursued. "Then I

suppose you'd like some bread to go with it."

With one hoof Lucius made six marks in the dust of the street.

"Oh, six slices. And some ale to wash it down with?"

Jones brayed approvingly, and Golias waved one hand. "We've got a road show, Shandon."

I could see that he liked the notion. As for me, my principal concern was to get out of a town where nothing much but bad luck had come our way. I was therefore impatient of the by-play between the others.

"Let's not stand around and wait for our pockets to be picked," I suggested. "Did you notice there was an inn on the next corner?"

After I had satisfied my needs, and food—in the comparative privacy of a stable—had been smuggled to Lucius, we left Parouart behind. Golias had exercised his skill with the dice in vain as far as our speed was concerned. Coach travel was out of the question. I was afraid that Golias might purchase horses out of his new wealth, but he himself pointed out that it would be more trouble to gear nags down to the pace of a donkey than it would be for us to walk along with one.

Jones didn't need to be led, but as we didn't want to attract further public notice, Golias bought a rope to tie around Lucius' neck. Trailing them down the narrow streets of one of Parouart's suburbs, I had leisure for compassion. Having been through it myself, I could see the scope of Jones' tragedy. Not least of it, I was aware, was that he was not simply a man in a donkey's skin. He was a man whose human brain and spirit were warred upon by the inevitabilities of his new shape. I knew that the power to resist such a seige weakened with time. I knew that this siege was being abetted not only by a fifth column of donkey instincts, but by a more terrible enemy. The steps to degradation are only three: the actuality of the shameful condition, the recognition of the actuality while feeling unable to do anything about it, and then acceptance of it as the normal state of affairs. It gave me the crod to see Lucius balk at being led around a corner. It wasn't that he didn't want to go. It was the jackass in him getting the upper hand.

About mid-morning of the next day we were ferried across the surging brown waters of Long River—nearly a mile wide, it must have been—at a point just south of Erech. Although from what we could see of it the place was considerable of a city, the country on the west shore was sparsely settled. Shortly after we turned off south our road was crowded by timber on both sides.

"That sign back at the crossroads said it was twenty miles to Troynovaunt," I remarked. "Do you think we can make it by dinner time?"

"Not if we don't do any better than this," Golias said. "Shake it up, Lucius, or so help me Shylock, I'll carve a chunk out of you."

To my dissatisfaction, although it paralleled the river, the road kept its distance. The country, as was to be expected, was flat. This made for easy but dull progress. Nor was the traffic interesting. We met only one person of note.

She was not alone; but you didn't watch any of her companions, nor did she intend that you should. She was as impossible to overlook as a full moon. She was as bright as the moon somehow, and as brazen as the moon on a winter night, and as hotly overwhelming as a harvest moon. She was luscious as she lolled in the little shack on her elephant, and she was poisonous. She was cold-hearted and sultry of eye. She was whiter and redder than she should have been, and the jewelry store in her black hair would have looked absurd on anybody else, but she was very beautiful. And not a harlot to be bought, either, but a bird of prey.

"God save all men without chaperones!" I said out of a corner of my mouth, as I stared up at her. She was nearer the river side of the road, so, the better to have a look, we had moved to the left to make room for the procession. "Who's that?"

"Some potentate making the grand tour." Golias was gazing at her, too, and couldn't spare me an eye. "I've seen her before somewhere, though—Semiramis! That's it, Queen Semiramis. We'd better get all the way off the road. Come on, Lucius. You don't want to get run over."

That could have happened, for there were camels as well as other elephants filling the highway behind the queen; and I could hear horses neighing. I stood with my hands in my pockets, highly pleased with the parade. Golias took off his hat as Semiramis drew abreast of us, and I was glad I hadn't when she looked down at him as if she were peering into a spitoon. Glancing to see how he was taking this, I noticed what Jones was up to. He was in the act of falling to his knees. From that position he bowed till his muzzle touched the ground.

That stopped Semiramis, who stopped her elephant, and the dazzling shebang of gaudy riders and gaily harnessed animals piled up behind them. While we gazed back uncertainly, she considered us.

"You have trained the animal?"

"Yes, ma'am." I had never said ma'am to anybody in my life, but I did to her.

"I think you lie," she decided. "When your own manners are so bad, how could you impart good ones to your beast?"

I thought it best to make no comment, but one of her followers scooped up the ball. "Assuredly, your highness," he called out, "it was a spontaneous tribute to your greatness and beauty."

That should have closed the subject, but Lucius chimed in. Inarticulate as the sound he made was, the inflexion was unmistakable. Then to my disgust he shut out doubt that he was agreeing by nodding his head three times.

For a moment she brooded, then she made up her mind. Stepping forth from her throne, she stood, tall, graceful, and terrible, on her elephant's head, and spoke to it a second time. An instant later she was on the ground.

I looked at Golias, but he shrugged; so we stood pat while she gathered several handfuls of greenery. Then if ever I wanted to kick a jackass, my foot itched for Lucius. He had risen and was waiting with outstretched neck as she approached. The morning before he had scorned honest hay and seen fit to gobble my breakfast instead; yet when she proffered a messy collection of leaves and dusty weeds, he ate it all. Then by way of dessert he licked her hand and forearm.

She liked it, too. Her face couldn't be said to grow tender, but it glowed less coldly.

"Nice boy," she purred. "Nice boy. You understand other things; do you understand that?"

In answer to this query Lucius winked, and I found myself growing more disturbed. "We've taught him to wink at all women," I muttered.

I had been amused at the withering way she had looked at Golias, but didn't smile when it was my turn. There was force and intelligence mixed with the most intense sexiness I had ever encountered. The compound enabled her to drive home the fact that she considered me lacking in the most fundamental attribute of manhood. After my flush told her that she had put it across, she turned to Jones once more.

"I don't believe you would wink at just any woman; I think you have too much sense." When he nodded his head in agreement, she chuckled deeply, caressing the white patch on his shoulder. "This heart here shows you have the gift, and would not waste it on unresponsive ninnies." While saying this she had commenced running her hand along his flank. "There are so few of us who really appreciate strength, and you are so strong."

When Lucius gave an ecstatic wriggle, I couldn't stand it any longer. I hadn't known that I could be scandalized, but I was.

"You'd better leave him alone," I warned. "He might kick you."

She laughed, and Jones hee-hawed in chorus with her. I was blushing, and the knowledge that I was doing so angered me past discretion.

"God damn it, Lucius! Cut it out!" I yelped, catching at his lead rope and trying to drag him away. He balked, so I tried persuasion. "I know you're as good as anybody else, maybe, and I guess a donkey's got to take his fun where he finds it, but this won't do."

"That is something for Lucius and me to find out," Semiramis stated.

Her shamelessness infuriated me still further. "Well, you're not going to!" I roared. "This is our jackass."

"He's going to be mine," she announced. "Would you rather have me buy him or take him?"

"Oh, you can buy it," Golias told her, "but it's a high priced animal, and the rope doesn't go with it."

"Name your price, and I'll double it," she declared, turning to signal, apparently, to whoever had charge of her cash. "And I don't want the rope. He'll follow me without it."

I knew she was right, and I didn't see what could be done. The bestiality about which I had been so concerned was now unimportant compared with its overall consequences. Jones was my friend, and he was condemning himself to remain misformed the rest of his life.

Despondently I watched Golias draw his knife. In his eagerness to be free of the halter Lucius had turned towards him, so that he was now facing off the road. Severing the rope, Golias whipped it away, whirled it high, and snapped it down to catch Jones on the rump. With a squeal he sprang forward, and Golias fell in behind him, swinging hard and shouting.

"Hermione!" he yelled. "Run, if you ever want to see Hermione again!"

Perhaps the pain broke the spell of the lust, and if so, it won't be the first time on record. In any

case the import of Golias' words reached Lucius.
He dashed ahead, which is to say toward the river,
of his own accord now. I was already following
Golias, and we didn't lack for company.
Semiramis shrieked, and, glancing over my
shoulder, I saw her being lifted from the ground
again. Then elephants, camels, and horses, they
were all after us, trumpeted, snuffling, and whin-
nying as they crashed through the woods.

By then I was running less for Jones' salvation
than my own skin, but I couldn't gain on the other
two. "You can smell better than we. Make for
water!" Golias gasped to Jones. So the latter was
our guide for the rest of that mad chase through
the twisted trees of the bottomlands.

It was hard going for us, but the muddy footing
which we soon encountered was worse for our
pursuers. The elephants and camels began to bog
down, and even the horses, which otherwise
would have caught up with us, were sinking
halfway to their knees.

By virtue of this handicap we still had a small
lead when we reached the river's edge. Lucius
hesitated on the steep bank, and Golias, who had
dropped the rope, booted him.

"Go on, damn you! Take to the water!"

Down we slithered through a tangle of vines
and shrubbery. "Hug the bank and keep your
noses under," Golias instructed us. "It's our only
chance.

"No!" he contradicted himself, as we plunged
through a clump of bushes to the brink. "Look; it's
the raft! Shandon, the painter's by you. Cast off!"

XVIII

⚙ Travel De Luxe ⚙

LOOSENING THE ROPE from the root to which it was hitched, I jumped for the raft. As Golias was already shoving off, I landed short of it. Lunging for it, I pulled myself aboard. Shouts told me that our pursuers had gained the bank; but though they could hear us, they couldn't yet see us. Fortunately they were as loth to use their feet as automobilists and chased around looking for a grade down which they could ride their horses.

"Get Lucius into the wigwam!" Golias panted.

The shelter to which he referred was a tent-shaped structure on one end of the raft. Clinker built of rough timbers, it looked sturdy but hardly big enough to accommodate a sizable jackass. Lucius thought so, too, and laid his ears back.

"He ain't going to fit," I objected.

"He's got to fit. Shandon, I mean it! Are you ready?" He jabbed Jones' already irritated rump with the point of his knife, then ducked as he drew a heartfelt donkey reaction. In kicking, however, Lucius was momentarily supported by only his two weakest legs. I tackled these, had him unbalanced before his hind legs came down, and Golias hit him aft. By the time he recovered from the shock of the fall we had him by the tail, mane, and ears. As he couldn't rise and found it unprofitable to kick, we succeeded in cramming him into the wigwam.

"Now if the raft doesn't swing around to leave us vulnerable," Golias said, as we squeezed in more or less on top of Jones, "we ought to be all right."

There was a knothole in the back, which I reached by a little ruthless squirming. Peering through it, I could see that the current was taking us toward midstream. This meant that we were getting farther from our enemies, but it also meant we would be visible to them once more. Just after I fixed my eye to the knot hole, a shout told me that the raft had been seen, and the fierceness of its quality showed we had been identified with it.

Before they could decide what to do, the queen's elephant appeared, and Semiramis sprang to stand upon its head. "Shoot! Shoot!" she screamed. "Kill them or die yourselves!"

She got action. Some stayed where they were, sending arrows as swiftly as they could draw them from their quivers and nock them. Others surged along the bank to let fly when they were parallel with us. A few who either didn't know about big rivers, or who thought they were less dangerous than Semiramis, scrambled down and jumped their mounts from the brink. I didn't worry about them, for no horse could choose its course breasting that current. The arrows made me nervous, though. Those fellows could shoot. After a little it occurred to me that one might score a bull's-eye on the knothole, so I ducked my head. For a few minutes arrows were striking so rapidly that it sounded like a woodpecker with a bass drum. A lot bounced off, but plenty of them stuck, and quite a few heads came all the way through the thick boards.

If the raft had ever turned so that the open side of the wigwam faced the west bank, we would have been goners, but, though it swung nerve-wrackingly, we were never quite exposed. Nor was that all the river did for us. The channel, which is as much as to say the main force of the current, was sweeping south and east to a point where it would bite the far bank. In less than ten minutes we were out of effective range.

Semiramis had so impressed us, however, that it wasn't until we were past midstream that we emerged. She wasn't in sight, though a few horsemen were still churning along the bank, looking for a place where they could ascend it. While we watched, one of them disappeared into the foliage, having probably discovered the mouth of a creek. When the last of them followed him, we were free to discuss the completed incident.

"Just so I won't ever make the mistake of going there," I said, "what district of the Commonwealth does she rule?"

"Oh, some place south and east a stretch." Golias looked at me, started to laugh, then lay down, guffawing. "If you could have seen yourself when you were trying to save Lucius from his baser nature."

I reddened. "Aw, it wasn't Lucius. Nobody ever had any excuse to compare me to the old lady of Dubuque before, but some things aren't—" I stopped, because I realized my argument was based on feelings only, whereas I had always prided myself on leading from reason. "Well, hell," I went on, "some things just aren't suitable, especially from a woman."

"Sure," he smoothed me down. "Beauty should act in kind, though it doesn't always get all the help it needs. Let's look this hooker over."

Glad to change the subject, I rose to join him in the inspection. I had noticed some stuff stowed in the back of the wigwam, and it was of this that we first took inventory.

"Well," I said, "the hooks and lines may be useful along the way, but I wouldn't know what to do with that muzzle-loading gun."

"I can handle one." Golias was inspecting some sacks of provisions. "Cornmeal, coffee, salt, beans, rice, and—yep, there's a flitch of bacon wrapped in this oilcloth, and molasses in the jug."

"We can shake up some sort of lunch," I commented, "and maybe it'd be a good idea to take a ration or so with us. With the knack Jones has for getting us into trouble, we may be chased off the road again before we find an inn tonight."

"Road!" Golias looked at me incredulously. "Why the devil should we chew dust and argue with Lucius when this raft will take us the long half of the way to our destination in peace and comfort? We'll make better time than we can walking, too."

Feeling that I should have had sense enough to

think of that myself, I saw fit to object. "Yeah, I
know," I said, overlooking the fact that the question of ownership hadn't previously bothered me,
"but how about the fellow the raft belongs to? He
must have been planning a trip himself to have
put all this stuff aboard."

"Unquestionably." Golias was inspecting the
mechanism of the gun. "He had some sort of
getaway in mind."

"Then don't you think we should tie this thing
up in some spot where he can find it if he goes
looking?"

"And kick providence in the face?" Looking
pained, Golias put the piece down, so he could jab
a finger at me. "I'll be party to no such Delian
sacrilege and general damned foolishness."

As long as we were going to stay aboard it for a
while, I examined the rest of the craft with added
interest. It was twenty feet long by about twelve
wide. Made of two-by-twelves nailed on huge
logs, it was both buoyant and sturdy. Balancing
the wigwam there was a clay hearth for cooking.
Beside it was a pile of wood and a chopping block
with an axe stuck in it.

"If we only had water, we'd be all fixed," I said.

"If you drink Long River dry, you'll be the first
one to do it," Golias informed me. He had brought
the frying pan and the coffee pot out with him,
and he dipped the latter in the turgid water. "Can
you use an axe?"

"Some," I admitted.

"Split some of that wood, then, and I'll fix us
some hoecake, bacon, and java."

Eating that meal, I began to relize how complete
we were. To improve our diet it would be neces-

sary to do a little hunting, but otherwise we were
independent of the shore. Meanwhile, and with a
minimum of effort, we were accomplishing our
purpose.

To make things better, there were a couple of
corncob pipes and some tobacco aboard. I hadn't
seen Golias smoke before, but he joined me after
lunch. It was hot, and we had already peeled off
our shirts. Some time later we worked the raft into
slack water with a pair of long poles and took a
dip. When we climbed back aboard we didn't
bother to dress again.

All the effort required of us was to see that the
raft stayed in the current and didn't get hung up
on a sand bar or a snag. For this purpose one of us
was on watch throughout the night. That was no
hardship, for we could deal out time to suit ourselves. We had complete freedom and yet were
warmly wrapped in boundaries. The raft was a
continent, and yet it held us as snugly as a tire
holds a wheel.

If the raft was a continent by day, it was a planet
by night, gliding down the milky way of the
mist-whitened river, the peer of Mars and Mer-
cury, and all the stars of the wheeling constella-
tions. In general the most we could see of the earth
was the dark and jagged outlines of trees, which
we were forever approaching and leaving, as the
current shuttled us from one bank to another.
Occasionally there were the lights of some town,
and while it was still dark early the first morning
we passed Troynovaunt.

Golias waked me just before we got there, but
only in part to point out its great towers, black
against the fading stars. There was a bridge, and

we had to find slow water or risk being dashed against one of the stone piers which supported it.

It was two days later that we came to the only other bridge I saw. That was the one at Valentia. As we rounded the bend and drifted down the straightaway toward it, I observed men swarming over the spider-legged structure. The sound of the blows they struck, deep and hollow, reached us clearly.

"They must be just finishing it," I said.

"Sometimes finish and end don't mean the same thing," Golias retorted, "Those sound like axes, not hammers."

He was right, now that I thought of it. I peered downstream, puzzled.

"What's the sense of knocking this bridge down before they've built another one?"

"You might just as well say what's the use of building another one until this is down." He spoke somewhat impatiently, and I noticed that his eyes were watching the west bank. "They've got a reason, and if we're lucky, we'll spot it."

Up to that point we hadn't been able to see the right end of the bridge, but within a couple of minutes it came into view. I then saw that I was wrong in attributing all the noise and shouting to the wrecking crew. There was plenty going on at the other side, though the excitement was of a different kind. Men in armor flooded the approach there and spilled over to line the shore. Back down the road they stood in ranks as far as I could distinguish men, and beyond that point I could descry flags taking the wind. This was an army to make the force of Brodir and his allies look like a platoon.

One of the best things about rafting is that when you pass something going on ashore, you have plenty of time to watch the action develop. In this case we had seats on the center aisle. With the delighted interest of a man watching a four-alarm fire, I shifted my gaze from the invaders who wanted to use the bridge to the group straining to destroy the approach to their town. The only thing which wasn't clear was the reason for the army's delay, but I soon figured it out. The invading commander had decided that the structure was already unsafe.

That thought sponsored an idea which bothered me. "Suppose they dump the thing in our laps," I suggested.

"Huh?" Golias was so absorbed he didn't turn his head. "Nothing we can do about it."

That was so. We could work the raft ashore more or less where we wanted to if we made up our minds far enough in advance, but landing short of the bridge was now out of the question. The most we could do for ourselves, if we could manage that, was to fend ourselves off from the wooden piles on which it rested. I rose and picked up a pole in readiness.

"You'd better give me a hand, Golias."

"Wait a minute. Look!"

Complying, I saw the biggest man I had ever set eyes on step from the ranks. It was only at that instant that I realized that the three men I had observed lounging at the western end of the bridge were not MPs of the invading force posted to warn troops off the bridge. Instead they were defenders set to block the big fellow's way. I whistled as I saw so much more than that. These three, bracing in the narrow passage, had blocked and were still blocking a vast army while their buddies sweated to obliterate this one point of vulnerability.

Previously I had viewed the spectacle with nonpartisan excitement, but now I knew whose side I was on. "The bigger they are, the harder they fall," I said, but I wasn't very optimistic.

The giant, for he was nothing less than that, had a sword nearly as long as an ordinary man. It seemed to me that he could finish all three of the defenders as easily as reaping daisy heads with a stick, and it was evident that he felt the same way. We were near enough to see him grinning.

"Gang him, you fools, gang him!" I said aloud. Instead only one man tackled the man mountain. The latter promptly knocked him spinning with a sweep of his sword, and both he and I thought it was all over. It just about was. While the big boy was winding up for another devastating swat, the man he had wounded sprang inside his guard, jumped up, and pushed his own sword through the giant's face.

"Timber!" I exulted. Then my cheer turned to a squawk. "Oh, my God! Golias, help!"

Watching the fight, I hadn't watched where the river was taking us. It was now apparent it was going to slat us against a pier. The reason for the town was the bridge, and the reason for the bridge was that the river was uncommonly narrow there. In consequence the mighty current raced through at double speed. Golias sprang to my assistance, but all we could do was to ease the shock of the collision. As it was, one corner of the raft struck the clump of piles with splintering force, spin-

ning us around and knocking Lucius off his pins.
When the raft spun, it removed the pressure
against which we had been thrusting and spilled
us to the deck, too.

When we recovered interest in what was happening on the bridge, the situation had changed.
Only one of the three guardians—I think it was the
one who had killed the giant—remained at his
post. The other two, having evidently got word
that the bridge was about to go, were nearing the
town side. Of course, if it still held them, it was
still possible for it to hold enemies; but the man
who remained had let himself in for it.

I was about to express my worry over this de-
velopment when, with a cracking sound like
monstrous static, the eastern end of the bridge
collapsed. In the water it collaborated with the
current to drag the rest of the structure down.
Interdependent, the wooden piers could not
singly hold the weight they carried and stand
against the river. One by one they tilted, and the
superstructure peeled off.

It was lucky for us that we were downstream
and going away from that furious stirring of water. Even at that a chasing wave rocked us, and
Jones, who was having a hard time of it, skidded.
If Golias hadn't caught him by the tail, there
would have been a donkey in the drink. Having
seen that he was safe, I turned to watch what the
army would do to the lone hand who had so
balked them. I looked just in time. Armor and all,
he dived into the stream.

It appeared to be a choice of suicide over capture, but to my astonishment he bobbed up and
started swimming. "Do you think he can make it
with all that hardware on him?" I asked.

Finding that he still had hold of Lucius' tail, Golias dropped it. "There'll be a long walk waiting for him on the other bank, but with a stroke like that it looks like he'll put it through all right." He chuckled. "Shall we tell Lars Porsena he might as well go home, or shall we let him figure it out for himself?"

In another few minutes both the town and the frustrated invaders were out of sight, and the woods closed in on the river again. Seeing that Jones was lying down, Golias and I leaned against him, lit up our pipes, and watched with detached approval while the world went by. Sometimes the raft would be facing toward one bank, sometimes toward another. Then again it would swing so we faced up or down stream. By turns we visited both shores and rode the middle of the river, and our talk was loose-footed as our progress. We had the freedom of every port on the chart of thought and took advantage of it in a good few cases.

Even in the Boss of Arden I had never been so comfortably aware of my natural relation to the elements as I was during the days which followed. The air we breathed reeked of trees and earth as well as water. Nothing stood between us and day and night in their fullness. Under the sun a breeze tempered the heat. When darkness came, it was technically a little cooler, but the breeze dropped, leaving the air still attuned to our naked bodies. Having abandoned clothes, we deemed it silly to hide from the warm rain. Usually we slept out on deck, seeking the shelter of the wigwam merely when a storm interfered with our rest.

We went ashore only to gather wood and to do a little hunting. About the fifth day, for example,

we maneuvered into slack water inshore so that
Golias could land and bag us something for supper. He was going through the business of loading
the old rifle when we heard a voice.

"You surely intend no such barbarity as to mor-
tify the tender ears of God's fishes with that mur-
derous blunderbuss, do you?"

Glancing up, we saw a man with a rod, landing
net, and creel on the bank above us. In spite of the
heat he was carefully dressed, from buckled shoes
through knickers to a high crowned hat. A small
man, he had, allowing for his moustachio and
goatee, the face of a happy saint. He was in earnest
in what he said, I should judge, though a smile
made his impertinence acceptable.

Golias smiled back at him. "I assume," he said,
"that although God's fishes have tender ears, they
don't have tender mouths."

As if pleased with the contention, the stranger
seated himself on the bank. "Why to be truthful
with you, friend, there are those who have and
those who haven't. One of the dispensations
which makes angling the most delightful of arts is
that one which supplies creation with leather-
mouthed fish such as the chub or cheven, the
barbel, the carp, and the gudgeon on the one
hand, and balance these on the scale of variety
with the pike or luce, the perch, or the trout,
whose mouths will spew a hook where dexterity
isn't at the other end of the line. But if, and your
remark could also be taxed for this interpretation,
you imply that the hook pains the fish, I could
reply that none is on record as complaining.
Speaking less equivocally, I could grant that such
is the probability, or I could declare that it is no

more possible to conceive of a fish having feelings
than to attribute them to trees. Even less, I should
say, for it had frequently been asserted that each
tree once had a spirit winsomely incarnate in a
dryad, who suffered and died with it. Of course,
these were not possessed of the beauty and other
pretty qualities which graced the sprites of diverse bodies of water, fitting them to be loved by
gods and to give birth to heroes and anglers. Can
you answer me a question?''

"Probably not at such length," Golias admitted.

"Not all subjects permit of discursiveness." The
fellow smiled again. "Nor do the addicts of most
pursuits have the leisure to develop it. It could
even be argued that they are not capable of sending their minds on voyages of inquiry, elsewise
they would naturally gravitate toward angling.
And that returns us to my question. Why should a
man, one whom I can observe to have mental
address, plan to run, shout, set off explosives,
make a stink in the air with gunpowder, scatter
blood, and jangle the nerves of the forest, when
the subtler pleasure of killing fish is at hand?"

"Passing over the fact that you do not run and
shout if you wish to catch up with a wild turkey,"
Golias retorted, "I see no difference in the nature
of our activities."

"Do you not, Venator? Why it is a difference as
great as that between the footpad who sneaks up
behind you and hits you over the head and the
coney catcher who will get your money only if his
wit is superior to yours. Moreover, it is a difference of the spirit. In the case of hunting, the bullet, the arrow, or the dog is, to put it mildly, forced
upon your victim. In the case of angling, it is the

fish's free choice whether or not he takes your hook, which skill must make alluring."

"That's a good point, Piscator," Golias agreed, "But there's no trick to seducing a Long River mudcat. It'll swallow anything."

"A mudcat!" The words were shocked out of the man. "Catching a mudcat isn't angling, and all the arts of Trimalchio's chef, considerable as I will concede these to have been, could not make one palatable. Why not put aside that piece and watch me catch you something good enough for even an angler to eat? I came here to duel with a pike, but as I doubt that you have the necessary condiments to fit him to your palates, we'll go a mile or so downstream, and I'll kill a bass for you."

This man took my fancy. "I'll be glad to go with you," I volunteered, "even if Golias here doesn't feel like it, Mr. Piscator."

"Come aboard the raft," Golias invited, "and we'll all go."

"Why, a thank you for your courtesy," Piscator said; and without further discussion he came down the bank and jumped to the deck. After I had put his rod in the wigwam so that Jones wouldn't step on it, we shoved off. The channel was some distance out, but, rather than exert ourselves in the heat, we let our craft make its own way through the slow water. Our sluggish progress dismayed our passenger no more than it did us. He had a pipe of his own, and soon all three of us were smoking contentedly.

"This craft is too good for any but fishermen or other wise men, so I hold you to be men of wisdom," he said at length. "Indeed, having found you wise enough to take one excellent suggestion of mine, I am encouraged to ask that you accept a second."

"What's that?" Golias demanded.

"Why at the gait we're going it will be some while before we reach the fishing grounds I have in mind, so let's use the time for the next best pursuits and treat each other to songs."

"How about the fishes' tender ears?" I enquired.

The other laughed. "While I'm no Arion to charm fishes, I count on them to take no harm from my song, in as much, especially, as I will sing nothing lewd or otherwise unfit to pass from my mind to that of any hearer whatsoever. Will one of you begin?"

"No." Golias gestured toward him. "As our guest, start off, if you don't mind."

"Not in the least," Piscator assured him. "In fact, next to a day of fishing I can think of nothing that pleases me more than a good song served up in my own music. Combining the two pleasures, I shall now sing of angling.

> Angling is the only fashion
>   Of gaining good;
> For men of sense and gentle passion
>   Right livelihood
> Is following the water well and knowing
> Where salmon swim or muskelonge are wait-
>   ing,
> And judging how much line to give, and
>   throwing
> A hook where careful skill has done the bait-
>   ing.

Every mind is like a river,
    One nobly stocked,
Where thoughts, like trout with fins aquiver,
    Lurk, shadow-locked.
Great, shining beauties, they won't leave
    their hiding
For bare hooks or stale lures tossed out of
    season;
Only the cunning cast will draw them gliding
To fight the line which brings them into
    reason.

"I see you fish farther than most," Golias commented, "and I like the way you give your heart to a song. Well, I'll sing of a river, specifically this one, too; though I won't entirely neglect fishing, either."

From source to mouth there's but one ford—
    And that cannot be crossed—
Where Ferdiad was gripped and gored;
    His best friend won and lost
        The water's red from brink to brink,
        The Morrigan comes down to drink;
        And the river goes on south.

Right close in shore, to ward off cold,
    An angler sucks a jug.
The water seals and gets its hold;
The angler feels and gives a tug.
        Above the ice he's having fits,
        Below the ice a long tail flits;
        For the river takes it south.

Steeped in the vacuum of her dreams,
A mirror's empty till

A man rides through it. Once she gleams,
And once she moves, then she is still.
> The filament snaps in the light,
> But yet she is a lovely sight,
> As the river bears her south.

The gold a dragon could not keep
Came to a woman's hand;
Then thieving kinsmen, diving deep,
Found out a safe in sinking sand.
> Dying, they would not tell the place,
> Nor does the water yield a trace,
> As the river sweeps on south

"Nobly sung," Piscator applauded, "and I have no doubt the river runs through much history, which could be profitably studied in the non-fishing months, if there were any, which, praise be, there are not." He nodded to me. "It's your turn now, sir."

"I don't know any songs that'd be suitable," I said.

Piscator eyed me as though I was a scholar who had flunked his lesson. "If you can't appropriate anything from better men, as I do half the time, why put one together yourself, as I do the other half."

"I can't do that," I confessed, feeling my inadequacy. "I tried last night, and—"

"You did!" Golias, who had been gazing downstream, snapped his face toward me. "What was it about?"

"Oh, nothing much," I said, wishing that I hadn't mentioned it. "But last night, when I was taking my watch, the moon set the river mist glowing, and the trees, where they came out of the

dark at all, seemed wading in it. You could see a
long ways, all soft lights and blackness, and you
could hear everything from the wings of night
hawks to the call of wolves; and yet it was very
quiet. I sort of thought I'd pass the time putting it
into a poem, but I didn't get to first base."

"Why didn't you just go ahead?" Piscator
wanted to know. "Making a song is like tying a
fly. Granted the proper materials—and it seems to
me that you had them to hand—all that is necessary is skill, which is only to be acquired with
diligence."

"Yeah?" I said, beginning to feel a little
peevish. "I sweated at it for hours, and all I turned
out was 'The river is'; and then I never could
decide what."

Golias continued to look at me. "We'll have to
see what comes of that," he said finally.

Not sure what he meant, I didn't comment,
though nothing came of it that afternoon. We had
a pleasant time, and old Piscator turned out to be
as good with a rod and line as he thought he was. I
never tasted fish to equal those we broiled over
coals on the raft that night.

XIX

❧ Big and Green ❧

THE ONLY SOUR THING about our life on the raft was
our relationship to Jones. This troubled us less
than it might have for the reason that we inevitably came to take it for granted. If clothes don't
make the man, a man's status cannot be disregarded. No matter what his potentialities, what he
actually does with his time is the index by which
he is classified. Lucius put in his time being a
donkey, and it became increasingly difficult to
think of him as anything else. He could not talk, so
we got out of the habit of addressing him. On his
part, he felt the chasm of which we were generally
oblivious and except at meal times avoided us as
much as the limits of the craft permitted.

But though that gave us concern when it
crossed our minds, Golias and I were happy. "I
hate to think of abandoning ship," I told him, as
we were having an after-supper smoke a few days
after our meeting with Piscator. "You say we
ought to reach the road to the Oracle tomorrow?"

"Some time in the afternoon by my reckoning."
He puffed on his pipe a moment. "It's not much of
a road; just wheel tracks leaving an old landing.
We'll have to keep our eyes skinned."

"Then how do we get back?"

He shrugged. "The best way we can, but don't
start to worry about that yet. There's a hatful of
parasangs between the river and the Oracle, and,
as I believe I've told you, the Warlocks are rugged."

"A mountain range figures to be rugged," I remarked, "but if a road runs over it, it shouldn't be
too bad a climb."

"Oh, the terrain is the last thing you worry
about in that part of Broceliande," he informed
me.

Some time later he lay down to sleep, leaving
me to keep watch for snags and sand bars. At least
there had been nothing else to watch out for on
preceding nights. For that reason I was caught
short when a boat hove into view.

River acoustics are peculiar. At times it's possible to hear small sounds for incredible distances,
while at others you can't hear two claps of thunder having a knock-down-drag-out just around
the bend. That's the way it was with the steam-
boat. As far as I was concerned, it had made no
sound until just before it came into sight, shooting
sparks from its funnels and lighted up like Satur-
day night.

With the whole river to swim in, there was no
reason why the ship couldn't give us plenty of
room; but our helplessness made me nervous. It
might be possible to find bottom with a pole and
maneuver us to a certain extent; yet if I altered our
course, I might be moving us more into the path of

the vessel. In the end I decided to depend upon the pilot to spot us and steer around.

I wanted to wake Golias, but it seemed foolish to rouse him to show him a steamship. He would know, of course, that I was doing it for moral support; and it was this that determined me. Even when the boat started to cut across the river toward us, I didn't say anything, for I knew it was only following the channel. It was therefore only at the last minute that I yelled.

"Hey, you sons of bitches, look where you're going!"

My shout roused Golias. "Come here and help!" I cried, trying to shove the raft out of danger; but instead of joining me he sprang to where Lucius was shying away at the farthest corner from the onrushing ship.

"It's too late!" he barked. "Jump for it!"

In the moment it took me to consider his advice I saw him catch Jones by the hind legs and tip him overboard. No doubt he followed an instant later, but I didn't watch. The boat wasn't going to miss us, and I was on the side nearest it. I dived, and dived deep.

Luckily river shipping is shallow draft. Ordinarily that would have been more of an underwater swim than I could manage, but the river and the vessel's engines were collaborating to give me clearance. I was well astern of the boat when I surfaced. Finding myself in no danger, I began treading water, yelling for Golias. He didn't answer, and the current was sweeping me rapidly away from the zone of the accident. When I had rested my lungs, I commenced working my way toward the west bank.

I had made a mile or so of southing before I got

ashore and clawed my way out of the river to the
comparative dryness of the bottomlands. Aside
from being wet, chilly, and tired, I looked forward
to daylight without optimism. I felt sure that my
friends would make for the west bank, too, but
there certainty ended. I couldn't be sure Golias
had succeeded in staying with Jones. Never having given it a thought, I had no idea how well a
jackass could swim. And I couldn't guess whether
they would land above or below me.

When it got light, a thing it took its time about
doing, I began to search. The tangled growth of
the bottomlands was hard on a naked man. I persisted with little rest, though, and around noon I
saw most of the raft hung up on a sand bar not far
off shore. It was pleasant to eat again; but once I
was aboard I felt the loneliness acutely. There's
hardly such a thing as being lonesome outdoors,
but a house or a boat with a cabin—even the raft,
as long as it had the wigwam on it—was made for
company. By next morning I had a case of nerves
and decided not to wait any longer.

As Golias hadn't come by then, I felt sure he
would not. My best chance of seeing him again, as
well as the only thing I could think of to do, was to
try to find the Oracle. Working the raft over to the
bank, I dressed, made myself a food package,
belted on Golias' knife, sailed my fancy, white
plumed hat into the river, and set out.

Probably I would have been wiser to plug along
down the bank until I came to the old road Golias
had mentioned. I was, however, sick of the thick
underbrush, squashy footing, rank air, and numerous snakes of the bottomlands. Free of them, I
began to climb. At first the ascent was a steady

sweep out of the valley, then the ground crumpled into hills.

The next day I ran into grief of a sort that I might have anticipated but had not. Out of the foothills and in the Warlocks proper, I found that I had left summer behind in the valley. Fall had hit early in this high country, and it grew steadily colder as I climbed. Whenever I stopped to rest the chill reached me; and the forest was dismal. Oaks predominating, there were dangling leaves to cackle in the wind; but many branches were bare. Around three, maybe, clouds put the sun out. Then the ceiling started to drop. At worst, a sheltered place to make camp was necessary to survival, and I pushed myself to the limit. Yet hard as I drove myself, I wasn't keeping warm.

It was almost dark in the woods when I reached the first downgrade since leaving the foothills. Glad of any relief from the cutting wind on the ridge, I rapidly descended. The way was steep, but there was a deer run, more or less following the course of a brook, to guide me. The stream itself was black with cold water which snarled as it pitched from one level to the next.

The reward for my hurrying was a piece of scenery that gave me the creeps. Just as a house can be far more lonesome than the outdoors, nothing in the woods can be as desolate as a clearing. Above the wan trees fencing this one I could see rocky knobs with the general appearance of warts. Viscous clouds slid across their tops, endless as flowing water. They were nearly as dark and chill looking as the brook.

That stream, which I had eventually crossed, swept around behind me and reappeared as a falls over to my left. Where it did so there was a grassed-over rise resembling a sawed-off Indian mound. Beyond it, which is to say, on the other side of the falls, there was a jumble of boulders.

Those rocks seemed likeliest to offer a sheltered place to camp, and so, although not liking the idea of staying in the vicinity, I approached them. I was in the act of passing the mound when I noticed a hole in the side toward me. Investigating farther, I found first another hole and then a crude doorway. Nobody answered when I called out, so with some misgivings I entered.

At first I only observed that the wind no longer reached me. As my eyes grew used to the dimness, though, I found that the place had other and most unexpected virtues. The faint light supplied by the several air vents showed me a fireplace with a fire all laid. When I got this going, which took time because of my stiff fingers and because I wasn't handy with flint and steel, I discovered new wonders. There was a balsam bunk in one corner, with a bear robe to use as a cover. There was a small supply of food, including part of a ham dangling from the ceiling, a bottle of wine, and a few cooking utensils. Most surprising of all there was an altar, whose candles supplemented the firelight nicely. By their light I was able to read what was carved on the altar's base: "The needy are welcome to the High Hermitage."

I qualified. There was no doubt in my mind that whoever had conceived the practical charity of erecting that wayfarer's hostel had saved my life. It was an hour or more before the fire and wine could drive the chill from my bones. Meanwhile the wind increased to gale strength; and when I went to the brook for water, I felt snow on my face.

Exhausted by exercise and exposure, I turned in as soon as I had eaten. I was in no hurry to get up in the morning, but full day—another cheerless one—had just found its way into that nick in the Warlocks. The snow hadn't amounted to much and had drifted clear of the rocks and bare earth near the hollow mound. When I stepped outside after breakfast, therefore, there were no tracks to indicate whence the man I found waiting had come.

"I thought I noticed smoke," he remarked, "though hard wood doesn't throw up much you can see on a day like this."

"No," I said, I wanted to be polite to him, but I didn't feel like conversation. He was, and I checked my vision by making sure other things retained their normal hues, a bright green. I don't mean the clothes he wore, although they were also, but the man's hide was shamrock colored. So was his hair, which he wore in a Buffalo Bill bob, and his beard. A full grown, green beaver, it sprayed out to cover his chest.

I would have felt better about it if he had been a smaller man. He was some eight feet tall, every inch of him built for speed and power. Moreover, he sported a battle axe with a massive head climaxing five feet of shaft.

"You haven't seen anybody around, have you?" he asked, when we'd looked each other over.

"There's been nobody here but myself." I cleared my throat. "And I'm just about to leave."

"It would be worth your while to stay," he said.

I wasn't sure whether he was suggesting or giving a command and didn't quite feel like finding out. "What's going on?"

He had been twirling that huge axe as easily as a

policeman twirls a billy. Now he stopped and leaned on it.

"It's a serious thing to do," he said, half to himself, "and I wouldn't do it except under orders; but right here a man is going to be plumbed and sifted."

I was reasonably certain that he wasn't talking about me, but I wanted to know it. "How?" I demanded.

"With this." He lifted the axe from the ground and set it down again. While he did so he continued to stare at me, and something he read in my eyes made his green lips twitch. "I doubt," he said, "if you'd have had the nerve to chop off my head."

The gratuitous sneer got to my pride. He wasn't the only one of us that had used a battle axe, though there was no reason for letting him know that I had done so but once.

"Oh, I've killed with those things in my day," I bragged, indicating his weapon.

"You have?" He looked at me some more, then he glanced in the direction whence I had entered the clearing. "He's not really due yet," he declared, "but we'd better go behind the chapel to be safe."

"Who'll be safe?" I enquired.

"You will." He wasn't rough when he took my arm, but I knew I couldn't pull away from that grip. "Now," he said, when he steered me behind the mound, "you seem to know all about battle axes. What would you say if a man invited you to swing one at him?"

I tried to hide my uneasiness behind a laugh. "There's no hitch to dishing it out with an axe; it's taking it that hurts."

"Exactly," he said, as if admiring my judgment. "Now as long as it's so easy, chop my head off."

It did not raise my confidence when he thrust his weapon into my limp hand. On the contrary, I felt more nervous than ever.

"What's the gag?"

He laughed. "Nobody's hurting you or even threatening to, but you're frightened to death, aren't you?"

Because he was so right, I became angry. While I was trying to think of a retort, he reached for his axe again.

"Very well;" he said, "as long as you're afraid to behead me, give it here."

I jumped back. If I surrendered the axe to anybody as crazy as he obviously was, I might be committing suicide.

"Keep away from me, or I'll let you have it," I warned. "Stand back, damn you!"

He crowded my retreat along the rear of the hermitage until the brink of the brook was a step behind me. My mind had room for only two convictions. I wasn't turning the axe over to that green madman, and I wasn't going to risk pneumonia by getting a soaking on that wintry day. There was but one alternative. Bracing myself, I swung.

My blow, designed to scare him into giving me space, was a sweeping one aimed more or less at his hip. It didn't catch him there, because he did a deep knee bend. The heavy bit went through his neck, balked at the strong bone, and then continued. The head bounced off and rolled toward me. Horrified, I kicked it away.

"You asked for it, you hundred proof idiot!"

As I voiced this self-justification, I was glad to

have the axe to lean on, but my victim asked no such support. Leaning forward, he picked up his head and dusted the right cheek. Then he stood at ease, holding his head by the hair. The eyes popped open.

"Nervewracking, isn't it?" I couldn't have said it, even if I had thought of anything to say. "The only point in this business," he went on, when I was silent, "is to make you appreciate the man who is coming. As long as you happen to be here, it's due him for you to know what he has done and is doing. Oh, brace up! I was the one who got hit, remember; and I told you you'd be safe."

"Yeah," I admitted, unable to take my eyes from the detached head.

"Suppose it had been otherwise. Suppose you'd bargained to let me hit you back, provided I was able to, and then you had seen me pick up my head."

My mind stumbled over imagining the horror of such a situation. "That wouldn't have been a fair bargain, if you knew you'd live, whereas the other fellow'd be killed."

The head raised its brows. "The point is, I think, not whether a man has been taken advantage of, but simply whether it's worth while to keep an agreement."

"What in hell's the use of an agreement to a guy in two pieces? Dead ones, I mean," I added as an afterthought.

He lifted his head to the stump of his neck. The blood, which had welled but not spouted, seemed to act as glue to knit the matching parts. After wagging his head a couple of times to test its security, he stared down at me broodingly from his restored height.

"You give yourself away by looking so defiant," he remarked. "Now I allowed the fellow in question a year to think it over—and it's astonishing how much sophistry an industrious mind can crowd into a year—but he always came to the same conclusion. I'm expecting him here, and he's expecting me to behead him."

"My God! You mean to say he's had this to think of every day for a year?"

"I just want you to know what this man—Gawain is his name—has done. He's had to come looking for me, spending a couple of rough months in the process, and—How would you have acted, for instance?"

"Shucks, that's easy. If I saw by the way people looked at me that they thought I was yellow if I didn't go, I'd have just hid out somewhere, then come back grumbling because I couldn't locate you."

"I might do the same thing," he admitted. "I wish I knew, but I hope I don't have to find out. Yet I happen to know that Gawain has reached the vicinity and has actually asked to be guided here."

"Maybe he'll get cold feet at the last minute," I suggested.

"It eases our complacence to see our cowardice shared, doesn't it?" He was silent a moment, then he shrugged. "However, my information is that he hasn't so much as sought sympathy by telling why he's on his way here."

He spoke with such admiration that I got up the courage to expostulate with him. "If you think so much of the guy, why are you going to kill him?"

"I'm not; but having been carried this far, the test can't be left inconclusive." He took the axe from me and examined it. "You nicked the edge, biting through that tough neck of mine. Come on and help me get it sharpened."

Still unwilling to refuse the commands of anyone so formidable, I followed him. Vaulting with his axe, he made the brook in one jump, but I was glad to find stepping stones. On the other side he climbed up to the great rocks I had noticed the night before. Several were so placed as to form a cave, which opened out comfortably once we had passed the narrow entrance. It was evidently used as a tool shed for the chapel, and, among other utensils, it sheltered an outsize grindstone.

"See if there's any water in that old tankard," my companion said, as he plumped himself in the saddle.

"You mean this can? It's nearly full."

"All right, wet the stone down—oh, more than that; never mind if your hands are cold—then start turning easily. No, don't put the water down. Keep dribbling it as you turn."

At first he didn't exert much pressure; but when he did, the axe yelled like a saw cutting steel. The rocks made a fine sounding board, and whenever he lifted the weapon I could hear the echoes bouncing around the crags framing that sorry hollow. The racket was so loud that I heard nothing else, but the green bird held his axe up with one hand and with the other motioned me to stop grinding.

"If anybody here wants anything of me," a voice was loudly announcing, "he must speak up now or never."

"Wait a minute," my companion roared, "and you'll get what's coming to you right enough! No, faster," he whispered to me; and the din became louder and more sinister than ever.

A man of weapons could not have failed to interpret the sounds. I recognized that I was accessory to an assault on the nerves of an already overburdened man. At the same time I had begun to share the green fellow's fascination with the problem of how much Gawain could take. While the latter couldn't see us, above him and in the dimness of the cave, the upper half of his body was visible to me whenever I looked up from wetting the wheel I was cranking.

Gawain was in full armor like Calidore. After a while, though, he swung his shield back out of the way behind him, took off his helmet, and tossed it on the ground. The way he did it convinced me. With a similar gesture I threw the can of water from me, and stopped grinding.

"You've got to do more than make noise if you're going to buffalo him," I said, as I straightened.

The green man nodded, yet he hesitated. "Did you ever have anything so good you were afraid to use it for fear it wasn't as wonderful as you thought it was?"

"No," I said, "but if you're worried about that fellow, five gets you ten he won't back down."

He patted me on the shoulder. "I hope you're right, and if you are, we'll all go over to my place and enjoy ourselves."

While I was trying to think of a noncommital response, he left me. Watching, I saw Gawain bend over, bracing his knees, in the literal position of sticking his neck out to have it chopped. The green fellow was talking a blue streak, but the noise of the brook prevented me from hearing him. Besides, I had just remembered something.

That cave, as I had noticed when we entered it, had a back entrance, and now I jumped to see what was beyond it. A path came down from the slope above the cave, and at that point switched off to parallel the brook on its downhill run. It was all I needed to see. I didn't go slow either. That big, green guy had done me no harm, so far, but I preferred company I could deal with on more even terms.

I had been chilled through when I started, but exercise was not the only thing which warmed me up. A couple of hours of steady descent took me into a milder zone and out from under the clouds. Frost had turned the leaves, but the temperature was that of Indian summer. Forgetting my problems, I loafed along, soaking up the soft warmth.

Had I been hurrying, I would have made too much noise treading the dry leaves carpeting the path, to hear small sounds. As it was, this one just reached me. I took a few more steps before I remembered what it reminded me of, then I halted. Not seeing anything, I was about to go on when it was repeated. Leaving the trail, I commenced peering behind trees.

She was crumpled behind a rotting deadfall, so wrapped in her grief that she didn't hear me. I watched her while she shivered with a few more squeaky little sobs. I couldn't stand it if I stayed, and I couldn't quite make myself leave. I coughed.

She lay very still. Next she looked up, then she jumped up. What she saw as we assayed one another I don't know, but my findings can be itemized. For a second I could have sworn she was Rosalette, before I realized her features were quite different. At the same time the impression of a resemblance remained. The other thing I saw was the source of her despond. She had been pregnant for some months.

If any man could help her, it was the one who had helped to get her in that condition. Wishing I had minded my own business, I was fumbling for an exit line when she spoke.

"What do you want?" she demanded, backing away.

"I was just passing by and happened to hear you," I mumbled, "and I thought maybe you were in trouble."

As soon as I had said that, I wished I had kept still. She turned as red as the frost-bit maple leaves above her.

"Well, you can just go away, because I'm not in trouble at all."

"That's swell," I said, trying to look as if I believed her.

"I'm not!" she insisted. "Married women have babies, too, you know; and I'm married—that is I would be. O-oh!"

She had started to cry again when she turned to run. I would have let her go, but she tripped over a root and fell. I was worried when I picked her up, but no apparent damage was done.

"Thank you, sir," she said. "I always forget I can't run any more. Let me sit down here. Just the wind knocked out of me, I reckon."

I seated myself on the fallen tree beside her. "Hadn't you better go home?"

Still breathing heavily, she shook her head. "I wouldn't have the courage to come back," she said at length.

She still hadn't given me a chance to leave her,

but I hadn't given up trying. "It'll begin to get cold again in a few hours, and it'll be bad for you here."

"I don't care whether I die," she declared, "if I don't have Tamlane."

It struck me she was a little out of her head. "If you go on home," I coaxed, "your boy friend will know where to look for you, but you won't find him traipsing around these woods."

"But he *was* in these woods. I saw him this morning, and—" Reading my glance of pity, she straightened. "It's not like you think," she cried. "He would so marry me, but he's under a spell."

"I thought I'd heard them all long ago," I remarked; but she didn't notice the dryness in my voice.

Taking a handkerchief from the bosom of her blouse, she wiped her eyes and tried to smile. "Of course, I'll get him back tonight and everything will be wonderful."

"Then what's the fuss?"

Her chin began to tremble again. "It's just that I'm so scared to go there alone. They're all enchanters and wizards; and anything could happen, though Tamlane says all I've got to do is to hold on to him."

"Enchanters, eh?" I saw that I had been doing Tamlane wrong. "And just what have you got to do?"

"Intercept them at Miles Cross at midnight tonight," she whispered, looking as if she was already facing the ordeal. "My baby's got to have his father."

If she hadn't reminded me so forcibly of Rosalette, I wouldn't have said anything. But she did, and I don't believe she was any older. It seemed a hard thing that such a girl should have to go scrabbling among wizards for a husband, with nobody to back up her play. Before I knew it I had put my foot in it up to the hip.

"Look, kid," I told her, "if you can't find anybody else to go with you tonight, you can count on me."

XX

⮜⮞ Meetings at Miles Cross ⮜⮞

JANET, as she told me her name was, was so grateful for my offer that I was moved to take further care of her. I therefore sent her home to get as much rest as possible. When she was gone, I found a likely spot to bivouac and stretched out myself in preparation for being up a good part of the night.

I felt very virtuous, and, now that I had time to think of it, there was a practical side to the business. That girl and her fiancé didn't know it yet, but one of them was going to have a guest before morning rolled around. Then when I was rested they could orient me. Or they might even know just how to get to the Oracle.

Satisfaction with my plans did not long survive my waking, however. The sinking sun was allowing the Warlocks to assert a character that hadn't been obvious at mid-day. When I went to gather wood I couldn't shake off the impression that some of the trees were stalking me. Walking about was like being "it" in the old child's game. When I

stopped and turned, those trees froze and faced
me down. When I moseyed on, they came cat-
footing after. By marking a few, I proved to myself
that it wasn't so—and it didn't help a bit. Once the
imagination is convinced, reason might as well
take the afternoon off and go to the ball game.

That was but one facet of an atmosphere which
was swiftly giving me the willies. If the trees
didn't actually move, it is certain that they looked
unpleasant. The knots in them were like so many
malevolent eyes. I could feel them boring into my
back as I huddled by my fire, grumpily eating.
Then I couldn't decide which was worse: when I
heard strange noises or when there was a silence
like something—unimaginable but never my
friend—holding its breath. In addition there was
the jaunt to Miles Cross to think about. I thought
about it.

A hundred yards away in the restless dark was
the trail. I could find it by following the little
stream by which I was camped, but on general
principles I had hidden my fire so that no one
using the patch could see it. To get down to cases:
if I stayed put, Janet couldn't find me and ask me
to make good on my promise.

The fulfillment of that promise no longer en-
ticed me. It entailed leaving my fire and following
the trail a mile or so to the little clearing where
Janet was to meet me. Thence she would guide me
to Miles Cross. The good sized moon which was
due made this practicable, but I could think of
nothing that made it desirable.

My altruism had died of a chill long before it got
full dark. If I had had any personal interest in the
girl, I would have had some impelling motive. As

things stood, I couldn't see why I had been idiot
enough to volunteer in the first place. Once before, in the instance of Rosalette, I had been
moved to try to help a girl; but the case had differed. My motives had been largely generous, yet
they had had just enough of an erotic flavor to
make them taste good. If I had expected no return,
either emotionally or sexually, the possibility had
not been excluded. In the case of Janet there had
been nothing to gain or that I wanted to gain. I had
simply got up a head of steam and chugged off
into the misty waters of idealism without a port in
mind or a cargo to bring back.

I had a better cause for unhappiness. The mysterious quality of the woods boxed me in just
outside the nook of light and comparative safety I
had made for myself. What I had contracted to do
was not only to leave my haven, but to challenge
beings who were of a piece with the power daunt-
ing me.

So far, then, I had no reason for going to meet
the girl, and an excellent reason for not doing so.
As a supporting factor there was the knowlege
that I could shrug off my poltroonery in private.
Janet would know I had welched, but as I
wouldn't see her again, she couldn't make me
uncomfortable. The uncaught louse is only half a
louse; and besides, I could justify myself when
you came down to it. I had made a foolish decision
on impulse and had changed my mind upon ma-
ture reflection. If I felt a little bad about it, that was
my just punishment for making a fool of myself by
talking out of turn.

During the next few hours I laboriously worked
the problem over a dozen times, always with the

same results. Each time the answer would leave
me satisfied—but only for a few minutes. Then I
would begin again. Finally the rising of the moon
interrupted me in midmonotony. By and by it
wrought all the changes in the night of which it is
capable, but that wasn't why I watched it. When it
soared past a certain point it would be too late for
me to do other than to stay where I was.

Well before it gained that crucial mark I sighed
wearily, cursed Gawain, and rose. What had come
between me and the comforts of rationalization
was the recollection of that man taking off his
helmet and throwing it on the ground at the conclusion of a long search for peril. If he could do
that where death had been promised him, I could
take a chance when I hadn't been so much as
grazed by the direct threat of harm.

Yet if I was attempting to match Gawain in his
determination to keep his word, it cannot be said
that I even tried to match his boldness of bearing.
The moon made it easy to follow the trail, but it
did not cheer me. The light had the quality of fog
in that I couldn't be sure that anything suspended
in it was fixed or moving. And places which the
light avoided were as black and living as the en-
trances to giant rat holes.

Only one thing actually materialized from this
matrix of possibilities. Picking my way over a
boggy spot, I had my eyes on the ground. When I
raised them a man was about to cross the trail a
few yards in front of me. Hearing me, he stopped.
Seeing him, I did likewise. Although I felt like
retreating when he turned to approach me, I stood
my ground. A second later I was staring back at
him as he peered at me with the eye which didn't

have a patch on it. The shadow thrown by the brim of a slouch hat made his other features indeterminate. A long cape blurred the lines of his figure, too, but he was a tall fellow with good shoulders. Upon each of them sat a huge crow.

"You're not the man I want," he announced at length, "but I wish you'd do me a favor."

"Glad to," I said, meaning I was glad our relations were amicable.

"My own hair wouldn't show up so well," he proceeded, "but a strand from that silver lock of yours would be just the thing." Without further ceremony he yanked one of my white hairs out by the root. Next he slipped a long sword out from among the folds of his cloak. "I have been working on Tyrfing," he said, "and I think he's ready; but I want to be sure."

It was impossible for me to discern the weapon's twin edges, but he gave the impression of being able to when he ran that singleton eye up and down the blade. I looked at it, too, because I couldn't help it. The steel sucked up the moonglow. When the fellow twisted it from side to side, it seemed as if he was examining a bar of cold light.

"Here's for a trial," the man muttered. Opening one hand at shoulder height, he let my strand of silver hair fall. Gravity was gentle with it, and, glowing like a tiny cylinder of neon, it sank unhurriedly to where the sword waited at hip level. There broke in two, and the crows gave a hoarse cheer.

"He is ready," the man murmured. "Now to find the hand for him." The sword went into the cape again. He himself stepped into the shadows and was gone.

I on my part could not go on for a second. All terrors have death for their last name, and in the person who had just left me I had recognized the embodiment of my fears.

The clearing, as it turned out, was not far ahead, and yet I had worked up a sweat when I got there. Waiting was harder than moving, although it gave me a chance to control my breathing before Janet arrived. Much as I wanted company, I was careful to inspect the company this part of Broceliande had to offer. She was within a few feet of me before I was sure enough to step out of hiding.

"Hi, there!" I said, so glad to see her that I sounded almost hearty.

She gave a shriek, then clutched my arm. She had been traveling faster than anyone in her condition should, and had trouble making it when she spoke.

"I think—I would have died—if you—hadn't been here. But, of course—I was sure—you would be."

"You were, were you?"

"Oh, yes. Anybody who would—deliberately camp out in the forest—wouldn't be afraid—of what's here at night."

As it dawned on me that she thought I was taking this business in my stride, I couldn't decide whether to be flattered or indignant. She would never know how much I had gone through on her account.

"Well," I said, "I may not be afraid, but if any of those enchanters start chasing us, don't make the mistake of getting in my way. Where do we go from here?"

It developed that just past the clearing, down

the way she had come, there was an old road. It was so overgrown with bracken that you could see it no more than you could feel it with your feet, but by keeping your eyes a few yards ahead you could follow it. I broke trail, making it reasonably easy for her to come after me, but I couldn't fend off the dew which soon soaked her dress as well as my breeches. Our progress was uphill, but zigzagging softened what would otherwise have been a sharp gradient. We must have walked nearly a mile to ascend a knoll a few hundred feet high.

At the summut there was another little clearing. Within it was a monument which Janet told me was Miles Cross. Whoever Miles was, his notion of what was cruciform differed from my own. It was a cross only in the sense that a capital 'T' is one, though in this case there were two vertical columns. Actually all the thing was was a big slab of stone supported by a couple of shafts of un-tailored rock. It could have been an accident of glaciation, yet one glance assured me it was not. Nature's work may be uninviting, but it cannot look abandoned. This structure smelled as strongly of the past left in the lurch as a haunted house does.

The clearing was overgrown, with twisted shrubbery looming here and there above coarse grass, gray in the moonlight. In a huddle around it were spruce trees, looking as if they had just arrived to take a look at the body. Where we stood it was silent, but somewhere downhill a stream imitated faint, croupy laughter.

"Which way are these birds supposed to be coming from?" I asked, when I had cased the situation.

"I don't know," she whispered. "All he said was that they'd pass right by Miles Cross."

Seeing no reason to be conspicuous, I chose a resting place for us under the overhang of a large bush a few feet from the monument. Aside from providing us with both a vantage point and a haven of deep shadow, there wasn't much to be said for it. The ground was damp, dew fell from the leaves above, and, now that we had quit exercising, the chill got to us.

"What do you want me to do when they show up?" I demanded.

She squeezed the hand I had given her, as much to bulwark my own nerves as hers. "Nothing, thank you. Getting a man is something a woman must do for herself, and so is holding him. I won't be scared when the time comes—or I don't think I will; and you've done all you can by coming here and waiting with me."

Relieved, I peered out at the empty clearing once more. "But how about you? Aren't you in any danger from these varmints?"

She caught her breath. "I don't know, Shandon, but if they stop me from getting Tamlane, I don't care what else they do."

The only thing that happened in the next half-hour was that we grew more depressed as well as more miserable physically. At the end of that period I smelled the cold turning point of darkness, which usually comes around midnight. There had been no breeze, but now one commenced to gasp in the spruce tops. It brought other sounds.

I couldn't identify them, but the girl did. "Bridles jingling. They're coming!"

She cringed against me as she spoke. "You'd

better lie doggo," I advised her out of my own nervousness. "You can't make any headway against wizards and what not."

My words seemed to stiffen her backbone instead of softening it. "I couldn't look my child in the eye if I hadn't tried." She was crawling out from under the bush as she made this statement. Then I saw her take an object from inside her cape. "This is holy water. I don't think they'll see you, but would you like some just to be safe?"

I wanted some, but I didn't take it. "You're the one on the firing lines. Use it all yourself."

She started sprinkling it in a circle around her, praying as she did so; but for the moment she was getting only the leftovers of my attention. The jingling was getting closer, and there were faint accompanying sounds. It seemed to me that horses should make more noise than that. As it turned out, though, she was right. She had hardly finished her preparations when riders began to appear.

They came out of the woods like smoke, their horses making easy work of it because they no more than brushed the top of the tall grass. That was not the only thing that astonished me. Although the moon was on the far side of them, neither the riders nor their mounts cast any shadows.

Careful not to make a sound, I watched the first draw near to where Janet waited. It looked as if the nigh horse would run her down; but she stood fast, and it shied around her. None of the riders showed any inclination to bother her, so, feeling better about the whole business, I turned my eyes toward the woods again.

A second straggling echelon of three or four was almost on us, and behind there came another. The inside horse of this third group was the only white one in the parade so far. Following standard procedure, it started to give the girl, or perhaps the holy water, room; but with a passionate cry, Janet went into action. Riding the grass tops, the fellow in the saddle was out of reach. He wore a long cape, though, and she got both hands on it when she lunged. Bracing herself, she brought him to the ground, wrapped her arms around him, and hung on.

Her second cry, a strangled mixture of love and triumph, stopped the parade. "Tamlane's freed!" someone called.

Up until that instant I hadn't known that any of the riders was feminine. The screech I then heard showed the presence of at least one. If there was grief in it, it was the grief of jealousy, not of loss. Mostly it sounded to me like a war cry, and Janet read it the same way.

"He's mine!" she defied them.

It was noticeable, even if I was too excited to notice it much, that Tamlane had neither helped the girl nor resisted her. Possibly this neutrality was the result of wanting to be with Janet while still under control of the enchanters with whom he had herded. At any rate the latter still had the Indian sign on him and proceeded to use it, holy water or no holy water.

One of the things which made it peculiarly terrifying was that they operated by remote control. Nobody did anything as far as I could see, but when Janet screamed I saw that she was holding a snake instead of a man. Even when it struck at her

she didn't let go, though, and in another minute it
became a monstrous frog or toad, trying to kick
loose and grunting horribly.

They had plenty of tricks, but in Janet they were
up against a determination they couldn't face
down. She squealed with fright, she sobbed, she
wailed, she begged them to cease their machina-
tions. In fact she showed every symptom of being
a quitter except that she didn't quit. A man and a
father for her baby were what she wanted, and
short of killing her they couldn't make it too tough
for her to take.

In the end they got tired of trying. Suddenly
Tamlane changed from a buck deer to a buck
naked man. She threw her cape around him with a
crow of victory, and he stopped standing there
like a dummy. Their shadows, for now he had
one, too, came together as he got a good grip on
her.

She was dead game, that girl, and deserved a
kiss, but everybody wasn't in the cheering section. "You're welcome, my dear," a woman's
voice said. A rider on a second white horse had
drifted up and sat looking down at the pair. "I'm
quite through with him."

If that blow landed in foul territory, so did
Janet's counter punch. "Thank you; and I hope in
time you'll learn enough magic to hold on to a
man."

Talmane had sense enough not to say anything,
but now the rider turned to him. "If I had known
your eyes were so bad that you couldn't distinguish burs from blossoms, I'd have scratched
them out for you. Now leave, both fools!"

They took that advice, which was sensible, although it upset my own plans. Undoubtedly Janet had forgotten me for the moment, and I didn't feel like calling attention to myself while indignant wizards were present. My visions of spending the rest of the night in comfort vanished as the young couple hurried to the edge of the clearing. When they had gone, I gave my head a regretful shake, carelessly stirring the branches beneath which I crouched.

Having watched them go, too, the night rider near me was in the act of turning her mount. Now she halted.

"What moving brightness could the moon find there?" she wondered aloud.

When nobody answered, she slipped from the saddle. "Whatever you are that gleams so, come out."

Unwilling to wait until I was exposed, cringing in hiding, I crawled forth and got stiffly to my feet. Her eyes went over me.

"What a fine glow worm to pluck from a bush," she congratulated herself. Standing above me on the grass tops, she reached out and touched my white hair. "Who are you with this vein of silver?"

I was uneasy, but more than anything else I was disgruntled at having been caught skulking. "Nobody you know," I growled. "Just a man."

She read me and had fun doing so. "Oh, a man?" she said. "And huggermugger under a bush like a rabbit. I must pay more heed to the shrubbery in the future."

Meanwhile she hadn't been the only one to take notice of the other. She was, at least by the favor of moonlight, singularly attractive. Moreover, she was certainly not being unfriendly. I quit being truculent.

"It mightn't be safe for you," I ventured.

She didn't hesitate; she paused for effect. "Or you," she put it to me.

Moving closer, I could see that she was even lovelier than I had thought. Her voice matched her looks, and so did her fragrance. As yet neither of my other senses was gratified, but both knew a foretaste of ecstasy that couldn't share the same body with caution.

"Let the others go on, and we'll make a test of it," I urged.

"I'll send them on," she said, giving me my first intimation that she bossed the outfit. The rest had gathered into little groups, but at a word from her they broke it up and commenced gliding into the woods again.

"Wait under one of those trees yonder at the rim, and I'll join you as soon as I've arranged for somebody else to take charge of what must be done," she whispered, as she turned to remount.

Her horse shifted, offering us a modicum of privacy, and I thought it time to take some charge of proceedings myself. Snatching her off her feet, I swung her face in line and kissed her. That kiss made connection with rejoicing nerves throughout me. The impact was such that I felt lightheaded when I released her, and I laughed a little.

She laughed too. "Now I know you will wait for me."

I thought that an odd comment, though my attention was quickly diverted to things I found far more remarkable. For as I walked away at a tangent to the route of the riders, it was no longer necessary to slog through the thick, wet grass.

Instead I stepped lightfooted atop it; and no shadow matched strides with me.

It was immaterial to me how long I waited for her. The purpose of existence was in escrow until she returned. Meanwhile I leaned against a tree—gratified rather than astonished to find that I wore different clothes, and dry ones—steeped in contentment.

So I don't know. In five minutes or a couple of hours she came to find me, singing as she rode. It was not just a voice, it was her voice, and I listened enraptured.

> There's no other sport so fine,
>   Never out of season,
> As this lovely game of mine,
>   Stealing men from reason;
> Taking them into my will,
> Holding them with might and skill,
> Mine to damn and mine to bless,
> I their hell and holiness.

I couldn't yet see her, but with the next stanza her voice grew so merry that I smiled myself.

> There's one now fixed in my spell
>   Like a moth in amber,
> Lust for me his darling cell
>   Whence he dare not clamber.
> Let him freeze or let him burn;
> Thrust him out and he'll return,
> Deft chameleon to my mood,
> My commands his drink and food.

By the time she had sung the last line she had halted beside me. My desire alive again, I clutched her to help her from the saddle, but she chuckled and shook her head.

"Mount up behind me, sweet my heart."

It happened that my closest previous dealings with a horse had been hanging around stables as a boy visiting in the country. Yet if she wanted me to ride with her, I certainly wasn't going to demur. I got aboard, making easier work of it than I expected. Then I held her so that my right arm was snug up under her breasts. To complete the intimacy she leaned back against me. A portion of my cheek found its way through the soft scented hair to burn deliciously against her temple. My eyes were closed, because they weren't in position to see her, and nothing else seemed worth looking at.

"Start him up," I suggested.

I remember how Nimue felt in my arms, as well as her hair fluttering across my face. That's about all I recall of most of that ride. The wind whizzed past us; but the horse's ground-skimming gait didn't jar us, and he somehow avoided whipping us into any branches. Although I didn't pay much attention, I do recall that when we came to a certain hill, he rode right into it. Opening my eyes from time to time, I noted without concern that it was pitch dark within. There were roaring noises like surf on a stormy day, but they didn't make much of an impression, either. I could hardly hear them above the pounding of the pulse that signified the building up of my passion.

When we emerged into the light again, it was neither moonlight nor dawn but full day. Blinking, I gazed upon meadows whose lush grass was glossy with sunlight. Peeping out of the grass were flowers of every color, and here and there were trees whose leaves had the green of spring rather than of late summer. They held their branches, laden with blossoms and bright singing birds, over a pair of winding streams or the clear pond into which these flowed. Beyond the little lake there were more trees and grass and flowers, but with a difference. In and out of sight amidst them was a road. Nobody was on it, but anyone who cared to could have followed it to the shining city whose towers broke the horizon.

To a man filled with unslaked desire all beauty is an aphrodisiac. Not only what I saw, but the sweet calls of the birds and the smells of grass, flowers, trees, and clean water were confused in my mind with the body I held and wanted.

"Is this the place?" I pleaded. "Is this the place?"

She didn't answer, though her breathing was almost as fast as mine. Snuggling closer against me, she let the bridle drop. The horse had slowed to a walk, yet he kept on to where a tree made a canopy of blossoms which touched the fresh, tall grass. In a moment then we were standing in that perfumed shade. It was my first full look at her, and I found that, lovely as was the sketch of her which the moonlight had shown me, it was no more than a slander on the reality.

She saw the way I felt and smiled before she closed her eyes. Her head was thrown back, and her arms hung limply.

"Take me, Shandon," she commanded.

XXI

❦ Avarta's Nag ❦

THAT COUNTRY was always fragrant with spring. The smell and the feel of it were never absent even from the gay, clean city where we lived in luxury. Not that I would have cared if the surroundings had been less fine. Nimue was glorious, I was her joyous stud; and there was my happiness without looking farther.

It was only occasionally, in the rare intervals when we spent some hours apart, that I so much as thought of anything else. Then I recalled Golias and Jones, but with no feeling of immediacy. I merely wondered how they were getting on, just as you might speculate as to the whereabouts of old schoolmates you never expected to see again.

Then, when I had been there a while, Nimue went on an expedition, leaving me behind. I thought myself miserable, but I didn't know what the word meant until she returned. She had a fellow called Tom Learmont with her, and I was relegated to second string. From that point on I weltered in a sort of feeble-minded madness.

I wanted to kill him but had no power to lift my hands against him. I wanted to hate her but could only continue to desire her. Time away from her might have helped; but it wasn't in her nature to be willing to lose an idolater. She let me see her, and caress her occasionally, just often enough to make sure I wasn't getting out of hand.

In between times I infrequently saw that my salvation was escape, but I couldn't imagine a course of action. Having lost Tamlane by taking him on one of her expeditions, Nimue kept me on the premises, wherever they were. I only screwed up the courage to ask how to skip the country once. The fellow I asked got a queer look in his eyes and told me Nimue was the leading authority on that point.

The sole person who could possibly have helped me I didn't like to ask. I never understood too much about the political set-up, but I did grasp that the authority of Nimue, as queen, was matched by that of her husband, Gwynn Uriens MacLir. His ideas of what constituted a marriage were as liberal as her own. You might think she would have been glad of it, but she hated him for being free of her power. This didn't faze him, nor did anything as far as I could see. A jolly chap, he might have been willing to give me a hand if my emerging consciousness hadn't dredged up a grain of pride. I couldn't quite bring myself to ask a fellow I had cuckolded how to get out of his wife's clutches.

Yet most of the time I couldn't conceive of wanting to; and the town was such a concourse of happy lovers that I couldn't stand it. On those days when Nimue had no time for me, therefore,

I used to hurry outside the city limits. Those scented fields were a constant reminder of lost joy, but at least I could find a place there where my misery wasn't scandalized by the contentment of others.

Yet once as I drank gall in a stupor of wretchedness, even privacy was denied me. "He's right around here," a voice said. "I watched him tear out of town while I was breakfasting on the balcony this morning."

"And you're sure it's the one?" That was Golias' voice, yet I lay where I was, face down in the deep grass.

"I couldn't swear to it. All I know about him is that he's one of Nimue's culls." When he spoke the second time I knew him to be King Gwynn. They were closer to me, and I held my breath.

"He must be having a bad time of it," Golias said.

"Nah, he just thinks he is. Suppose she'd put him under a rock like a grub the way she did with old Merlin. Then he'd have something to squeal about; but all that's happened to him is that she hung somebody else's pants over the foot of her bed."

"Well, I'm glad she's through with him anyway."

"You don't know Nimue," Gwynn chuckled, "if you think that." I could tell from their voices they were cutting a circle around me, and I scrounged closer to the ground. "She's never through with anybody—anybody masculine, that is—and I know from experience they never quite get away from her either." He chuckled again. "Unless Nimue has had a yen for you—"

"Or to kill you," Golias offered.

"That's right." Gwynn laughed delightedly. "Remember how she sicked that young what's-his-name on me?"

"Accolon."

"Yes, that's the fellow. And I don't forget you're the one who found out about it and tipped off Uwaine."

"Oh, you'd have been able to take care of yourself."

"Maybe. Anyhow Nimue's quite a girl. Someday we've got to make up and have a—Oh, oh. I was so busy gabbing I nearly stepped on him. Is this what's left of your friend?"

Crouched down beside me, Gelias didn't answer him. "Shandon," he said, shaking me when I refused to look up. "Shandon!"

Because his persistence irritated me, I finally raised my head. "What in hell do you want?"

He paid no attention to my testy greeting. "Come on; we're getting out of here."

"You are?" I retorted. "Good-bye."

"No, you, too. Lucius is waiting for us—counting on us."

I avoided looking at Gwynn, but out of the corner of my eye I could see him watching me quizzically. That annoyed me more than his indignation would have done.

"Give Lucius my regards when you see him," I told Golias. Then I put my head down and folded my arms around it.

After he had tried a couple of more times, I could sense that Golias rose. "Just so I'll know what the score is," he said to the king, "will Nimue stop him from leaving?"

"Not when I say he can go," Gwynn asserted. "Speaking of pants, as we were a moment back, I still wear the only pair that's in the family legally. Of course, there'll be ructions."

"Thanks, Gwynn."

"Glad to do it if only to get him out of my sight. I don't mind a moping bloodhound looking like a moping bloodhound, but my tolerance doesn't reach as far as a man."

"It would be easier if he was willing." Golias' voice was troubled. "Got any ideas?"

"Let's see, Amergin. No, that wouldn't do." The king was silent for a minute. "Do you happen to know Avarta?"

"He was pointed out to me the last time I was here. I don't know him personally."

"Well, on the way back I'll show you where he lives. Wait for him if he's not around and tell him I said you were to have his nag for as long as you need it."

They left me then. I meant to find another hiding place when they were gone; but my mind turned to Nimue again, and I forgot about them until they came back. At least Golias did. I could tell by his voice that the fellow with him wasn't Gwynn.

By then I was worn out with reviewing my grief. I was therefore resigned rather than combative when I sat up to talk with them.

"Hello, Golias," I mumbled.

He brightened at finding even that much reception. "You seem to be feeling better, though you still look like a hangover in an earthquake."

I glanced at his companion before I took the trouble to answer. A tall, handsome galoot, he was stroking the muzzle of a horse. He had to reach up to do this, and the horse had to bend his neck to let

him. It was a monstrous, hideous, boney beast
with hair like a mangy camel's.

"I'm all right," I said at length.

"Sure you are," Golias agreed. "But you'll be
better when you get out of here, won't you?"

As I had reached one of my occasional semi-
lucid periods, I knew almost as well as he that
everything was wrong with me. I knew Golias
might be able to help me, too. But the thought of
what he wanted to do for me brought my mind
back to Nimue, and I was off again.

"I don't want to get out of here."

"Well, suppose we go for a ride, just for a
change of pace."

If I had been anything of an equestrian, that nag
still wouldn't have attracted me. And it didn't
have a saddle to shield a man from the spiny
ridges of his back.

"I may be in bad shape, but I haven't got that big
a hole in my head," I told him. "You ride him."

"I aim to." Golias stopped wheedling and stuck
out his chin at me before he addressed his companion. "Will you give me a hand, Avarta?"

Taking in the implication, I began to smoulder.
"Don't be a damned idiot," I warned him, as I got
to my feet. "I can knock your block off, and I'll be
glad to do it if you start fooling around."

Lowering, I turned with him as he circled me. I
was keeping an ear posted for Avarta, but it turned
out to be inadequate security. I didn't know he
sneaked behind me until he had pinned my arms
to my sides.

I couldn't get free, and I missed my try at kicking Golias in his grinning face. The only thought
in my brain was that they were trying to take me

where I would never have a chance to win Nimue
back again. The hope of regaining her favor was
all I had to live for, and anybody who tried to
scotch it was my mortal enemy. My rage would
have made me deadly in fact to anyone less powerful than Avarta. Against his strength, however, I
could do nothing.

In spite of my struggles, oaths, and threats, he
dragged me over to the gigantic horse. Then he
picked me up.

"Maybe you can put me on his back," I said,
"but you can't make me stay there."

"We'll try anyhow. Ready, Amergin?"

"Heave him," Golias responded; and Avarta
took that literally.

The toss he gave me landed me squarely on the
brute's back. My intention was to slide down the
other side, so as soon as I was astride I tried it. It
was no go. First I discovered I was butt-fast, then I
found I couldn't pull my hands free from where
they were braced against the nag's spine.

From then on it wasn't anger that gripped me.
It was the insane panic of a dope addict faced with
the iron cure. They were taking me away from
Nimue, and she was necessary to my existence. It
didn't matter that she was tired of me now. She
had loved me before, and she would again,
because—well, because it was unsupportable to
think she wouldn't. I tried to explain it to them. I
pleaded with them. Then when they wouldn't
listen, I broke down and screeched my agony.

While I was putting on that performance, Golias
and Avarta were exchanging friendly farewells.
Finally the latter gave the former a slap on the
shoulder, gripped him below the arm pits, and

gave him a basketball throw. I couldn't free a hand
to hit Golias when he landed just in front of me,
nor was my prayer that the beast would prove
balky effectual. With a snort the nag lunged forward and started rocketing over the grass tops.

I was still trying to throw myself off when we
dashed beneath a small but low-hanging cloud. It
was a good thing that I couldn't lose my seat, for
our mount gave a great leap. By that I don't mean
that he merely jumped from one place to another.
He took off into the air, soaring until he pierced
the bottom of that cloud, which turned out to be
considerably more than so much uncondensed
vapor. Inside it there was absolute water; and still
we went swiftly up.

Perhaps the combination of madness and fright
put me on ice. At any rate I didn't suffer for lack of
breathing while that horse mounted through vast
depths. Another circumstance worth noting had
to do with my shadow. Where we had met, Golias
alone had owned one; but when the nag broke
water and clambered out of a pool, I had one also.
The horse alone was shadowless as it stood drip-
ping in the sunlight.

The beast was apparently waiting for directions, for Golias was gazing about as if to get his
bearings. "This must be the place Kydnon took
that beating," he muttered. "It fits his description
exactly. West with some southing but not too
much," he then said to the brute we straddled.

While he was getting oriented, I was making
discoveries of my own. My shadow wasn't the
only thing which had come back to me. My old
clothes had for one thing, though that wasn't important. What did matter was that I was in posses-

sion of my will again. That doesn't mean I had forgotten Nimue. Whenever I thought of her I still wanted her. The big thing that had happened was that I found I could stop thinking about her.

First my control was tremulous; but the farther away from her we got the better I felt. The wind made by our steed as it rushed over the ground blew the pain out of my brain and swept out the dimness. The process was steady rather than episodic, but it can best be described in stages. First I was fearful that the absence of Nimue from my thoughts would leave an unfillable vacuum. Next I began to wonder why I had let anybody so dominate my being. Then I felt a revulsion of shame. It seemed likely to be permanent, but it wasn't. In the end I found that I could put that in its place likewise. I had had a fine time with Nimue—and I had loved it. I had a bad time—one I didn't like to remember, but would occasionally. Both were neither more nor less than a part of me, and neither stood in the way of whatever the future held.

Before thrashing that out with myself I couldn't talk to Golias; and when I felt that I was able to, I still hesitated. After all when he had last addressed me, I had made a deliberate effort to kick his teeth in.

When I did speak, I was careful to be impersonal for a starter. "Where'd you leave Jones?"

To my relief he was smiling when he looked over his shoulder. "Oh, you're there now. Good. Why, I left him with Degare, in whose keeping I knew he'd be safe, which you can't say of everybody in the Warlocks. We'll be at his holding directly."

With an effort I got it out. "You were a good
fellow to come and get me."

I implied in my tone if not my words that I
was sorry for having acted like a dope when he
arrived. His look told me he caught it, while his
words dismissed it as something that was done
with.

"What happened to you after you jumped in the
river?"

When I had sketched my experiences as far as
Miles Cross, he nodded. "Bercilak's quite a fellow, isn't he?"

"Who?"

"The green lad. I'm sorry I missed him this trip,
but Lucius and I found a pass well south of the
hermitage. We missed the raft, too—probably because we landed below where it hung up—and as
I thought it was wrecked, I didn't bother to look
for it. Incidentally, if you want to wish somebody
hard luck, wish that he has the job of steering a
jackass out of a wide river with steep banks at
night." Golias shook his head at the recollection.
"When we didn't see any sign of you, I figured
that the best course was to hit out for the Oracle.
Jones wasn't bad off, but I was naked as Conaire on
coronation day and hungry as a valraven. Luckily
we ran into Leoline down in the foothills boar
hunting. He fed me and gave me this nifty outfit."

He kicked out first one leg then the other, so I
could admire the respective blue and yellow in
which they were cased. "We'd been on a south-
westerly course that brought me to the old road a
couple of days after we left Leoline. A little
searching satisfied me you hadn't preceded us,
but I decided to keep going and chance it that you

would find some other route to the Oracle."

"What changed your mind?"

"Nothing until I ran into Groa. She loves to talk in riddles; but she's a savvy old girl, and don't forget it."

Golias looked at me to make sure I was impressed. "I ain't arguing." I told him. "Go on."

"On the chance she might have the answer, I reminded her I was a friend of Svipdag's and asked if she knew where you were. She talked in her rigmarole, but the gist of it was that, although you hadn't just vanished like Kaikhosru and hadn't learned to fly, you weren't on earth. I knew pretty well where to look for you then, if I could only get there; and that's when Lucius caused more trouble. I had to leave him; and I had to be careful where, or I'd come back to find some witch using him for cat meat. So I looked up Degare, who's not only a reliable citizen but tough enough to see that other folks are reliable when he's looking.

"Lucius wasn't much pleased at the delay, but as you'd got into a jam on my account, I had to get you out. Still it's one thing to want to go to Avalon and another thing to get there. I covered the Warlocks from Mount St. Michael to the Venusberg but had no luck until I stumbled onto Laeg. He was doing some scouting for Cuchullain and had just found one of the routes used by the people from down under. I tagged along when he infiltrated, and—there's Degare's place just ahead."

There was Jones, too, munching grass by a ditch surrounding the castle in a manner suggesting that he had never been convinced it was food. I was wondering how we were going to hoist him

on the horse's back, but at a word from Golias the
nag solved that problem. Lucius had barely had
time to notice our arrival when the huge beast was
on him. Picking him up in his teeth in the manner
of a cat with a kitten, it set the donkey athwart its
withers. From the way Jones laid back his ears and
brayed, it was clear that he didn't like the idea, but
there was nothing he could do about it. He was
stuck, just as I was, and couldn't kick.

"Take it easy, Lucius," Golias advised him
when he rolled his eyes toward us. "We're on our
way to find out how to snake you out of that
jackass skin."

We were really on our way. That nag was making time to shame a diesel engine on level tracks.
Fortunately its method of travel didn't kick up
any dust. When I turned my head away from the
prop-wash, I could observe the country through
which we were racing; and now that I had shaken
off Nimue's influence, I was interested enough to
take a look.

In a little while we broke out of the woods to
course through a curiously divided land. We
ourselves were streaking across a prairie which
extended to our left as far as the curve of the earth,
at least. Not far to the right, however, the terrain
was obscured by mist. In the main it was too
thick to see through, yet every now and then it
lightened enough to let me know that here was a
different country. I don't simply mean its geo-
graphic features, for I never got a clear view of
them. What impressed me was that it was developed after a fashion unique to my experience
with the Commonwealth.

Occasionally I caught blurred glimpses of skyscrapers and factory chimneys, and twice I made out aerodromes. Yet it was the sounds—even the sounds of machine gun fire that I heard once—which made me homesick for the familiar. There was the purposeful racket of a riveter. There was the sweet hum of power plants. There were engines purring softly in the ground and roaring mightily in the air. Finest of all, there was the wailing whistle of a rail train in passage.

We must have cut by one corner of the district, for in a little while we were leaving it behind. Absorbed, I had forgotten where I was until, as I turned from looking over my shoulder, I noticed Golias. He was gazing back also.

"What's that country?" I asked.

"It's the New Purchase, Shandon." I could tell from his voice that he was as interested as myself. "Looks all right, doesn't it?"

"Couldn't we take a look at it? After we get Lucius all fixed up, that is."

He shook his head. "It's not a part of the Commonwealth yet, though, of course, it's going to be."

"Well, who lives there then?"

"Oh, a bunch of squatters as usual," Golias reached forward and chased a horse fly away from Lucius. "Some of 'em will be permanent settlers," he went on, when he had straightened up, "but you can figure that most won't be able to stick the competition after Annexation Day."

"When's that?"

"I couldn't say exactly," he shrugged, "but you can bank on it that I'm going to have a lot of fun and trouble there—maybe next trip if I'm lucky."

The prairie gave way to a cedar forest, which in

turn yielded to hills covered with vineyards and scrubby little orchards of what Golias said were olive trees. Most of the fruit was gone, but as I had never seen an olive outside of a jar or a martini, I found this a novelty. Nor had it quite lost its shine when we reached the edge of a copper beech grove on a lookout over the sea.

"Whoa!" Golias commanded.

The nag deposited Jones on the ground. Finding I was no longer stuck, I slid down the great flanks and dropped to earth beside Golias.

"Wait here for us," the latter told Lucius. "I don't think it'll take long, though it may if we have to wait for a seance. Here we go, Shandon."

Although the sun was just going down, it was already twilight under the interlocking branches. The gray holes suspended from the thatch were not menacing; but they were so aloof I would never have dreamed of touching one. The indifference toward life that is one of the qualities of dusk in the woods flavored the atmosphere. A few birds sang, as they often do at sundown, in a way that is more cheerless than no song at all.

Golias was walking more slowly than was normal with him, nor did he hurry when we turned into a path. A couple of minutes later this brought us to a facade in the side of a knoll.

There was still enough light to see that the stone was adorned with carving. In fact the entrance piercing the rock was a centerpiece from which groups of men and animals radiated. If some of the forms and activities struck me as curious, all the work was beautifully done. Yet what held my eyes was the blank dark of the doorless entry.

"Are we going in there?" I asked.

"It's a cinch Deiphobe won't come out to us."
Golias' voice was as low as my own. "You ready?"

I vainly tried to peer through the doorway. "No,
but let's go."

Inside, as soon as we had advanced a few steps,
we could see something after all. The stone beneath our feet was still lost in darkness, and the
corridor through which we walked might as well
have had no walls; but directly ahead of us I could
make out a faint glow. It wasn't as far away as I at
first thought. Soon it took form as another doorway, and in a minute we had crossed its threshold
into a cavern.

The light which flooded it was provided by
pools of some smokeless liquid held in silver con-
tainers. These did not suffice to show us the ceiling; and the far wall was likewise in shadow.
Except for the lamps, if you could call them that,
the place was unfurnished. It was also unoccu-
pied.

I was just about to suggest to Golias that as long
as nobody was there, we might as well leave,
when he called out: "Deiphobe, we would hear
the voice of the Delian."

To my dismay the answer came from all directions at once, including behind us. "Who comes
to seek word from the Delian, and by what right do
you trouble him?"

"We are Demodocus the Maker and Shandon
Silverlock," Golias called back, "and we have no
claim against his kindness save that of men helpless without it."

There was silence for a few moments. "The
voice of the all knowing one will come to you,"
we then heard. "It will give the solution to what-

ever problem absorbs each of you. That and nothing else."

"We've got to concentrate," Golias whispered. "Keep your brain nailed down to just what we want, and we'll find how to get good old Lucius straightened out."

In the stretched minutes which followed I tried to do precisely that. Yet it turned out to be more than I could manage. I started out all right by wishing Lucius could be turned into a man again; but after it was jerked back into line a few times, my mind pursued its natural course of skipping from one point to another.

My chain of thoughts in this instance had a logical sequence. From bearing on Jones' release from donkeydom, the next jump was in the direction of his ultimate goal. If he achieved that, which is to say his marriage to Hermione and settling down to the management of his affairs in general, our scheduled connection with him would end. That raised the question as to what would happen next, which in turn promoted the query: what did I wish to do? With that query all the inchoate desires which had visited me during the quiet of nights on the raft revived and took over my mind. If they were complex when separately considered, they teamed to give a simple answer. Like all travelers in a country which interests them, I longed to be an initiate instead of a neophyte.

I had just arrived at that conclusion when Deiphobe finally came to stand on the edge of darkness. So placed, only the highlights of her features were visible. They outlined a face as impersonal as time. I could see only the sockets of

her eyes, but it overawed me to be aware of the
passionless knowledge they must contain. Nevertheless, I could not look away from them, and in a
moment they stopped the clock on my thinking.
Until they should turn away from me, my brain's
only function was to be a receptacle for what she
might have to say.

So I was not really disturbed when she went
into a fit. She writhed and slavered, but as she did
not take her eyes from us, I waited, neither pa-
tiently nor impatiently, until the frothing lips
began to bark words.

"Demodocus the Maker," she yelped, and the
chorus of echoes took it up, "the Delian answers
the questions which trouble you. Your friend who
is now an ass can regain human form only by
eating fresh rose petals. He will find the secret of
his paternity and the woman he desires for his
mate at Chapel Perilous."

"I thank the great Delian," Golias said with a
bow. "It's time to go." He plucked me by the
sleeve as he whispered the words; but I didn't
turn, because I knew I must wait.

"Shandon Silverlock," Deiphobe now cried in
her harsh high monotone, "the Delian answers
the problem which troubles you. His decree is that
you attempt the pilgrimage to Hippocrene."

As soon as she was silent, she stopped shaking,
swaying, and slavering. "Leave," she ordered us,
and I discovered I had the ability to comply.

I was careful not to look at Golias for a minute
after we stepped from the blackness of the passageway back into the gloom of the grove. Something had to be said, though.

"It's a good thing one of us kept his eye on the

ball. Lucius would have stayed a jackass for any help I gave him."

"Oh, as long as we got the job done, that part of it's all right." Even in the poor light I could see how soberly he looked at me. "It's you that I'm worried about now. You don't know it, I suppose, but you just pushed yourself into a tight spot. The trip to Hippocrene is a rough assignment."

The seriousness of his tone impressed me. "Heck; if it's that bad, I won't try it."

He snorted. "That wasn't an option you were offered; that was the high command giving an order. It may be different outside the Commonwealth—I wouldn't know—but inside it such things as economic, moral, political, social, theological, sentimental, and scientific laws are vain pretenders to authority." Golias made a gesture of sweeping finality. "Here there is only Delian Law, and anyone rebel to it has swift burial and a water color epitaph."

Listening to him, I nearly bumped into a tree but sidestepped just in time. "Quit scaring me with generalities," I suggested, "and give me facts. What's so hard about getting to this Hippocrene place?"

"There's no use in going into that until we find out whether we're going to survive winding up Lucius' affairs." If his words couldn't be called cheerful, his tone showed me that he had temporarily shaken off foreboding. "Hey, Lucius!" he shouted, as we came in sight of the two animals. "Come here and get a long earful of good news!"

XXII

⚘ Activities at the Chapel ⚘

AMONG THE THINGS Golias had taken thought to procure from Gwynn Uriens MacLir was a small supply of food. It was so limited in quantity, however, that we agreed—Jones as yet having no voice—that as long as Lucius could get by on leaves and grass, he'd have to lump it. At that we were able to set aside no more than a snack for breakfast the next day.

While we ate supper we sat looking out over the darkened water, which Golias told me was the southwestern tip of Gitche Gumee, and discussed the project before us. "Where are we going to find roses this late in the summer?" I asked.

"You mean in the fall," Golias mumbled. He swallowed, then used the flask of wine to clear a path for further speech. "Damned if I know where to go for roses, but I figure we ought to start looking at Chapel Perilous itself. It's been seven weeks since we set out, and I—"

"Holy cow! Has it been that long?" Then I thought back. "I guess it has," I answered myself. "And Ravan said he might be back by now."

"That's our indicator," Golias nodded. "We've got to go there first to see what Hermione's situation is. As it's far in the south, there'll be roses in that vicinity if anywhere. Besides, I think that's what the Delian meant for us to do."

With the nag's cooperation we remounted and left the miles behind in the night. The wind of passage made me drowsy. If I didn't actually sleep much, I was between a doze and a stupor most of the night. It wasn't until day had been a fact for a couple of hours that I shook the feathers out of my mind.

About the time I did so the nag abruptly stopped. There was no apparent reason. Nothing was in sight but trees.

"What's the pitch?" I asked Golias.

"I don't know, but we'd better look around," he decided.

I was so stiff, when I followed him in his drop to the ground, that I fell down. The horse was in the act of plucking Jones from his back by the time I had picked myself up. Quickly but not roughly it set the donkey on the ground—and then the huge beast simply wasn't there.

"That should mean we're about where we want to be," Golias said, while I was blinking dazedly. "Now that we're afoot I can see open country."

The forest line was indeed only some fifty yards off. Where the trees stopped the country fell away to give us a view I didn't admire. Its chief natural feature was a little color to take the curse off the dead reeds, dirty pools and water-poisoned trees.

Buzzards, flying low to suggest carrion was handy, presided over this expanse of ugliness. Above and in the background was a dull sky.

Man's contribution to the scene was a building whose walls and towers climbed out of the very middle of the swamp. There was no use in asking whether that was the place we were going. I knew it.

"Let's eat while we still can," I said. "Though I must say I'd never tell the sight-seers that was a church."

"The chapel's just beyond." Golias was fishing our food out of a bundle largely composed of clothes for Jones and a whacking big sword. "We've got to go through the castle to reach it."

I watched one of the buzzards drop out of the sky. "It doesn't look like much of a spot for roses."

"It may not be," he admitted. "The only time I was ever in the chapel was with Lancelot, and we had other things on the docket. I wish we had some of that wine left."

"I wish we had a couple of stiff jolts of drinking whiskey," I said.

The approach to the castle was a road which we reached after a half-hour of downhill walking. Following it into a patch of woods, we discovered a thing which the trees had previously concealed. A considerable body of men, lounging amidst a gay assortment of tents, was encamped there. Some weapons were in evidence, but if it was a military camp, it was one untroubled by officers. Early as it was, quite a bit of boozing was in progress, although gambling was the principal occupation.

"All you need for success at this is a good eye,"

one professional shark was announcing. "The shells can't outguess you, and the pea can't walk off the table, you know. It's bound to be under one of the three, and a good eye—I'll admit it takes a good eye—can follow it and find it. Just lift up the right one, and it is no more possible for the pea to hide from you, than it is for the shell to conceal it."

Glancing around as he talked, the man suddenly waved a long, bony arm. "Hi, Golias." His voice was cordial, but his wild-eyed horse face was unsmiling. "Would you like to try this wonderful, new game of chance I've just invented?"

"No, thanks, Tyl."

"But as I was telling these gentlemen," Tyl persisted, "it's excellent training for the eye, it gives the mind practice in forming rapid decisions—"

"And," Golias took him up, "it is harmless to the lights and liver, doesn't stunt your growth, eases pay day itch, and is an education in itself. But just now I'd like to be educated along different lines. What's this camp for, for instance? They got company at the castle?"

"Just the arch king," Tyl drawled. "This roost is for the overflow of the free feeders he brought with him."

Golias exchanged glances with me. "Do you know why Jamshyd is here?" he asked the gambler.

"I do not," the latter informed him, "enjoy his majesty's confidence, or things would be run much better than they are. However, I am at liberty to disclose that there must be big doings today. Every fancy pants in the carnival made for the castle right after breakfast."

As we were starting on our way again, Tyl called after us. "You figuring on getting in there, Golias?"

"Yes, why?"

"Well, if they don't chop you up before they throw you out, I've got a proposition for you. I'll wait around."

"I don't like the fact that the king's here," I confided to Golias. "If Deiphobe was right about Hermione being on the premises—Well, if his nibs thinks as much of Ravan as he's supposed to, wouldn't it be natural for him to turn up for the wedding?"

"It would, especially as Jamshyd's sanction is the only thing that gives Ravan the nerve to be so high-handed." To spare Jones' feelings both of us had been speaking softly, but now he dropped his voice to a whisper. "If all the nobles had been summoned to the castle, as Tyl claims, it might mean that the wedding is due to come off today."

Low as we had pitched our voices, Jones' outsize ears had picked up our words. Golias had hardly expressed his fear, when with a startled grunt, Lucius charged full speed down the narrow causeway which connected the castle with solid ground.

"Hold it!" we chorused, but as it was obvious that he wasn't going to, we broke into a run also. Donkeys not being built for racing, he didn't get far away from us, but neither could we gain. Cursing and panting, we trailed him through the bog toward a danger we would have preferred to approach cautiously.

Nor was this all there was to aggravate us. Somehow there are few things that rejoice spectators more than the sight of men vainly pursuing a supposedly domesticated animal. Soldiers on duty on the wall above the castle gate saw us and were overjoyed. To my chagrin they commenced roaring with laughter, and to their delight I tried harder than ever to seize Jones' tail and stop the ridiculous procession.

"Three to two on the jackass!" one fellow cried.

"Which one?" another was careful to enquire.

"Eight to five silvertop there busts a gut," a third offered.

I didn't quite do that, but I had used up my sprint and began to fall behind. Seeing that, as well as the general futility of the pursuit, Golias slowed to a walk.

"Ease up," he advised. "We'll need our breath."

We were then close to the walls, and Lucius was right under them. I don't suppose it had occurred to him until that moment that he had no means of bargaining for entry. He had simply dashed ahead, driven by a vision of Hermione's danger. Having crossed the bridge leading to the gateway, however, he was visited with a full knowledge of his helplessness. He saw he could accomplish nothing, yet he had to make the effort. With a loud bray of protest, he threw himself against the mighty gate, to bounce back, half stunned.

I thought some of those guards would fall off the wall and fervently hoped so. My next thought was that we had no better chance of getting inside than the donkey. In the third place I sneakingly wished we wouldn't succeed. The idea of having those iron bars close behind me gave me goose-flesh.

"I don't know about the chapel," I said aside to Golias, "but I bet this is Castle Dangerous."

"Nope, Nigramous," he contradicted me. His

eyes were fixed on the laughing men above us. "If
the Porter is at his post, which one is he?"

At this formal appeal one of them checked his
mirth. "I, Glewlwyd Gavaelvawr; and I'm the one
to ask questions here, not you." He didn't succed
in his attempt to look forbidding, and I saw that
the whole crew had been hitting the bottle. "What
are you doing here? Nobody's to cross the draw-
bridge today without an invitation from my Lord
Ravan."

"We were just following our pet donkey,"
Golias said.

"He didn't look very tame to me," Gavaelvawr
declared. He nudged the man next to him, as he
made this statement, and they all howled. "I was
afraid he was going to wreck the portcullis."

It was apparent that Lucius' antics had made
them genial where they would otherwise have
been tough. Perceiving that, Golias made haste to
act before they could become tired of us. Whatever he whispered into Lucius' ear, it must have
had to do with Hermione, because Jones came out
of his daze and gave him his full attention.

"All right, Lucius," Golias said loudly. "We've
been told that the arch king is in the castle here.
What would you give to see his august and thrice
gracious majesty?"

For answer the donkey lay down, rolled over on
his back, and closed his eyes. "Oh, you'd give
your life and feel lucky to do it?" Golias pursued.
"But suppose you were still living when you saw
him. What would you do then?"

Scrambling to his feet, Jones went down on his
knees and touched his head to the ground, as he
had once done before Semiramis. The porter and

his subordinates laughed again, but now their mirth was appreciative rather than derisive. Golias put Lucius through a few more tricks before he tried to take advantage of this change in attitude. Finally, though, he turned and made Gavaelvawr a showman's bow.

"We're strolling entertainers who'd like our opportunity to amuse the glorious inmates of the castle—and to collect gloriously from them. What's the chances?"

"H-m-m-m, I'm not supposed to let anyone in without Don Rodrigo's orders," the Porter said, "but he's already given entry to a lot of minstrels and what-not."

"Aw, this is a good act," one of his men said. "I think the king himself would get a bang out of it. Besides, Ravan'll never know he didn't give his O.K. He's got something else on his mind."

"What's the sword for, first?" Gavaelvawr demanded, pointing to the hilt sticking out from the bundle Golias carried.

"Just one of our props." Golias drew the sword, threw his head back and, to my astonishment, lowered a foot and a half of the weapon into his gullet. "See?" he inquired, when he had removed the blade.

"Haul up the portcullis," the Porter ordered.

Within we found ourselves in a paved court yard surrounding a second wall. The gate to this was not closed, and the guards didn't so much as break up their gabfest to look at us. It was certainly a day of celebration when such laxness was permitted. Without consulting each other, Golias and I started walking faster.

"We'll try the pleasance for flowers," Golias

said, as we skirted the main inner building. "Of course, if the ladies are using it, it might be worth our necks; but I'm not sure that's saying much today anyhow."

The entrance to the wall-enclosed garden to which he led me was not guarded, and a glance showed us it wasn't occupied. "Inside, quick, before somebody spots us," Golias ordered.

Alert to the occasion, Jones trotted ahead of us. Yet it took only a minute to see we were taking a vain risk. I recognized, without being able to name them, a variety of late-blooming flowers, none of them any variety of rose. And what made our disappointment doubly hard to accept was a profusion of barren bushes to show how common the blossom we sought had been earlier in the year.

"We'd better try the church yard," I said, glad to be able to suggest getting out of there.

"Look, Shandon;" Golias said, as we left, "have you seen anybody stirring since we came into the inner court—anybody at all?"

While I was thinking, I realized why he had asked the question. "No," I replied. "There must be a gathering some place."

"Let's try the great hall first," he snapped, leading the way on the double.

The main building had much of the architecture and most of the atmosphere of a penitentiary. There was a man on guard when we reached the inner doors. At least there was a spear as well as a bottle beside him, as he sat slumped on the steps. He looked up when we came running, and we slowed to answer his challenge, if any.

"Is it all right to go in?" I demanded, when he merely stared at us.

"No, but you wouldn't want to anyhow."

"Why not?"

"Because there ain't nobody in there." The pathos of it was too much for him, and his voice broke. "They all went off and left me, and I'm alone all by myself."

From the way Jones groaned I knew he caught the implication as well as we. There couldn't be too many places for a crowd of people to go in this tiny island. If Ravan and his guests weren't in the castle, then they must be at the chapel. The poor donkey looked almost out of his senses as we started to run again. The only thing which kept him from dashing ahead of us was that he didn't know the way.

"You stick with us even when we get in sight of the place," Golias counseled him. "We've got to work together, or we're all sunk."

Following them out the second of two lesser gates at the rear, I saw that we didn't have far to go. The terrace between the castle walls and the swamp which so effectually protected them was narrow. Nearer than I wanted it to be, an ecclesiastical structure hunched under dead trees as gray as the sky. Three buzzards were on the roof.

"It looks like we're expected," I panted.

Golias didn't answer, and another few seconds brought us within the crumbling stone wall bounding the church yard. A glance did our business there. Except for faded grass, the only growth was a crop of pustulant toadstools. I echoed Jones' moan.

"There's nothing to do but see what's inside," Golias said. "Hang on to Lucius' ear, Shandon, and don't let him get away from you."

He flung opwn the door, and I gingerly crossed

the threshold, donkey ear in hand. Because
everyone was engrossed with what was going on
in the rear of the chapel, nobody noticed us. I
looked and listened with the dreadful conviction
we had come too late.

A pair of men and a pair of women were standing before the chancel rail while a parson, facing
them, raised his voice in the even cadences belonging to a ritual. A couple was being married,
and while I couldn't be sure it was Hermione in
the midst of bridal draperies, I was pretty certain
that the man on her right was Ravan.

Promptly after reaching that conclusion, I saw
that the moment of absolute crisis was at hand. I
hadn't concentrated on the minister's words, but I
suddenly heard Don Rodrigo—I remembered his
voice, right enough—say: "I do."

While I gasped, stunned, the vicar rushed on
with "Do you, Hermione," and so forth. Golias
was at my shoulder now, and I turned to look at
him despairingly. He wore the expression of a
man expecting to be hit in the stomach.

"She's the only one who can stop the train
now," he said.

Against all hope, she did so. "No, I do not!" she
cried, when the priest came to an enquiring
pause.

That was all she said, but it was effective. Ritual
is always thrown for a loss when it doesn't draw
the right answers. The minister peered at his book
as if he thought he must have read the wrong
passage. Ravan jumped, then whirled to glower at
the spectators, now suddenly noisy. The maid of
honor and the best man stepped hastily out of the
limelight which had become disturbing. The
bridesmaids got in a huddle to talk things over.

Only the man posted to give the bride away showed no signs of agitation.

"Father," he demanded, "why have you interrupted the service?"

"But, your majesty," the parson protested, "she said—"

"I heard her reply," the king asserted. "She said: 'I do.' Or is it your opinion that something is faulty with our hearing?"

"Oh, no, your highness!" In his eagerness to disclaim such a thought the minister ran a finger into one of his own ears. "I'm afraid it's my hearing that is faulty, sire. I'm getting old, I suppose."

"Too old to retain the benefice of Bray?" the arch king enquired.

"Why—why—no, your majesty! I should certainly think not."

"We might even find a better place for you," Jamshyd suggested. "But not until after the wedding. Please carry on from the exact point where you left off."

Everybody stepped into place once more. I thought Hermione's courage had lost the game to trickery, and looked at Golias again. From his expression I saw that he had thought of something.

"Your arch majesty, my Lord Ravan, and all assembled here," he shouted, "I put you under geas!"

While I held my breath and squeezed Jones' ear, everyone turned to stare. Everyone but Jamshyd, that is, who seemed impervious to shock.

"Who dares," he asked in a voice which barely showed his displeasure, "to put our royal self under geas?"

"A bard."

"I knew that. Nobody but a damned poet would have the consummate impudence. If it's Nornagest, I'll fry you over the same fire that eats your candle. Who is it? Say your name or lose your bid."

"Taliesin," Golias told him.

"Ah. Taliesin puts us under geas and escapes whole if he can. What are the terms?"

"No one here is to move from where he stands or to lift a hand until I've finished singing a song for this wedding."

"Sing then, and be cursed, since I can't stop you."

"Thanks, sire," Golias said through his teeth. He gave me a shove. "The bridesmaids' bouquets!" he hissed. "They may have roses in them."

I stepped forward, tugging at Jones' ear, as Golias sounded off.

> Birth and mortality
> Are only two of three,
> Mating's a mystery
>   Great as its brothers;
> Not less to be revered,
> More, maybe, to be feared
> As more the realm of Wyrd
>   Than the two others.

> Great Gunnar, noble Finn
> Blasted their might and kin;
> Conor did so begin
>   Ulad's undoing.
> Though they were high in name,
> Loss was their lot, and shame—

> Right pay, and theirs the blame
> For an ill wooing.

There was standing room only in the church, and Jones hadn't been able to see what was going on. Having heard Hermione's voice, he was eager to do something, but the crowd through which we were pushing obscured his view. Sticking close to me, he was unexpectedly cooperative. That, however, was the only comfort connected with my assignment. This place didn't have to be called Chapel Dangerous to make me know it. Because of the whammy Golias had put on them all, nobody stopped us. Yet from the way the men looked at us, I would have liked it better if they hadn't let us pass. It isn't getting into the trap that stumps the mouse.

What would happen when Golias ran out of song I didn't try to imagine, but he was still going strong when we had threaded our way to the wedding party.

> So I direct my verse
> To speed a working curse
> Bound to be cause and nurse
>   Of a miscarriage
> For what is being wrought
> Here out of evil thought;
> Let doom be hailed and brought
>   Down on this marriage!

Seeing Hermione, who had turned with the rest to stare at us, Jones stopped. I yanked at his ear savagely.

"The bouquets!" I implored him. "It's our only chance."

We went to each of the startled bridesmaids, wasting our time, as I would have known if I hadn't been so rattled, by going to more than one. Their posies were identical and roseless from first to last of the dozen. I left each knowing that a hope for life had failed me.

Doubtless Golias, following us with his eyes, realized this as keenly as I, though his voice rang out as confidently as if all were well.

> Fetch the wrath, Allecto!
> Megaera, pour out woe!
> Quick bane, and not the slow;
>   Don't spare or palter.
> Then may Tisiphone's
> Hand thrust the bitter less
>   Forced on Achillides,
>   Too, at the altar!
> Now, if you three assent,
> There is an instrument
> Sharpened for this intent,
>   Savagely biding;
> There's a man, having sown
> Blas' follies, so has known
> Kormak's blight, then been thrown
>   Into strange hiding.

I had finished with the bridesmaids. Hermione, a desperate glance told me, had no flowers. My last hope was the maid of honor. Her bouquet was dangling, petals down, from her left hand, the one nearest me. Trudging toward her with Jones in tow, I grabbed it from her. Then I dropped it as though it were hot.

"We're licked, Lucius," I rasped. "Let's make a break for it."

In my eagerness I dragged him a few feet before he balked. When I turned to swear at him, therefore, I was on the maid of honor's right. She was holding another bouquet—Hermione's. Naturally the bride wouldn't be holding flowers during the course of the sacrament, but I didn't stop to figure the wherefores out then. I snatched the bouquet, glanced at it, started to drop it, then looked at it again. My mind had been on the lookout for something red; but my eye had registered the shape of roses, even though they were white.

Lucius was forlornly mooning at Hermione, and I nearly jerked his ear loose before I could get him to look. The delay, brief as it was, infuriated me.

"Damn you, Jones, roses!" I snarled. "Eat 'em before I cut you open and ram 'em inside with my foot!"

I was holding them so near him that he probably couldn't see what I was offering. The urgency in my tone got to him, though, so his mouth opened. Golias saw that, and his voice was a chortle of triumph.

> He, by express command
> Of his stars, understand,
> Can have none, or the hand
>   Of Hawthorn's daughter.
> Judge if he'll fail you when
> He sees his man of men,
> On his two legs again,
>   Ripe to do slaughter.
>
>
> As once a vengeful force
> Crammed the skin of a horse,

One man could well, of course,
    Lurk in an ass's.
But where the roses bloom
He leaves that hiding room,
Finding a kinder doom
    As the spell passes.

He stopped, so his hex was non-operative; but I forgot to be scared. Along with everybody else I stood fixed, my eyes upon Lucius.

"Good gracious!" one of the bridesmaids squeaked. "What's happening?

She had reason for asking. Jones had no sooner swallowed that bunch of rosebuds than he stood on his hind legs, flexing his front ones and throwing back his head. His ears were shrinking like burning paper. When only the nubs were left, they flattened out on the sides of his head, and the hair peeled off.

From then on it was as if a rapid action caricaturist was showing how a few lines could change one thing into another. When the muzzle had been transformed into a face, humanity raced down the shortened neck and made arms out of the forelegs. The process was so enthralling to watch that I forgot I had any connection with it.

Jones himself was the first to react to the state of affairs. As his tail began to evaporate, he reached hastily for the bundle of clothes I held. Becoming aware of the necessity, I was trying to help him sort them out, when I heard Golias' shout of anger.

"The sword, Lucius! Damnation, you're not still a jackass! Shandon, give him the sword!"

Lucius compromised by stepping into his pants and letting it go at that. While he was snugging them to a no longer hairy waist, I unsheathed the weapon and had the hilt ready for his fist. It was time for that, for the spell of the marvel was being everywhere broken.

Don Rodrigo was ahead of the rest. "Why it's my putative young kinsman, stepping out of character," he announced.

Jones leaned on his sword. "My lord," he said, "when we last met, I made a promise to come to your wedding."

"Quite true," Ravan acknowledged. "At the time I issued the invitation it was sincerely done. But the king thought it best, in view of certain enquiries being made by my betrothed's kindred, to hold the ceremony in this far, new holding of mine rather than at court. And in my amorous impetuosity, forgivable, I trust, I forgot to notify you of the change in plans."

In spite of his mocking words, he was watching Jones keenly, and in the course of his speech he drew his own sword. It was done in an offhand manner, as if he had nothing on his mind. When his weapon was fully out of the scabbard, however, he leaped and lunged with vicious swiftness.

He failed to kill, because Lucius spun sidewise and sucked in his guts till they hugged his backbone. Before Ravan could recover, Jones stepped inside his guard and took his head off with a two-handed blow. The head bounced at my feet, like the green man's. Unlike Bercilak, though, Don Rodrigo didn't recover it. His body collapsed, spewing blood all over the floor, and stayed still as only the dead can.

Preparing for consequences, I caught up the

sword he had dropped, but for a moment no one moved except Hermione. "Darling," she said, swaying toward Lucius, "are you all right?"

He took his eyes off Ravan. The killing fury hadn't left them, but he managed to make his voice soft.

"Yes, my love."

"Then I'm all right," she assured him; and passed out in the arms of Golias, who had just pushed his way forward.

"Huon couldn't have done it better," he congratulated Lucius. "No, don't worry about her. It's just reaction, and the bridesmaids can take care of her. Come and get her!" he snapped at the bewildered girls. "I've got other things to do."

"Taliesin," the arch king said in his bored, easy voice, when Hermione had been taken off Golias' hands, "have you and your friends accomplished everything you had planned—with the possible exception of getting out alive?"

"Almost everything, your highness."

"Then let me point out to you that although some of your activities were remarkable, I find them in wretched taste at a wedding."

As he spoke, I could feel swords in my gizzard. Golias didn't like it, either, but he shrugged. "If you're concerned about the loss of the groom, sire, we can fix you up with a better one."

To my surprise Jamshyd seemed to be giving his words consideration. "A dead favorite is not a favorite at all," he finally observed to no one in particular. He glanced at me, then stared at Jones. "I've been king long enough never to have a man killed without finding out who he is."

Lucius stopped looking defiant and looked confused instead. "I don't quite know, your highness. That seems a foolish admission, but they tell me that the name I have always carried is not rightly my own."

"What name is that?"

"Lucius Gil Jones, your majesty."

"What?" His majesty looked mildly interested. "Next of kin to the old baron—and to the late Lord Ravan, for that matter?"

"The old baron's grandson and heir, sire," Jones flushed as he bowed. "But my legitimacy is in doubt."

"A bastard is as much a grandson as any other."

"Not if somebody else's son is the father." Lucius' voice was so husky he was all but whispering as he pointed that out. "It's what my grandsire came to question—at my Lord Ravan's instigation, I believe. I can't, of course, be sure, and my father is not alive to speak."

"That's so." Jamshyd looked reflective. "You know, I have always thought Don Rodrigo brought about your father's mysterious disappearance after he came to covet the person and property of your mother, whose widowhood, it is interesting to note, was terminated by death shortly after her refusal to him." He paid no attention to Jones' exclamation. "Put up your sword— you, too, you with the silverlock—and kneel to your soverign."

While I was still fumbling to stick my blade in its sheath, for I wasn't going to argue while there was any chance of arbitrating, Jones stepped over Ravan's body, knelt, and bent his head. I looked at Golias to see whether he thought good would come of it, but I saw he was holding his breath, too. For an agonizing minute the king stared down at the man at his feet. Naked above the waist, Lucius peeled well. He had a finely muscled back and a clear skin whose whiteness was only broken by that heart-shaped birth mark on his shoulder. After an interval his majesty put a finger on it.

"Get up," he ordered. "Some few years ago, when I was only a prince," he went, on when Lucius had risen, "I knew the old baron's son. In fact I was a very good friend of his—and he was my associate. I make this distinction for you, because you'll never have the royal opportunity to make it for yourself."

Jamshyd must have had magnificent features once. They still looked so at first glance, then with repulsion you realized that there was no more feeling behind them than exists behind the smile of a jack o'lantern. Watching his eyes as he spoke, I shivered, because I remembered where I had seen such a look of self-possessed deadness before. It was every time I had gazed in the mirror during the months—years, perhaps—prior to boarding the *Naglfar*. It shocked me to find something at once so familiar and disquieting in the Commonwealth. It also filled with vague premonitions of evil.

"You are young Jones," the king said, after his parenthetical observation. "As an intimate, if not a friend of your father, I know that a son, reckoning the normal period of gestation, was conceived on your parents' honeymoon. You are that son. I was present to cheer your father's anxiety when you were born and saw you before you wore your first diaper. Both the shape and the location of your birth mark check with your name—and I will inform your grandfather."

Before Lucius could respond, the arch king turned his back on him. "Get that girl on her feet," he commanded. "I came here to attend a wedding, and I'm not used to being thwarted."

WAY THREE

Down and Out to an Ending

XXIII

∽ Lorel's Passenger List ∽

I HAD A FINE TIME at the wedding celebration except when I looked at the arch king. Of course, Golias and I didn't overdo it. I don't recall that we drank a drop more than was held by any given bottle. At that it was three days before we eased back to normalcy. In the meantime Jamshyd had left, making it possible for others to depart. Lucius and Hermione had taken advantage of the opportunity to escape on their honeymoon.

If we had made any friends in the course of our whingding, they must have gone, too. "Cold sober," I said, as we sat at breakfast the fourth day, "I don't like this joint or the people in it."

"There are more cheerful places than Castle Nigramous most of the time," Golias admitted.

"Let's hit the road, then." Disregarding the fact that he made no rejoinder, I looked at him with cheerful expectancy. "Where shall we go?"

This time I noticed his hesitancy and the curious expression which went with it. "I haven't quite decided," he said at length. "About where

I'm going, that is. You're going to try to reach Hippocrene."

"Oh, yes, that business." The Delian's injunction had slipped my mind. Now that it was called to my attention again, I was only a little troubled; but I didn't like the way Golias was talking. "What's the matter with going together?"

He helped himself to some more ham and eggs. "The Delian didn't include me."

"Forget the Delian." I was irritated by his evasiveness but still inclined to be cheerful. "Make up your mind where you're steering for, and I'll tag along."

Golias hadn't been looking me squarely in the eye, but now he did. "I wish it could work out that way, Shandon, but it's not in the cards."

"Go to hell, then!" I snapped. "And the next time you don't want a man's company, tell him so instead of giving him double talk."

I was still indignant when we left the castle and retraced our steps through the swamp. A factor which increased my bad humor was that Golias made no overtures. Moreover when he found Tyl waiting for him at the end of the causeway, he held a long confab with the gambler—one which I wasn't invited to join—before he walked on with me. Puzzled as well as angered, I, too, kept silent until our arrival at a split in the road forced the issue.

"Well," I demanded, "which way now?"

He pointed down the left-hand road. "That's the only way you can go."

"Oh, rats! What's to keep me from going to the right, or back where we came from?" As I asked this, I looked in the direction of the swamp. We had reached high enough ground for it to be almost wholly in sight, but the fortress which had risen from its midst had vanished. With an exclamation I whirled to take the right-hand road, which ran east to the young sun. I did not advance.

I have known people who profess a physical inability to force themselves to walk across a high bridge. No matter how safe they know the structure to be, they claim they cannot make themselves walk so far up in the air. I had never fully believed that, but now I had a similar experience, more unsettling because it took place on solid earth. When I gazed down that road, I suddenly couldn't conceive of any possible course of action. Unable to contemplate so much as a second of the future, I was panic-stricken. When I turned to face the open country, it was no better. It wasn't until I had turned to the westerly road again that I regained poise.

"It's just the way Delian wants it," Golias explained. "So you might as well want it, too."

"Oh, well, it doesn't make any difference to me." It was a relief to have my faculties in order again, but I was resentful about yielding under pressure. "How far is this place, and what do I do when I get there?"

"To answer your last question first. Hippocrene's a spring."

"A what? Well, O.K. Do I get a drink out of it, or do I just peek in it to see how pretty I look?"

Golias expression showed me he didn't take to my jocularity. "You drink three times—if you can, and if you get there, which you probably won't."

"That's jake with me, too," I said, growing more jaunty as he grew more serious. "But why do I drink, and water at that, Tamborine?"

"So you won't stay a nit-spirited slug all your life!" I had wanted to anger him, and I had succeeded. "Listen, Shandon; you got this assignment, because the Delian read something in you that made it suitable. Didn't you once tell me you tried to make a song?"

"Yes," I owned up, "but it was no go."

"Well, you weren't qualified, but the Delian's giving you a chance to be. That's where Hippocrene comes in. The first swallow is the drink of recollection, so you won't forget what you've seen, heard, and done in the Commonwealth. The second is the passport drink, giving you the know-how to find your way back. The third is the maker's drink, no bottom limit to quality guaranteed, and no top specified."

I reviewed his list. "Two for a passport, eh? And how many for citizenship?"

"You won't have to worry about that," he assured me. "Unless you're born to it, there's no such thing. Now going back to your query about distance, I can't help you. I've been there, naturally, but there are miles on the way which can't be computed. That signpost gives no figures, either."

I ganced at the road marker to which he pointed. The arrows aiming west read:

Usher's Tarn
The Dark Tower
Gnipa Cave

"It doesn't say anything about Hippocrene," I protested.

"Unless you get by what you're bound to encounter, you won't care," he informed me with a coolness I found callous.

"I see. And it's final that you're not going?"

"It's out of the question," he declared, exasperated at my persistence. "I've told you, Shandon! This trip is one that a man must take by himself."

It seemed to me that he was telling me that he had other things to do beside attending to my affairs. Mortified at having asked him, I froze up.

"So long, bub."

"I'm sorry you can't understand." Golias caught at me as I turned away. "Wait. I've promised to help Tyl out with a deal he's cooked up, but if he doesn't land me in jail, I'll pick you up somewhere along the line, if it's possible."

I took the hand he offered as if it were slimy. "That will be fine," I told him.

My mood grew more sour as I went on. I had made shift for myself in the Commonwealth before, but only as a matter of accident. I had come to consider my partnership with Golias a pillar of existence. Now, inexplicably, he had walked out on me. At the outset amazement kept pace with indignation. It seemed incredible that our association should dissolve just after our fine triumph in pulling Jones out of his troubles. I myself had never felt the zest of good alliance more keenly than when we had stood together watching Lucius' wedding.

And now, for no cause, we were washed up. Other feelings made way for bitterness, as I remembered that when he had asked me to join him in assisting Jones—an utter stranger to me, be it noted—I hadn't failed him. But when I requested him to come along on a journey on which, by his own account, I would need all the help I could get, he had quit on me.

I cursed him for the way he had acted, and myself for caring. He had come to stand for integrity at any price, and now I had found he wasn't like that. The knowledge cheapened and rendered suspect everything I had discovered, or thought I had discovered in the Commonwealth. All my latent skepticism revived to jeer at me for letting myself be taken in. Yet if I writhed in a fury of shame at having been naive, I felt sad, too. The disillusion of the convert is a harder affliction than having no faith.

Because walking was the only outlet I had for working off steam, I kept on steadily, stopping only for a bite of lunch. Feeling as I did, I paid no more attention to such traffic as there was on the road than I did to the countryside through which it led me. When some sort of horse-drawn vehicle rolled up behind me about the middle of the afternoon, I merely gave it room without troubling to look at it.

"Stop the coach, please, driver," a feminine voice said. Even then I continued to face doggedly forward until the inmate of the carriage spoke again. "If you please, sir, can you tell me whether this is the way to Gotham?"

Unwillingly I halted. "You can't prove it by me." I waved my hand toward the descending sun. "All I know is that it's somewhere on the other side of the Titans."

Her small features were not especially pretty, but her face was made attractive by bright, intelligent eyes. They were giving me a going over.

"Excuse my curiosity, but are you out for the exercise?"

I knew why she asked that. Jones had given me one of Ravan's best outfits, a black velvet affair with silver trimmings, that made me appear very prosperous. Certainly I looked too well-dressed to be footing it on a dusty road.

"No," I grunted. "I'm just going from one place to another."

"Oh." Her voice was soft. "You're the kind of man who just goes from one place to another. it must be fun."

Starting to give an ironic rejoinder, I stopped as something clicked in my brain. Her eyes lowered when I stepped nearer, but a dimple winked at me. Then she met my look, and her own wasn't new to me. I had seen it on the faces of sundry girls I had known at home. It was the look of a woman who was too sharp an article to prize anything but her own impulses. In a moment my face wore its male counterpart, as it had not since the disastrous encounter with Circe.

"It can be a lot of fun with the right person," I said.

She seemed to consider that remark. "Would you think me forward if I offered you a ride? All this walking must have made you tired."

"No more forward than you'll find me as a rider," I volunteered. "and I'm not too tired."

That was the way it was with Becky Crawley. She wasn't the kind that bothered to take off her wedding ring when I entered her room at an inn that night. When I left early the next morning, she merely grinned sleepily and twiddled the fingers of one hand in farewell.

Everything between us was therefore easy, natural, and perfectly understood. But if there was none of the grief that had unsettled me after the loss of Rosalette, and none of the wild passion which had undone me with Nimue, there was also none of the ecstasy I had known with those two. One night of matter-of-fact lust was enough at a time. I saw Mrs. Crawley too clearly to wish further relations. To make sure she would not again catch up with me, I turned off the highway at the first fork in the road after leaving the inn.

Just the same, meeting someone who viewed human relationships with such a casual eye calmed me. I lost some of my indignation toward Golias. He had simply used me when he wanted me and discarded me when I was no longer useful to him. That was the way I myself had always acted. That was what I had always recognized, except for my recent period of mental aberration, as the normal in conduct. All I had to do to get my feet on the ground again was to cleanse my mind of irrationality.

Ever since I had left the causeway to Castle Nigramous the road had climbed steadily. By noon I could see ridges that I took to be the foothills of the Titans. About the same time my progress was halted by a canal. The bridge which had once spanned it had been down for years. Irritated rather than concerned, I looked around.

All day the scenery had been dull. Here it was downright silly. That is a state which can only exist with man's help. I was reminded of some of the broken-down rural stretches near Chicago. There were drab farms which looked as if nothing could be or ever had been raised on them. There were scattered houses, but no explanation of why anybody chose to live there or how they found it possible. Autumn had faded the leaves on the few, blighted trees instead of changing them. As a crowning touch, a sign on one scrofulous field bore the warning: "Hunters and trappers will be prosecuted."

The canal still looked usable, though the water was scummy. Off north to my right there was nothing on it for as far as I could see. To the south, however, something caught my eye. It turned out to be a mule-drawn canal barge, moving toward me.

Notwithstanding the countryside and their means of conveyance, the passengers were getting a lot of excitement out of their trip. They were shouting and laughing, pointing and gesticulating as they approached. Their appearance was as wild, I saw when they got close, as their voices and actions. Even their mules were wall-eyed and unkempt.

Because the animals were using the tow path on my side of the canal, I withdrew to give them passage. When I stepped forward again to hail the barge, more than half of it had already passed me. Folding my arms, I waited until the vessel showed me her square stern. The paint was peeling, but I could make out her name and home port. She was the *Menippus* out of Narragonia.

"Ahoy, *Menippus*!" I called out, much more loudly than was needful. Because most of the passengers were intent on something or someone on the other side of the boat, none aboard had so far noticed me. My shout changed this situation. Nearly all of them—and there must have been several dozen—turned to peer at me. Simultaneously they began to laugh, and some pointed to let me be sure I was the object of their derision.

"There's one!"

"Somebody tell the skipper."

"Where's Lorel?"

"Hey, stop the boat until the skipper's had a laugh, too."

That injunction was unnecessary, because the driver had turned to grin, and the mules had halted without being told. The result was that everyone could examine me at leisure; and I had the choice of standing my ground in the face of their mirth or of retreating out of eye and ear range. Not pleased by either alternative, I stood glaring at them. They were too numerous to assault and too noisy to allow me a come-back.

My wrath, thus short-circuited, was just about to blow a fuse when a diversion was created. A man emerged from the cabin and looked at the driver.

"Who told you to stop the ship?" he demanded.

"I did," a half-dozen passengers promptly announced.

"Sure they did skipper," the driver said, "but the mules got more influence when you come right down to it. They stopped when I turned to look at that one." Here he pointed to me.

The skipper, a gangling, horse-faced fellow, turned his gaze my way. Instantly he chuckled.

"That's the one, all right."

At that the top came off my restraint. In a few strides I caught up with the boat.

"What the hell are you talking about?" I snarled, growing more enraged when they all yelled with delight. "One what?"

He was unmoved by my fury. "What," he wondered, "would you say you were yourself, if you had a guess?"

If there was a way out of this ridiculous position into which he had euchred me, I couldn't find it while I was in a bad temper. Having no good answer, I settled for one I couldn't lose too much on.

"Just a guy, like you."

"Proud of it?"

He had left me a small opening, but I didn't have the heart to take it. His sardonic words, and his even more sardonic eye rubbed my raw grief. Nevertheless, I didn't feel like giving him the satisfaction of knowing he had scored.

"Oh, I'm doing all right."

"Named Ananias as well as Simon," he commented. "Lorel's my handle—C. Lorel, shipmaster and connoisseur of my fellow idiots. You look to me like a collector's item. Jump aboard, if you like."

I hesitated. Although this crew had got my hackles up, I was in need of guidance or at least a means of getting across the canal without plunging into the foul water which filled it.

"Where are you going?" I temporized. Then as I caught the gleam in his eye, I added hastily: "I know—where the canal goes; but would it take me anywhere near Usher's Tarn, say?"

"What difference does it make?" he wanted to know. "You won't find any friends no matter which way you head."

There he stuck his finger right in my new sore. At the same time the jauntiness with which he voiced the truth served as cauterization.

"You've got something there," I agreed, "but I'm looking for a place not a person." In spite of making the effort, I couldn't speak with conviction. "I've got a project."

"Oh," he said, pursing his lips. "There's something you want to accomplish. Think it will make you feel any better?"

"Of course."

"Up anchor and shake out every stitch of canvas!" he roared. "And while you're at it, hit those mules a lick. Here's a man with big things to do, and we're in his way."

Everybody laughed, but I didn't much mind, because I found myself joining them. Captain Lorel grinned over his shoulder.

"Put her in the wind and whoa!" he shouted. "I'm willing to admit you could walk faster than we can bully these mules into doing," he remarked when I had caught up again, "but what's the use in it?"

My only assurance that the road I had chosen was taking me toward my ordained goal was that I had found it possible to follow it. It now occurred to me that I might be able to outsmart Delian. If I couldn't walk except on the way to Hippocrene, perhaps I could ride on a divergent course. Then once I had broken the hex, maybe I could find a way to get out of this country that no longer appealed to me.

"No sense in it that I can see," as I jumped aboard.

He grabbed my arm to steady me. "Hope you didn't jar yourself when you came down from that high horse. Of course, it sometimes operates to get the gas out of you."

"Bet it wouldn't work in your case." This fellow wasn't bothering me any longer, and I wanted to let him know. "As for the nag you mentioned, there's no sense in riding where there's no purse."

"Talk 'em into starting up again," Lorel ordered

the driver. Then he shook his head at me. "If you know that much, I shouldn't expose my self-hypnotized innocents to your corrosive influence; but, anyhow, come up on my quarterdeck. As a newcomer, you have a right to examine the passenger list."

His quarterdeck turned out to be a small platform at the stern, which enabled him to oversee the boat, watch the progress of the mules, and look on down the canal. Mounting to this eminence, we seated outselves, dangling our legs.

"What's your set-up here?" I asked.

"Let's speak low, so as not to distrub the harmony of this cruise," he cautioned me. "You see, everybody aboard is a one hundred percent by volume, habitual, congenital, and non-convertible damned fool. And the best part of it is that although each ascribes that character to all the others, there's not a one of them who knows it's true of himself."

"Uh-huh." While not doubting that he was probing me for weak spots, I was beginning to get a brittle pleasure out of his company. I surveyed my fellow passengers. Four or five were playing cards. There were a few solitaries whose jaws worked in audible self-communion. The majority, however, were in groups of enthusiastic arguers.

"Are you going any place in particular?"

"Is anybody?" he countered. "No, we're just traveling through the country to study the fatheadedness of mankind. We really wouldn't have to budge, being loaded to the gunwales with it; but a traveled fathead is always convinced he's learned something." He sucked the flavor of his joke through his teeth. "Good, isn't it?"

I chuckled, hoping he wouldn't sense that up to

the day before I had been preening myself on my
own recent travels. Now with a man who spoke
my old language, I knew again that wisdom lay
only in clear eyes to recognize inanity.

"What do you get out of it besides fun?"

"They pay me!" He was so pleased with himself
he could hardly whisper. "They pony up hard
cash to be able to crawl under my microscope."

"I haven't got the fare and wouldn't pay it if I
had," I warned him. Not that I was actually broke,
but I wanted to show him I was not to be classed
with the others.

"Remind me to have you put in irons later. But
right now I feel I can afford the luxury of having
somebody to exhibit my specimens to." His eyes
ranged over the boat. "I love 'em all; but my favo-
rites are the rascals who'd swear up and down—
and believe it—that they're honest men."

It is always entertaining to see other people
making themselves ridiculous. "Which ones, for
instance?"

"Do you see that bearded old cluck bending the
ears of the card players? Never can think of his
name. I call him the cloud rooster, because he's
always in a high fog. He isn't kibitzing, as you
might think; he's just found some poor devils that
can't get away from him without busting up their
game."

I observed the wagging beard and the resigned
looks of the players. "What's he talking about?"

"Some rigmarole about just pleas and unjust
pleas if he's in form. He's a pistol. His specialty is
giving ethical advice that'll get you hanged if you
follow it. He's a social asset in the same degree as a
coral snake whose tail has just been stepped on,

but it's his positive conviction that he was delegated by Heaven to coach suffering humanity.

"Take Cave Burton, the one who's dealing," the skipper went on, after he'd paused to laugh. "The reason he's so glum, in spite of having won about all the money in the game, is that he's found somebody who can outjaw him; and that never happened before. Now if you were to ask him his status, he'd tell you he was a lawyer, although he has no comprehension either of the philosophy or jurisprudence or the mathematics of justice. Cave's walking proof that a man can be conscientious without having a conscience. Feed him a case, he gives all he's got, opening his mouth in the blind trust that either wiliness or wisdom—he doesn't much care which and couldn't distinguish between them—is bound to come out."

"And what does come out?" I asked with malicious anticipation.

"Meaningless noise and stale air—the same things you'd expect if the wind blew out of any other cave." Lorel nudged me. "There's one of my jewels, just coming out of the cabin. The one reading."

As this was the first book I had seen reaching the Commonwealth, I stared with some curiosity. "What's his racket?"

Instead of answering the skipper nudged me again. "See him bump into those fellows? That isn't put on. Bayes really doesn't know where he's going or what he's doing."

"You mean to say he can't read that book he's goggling at?"

"It's better than that," Lorel chortled. "He's that gem of jackasses, the scholarly illiterate. When he gets through that book, he'll be able to tell you every word in it without having the least idea what any two of them mean together. He eats books, and all that is left in his mind is what is left after the consumption of any other food—a shapeless crap that gives no clue to the structure, color, and life it once possessed. Funnier yet, he thinks he's a maker."

I had heard Golias use the term, and because it reminded me of him, my mind growled. "You mean he's a dope of a poet?"

"Never for an instant! To be even a rotten apple it is necessary to be the fruit of the apple tree. A puff ball can't qualify. Yet as he looks up from a page he doesn't comprehend and stares vacuously into space. Bayes thinks the soul he hasn't got is in a turmoil of creative frenzy.

"In some ways," the skipper continued while I was still chuckling, "I get more of a bang out of him than I do out of any of the others, though I've picked up a few who are of less account."

"That's hard to believe."

"Wait a minute, and I'll point one out. There." He flicked a finger to guide my eyes. "That fellow hunched up on a corner of the cabin roof."

"The pretty boy—the one who looks like a gigolo?"

"Naevolus is only a part-time gigolo," Lorel said. "Other times he's a pimp, a pandar, and a go-between. He has a fee for getting the young wives of old men pregnant, so the gaffers can brag to the world that they've still got what it takes. He has another price for keeping mum about it."

"It doesn't sound so funny to me," I pointed out.

"I haven't come to the funny part. The punch line is that the reason he's sulking is that he isn't admired for his talents. According to his way of thinking, he's a useful citizen—efficient, resourceful, and reliable—and he can't see why he's refused the standing given to other hard-working businessmen."

Lorel was laughing so hard by the time he had wheezed out the last sentence that he got cramps. "I've only collected one lower than that," he said, when he had caught his breath again. "I've been waiting till you could see him in action: the prissy barrow who's picking the pocket of the man behind him while he lectures the one he's got backed against the cabin. What would you figure he's sounding off about?"

"I pass, though he looks kind of like a deacon."

"Not a bad guess. Tartuffe is not only deacon, but vicar, canon, bishop, pope, and prophet of a religion whose only article of faith is that Tartuffe shan't have to work for a living. I'll give odds he's shaking that sucker down right now in the cause of holy charity. H. Charity is another name for Tartuffe; but he's acted his part so long he's forgotten he started out as a thief. Call him on it, and he'll jump back so that the lightning God sends to strike you dead won't salivate him, too."

XXIV

❦ Men and Horses ❦

CAPTAIN LOREL'S conversation not only fitted in
with my mood but outfitted my sense of humor
with shark's teeth. It flattered me to know that I
was the sole passenger whom he considered
worthy to be his confidant. From time to time, by
way of showing him he had made no mistake, I
gave him examples of my own bitter wit.

Sitting thus in mocking judgment, we dawdled
along the canal for some while. The scenery in the
meantime had changed without improving. Every
house had been reamed out by fire. The vegetation, such as it was, had also been seared by
flames. The trees held up no more tham stumps of
branches to a dull autumn sky. The few leaves
were shriveled. The men hanging from some of
the branches were, on the whole, in a better state
of preservation.

For a time we saw no live men, but eventually a
marching column appeared from behind a cluster
of burnt buildings and came slowly down the
other side of the canal. As long as the skipper
showed no concern, I wasn't going to, either.

"Do you figure this is part of the wrecking crew?"

"They're not near enough for me to see just what kind of fools they are yet," Lorel told me. "They're not all soldiers, though."

He was right. The fellow in front was carrying a crucifix much like the one Friar John had wielded so effectively. He and the men immediately behind him were dressed like John, too, being barefoot and wearing gunnysack gowns. In back of them was a squad of soldiers. Trailing them in turn was a chain gang, stark naked, marching double column. Bringing up the rear was another squad. The soldier wore helmets but not much armor and carried guns and spears.

Walking on the far towpath, they didn't have to swerve to avoid our mules. It appeared that they weren't going to pay any attention to us; but when their leader reached a point abreast of our bow, he shouted for a halt, planted his crucifix in the ground, and threw up one hand.

"Stop in the name of God and the Holy Inquisition!" he commanded.

"This vessel," Lorel told him, "only stops when those mules do, but I'll bring pressure to bear. See if you can have 'em whoa," he called to the driver.

By the time the mules had consented to oblige, we in the stern had drawn level with the cross bearer. In spite of his beggarly costume, I could see that he was a leader who was used to being taken seriously. Judging the skipper would have some fun with him, I lolled back, prepared to stick in my oar if I found a chance.

"Blessings on all there," the fellow now offered. "Who's in charge?"

"Blessings right back at you, and I am," the

captain said. "C. Lorel, master and owner of *Menippus* out of Narrgonia. Would you like to book passage?"

I nearly choked over that one, but the other didn't know he had been insulted. "No, thank you, my son; I simply want to know if you have any malefactors aboard."

Trying to guess what Lorel would answer to that, I looked away to conceal my amusement. "Why, yes," I heard the skipper say, "I've got one deadhead." His voice lost its sharp quality and became plaintive. "He won't pay his fare, father, though how he expects me to make a living when people take advantage of me that way, I'm sure I don't know, father."

Even when he put his hand on my shoulder, I wasn't able to grasp what was going on. "It seems to me, father, that that's stealing—just as much thievery as coming into a man's house and taking his money."

"It certainly is," the friar or whatever he was agreed. As he turned to signal to one of the soldiers, he had the satisfied look of a salesman who had just secured an order. "Take charge of the poor sinner, sergeant."

I was still befogged when soldiers strode over the gangplank gleefully furnished them by the other passengers. Lorel couldn't have meant to get rid of me, the one man who shared his wit and sanity among his boatload of fatuous doughheads. Because I insisted on arguing with facts, I made no effort to get away. It was only when several spearmen took rough hold of me that I fully understood that I had been betrayed.

As they started to drag me away, I made a

stunned appeal to Lorel. "But I thought we were
friends!"

He was still sniveling to the friar, but when he
turned to me his mouth was grinning beneath
crocodile-cold eyes. "Your chief trouble seems to
be that you always think wrong. For example, you
thought you weren't a fool."

He was having a tough time to keep from laughing outright. I tried to get at him, and one of the
soldiers slugged me. The next minute I was
hoisted over the side and shoved down the
gangplank.

"Tell those damned mules we have a fair
wind!" I heard Lorel shout.

The boat was already moving down the canal
when I stood before the man who bore the
crucifix. The only difference between the hard-
ness of his expression and the one worn by the
skipper was that it was unamused. Already furious, I hated him on the instant and let him see it.

"My son," he said, when we had taken stock of
each other, "do you believe in God?"

"My father," I answered him, "not when I look
at you."

I considered that a pretty smart crack until one
of the soldiers walloped me over the head with the
butt end of his spear. I thought for a minute I was
going out. While I was trying to pull myself together, I heard the friar speaking.

"Infidelity and malfeasance. Only the Inquisition can deal competently with such cases. Attend to him, sergeant."

I was attended to. They started to peel me, and
when I resisted, they got rough. I was battered into
senselessness, and when I came to they were

whipping me to make me get up. After a while the pain of the lashes forced me from my stupor. Naked and bleeding, I rose and staggered away from the punishment. They guided me with whips to the end of the chain gang, then jerked me into position. The prisoners were in pairs with the exception of a singleton bringing up the rear. In a moment I was handcuffed to him and shackled to the fellow in front of me.

"All right," the seargant snarled, "you bastards get moving and start singing 'Praise God from Whom All Blessings Flow.' "

We were singing it for the third or fourth time when we turned off the towpath into a road. As I shuffled painfully by, I glanced up at a signpost. My eyes were so blurred with sweat I couldn't read the legend at first, but after a second I made it out: "To the Dark Tower."

"A nice day, isn't it?"

It was a moment before I realized that the man beside me, a plump little elderly chap, had spoken the words. They had used the whips on him, too; and he had been in chains longer than I, as his scabbed wrists and ankles showed. Yet he was smiling as if he had just uttered some sensible commonplace. The rest went on singing, and under cover of their noise I felt free to answer him.

"What college of nuts gave you a degree?"

He beamed at me. "Why it's true that I'm a scholar, albeit not a graduate of the university you mentioned."

I couldn't make out who was pulling whose leg, though he looked to be in earnest. "Have you written in to the alumni association to tell them how you're doing?"

"Oh, being a philosopher, I can't do otherwise than well," he explained. "The very purpose of philosophy is to fit one to recognize and admire the wisdom and careful planning which have gone into the making of this, the best of all possible worlds."

I looked at the lifeless landscape, at the sorry remnants of man's building, at the men to whom we were chained, singing a song made idiotic because it was wrung from them by torture instead of joy. From these I glanced to the fellow beside me, stumbling along in wretched indignity. At the same time I felt the anklets grinding my naked flesh and the sweat running into the furrows cut into my body by lashes. In full comprehension of my degradation and helplessness, I gave a wild bark of laughter.

"So this is what you call the best of all possible worlds! I could could make a better one out of oyster eyes, skunk lice, and dog vomit. You son of a bitch!"

The last was a cry of pain and anger as a whip bit into my back. "Sing!" a soldier growled. And when I had caught my breath, I did sing. "Praise God from whom all blessings flow."

Progressing westward, and something north of west, I think, we reached the foot hills of the Titans the next day. That doesn't mean we traveled fast. Our chains prevented it, and the activities of our captors were an added hindrance. Sometimes we were halted so that a new prisoner could be added to our column of wretchedness. At other times the friars stopped to read prayers while the soldiers raped women whom they rewarded with evisceration. Then there would be further delay while the murderers confessed their sins and were lectured for their naughtiness.

We didn't get far into the hills, for the steep slopes got to us. The first two or three who fainted had to be dragged along by the rest of us; but when half a dozen were down, the friars called a halt for the night. Having had only a little over a day of it, I was in better shape than most of the others, or in no worse than a partial state of collapse. I was therefore one of those detailed to help make camp.

When they unhitched me from Pangloss, the little jigger who was my chain-mate, I thought he was unconscious; but he opened his eyes to smile feebly. "It'll be nice to sleep stretched out under the trees in the bracing air of these hills, won't it?"

"Go to the Devil!" I said, wishing my irons would let me kick him.

We were bivouacked in a grove a hundred yards or so from the gully whence we drew our water. As cook's water boy, I was herded to the stream by the soldier who had been appointed my keeper. The chain linking my handcuffs was so short that I could not let the two buckets hang at my sides. Empty, they could be held in front of me, but it was manifestly impossible for me to carry them full in that position.

"What do you want?" I said to my guard. "Would you rather have me chained, or are you going to carry them yourself?"

"I never handled this detail before, but it's a cinch I ain't going to do your work for you." He considered a moment. "Turn around and hold your wrists in close to you."

Reaching from behind, he had to work with one hand, fumbling at a lock rusted by the sweat and

blood of the poor chaps who had worn the handcuffs before me. At length he had to peer around
my shoulder to see what he was doing; and it was
then I whirled and crossed my wrists behind his
neck.

The cry he gave was a poor thing even for a
squeak, for the chain crushed his Adam's apple.
He beat at me, but I held him too close to permit
any damaging punches. Holding him so, I
watched him die with contemptuous detachment.
I did not think enough of him—or of myself—to
hate him. To me he was like a cockroach in the
kitchen: something that had to be destroyed before I could go about my own business of messing
up the place.

His death would mean that I might escape from
these vicious fanatics. Of course, I would be glad
to get away from them; but all the same I didn't
feel any upsurge of joy when I picked up the keys
from beside his lifeless body to unlock my mana-
cles and shackles. My feelings were more those of
a suicide, escaping from something unbearable
with no guarantee that worse wasn't waiting.

Confident that the friars and soldiers, lacking
dogs, would not be able to track me, I took to the
woods beyond the stream. The lateness of the day
was in my favor where pursuit was concerned. It
was dark by the time I had reached the crest of the
next hill and dipped down into the valley on the
other side.

By that time I had left one set of fears pretty well
behind. New ones took over. As I had not dared to
wait to take the clothes of the man I had slain, I
was naked in a country which the warmth of day
had deserted. It was fall in the hills, and even that

far south there might be a frost. There might also
be other things. I had taken my victim's spear, but
it wouldn't be much good to me against an attack
in the dark.

That night I lived as a brute whose only hope
was to see the sun again; and when it rose, I was
too miserable to be glad. I had only escaped freez-
ing to death by keeping in motion. Long before
morning I had sickened from hunger, weariness,
and exposure. I had stubbed the toes of my road-
broken feet, and branches and brambles had
found the whip scars on my legs. In stumbling
across a stretch of bog I had lost my spear. When it
happened, I was too far gone to care.

Just after sunrise I came out into open country
between the foothills and the Titans themselves.
There was grazing land, but what took my eye was
a field, with what I thought to be ripe wheat ears
showing above the rail fence around it. It turned
out to be oats, but I didn't care. The raw grain was
the first edible thing I had found since noon of the
day before. I commenced stripping the stalks and
cramming the stuff into my mouth, chaff and all.

It took a while to make a meal of such provender, but I stuck at it. As soon as the sun got high
enough to suck the chill out of me, I planned to lie
out in it and sleep. After that—well, my mind
wasn't capable of thinking beyond the next clump
of oats.

Weariness, in fact, had so numbed my faculties
that I didn't hear anything until I felt myself
shoved from behind. "Hey!" a voice said. "Get out
of that, you blasted Yahoo!"

In the state of my mind it didn't astonish me to
turn and find a large, dapple-gray horse. The im-

portant thing was that I had been pushed and
roughly addressed.

"Who the hell are you calling a Yahoo?" I demanded. Then I noticed two other nags bearing
down on me. "G'wan, beat it!" I ordered them.

My words had no effect. The beast who had first
addressed me reached out with a foreleg and got a
grip on my wrist. Meanwhile the others closed
in.

"A typical Yahoo trick," one of them grumbled.
"He's eaten just enough from every ear to spoil it
for anybody else. Is he one of ours?"

About then it really came home to me that those
horses were using words. Moreover, other things
were going on which didn't belong to the normal
order. The horse was supposed to be a domesticated animal, prone to take instructions from
man. These three did not seem to be aware of the
fact. Their attitude was rather that of policemen
who have cornered a petty thief. The whole business was upsetting, and I checked my impulse to
shout at them. They wouldn't obey me, and I
could think of no reason why animals so much
bigger and stronger than I should do so. I stared at
them uneasily as they examined me.

"You know, I could have sworn he actually said
words when I sneaked up behind him," the one
that had hold of me remarked.

"You better get the wax out of your ears," the
sorrel standing to my left advised. "I don't recognize the critter, do you?"

"He's some runaway," the black nag on my
right stated. "The boss won't let us really take the
leather to our Yahoos, though God knows most of
them've got it coming to them most of the time.

Whoever gave this one a lacing knew how to chop meat."

"Yeah, and look at his feet and the way his legs've been scratched up. He come through the woods all right."

"What do you suppose we ought to do with him?" the gray asked.

"If I had my way, we'd work him over until he got religion," the sorrel responded, "but you know the boss. He'll want to do everything legal and give him back unharmed to whoever the thing belongs to."

"Well, let's take him to the house and get it over with." The gray turned me around and rapped me on the prat. "Giddap!" he commanded.

I looked around wildly at my captors. It simply wasn't possible that I was being pushed around by horses. But I was. When the sorrel and the black sidled toward me, baring their teeth, I moved forward.

My wrath was my only comfort in my humiliation. Maybe I didn't know how to manage animals—hell, I hadn't spent my life wading around in manure—but wait till I met the man who owned these brutes. By Jesus, he'd hear something that would make him wish he didn't have ears. And if he didn't like it, I'd mop up the barnyard with him, beat out as I was.

Almost out of my head with fatigue, pain, shame, and rage, I gave insufficient thought to the most notable fact about my captors. It was undeniable that these horses talked. Aside from that idiosyncrasy, though, there was nothing to distinguish them from the normal run of domesticated hay burners. I was thoroughly unprepared, therefore, when those nags choused me to a mas-

sive log dwelling. It seemed strange to find a
white horse taking his ease on the verandah, but I
was still waiting for a man to step outside when
the gray spoke.

"Boss, we found this Yahoo scrabbling in that
field of second-crop oats we was just getting ready
to harvest."

"He don't belong to us," the black volunteered.
"We think he come from some spread on the other
side of the woods."

The sorrel chuckled. "Jake here thinks he heard
it talk."

The words gave my dumbfounded mind something to brace on. "God damn it, I can talk better
than you can!" I glared at the white horse. "Better
than you, too."

This outburst drew startled exclamations from
my three captors. The one they called Boss, however, didn't lose his look of polite detachment.

"Most interesting," he decided, after gazing at
me thoughtfully. "Now where did a Yahoo acquire the gift of speech?"

Suddenly it became all too much for me, and I
lost control of myself. "Quit calling me a Yahoo!"
I shouted. "I'm a man!"

Unperturbed, he considered that statement. "It
is true that Yahoo is our own name for you: we
have never hitherto known what you call yourselves. Yahoo=Man. Man=Yahoo. It doesn't
make any difference, of course. Things equal to
the same thing are equal to each other."

"They're not!" I shrieked. "That is, who cares
what a bunch of dumb animals think, anyhow?
Horses don't run men. Men own horses, and tell
'em what to do, and beat the devil out of them if
they don't toe the mark."

The sorrel gave a raucous laugh, and even Boss looked amused. "Really? And is it your intention to tell us what to do?"

"I don't want anything to do with you," I blustered. "But I could if I wanted to. It's the way things work. It's only right for men to—to order horses around."

"Shut up!" the gray commanded.

"No, let him speak," the white nag said. "I've often wondered what lay below the muddy depths of a Yahoo's—excuse me—a Man's intelligence." He stared at me with good-humored interest. "And just why is it right for men to direct horses? Do you think that they conduct themselves so nobly as to fit them to be the guardians and guides of others?"

In an effort to answer him in a convincing fashion my mind quieted dreadfully. What, in truth, had the world of men to boast of that I could be eloquent as its champion? Typical was the chicanery that had left me naked, browbeaten, and humbled. Typical also was the arrogant self-righteousness that had left me a patchwork of scars.

So I had no answer as those horses looked at me, the white one with kindly contempt, the other three with open derision. After a little I passed my hand wearily in front of my eyes. Now that I no longer had anger to sustain me, I felt that I couldn't stand. My knees began to give, and I swayed.

"We might have known it," the sorrel jeered. "Trying to think is more than any stinker of a Yahoo can take."

"Possibly he deserved it," the white nag said, "but he has patently been misused. You'd better tie him up, so he won't scratch or bite while you doctor those sores; then put him in a box stall, so the others won't bother him. Keep him on bran and milk for today anyhow. Meanwhile I'll try to find out who his owner is."

"Let's go," the sorrel said, "as long as you're smart enough to talk language. And if you try to make a break for it, I'll kick you into the afternoon of next Thursday."

A road ran between the house and the barns. As I started to stagger across it, the gray pulled me back.

"Watch it!" he said. "Can't you hear that wagon?"

I wasn't interested enough to look toward the vehicle. A sign, however, caught my attention as we halted. I had to blink away the lights that were dancing in front of my eyes before I could read it. "To the Dark Tower," it said.

My mind had hardly absorbed that message when the wagon drew abreast of us. Aghast, I glanced from the horse which held the reins to the several teams he controlled. Although they were digging in on all fours, and although they were shaggy and brutish looking, these were men I was looking at. No, not all men, either. The pendant breasts of at least two of them told me that there were women in harness also.

"A likely looking turn-out," the black commented.

Something had to give to make room for the horror which suffused me. For a moment I thought it would be my reason, or even life itself; but it was only my stomach. With a great sob I vomited.

"Trust a Yahoo to make a mess," the gray said.

He steadied me as I began to collapse. "Take hold; we'll have to carry the varmint."

My sanity stayed with me the first forty-eight hours largely because I was in a feverish daze most of the time. My conditions saved me from being given the carrion on which the nags fed the others humans in their keeping. It also spared me association with the latter, though I could smell them and could hear them shrieking and snarling.

But the immediate degradation wasn't the hardest thing to bear. The cancer which ate my mind, feverish or lucid, was the recollection of the moment when I had vainly tried to say a word for manhood. With Lorel I thought I had regained the armor of cynicism and the shield of being proud of it. In the clutch they had crumbled. I had longed to speak boldly for the moral strength and wisdom of my kind. Yet in the face of sneering enemies I had been crushed by my own silence.

Dreadful as my captivity was, I nevertheless needed the enforced rest. The grease the gray horse applied to my welts was healing and prevented infection. The milk and bran they gave me, while not the food I would order, turned out to be nourishing. When the fever left me I played possum for one more day, so I could get my strength back. That night I meant to get out of there.

Like the box stalls in most stables, mine, I had observed when they came in to tend to me, had a door which was held shut by only a pivot latch. The mechanical knowledge of the men they called Yahoos must have been limited indeed for this to be an effective restraint. Once I was ready to leave, it did not hold me five minutes. Working like the primitive animal those nags took me to be, I chewed a sizeable sliver from the sill of the small air vent. Then I thrust this between the door and the jamb and worked it up until it came in contact with the latch.

The Yahoos, luckily not nocturnal, slept solidly and noisily in their stanchions. I found the stable door locked, but I remembered enough about boyhood romps in barns not to be discouraged. After a while I located the ladder to the hay loft. I ascended and in due course felt my way to what I was searching for. Unlike the one below, the door to the loft was fastened on the inside. Lifting the bar from its brackets, I pushed and peered out. Seeing nothing to alarm me, I lowered myself as fast as I could and dropped to the soft mud of the barnyard.

I knew where I was going. There was only one bearing left to me in the Commonwealth—or in the world, for that matter. The sign showing the way to the Dark Tower had pointed left down the highway. It was easy to find the road, a ribbon of lesser darkness twisting away under the stars. Once on it, I fled.

When my wind gave out, I still pushed myself as hard as my strength would allow, although confident I was safe from pursuit. It was not that I wanted to get to the unimaginable tower as such. Instinctively I dreaded the place. And yet it had come to represent a sanctuary from even more appalling evils. It offered me a possible toe-hold in chaos, for the simple but all-powerful reason that I could conceive of no other.

XXV

❧ A Guide of Sorts ❧

WITHIN AN HOUR the road started to wind up into the
Titans. A cold wind nagged me, once I was clear
of the valley, and I was glad to wrap myself in the
stinking Yahoo blanket with which the gray always covered me at sunset. Before the sun rose
again I was over a shoulder of the first mountain,
crossing a gulley-chewed plain. Daylight showed
me that I was on a mesa covered with bunch grass,
tumble weeds, and spiny shrubbery.

It seemed to me that educated nags, such as the
ones which had held me captive, would find the
foraging too rough for them here. Nevertheless,
when I saw some on the horizon, I approached
with caution.

Having reached a vantage point, I surveyed a
ravine containing that treasure of an arid country,
a large spring. It could have watered, I should say,
a considerable herd of stock. No cattle were drinking there, however, and the ones I could see
would not do so again. Even the buzzards had got
tired of them.

The buildings of what must have once been a prosperous ranch looked much like skeletons, too. Some were roofless, and the adobe was melting. Part of the ranch house itself had caved in, although the section from which smoke was rising looked dismally habitable. If I hadn't been so hungry, I would have visited the spring only. Being starved, I next followed the weed-smothered path to the residence.

When I had knocked a few times, a voice told me to enter. A bearded man in a loin cloth was hugging a fire at one side of a large room. The fireplace was without a chimney, leaving the smoke to find its way out of a hole in the roof. Windows opening on a patio were the principal sources of light in the room, which was scantily furnished.

After a minute the man slowly twisted his neck so he could look at me. My eyes had become accustomed to the dimness of the interior, and I was scarcely able to repress a gasp. Above the beard his face was a mass of boils. Next I saw almost every visible inch of him was tortured by the same affliction.

"Good morning," I said, when he failed to greet me.

"Maybe for you," he replied.

There was no use in explaining to him that it wasn't. "I just came out of the valley, and this is the first place I've seen after walking all night. Would it be possible to get something to eat here?"

There was a sleepwalker's air about him, as he swayed back and forth, apparently thinking that over. "Yes, we still eat here, though I couldn't say why. Food will be brought to me here in a while, and you will be free to prolong your own existence, if you see fit."

"That's fine," I said, though he made it sound silly to eat. There was another seat by the fire, and I commandeered it. "It's cold outside this early in the day."

"That isn't much of a coat you have," he commented after his usual delay.

"No, but it's the best I've got." I thought talk had died there, but in a little while he pointed to a cape or cloak hanging from a peg on the wall. "You're welcome to that one of my son's."

"Thanks a lot," I said, adding as a matter of routine: "I hope he won't mind."

"There is little chance that he'll tell you about it," the fellow assured me in his dull, measured tones. "He's—all my sons are dead."

I was glad to be able to cover the gash in conversation left by that remark by reaching for the garment he had offered. It was a long camel's hair cloak, light and warm.

"This is great!" I said with a false heartiness I promptly wished I hadn't attempted. "By the way, my name's Shandon."

He left me hanging before he turned his disfigured face toward mine again. I wasn't ready for the anger in his hot eyes, though I knew instinctively it wasn't directed at me.

"Job," he said.

Forgetting about his boils I put out my hand, but he was already looking elsewhere. It was plain that he wasn't anxious for company, but I wasn't going away without that meal he had promised.

"Well," I said, "thanks again, Mr. Job."

"Just Job. The name is the one thing that hasn't been warped or taken from me." He didn't acknowledge my thanks, but he did a better thing. "I'll get you sandals before you leave," he declared, picking up a piece of wood to prod the fire with.

Watching him, I saw that his poker was not just a chunk of split kindling. It was a board. Part of it was burnt away, but there was printing on it. The letters were upside down, but having nothing else to do, I began spelling them out.

"The Dar—" was all that was left to be read. I sat up. "Was there 'tower' on that stick when you first saw it? Did it say 'The Dark Tower'?"

"Why yes, it did."

"Where was it," I persisted, "and which way was it pointing?"

"I found it nailed to an old cottonwood when I bought this place." He pointed a finger lumpy with boils in the direction of the road. "Then after the plague wiped out my herd and things started going to pieces, the poker somehow got lost, too. So we began using this signboard. Unlike the native wood of these parts, it's reasonably durable."

"But which way was it pointing?" I repeated.

He oriented himself, slow-motion. "Along an old trail that runs up the shoulder of that peak behind the house."

At that moment a dejected-looking woman came in with a bowl of stew. In response to Job's request she brought me a dish of it, as well as the pair of sandals he had offered.

"Have you ever been up that trail?" I asked when she had left us.

"No farther than my boundary, which ends half a mile above timber line." He sipped painfully. "I used to ride there pretty regularly when I had stock—and when I could ride."

I had too many troubles of my own to be concerned with his, but I thought I ought to show a bread-and-butter interest in his hard luck story. "You've sure been striking it tough," I said with a great show of sympathy, "haven't you, old timer?"

Once more I was aware of the barely checked anger in his eyes. "I'm merely experiencing the common misfortune of being alive."

It made no difference that I felt the same way. There is an idiotic streak in men that makes them want to encourage others to make the best of their circumstances, even though they claim the privilege of making the worst of their own.

"Oh," I said, "it can't be that bad."

At this, his passion broke loose. Glaring at me, he commenced speaking with such furious speed that a froth of saliva gathered at each corner of his mouth.

We are born, and we suffer until we go;
We live till we die, and that's all we know,
Neither what the purpose nor whose the game
To make us break us with pain and shame.
We are brought to a board where there's all we
    wish—
But the cook's gone mad and has fouled each
    dish:
We can plan and make; we can think and do—
But the prize is a husk, worm-eaten, too;
Our minds are a marvel, as all agree,

And our bodies as well, but the two don't gee,
So they live in a permanent tug of war,
To each the other a scab and a bore;
And we have two sexes, fashioned to mate
In the flesh so well, but their spirits hate,
So the joy of a body is no part
Of the soul's delight and dies in the heart
Of a gangrenous blight. Yet we plant the seed
For the force of our lust and callously breed
A brood to inherit our rotten lot
And to scorn and hate us, as why should they
    not
When we act the lunatic Judas goat
For the miserable get on whom we dote;
Though they are as silly and warped as we,
As doomed to despair and futility,
As bound to be robbed of whatever they crave,
As lucky in finally finding a grave.
But we blather to them what was blithered to us
And babble our praise of the barbarous,
So that they in turn can swindle their kith
With a pitiful, sniveling, coward's myth
Of the wisdom and plan behind it all.
"Sing praise and let the hosannas fall!"
Is the constant bellow of dupe to dupe,
The idiot maundering of the group,
All bleating their fables in coined belief—
But leave an adult to his knowledge and grief.

As quickly as he had flared up, he ceased to
flame. He returned to his food in such silence as
might be expected of a man in the death house.

I on my part had nothing further to say. Some of
the things he had said expressed the more or less
disconnected feelings and thoughts which had

dispirited me since leaving Castle Nigramous. But he had gone much further in his thinking; and in his tirade he had assembled the whole into an indictment which clarified my own case for me. At the base of my woe had been the realization that I had grown for half of my natural life without sinking any roots or putting forth any leaves—without finding a man or a woman who valued my society. Now I saw plainly that it was worse than that. It was not merely I alone who had nothing of value. Nothing worthwhile was obtainable under the terms of our being.

I had intended to ask Job to let me rest there a few hours; but sleep had become unthinkable. The only urge left to me was akin to the fascination that a man's own wounds and sores hold for him. I had to try to find the full dimensions of evil, and I was fatally sure I knew the place where it could be measured and plumbed.

My host had been paying no attention to me, but he looked up when I rose. "Do you still want to go there?" he asked, gesturing toward the charred signboard. "It won't do any good. You can't escape."

"I know." I spoke as quietly as he. "I'm just going toward something before it comes and gets me."

It was a hard pull climbing through the steep grazing land, the tall firs above it, and finally over the bare rock in the clouds on the crest. There I lost the trail, but down on the other side I picked up it or another one. This led me through a belt of scrub balsam, and thence through a hemlock forest to a road.

Emerging soon from the woods, I found myself

in a country of bleak vistas. The overcast sky had
the aspect of a natural attribute. Although it was
fairly warm, it did not appear possible that sunshine had ever softened that rugged region. Yet it
was a land which had once been settled. There
was hay dying on the stalk among the patches of
juniper and outcropping rocks with their dirty
lichen pelts. Some of the trees, leafless for the
season, and long past their prime, had obviously
been planted to throw shade. Now their rotting
branches hung over the holes in the ground which
were all that remained of what had once been
homes. Occasionally there was a fence of roughly
piled stones. What they had been built to keep out
was not clear. They hadn't kept out desolation.

Except that the country looked more and more
forbidding as the afternoon wore on, there was no
change in the state of things until sundown. Descending one of the ridges over which the road
humped on its way to the next range of Titans, I
saw I was approaching a crossroad. It would be a
misuse of words to say I hoped for anything, but I
thought I might find another sign there. When
this expectation was disappointed, I simply stood
where I was, gazing vacantly up and down the
highway.

My first intimation that I wasn't alone was a
curious sound behind me. Pulling myself together, I turned to see a man fitting to the region.
The peculiar noise which had startled me was the
sound of his crutch thudding and dragging in the
dust of the road.

In the habit of connecting tattered cripples with
beggars, I snapped at him as automatically as I
would have if he had intercepted me while I was

hustling along the Loop. "What do you want?"

His smile was unpleasant as my tone. "Maybe you'd better tell me what *you* want," he said in a rasping voice. "From the way you acted when you hit the intersection here, I'd say you were lost."

Everything about him irritated me, but as he might prove helpful, I made an effort to be civil. "Well, I didn't find any signpost."

He spat and shuffled his crutch. "Which way're you heading?"

A desire to thwart his curiosity was struggling with an anxiety to get my bearings. "I'm not sure of the direction," I temporized.

He hitched nearer and thrust a dirty face up toward mine. "You know where you want to go, don't you?"

"Naturally." My hand forced, and, resenting it, I paused. "I've got several places in mind," I said finally, "but the Dark Tower will do."

He gave a cackle of laughter. "Small fry with big ideas, eh? And what do you think you're going to do there?"

My fist clenched, then relaxed as I remembered his condition. "None of your damned business! Do you know where it is, or don't you?"

"Sure, I know." Not the least disconcerted by my anger, he continued to look at me with amused malice. "You mean the old place by the tarn."

I had thought he was lying to me, but at this sign that he knew what he was talking about, I cooled down. "Yes, that's it."

For a moment he scratched in the dust with his crutch, as if he was doing something mean that he enjoyed. "I asked him," he said then, looking up slyly, as if addressing some third party, "but I couldn't get an answer out of him."

"Oh, all right." Seeing that he knew as much as he seemed to, I was willing to find out what he could tell. "I don't know what I'm going to do at the tower myself. What I have to, I guess. Now do you know anything about a hole called Gnipa Cave?"

He looked down again, but his crutch didn't move. When he glanced up again, his eyes were fiercely intent.

"Are you going *there*—inside?"

For the moment the complexity of my problem was squeezing bad temper out of my mind. "I don't know that, either. Maybe I just have to touch base. You see, my ultimate goal is Hippocrene."

"Then it's in the cave for you," he said with a crispness his voice hadn't owned before, "but you'll never get in by yourself—not alive, at least."

He spoke with such certainty that I more than half-believed him. I lifted my hands from my sides and dropped them again.

"But I've got to go there."

"It's the only reason anyone does," he declared. "Look at me!"

With the words he let go of his crutch and straightened up. In that position he was taller than I, a lithe figure with a hard, confident face which no longer seemed dirty. Next he tossed away his tattered cloak to disclose a leather jacket belted over neat-fitting tights.

"I'm Faustopheles," he said, in answer to my stare of amazement, "and I'll take you to the tower and beyond—for a price."

"Of course, for a price." I shrugged, then gazed around while I tried to make up my mind. I wasn't sure I liked the fellow any better for his transfor-

mation, but I certainly needed some sort of guide.
Twilight had just so long to go before it was followed by a night such as only heavy clouds can
bring about. "What's your bargain?" I asked, turning back to where he was eyeing me alertly. "I
haven't any money."

"And I don't wish any," he said. "I'm going to
put it to you straight, because I don't want to
waste my time on you unless you mean business.
What I'm asking is a pledge I think you'll be afraid
to make."

Actually I felt beyond the fear of anything at
that moment, but my professional instincts made
me wary of being flim-flammed. I narrowed my
eyes.

"Unwrap it and let's take a look at it."

"Right. I want your word—and once you give it,
I'll see to it that you keep it—that you'll go where I
lead you if it's to the Abyss itself." He tapped me
on the shoulder, and a shock went through me.
"And just between you and me, it will be."

"Will where you lead me be on the way to the
place I want to go?" I pinned him down, when I
had thought his proposition over.

"As far on the way as I can go," he nodded, "and
the contract canceled the instant I deviate."

On the brink of decision, I did know doubt and
fear. But more compelling was the realization that
if I turned down his offer, I would have no idea
what to do or where to go.

"Done," I said, then with a feeble attempt at
humor: "Do you want it in writing?"

"In blood," he replied. "Hold that arm still!"

Before I knew what he was about, he had drawn
a knife and nicked a wrist I wasn't strong enough

to wrench from his grasp. Dipping a finger in the welling blood, he wrote something on the air.

"Come along," he then ordered, and I fell in step with him as he swung down the left-hand road.

If the country had looked forlorn before, it was now despair modeled in landscape. The trees we passed had an agonized throw to their branches, and their knots were so many eyes washed hollow by grief. Most disturbing of all was something I saw uphill and ahead of us. Even after I was sure it was merely the crossed trunks of two birch trees, it still looked like a naked man spread-eagled in pain.

Precisely at this birch formation a path left the road. Without troubling to warn me, Faustopheles switched into it.

"Don't trip over the skeletons, Silverlock."

I didn't ask how he had come to use the nickname Golias had once picked for me. As for his advice, it was good but inadequate. To my mind the whole district into which we now stepped was a skeleton which hadn't quite lost all its hide and hair.

The evening being oppressively warm for the season, I was sweating. Yet, possibly because Faustopheles willed it so, I did not experience hunger or weariness. He walked at a tremendous pace, and I kept a step behind him, losing ground only when I jibbed at fording a vile-looking stream. When I did plunge in at my guide's command, I was aghast to feel unknown objects stir in the slime beneath my feet.

"The inlet to Usher's Tarn," Faustopheles explained. "We'll see it in a minute."

We were almost on it before I did see it. The water of that rank pond didn't pick any light out of the dusk, as lakes usually do. I could guess at the shore line only by noting its broken fringe of trees. We stopped under one of them, a thing made monstrous in the half dark by the vines which were throttling it.

"There's your tower," Faustopheles said, and I found I had been looking at it without perceiving what it was.

I had been expecting something vaguely on the lines of the Washington Monument. What I saw was a dim, squat structure, whose top looked like it had been bashed in, rising above the mass of trees surrounding it. Its very simplicity of outline left you free to guess what it contained. Within limits my mind had no question though. That place might hold many things but never one that contributed to joy or confidence.

I would have spoken less airily than I did, but I was conscious that Faustopheles was watching me to see if I would wince. "Anybody live in that box?"

"That's debatable," he said.

There had been rumblings of unseasonal thunder when we approached the pond. As he led the way around its rim, the storm swooped near, then broke. For me that completed the darkness.

"Do you know where you're going?" I demanded, when my companion jeered at me for suggesting a halt until the rain had stopped.

"Yes. I've been there for a long time." There was a quality in his voice to match the strangeness of his phrase. "Put your hand on my shoulder if you can't see to follow."

How he himself could find the way I don't

know. My own eyes were no good to me except when the great jags of lightning cracked the night and whipped earthward. Then I could see the tarn and the structure toward which we were moving.

The tower, I eventually made sure, stood on a little island just off shore at the far end of the pond. A short bridge connected the isle with the mainland. That relieved me, for I felt I could never nerve myself to plunge into the foul-looking water even to achieve a goal and to find shelter. Of the two the latter had become temporarily the most important. It was not only the torrential rain. I had never been uneasy about storms before, but the lightning was hunting to kill. I saw one tree blasted and heard other crashes which meant that bolts had wrought destruction.

Then at last we were within a few yards of the bridge. The flash which slowed us that was unusually big; but it was just a pilot fish for the shark of a bolt that followed it. Hurtling out of the sky, it plunged directly at the tower.

There was a detonation at impact which deafened and blinded me. More frightening, however, was the shriek of a panic-stricken man. For a few seconds after my vision felt clear again I gazed helplessly into the blackness before a third flash came to my aid. There was no tower any longer, nor was that all I discovered. A wild runner, his features twisted and fixed by horror, was dashing over the bridge away from the ruin.

That was our only sight of him. The stunning roll of thunder made it futile to call out, and I don't believe he saw us. When the next flash came, he had vanished.

I couldn't decide whether he was better off to

be lonesome in his terror than I was to have company in mine. Faustopheles could either see my expression, the darkness notwithstanding, or he could read my mind. When the cloven welkin had rattled together again, I heard him chuckle.

"You asked me whether anybody lives there. I now feel in a position to tell you 'no.' "

"What are we going to do?" I asked, too shaken to take offense at his sarcasm.

"Cross the bridge."

It did not matter that neither motive which had once made me willing to do so was left to me. I was past thinking in logical terms. What did concern me was the face of the fleeing man we had seen. It had taken more than the threat of physical destruction to smear his features with a fear close to madness. There are disintegrations more dreadful than that of the tower; and a man who looked as he did had either seen them in others, sensed them in himself, or both. I loathed the idea of approaching the place where he had experienced—whatever it was—and hung back.

"We'd better not."

"Do you think I'll let you do what I did not do for myself?" A flash showed me his face, but even distorted by the rain, it was less harsh than usual; brooding rather. "Suppose I freed you of your oath: could you go back whence you came? I have reason to know you cannot."

Overcome by a sense of inevitability, I argued no more. "Well, if we're going, lead the way. Let's see if there's a shed or something left to give us shelter."

"The weather is the one thing you will be sheltered from," he told me.

We had stepped on and off the little bridge and had made some progress beyond it before another flash of lightning came. I then had a view of the rubble which was all that remained of the tower. There was scattered masonry on the ground; but most of it was below ground level, as if the structure had tumbled into some great hole beneath it.

"Even that disappeared when I tried to reach for it," I muttered.

Faustopheles said nothing until, a moment later, he halted me. "Face this way. No, a trifle more to the left. Now keep looking somewhat in front of your feet."

When the next flash came, I was staring at what had been one of the walls of the tower's cellar. A section of it had crumbled away when the building collapsed, disclosing the bedrock behind. In this rock there was a man-high opening under two lines of inscription. The light left us too swiftly for me to be able to read them, yet I thought I knew what I had seen.

"What did it say there?"

"The big line straight across," he answered, "says: 'Gnipa Cave—Beware of the Dog.' The smaller one hugging the opening reads: 'Abandon hope all ye who enter here.' "

My knees were trembling, but I managed to hold my voice steady. "I have no hope to abandon."

Because it is a fact, complete in its own identity, even a miserable conviction feels entitled to respect. He greeted this one with a bark of laughter.

"Liar!" he cried. "All men and devils have hope—even if it's only the hope they will cease to be. Hope is the meanest evidence of the infinite

genius for cruelty that is the hallmark of Heaven.
Imagine the devious will that can steep us in the
torture of our lives while at the same time craz-
ing us with an opiate which makes us believe that
another day may bring better fortune. Nothing
sensate is free from this insane affliction at any
waking hour. As for you, who know yourself to be
without anything that makes life supportable, you
yet at this instant hope you won't have to go into
that cave."

I didn't need light to see that entrance. That
hole in the rock might as well have been a hole in
my brain it was fixed there so firmly.

"Do I have to?" Amidst all that water my mouth
was dry. "Is it on the way?"

"You do, and it is."

"But where does it go to; what's inside it?"

"It leads to the poisoned core of creation,"
Faustopheles responded, "and nothing is ever
found in a worm-hole but worms and gall."

Yielding to blind panic, I was turning to run
when he gripped me above the elbow. The next
instant I was being jerked through the air. When
we alighted, the rain no longer beat down on me. I
was in the cave.

XXVI

❦ Into the Pit ❦

THE SLANTING FLOOR, steep as a woodchuck burrow,
gave me no chance to brace and balk. Faustopheles still clutched me, and I stumbled downward after him until, at a level spot in the earth's
midriff, he chose to halt.

If I had tried to run from an imagined danger,
fatalism stiffened my backbone when I found myself helpless to avoid the actuality. I shook off my
companion's hand.

"Keep your hooks off me," I snarled to counter-
balance the fright I had let him see. "I can make it
under my own power. And if you want to show
me what's here, don't piddle around like a man
waiting for the house to buy. Let's go, in the
Devil's name, and get it over with!"

"We will do that," he said. Then he shouted:
"Open and hold Garm in check!"

It was not until the doors swung back that I
knew of their existence. There was light behind, a
sort of luminous dusk. That was only the first

thing I noticed; not the most startling. When my eyes stopped blinking, they discovered that the bulk in the foreground was not a mound covered with blackened grass. It was heaving, in fact it was breathing; and having decided that much, I could see we were approaching the tail end of a colossal canine-like animal. "Beware of the dog," the inscription had advised. This one was twice the size of a bull whale.

I glanced sidewise at Faustopheles to find he was looking at me with amusement. "Don't worry; Garm's only loosed upon those going the other way—those trying to escape. His time hasn't come to face around yet."

We were giving the monster plenty of room, but I was holding myself ready to dodge if it made a sudden move. "Do you mean it's going to be stationed so as to keep people out of here instead of holding them in?"

"No," he said with sudden heat, "I mean that he'll face around to go forth himself, unchained and frantic to kill and destroy."

"My God!" I shuddered.

"There'll be no use in calling upon your god then," he cried. "Whoever he is, he won't be able to save himself on the day Garm and his mates leap up to snap the stars out of the sky and curdle the Milky Way with the slaver of their madness."

"But can't they keep him chained?" I didn't know or ask about Garm's associates; the sight of the terrible dog alone was enough to convince me of the possibilities. "Who will let it go, and who let it be raised in the first place?"

"Who?" My guide's face was as wildly savage as his prophecy. "Do you think corruption has no power to generate forces to avenge itself, or that they can be leashed forever? The bonds which arrogance has forged for them are daily being eaten by the acid suppurating from the rottenness of creation; and they'll be broken, I tell you, they'll be broken!"

We were soon passing under one of the enormous chains which restrained Garm, and I examined it. It was rusty, but it still looked reassuringly strong.

All the same I hurried a little. "Will mankind be destroyed?" I whispered.

"You can't bear the thought, no matter how detestable you find life to be, can you?" Faustopheles laughed. "Do you think that when the seats of Heaven crumple and gods are eaten, that the homunculi they put through their tricks like trained fleas—and crack like fleas when they are tired of them—will be preserved?"

It was as he had said. The thought of the non-existence of man was more awful than the contemplation of zero. My mind could hold the idea for only a moment before the fear of madness made me drop it and kick it out of sight. I put a hand to my head, which had started to throb because of the mere instant of aberration.

"It can't be!" I protested. "Some must be saved."

"Oh, you've heard that gossip, have you?" He had used up his mirth and was intent on the problem rather than on needling me. For a few paces he walked on in silence. "They do say that two whom even the dog won't eat will live to see a new dispensation," he then said harshly, "but I—"

A growl as loud as any thunder we had heard during the storm interrupted him. Glancing backward, I saw that we were far enough ahead of Garm to be in focus for the monster. His jaws, flashing teeth as tall as men, were open. There were screeches from grinding metal as he sprang to his feet and strained against his chains.

"He's just making noise. They won't let him bother you, as long as you're not trying to dodge the Pit," Faustopheles said.

His chance of comforting me was slight at best, but at that moment Garm gave out with a full-throated bay. The hot, stinking breath of it knocked me flat—but not for long. If ever a man bounced, I did, and when my feet were under me again, they really moved me. Off to the left the rock yielded a narrow passage. I picked it out and made for it as instinctively as a mouse makes for a crack in the woodwork.

"Stop it, you fool; he's not coming after you! Wait, I say!" Fast though I was running, Faustopheles caught me. He had recovered from his somber mood and grinned at me as I shamefacedly caught my breath. "If he was free, you could no more evade him than a scuttling bug can save itself from being stepped on. However, you were at least going in the right direction. Our way lies through that passage; but I feel it my duty to warn you that the region beyond is no place for headless-chicken running."

"Aw, quit being so damned full of wisdom," I retorted. "You're right; of course, you're right. I know reason and resignation are one and the same; but I'm going to forget it every time I'm threatened with doom, so get used to the idea."

"I've been used to it for a long time," he said
with one of his odd changes of pace.

Not sure whether the was talking about himself
or me, I didn't answer. We had reached the passageway, and I saw that it led to steps cut in the
rock. Spiraling downward and out of sight, they
were worn by the usage of years—centuries,
perhaps. Faustopheles led the way, and in the full
knowledge that retreat was impossible, I began
the descent.

The stairs were broad and cut at an easy grade.
My guide negotiated them swiftly, and I crowded
after him, unable to conceive what I would next
see. In the withdrawn state of my mind it was
difficult to judge depth and distance, but we must
have left thousands of steps behind us when we
came to a landing. At this point Faustopheles
halted.

"One of the few windows to the universe," he
said, as casually as if he were showing a stranger a
good view of Lake Michigan. "Have a look."

With the words he stepped from between me
and the opening to which he referred. It was an
embrasure three to four feet square cut through
the rock. I glanced out without being able to see
anything. Then bracing myself on the sill, I poked
my head forth and peered down.

Whatever the elements were up to at the spot
where we had entered the earth, there was no
darkness here, nor were there clouds or any other
impediment to the vision. That air was as clear as
distilled water, and I could see nothing. I
examined the emptiness above, straight ahead,
and to my left and right before I gazed down
again. My sight went so far in a vain quest for a

resting place that my eyes felt like they were being drawn out of my head. Next my body felt as if it was being sucked into the quicksands of space. Shakily I drew back.

"There's nothing down there!" I exclaimed, looking at Faustopheles as if it were all his fault. That I could see nothing in other directions didn't disturb me; but I was unnerved to find emptiness below, so it was of this fault that I complained. "An airplane flies over something, even if it's only a cloud or the rump side of a rainbow, but one couldn't find that much here. It—it just falls away."

"Forever and endlessly," he agreed. "It's the Void, you know."

I didn't know, but I calmed enough to want to confront this challenge to my reason. "The what?"

"The Void," he repeated, half broodingly and half in enjoyment of the shock he had given me. "You ought to become acquainted with it, being akin to it. Containing everything, it is the fosterer of all matter."

"Oh," I sniffed, "if you want to take the line that because air is around everything, it contains everything, why have an analogy on me. When the wind blows right the city of Chicago is contained in the stench of the stockyards."

He disdained to answer in kind. "This isn't air, though the seeds of air are in it. You say it holds nothing?"

There was an appalling lack of color about what he called the Void. "Hold anything!" I derided him. "It doesn't hold so much as a sliver of a sunbeam, let alone a fleck of dust."

"Nothing so big," he informed me, leaning on the sill as if he was considering visible objects. "Yet in it are suspended infinitesimal particles of all things. I said 'suspended,' but that is wrong. The first beginnings of matter drop through it faster than the imagination can span distance."

I hesitated before I felt convinced that I had run across something familiar. "Do you mean atoms?"

He twisted his head around at me, smiling sarcastically. "Why, as you heard, in my simple way I call them the first beginnings; but if you're on such familiar terms with them, use your influence to make some of them put in an appearance."

"You're the one who believes they're there."

"Put out your hand, and I'll show you why." I hugged the side of the embrasure and refrained from looking down. Yet, having learned that it was useless, I didn't struggle when he thrust my hand out, palm up. "Hold it there and watch," he ordered.

For a while I was conscious of nothing. Then I felt something like the beat of very fine rain drops. Somewhat later I made out a couple of motes scarcely less colorless than the Void itself.

"Stopped in flight by something solid, the first beginnings get together like monkeys," Faustopheles commented. "That's when they become visible. It's too early to see what you've got; but the nature of the result will be determined by the first element to get on the field in any quantity. They only pair and congregate with their own kind."

Interested in spite of myself, I kneeled so I could support my arm on the sill. The specks grew rapidly more numerous, but I don't want to give the impression that they stayed in my hand. Rather they performed dizzy maneuvers above it in the manner of gnats hovering over a pool of swamp water. They danced up and down and in out and, frequently colliding and bouncing free of each other again. Some, I noticed, were bumped clear of the throng. Falling outside the barrier of my hand, these vanished.

Meanwhile some of the motes were getting larger. Eventually one of them attained such comparative bulk that it grew sluggish, then settled in my palm. From then on the character of the maneuvers changed. In place of being like the war dance of gnats the action resembled the swarming of bees. The weeding out process still went on, but those which survived it flew in an increasingly denser whorl whose focal point was the grain of stuff in my hand. In time they had all merged to form a unit.

"If you live long enough, you see all there is." I spoke casually to conceal the awe I felt. While doing so, I examined the tiny accretion in my hand, which lay as inertly as if none of its parts had ever moved. "You wouldn't think that all those high jinks would go into the making of a lump of clay."

"Don't be scornful of it," Faustopheles warned me. "The seeds of your own being were once adrift in that same impersonal matrix. Yes, and those of your god or gods, too."

"Possibly," I conceded, "except for one thing."

"What's that?"

Because he sounded so challenging, I took the more pleasure in making him give ground. "Life," I said, tossing the pellet of clay away and wiggling my fingers for emphasis. "It's one formula that isn't in the chemistry book."

"You haven't studied the right text. I was satisfied until I did." He seemed to be remembering something he hated to when he made that remark, but in a moment he came out of it. "Wait a second," he said briskly, seating himself on the sill in a way I would never have dared to do, "and I'll see if I still have the touch."

I hadn't noticed what long fingers he had until he moved those of one hand through the Void, occasionally brushing the other four with his thumb. "I've got a couple of the right sort of first beginnings," he soon announced. "It won't be anything fancy, but we'll get something out of them."

The same kind of creative gyrations that had taken place over my palm then took place above his. The result was not inspiring in itself, but it was stunning to me. The microscopic sub-grub he submitted for my inspection was undoubtedly alive.

"So with this worm, and so with you," he said. "Gaze into the Void and call it mother."

"But that's an animal!" I protested. "You can't compare its life with that of a man."

"Can't I? I suppose you will say that other creatures have merely a spark of vitality, while man has a soul, hand-forged by deity, which can be slipped in and out of him like a knife with its sheath."

"Well," I said, embarrassed and troubled, "I don't know that I believe in a soul exactly."

"But you like to think that there's something so precious about you that the cosmos can't spare it. You know your body won't survive, but some-

thing tells you that your own private unit of life
will be picked in Time by the cherishing power
that made it." He nudged the Void with his elbow.
"This is your creator. Find love and warmth in
it if you can, for in the end you're going back
to it."

I looked backward up the steps leading cheer-
lessly to my past, then out at the bleakness which
stood for the future. Whether he takes the trouble
to reason about it or not, or whether he wants to
believe in it or not, it is the nature of man to think
there's a chance of escaping oblivion. The denial
of that chance did not stir my emotions, however.
I merely felt like someone, already destitute, who
discovers there's something else for him to lose.

"That's all there is to it?" I said quietly.

"Every bit of it." He stirred the little grub in his
right hand with a finger of the left. "If you want to
claim that the life in you is a soul, salute your
spiritual equal here; for the animating impulse
which sets you both in meaningless motion is one
and the same."

My shrug was honest evidence of the way I felt.
"Why tell me about it?"

"Why! Because once you understand that man
is no pet of uncaring divinity, you can appreciate
the absurdity of men's moral pretensions. How
they love them and strut beneath the burden!
Even those who lay claim to skepticism where
deity is concerned—they often more earnestly
than the rest, as though to make up for it—will ask
whether man is living up to his responsibilities
and will soberly use such phrases as 'the destiny
of man.' "

With a snap of his forefinger he launched the

grub into space. Thinking of that endless fall, I couldn't help wincing. He saw that and grinned.

"There's your destiny of man, and your responsibility is neither more nor less than that of the Void, which made you and will redistribute your dead particles, alike with fish-eyed indifference."

Not because I disbelieved him, but because he was enjoying himself where I could not, I glowered at him. "Is this what you brought me in the cave to see?"

"Only incidentally. You had to comprehend that humanity was created soulless before you could savor the irony of people whose chief affliction is the belief that they are spiritual beings." As abruptly as if I had been causing the delay rather than he, he grasped my arm once more. "It's time to see the citizenry of the Pit."

The countless stairs were the stairs of a jail; but in the grim fashion of prison architecture they offered security. Not so much could be said of the path at their foot. Without preamble it dipped over the rim and down the inside of a vast cylinder.

To envisage something of my unhappiness, it is necessary to envisage descending into a volcano by means of a trail carved sparingly from the stone lining. Ahead all I could see was the path coiled downward until it disappeared in smoke. From somewhere below there arose a confusion of noises. Some I was unable to identify, while others sounded like human shrieks and shouts.

Although I did not like standing on so narrow a ledge, I can luckily do such without losing control of my faculties. The Abyss in itself, possessing dimensions, was less terrifying than the Void. I studied it as well as the limited visibility would permit, then looked at Faustopheles. He in turn was watching me keenly.

"Do many people live down there?" Determined to give him as little satisfaction as possible, I spoke coolly.

"A good few."

"I can't say I blame them, but they don't seem to enjoy it."

His eyes clouded, and I could see that he was concerned with his own thoughts rather than mine. "They do not, Silverlock, but you can't blame it all on the accommodations. Put a halo on one of these; lap them in the sweet air of Elysium; let divine maidens serve them and love them—or if they themselves are women, let them be Houris or Valkyries; and still they would not be happy." His expression grew sardonic. "And do you know why that is?"

I wanted to be flippant, but couldn't quite manage it. "No."

"Because they wouldn't even know where they were. They don't know where they are now; and if you asked an inmate of the crowded dungeons we're about to visit, he would swear he was in solitary confinement. Can you give me the answer to that one?"

"No," I repeated.

"Because they've reached the dead end of being, which is to be able to think of nothing but oneself. Let's descend now."

Keeping a shoulder to the wall, I followed him as he circled downward. Soon I was breathing fumes; but my lungs seemed to have the power to digest them, for I didn't cough. Nor did my eyes water, in spite of the fact that the smoke was thick enough to be opaque at a moderate distance. It was this which prevented me from seeing how a vast loft had been cut into the rock until we were on a level with it.

Obeying my guide's gesture, I left the path and paused with him to look around. Not much of the smoke which billowed in the Abyss entered here, so I was able to see that what I witnessed close at hand was in mass production on a huge scale. The sight was such that I would have fled to escape it, but Faustopheles grabbed me. Sick with horror, I accompanied him.

Seated on each of the blocks of stone scattered at intervals throughout the place was a man or a woman. They sat with their heads in their hands, gazing at the floor and mumbling to themselves. Except when they were subjected to torture, that is. This was administered by one of a corps of demons, red and naked, tailed and horned. One would step behind a man, say, and begin drilling through the top of his head. The victim did not struggle, though he usually stopped mumbling and sat up, wide-armed and sightless. He would hold this mesmerized pose until his torturer removed the drill and poured something into the hole that had been made. Whatever it was, it had the effect of nitroglycerine on the door of a safe. It burst the lid of the skull, so that the four parts stood erect to display a red hot and pulsing brain. When this happened the victim screamed and commenced babbling some wild confessional. At its conclusion the top flaps of the brain pan would close and knit again. Then the sufferer would quiet and go on talking to himself.

I couldn't help continuing to show my dismay, and as usual this put Faustopheles into what with him passed for a good humor. "This is the roost for birds who have done something which makes no sense when viewed with the rest of their lives in mind, and which, by the same token, renders the rest of their lives senseless." He chuckled. "We'll pick one out and hear it sing."

At this callous proposal my repugnance became anger. "No!" I shouted. "No, damn you!"

Instead of taking offense, he snatched me to him and laughed in my face. "Listen, mannikin; I've been damned by an expert; and besides, you should never waste a curse on anything too big for it." After giving me that advice, he peered about. "This one here," he said, pointing to a lanky, handsome, young fellow seated on a nearby rock, "ought to serve our purpose as well as any."

Rather than be forced, I accompanied him, as he walked over and grabbed the youngster by the hair. "What's your name and what are you in for?" he demanded, jerking up the head, so that the fixed eyes could focus on him.

After a while they did. "You know me—all about me. You've talked with me before."

"Do you think I can keep you all straight? I can tell a pair of pants from a shirt, but aside from that you look as much alike as lice to me," Faustopheles told him. He gave the fellow a shake. "Why are you here?"

"But you're bound to remember me," the other protested. "Everybody knows, or suspects and soon will know. I'm an atrocious villain."

"You're a first-class braggart," Faustopheles stated. "Not many men have the consistency of purpose to be villains, and the gumption for it never lurked behind those stricken-doe eyes." He released the hair to let the head flop down again. "Wait a minute," he said to me, "and I'll see if I can get us some service."

I could see why he used the phrase. Nearby, engrossed in conversation, there was a gathering of demons, close cousin to a group of store clerks chewing the fat while the customers vainly waited.

"Who has charge of this case?" Faustopheles demanded.

Nobody paid any attention; and he suddenly roared, "I'm asking—I, Faustopheles!" Echoes picked up the tremendous voice, and the shrieks of the inmates were smothered by a rumbling "Stopheles, Stopheles." Before those syllables could be thrown back, however, the demons my guide had addressed had leaped to stand in front of him. They were trembling and black with fear.

"That's better," Faustopheles told them, after letting them sweat it out a minute. "All I want for the present is to have this fellow treated. Now!" he yelled, as they looked at the prisoner, then at each other.

They stumbled over one another, but finally cleared out to leave one of their number at work. There followed the noise of the drill biting into bone, the hiss as the liquid was poured from a phial, then the dreadful tearing as the sutures of the skull gave way. When they did so, the young man rose with a scream.

"I am Rodya Raskolnikov, a man of culture, a student of philosophy, heir apparent to the wisdom of the ages. That wisdom was to have been dedicated to the service of humanity, but all it led me to was the murder of an old woman for her money."

Faustopheles stifled a yawn. "I remember something of your case now. She was a cruel, miserly old bitch, wasn't she—a vile, packrat of a woman?"

"You know." Raskolnikov dropped his voice. "I was sure you did. But then you know, too, that her sister, whom I also killed, was none of these things. She was a poor, harmless creature, too witless to try to protect herself when I struck her down so that she could not report my guilt."

"That was only good sense," Faustopheles said. He gave me a confidential wink. "Would you like to ask him anything?"

Given the opening, I couldn't resist. A morbid interest in the details of any crime is part of the make-up of humanity.

"How much money did you get?"

"I don't know," the fellow answered me. "There was a purse, but afterwards I couldn't bring myself to look in it."

"What!" Faustopheles cried. "Murder to rob, and then not even bother to tot up the swag? I don't believe it!"

I myself was disappointed at such a tame and pointless end to burglary, but Raskolnikov had no interest in our reactions. "It wasn't just the money, you see. I wanted to prove to myself that I was capable of acting to change my destiny."

Faustopheles stopped looking so contemptuous. "That's been done," he said in a hard voice.

"I didn't do it," Raskolnikov declared. "Instead

of altering my life, by that act I stopped it in its
tracks, so that ever since it has done nothing but
mark time there."

The last words were blurred by the groan he
gave as he reseated himself on his block of stone.
There was a sucking sound as the skull bones
closed and reknit. Raskolnikov bowed his head
and resumed talking to himself.

"What do you think of a fellow," Faustopheles
laughed, as we stepped out on the path and
walked farther down into the Pit, "who'll chop an
old hag up and then develop an *ex post facto*
scruple that will prevent him from using the
money he stole from her? You'd think that an
ordinary sense of obligation to the corpse would
make him want to spend the cash, wouldn't you?
How do you like that for comedy?"

It was not comic to me. "Many people do things
they think better of later," I offered.

"Surely," he sneered. "And next you'll add that
his remorse quickened the meat around the old
mare's bones and repeopled her veins with cor-
puscles.".

"It won't resuscitate her," I admitted, "but he's
paying, damn it! Can't you see that?"

"I can see that he's an egomaniac who's convinced that the rest of the world has nothing better
to do than to worry about whether he's committed
a crime or not." Faustopheles turned to look at
me, and I hunched against the wall while I waited
for him to go on. "Didn't you hear him? He
couldn't make up his mind whether he was confessing his depravity or boasting about it."

Unexpectedly, I found myself seeing Raskolnikov's point of view. "He wasn't boasting. It's just that he's still trying to explain to himself why he let go of his controls."

"And does it help to beat your chest and moan and tell everybody what a sinner you are?"

"Nothing helps," I said, as a few deeds I had rather forget stirred uneasily in my recollection.

"There's only one act beyond helping." My guide was proceeding, but his eyes glittered at me over his shoulder. "The only trouble with that grove of weeping willows is that they take themselves seriously. All they need is to forget about whatever they did, and they're cured. It's as simple as that."

"But it can't be done!" For the first time in days I felt a faint surge of pride in my being. "What a man does is too important for that. His actions aren't excrement to be cast off and left behind. They stay with him and go into his making. They've got to."

"Why?"

"Well—I don't know." As quickly as it had come, the flash of spirit left me. Considering my own sorry estate and my attitude toward a world in which I moved without joy or aspiration, I couldn't see that it made any difference, either. "It's just that way," I said, "but I suppose it doesn't matter especially."

"Exactly what I've been telling you," he said. "Here; step aside and see what we have on this level."

XXVII

❧ Going Down ❧

THERE WAS MUCH going on in the cavern we now entered, though it took me a while to unravel the action. When I had done so, I found that I was looking at a series of desperate flights. Here and there throughout the premises a lone man was being pursued, sometimes by only one person but more often by a group. The hunters were a startling lot, in as much as most of them were bleeding from knife and bullet wounds in mortal places. A few carried their heads in their hands or ran with them twisted away from the hangman's knot under their left ears.

"You are watching the dance of those who betray others for spite and for gain," Faustopheles said in answer to my questioning look. "Curiously, the two are seldom unpaired. All right, we'll join this chase. Tally-ho!"

Starting because I felt compelled to go where he wanted me to, I soon felt the heat of the hunt. The more our quarry turned and twisted, the more I enjoyed it. It was all the better because he was a powerful, strong-faced man who didn't look accustomed to squirming flight. He doubled and dodged, growing more frantic by the second, while we of the pursuit shouted in the lust of our implacability.

This is not to say that Faustopheles and I were leaders in the hunt. Rather we swelled the chorus of the ruck. The ones who followed close and turned the fugitive every time it looked as if he might have a chance to break away were long, bloody men in the shreds of armor.

In the end they worked him into a corner and there blocked him off. When we two caught up and pushed our way to the front rank, he looked as if he needed the wall in back of him in order to stand.

"Why do you hound me?" he was asking.

At this the biggest man among the ten or a dozen of his chief pursuers laughed, spurting blood from his broken temples. "I shall not bring the charge, nor will my brother Oliver, lest it be put down to malice." Lifting a horn made of an elephant tusk, he pointed the nozzle at a burly, middle-aged man. "You do it, bishop. Nobody will doubt that you speak for anything but Charlemagne and the good of the realm."

"And God," the bishop reminded him. He stepped forward, thrusting assorted bowels back into a big tear in his abdomen. "Ganelon, the charge is treason."

To my surprise the accusation had the effect of stiffening the fugitive's backbone. Ceasing to tremble, he straightened angrily.

"It's a lie! I'm as true a Frank as any of you."

A head held under the arm of its owner spat

scornful contradiction, but quieted when the bishop gestured. "No one denies," the latter said, "that you long held the right to such a boast, but we standing here know you changed."

After hesitating, Ganelon took a new tack. "To be hostile toward you was not to be hostile, let alone traitor, to the realm. You are my enemies."

There was a rumble of comment from his accusers. The bishop silenced this also.

"Agreed, but was it necessary to strike at us at a time when we were in the field against the realm's foes?"

"They wouldn't be our foes if it wasn't for you—if you didn't keep sitrring them up. It is you who are the realm's enemies, and not I. It was to make peace and save our country from the destruction of war that I wrought as I did, risking what you might do in reprisal." Ganelon folded his arms. "You have the power to kill me, and I don't fear death; but you can't prove treason where it didn't exist."

The blood spurted horribly from the temples of the man who carried the ivory horn, as he laughed a second time. "Where were you taking this risk of what we might do to you, while we were going down before the hosts you sicked on us?"

"In my place at the emperor's side."

"Having told him of your dealings?" the bishop suggested.

"Naturally not. I didn't want his foolish preference for you to interfere with his own or the realm's good."

"Of course, you intended to tell him later—and would have if he hadn't made it awkward for you by hurrying to the pass and avenging us?"

"There was no sense in telling him after my

good work had been undone." Ganelon spoke more slowly than he had before, as if giving himself time to think. "But I wouldn't have anyhow. It was no part of my plan to take credit for serving the realm."

This was too much for a man holding his unattached right hand in his left. "Not credit, but profit!" he yelled, holding out the severed member so that its stiffened fingers pointed at the accused. "Who, next to the emperor, would be the realm's most powerful figure after we were done away with?"

The other licked his lips. "An incidental and unavoidable advantage."

"Like the reward you accepted from the enemy!" The bishop had been speaking calmly throughout, but at this point he shouted. "Like the treasure you took; the money you were paid to hand over our lives while we were in the very act of defending the realm and the emperor. By God the Savior, and by God the Damner, Ganelon, you did not just betray us, you sold us!"

At that something of the nerve and aplomb which had carried him through so far left Ganelon. "No!" he said. "I—I admitted everything else, so you know I'm not lying. They offered me money; I don't say they didn't. But I wouldn't touch it."

"You'll have another chance!" the bishop cried. He turned to his friends. "Let him see it!"

With the words he reached around and unhooked a sizeable bag from the back of his belt, and they all followed suit. With one gesture they raised the bags and with another cast them on the floor at Ganelon's feet. There they all exploded like paper torpedoes, spilling out a mixture of gold pieces, blood, hunks of flesh, entrails, eyes, and some stuff I took to be brains.

The look on Ganelon's face made it unnecessary for him to confess that he recognized it, but he did so. "It's the price!" he moaned, as his knees let him down amidst the money for which he had sold them and himself. "I didn't think you really knew about the price."

For the third time the fellow holding the elephant tusk laughed. "Since he's shown himself so greedy for it, I vote not to stand in his way. What do you say, gentlemen, my comrades?"

"Let him eat it!" they growled. Or rather we did, for I heard the words issuing from my own throat.

It was not a funny sight to see that man writhing and protesting in their gripe; but Faustopheles whooped at something—the last thing the fellow mumbled before they stopped his breath with the first bag of blood-slick coins. "Did you hear what that rascal was saying just as they pried his mouth open?" he chuckled, as we started spriling downward again.

The glow of the pursuit and the interest aroused by the court martial had left me by the time they let Ganelon fall stiff and stuffed as a sausage. "No," I shrugged, "I didn't get it."

"Well, you wouldn't think a man would have an eye for whimsy at at time like that." Faustopheles looked back to show me the sardonic mirth in his own eyes. "But he said: 'Don't tell anybody.'"

"You're going to step off into smoke if you don't watch where you're going," I growled.

"I did that long ago," he declared; but all the

same he faced forward. "You don't grasp the drollness involved in those words, do you? Here's a man who deliberately satisfied his malice and as deliberately profits by it. Such a one you would naturally judge to be above the superstitions of morality. Instead we find that his dying concern is for his good name. Still, that's typical of the place."

"What place?"

"The place he was in, dolt. The traitors' ward. Up above, where we found young Raskolnikov, the chief thing that bothers them is that they themselves are aware of misdoing. Your traitors, however, taking them by and large, aren't gravely disturbed until their guilt becomes public knowledge. Curious, isn't it?"

"I guess they're both eaten by the same bug, though," I said after thinking his words over. "Even people who are professionally vicious like to be thought of as good fellows when they're off-duty."

"I know they do; and that's what's so funny. What difference should it make to one victim of an idiot destiny what another victim thinks of him?"

"Oh, I suppose it's because every man knows he's a remarkable piece of works."

"Including you?"

The way he said it struck a spark out of me that proved my point. However meanly I might think of myself, I didn't take to disparagement by others. Giving it thought, for once, I was acutely aware of the marvelous set of qualities which had gone into my making. To be sure, the parts didn't always move to the best advantage, but the capabilities were of a nature to be respected.

"There are people worse off than I am," I snapped.

"If so, they're all here, too. Let's pause to study some of your gifted peers."

What I saw when I followed him into this next ward was, at first glance, not at all disquieting. There were people seated, standing, or walking about at will, although it was noticeable that these last had an odd fashion of halting occasionally in mid-stride. Then I looked closer.

Each of these persons had a figure sketched in haze standing or walking behind him. If the man or woman it was following ran, it would run. If he or she sat down, it stood by. Its presence did not prevent such solitary recreations as singing, humming, or whittling. It never assaulted or seized the one to whom it was attached. It never so much as spoke. What it did do was to reach out at brief but irregular intervals and tap its victim on the shoulder, as much as to say: "Look, I'm still here."

Those touched never actually looked; it was clear they didn't have to. But the whittling, humming, and singing stopped. The walking and running stopped. The seated and the standing stiffened. Next they would go into a spasm. The form these seizures took varied, but they were uniform as to meaning, and as simple to interpret as the touch of the shades which haunted them: "There is, there can be, there never will be anything in the world for me but this."

"Who are these poor devils?" I asked, when I had taken it all in.

"They are those for whom somebody else's death has become more important than their own life," Faustopheles answered. "Notice the treatment? They play them like trout, giving them line, then making them feel the hook just when the think they may be going somewhere."

I looked at him sourly. "Sure," I said, "it's fine. Well, we've seen it, so let's get going."

"Not before you make closer acquaintance with a brace of the inmates." He took my arm, counterfeiting the smile of a man anxious to introduce one friend to certain others. "You have all the time in the world, and it will be well worth it to see the couple I have in mind."

It was indeed a couple to which he led me, yet they were anything but a pair. Nor did they maintain the same pose. The one standing was a man of mature years. Time had wrought well with his face. It was the countenance of a man who had worked hard and believed in what he was doing. At the moment he seemed engaged in working out a problem of which he had already glimpsed the solution.

The one seated near him was an athletic-looking young man with likeable, intelligent features. In contrast to the loose, white robe worn by the older fellow, he was dressed in snug-fitting, colorful clothes. He was reading as we approached, and his expression showed he found the occupation rewarding.

One preoccupied and the other absorbed in his book, they paid no attention to us. With a gesture Faustopheles halted me short of them, albeit not so far away that I failed to discern a shadowy figure behind each.

Unable to imagine two more respectable looking people, I glanced at my guide questioningly. "What could these two have done?"

"What," Faustopheles asked in place of replying to me, "would you say was the nature of sin?"

"Nuts, I don't know!" Nevertheless, as he continued to stare at me, I tried to come up with an answer. Originally I was in hopes of avoiding sounding like a line from a child's catechism, but I gave up on that. "I suppose it's—oh hell, it's just deliberately doing what you know is wrong."

"Near enough. Now if," he went on, his eyes gleaming recklessly, "I ever intended to sin, that's what I would do. But I tell you, Silverlock, these men have done no such thing. Neither one of them has ever been guilty of wanton malfeasance, yet they grieve for their conduct more than most of the men who have. If you don't believe me, watch."

He stepped forward, clearing his throat to gain the older man's attention. "What's troubling the pride of Cadmus' line today?" he asked.

The other came out of his trance, smiling to show he liked the flattery but didn't take it too seriously. "Why it has just ceased to trouble me, or I think it has. One thing, you will comprehend, that has been giving me concern is the matter of succession. My two lads both aspire to reign after me, but the important thing is not what they want. It is what is best for Thebes. You see," he continued, his face kindling at his own thought process, "if I will it to either outright, the odds are that the other will challenge the bequest; but it has but now occurred to me that I can avoid exposing the city to civil war by having my sons agree to reign alternately. Don't you—"

He didn't finish, because at that instant Faustopheles snapped his fingers. As if obedient to a signal, the ghost or whatever it was that stood behind the prisoner reached out and tapped his shoulder.

Immediately his expression changed from one of keen self-possession to one of frenzy. "Ask him why he is so haunted," Faustopheles ordered; and although I hated to so so, under the compulsion of his will I obeyed.

"Er—why is it that the—thing behind you bothers you so?" I enquired after several false starts.

Until then he had suffered in silence, but that touched him off. "Because," he cried, "he is the if-it-hadn't-been-so of my doom—the main arch supporting the bridge of sighs on which I limp toward my destiny. Yet it *was* so; and I, who thought myself the city's first citizen by a better right than that of being its king, did things which make me its vilest inhabitant. I who set myself up as a model and as an arbiter of ethics, found that the man I once killed was my father and that the woman who bore me children was my mother!"

He had been wringing his hands as he talked, but at this climactic declaration he found another use for them. Reaching up with horrid swiftness, he gouged out both of his eyes and threw them on the ground.

Moved by the nature of his confession, as well as by his shocking act of contrition, I thought I was going to be sick. Yet when I turned from watching the poor fellow reel away, the shadowy figure still stalking him, there was no sympathy in Faustopheles' face.

His mean grin not only helped to pull me together but drove me to argue with him. "That man," I pointed out, "has really got reasons for feeling that he's through."

"Why?" he asked with a coolness to match my heat. "Item, he killed a man to escape getting killed, which is strictly sensible, and whether it was his father or not is an irrelevant issue. Item, he cohabited with his mother, which must have been pleasant, for he worked at it for a good few years. It isn't saying much, I grant you, but his children, averaging them up, are no worse than other people's. Moreover, he didn't set out to make them the get of incest, so he ought to just shrug it off."

Hating and helpless, I now knew what he was doing to me. If I was bereft of everything else, I had not quite lost the quality which divides manhood from brutishness. This is the belief in the value of some sort of standards of conduct, both psychological and physical, as a wall against resignation to bestiality. Losing it, I might as well return to the hog wallow on Aeaea.

But although I recognized that I ought to make one, I wasn't prepared for much of a rebuttal. "You know as well as I do," I muttered, "that a man would hate to think of doing things like that."

"Why?" he asked again. "There's more reason for killing your father than any other man, because he begot you. As for copulating with your widowed mother, if you're lucky enough to have a handsome one; well, if you have something good, why let it go out of the family? Where's the cause for any tragic self-torture?"

Observing the confusion on my face, he chuckled. "There's the Q.E.D. to the proposition, if you have the brains to see it. That fellow Oedipus is Exhibit A in the support of my charge that man's chief ailment, next to being alive, is delusions of moral grandeur."

"But," I floundered, "I—"

He put up a hand to silence me. "Before we go any further with this discussion to which you've contributed so much pithy wisdom, let's turn to Exhibit B here." He drew me to where the young man, so engrossed his his book, apparently, that he hadn't heard what was going on, was seated at his ease. "How are you today, my prince of scholars?"

"Merely a princely scholar," the other said, looking up with a twinkle in his eyes. "Unfortunately that's not the same thing."

"Still it pays better," Faustopheles reminded him. "What are you reading?"

"Oh, a collection of tales, old but very interesting, with quaint, long-winded titles that have half the nature of synopses. I was about to turn to another one, so if you don't stop me, I will read it aloud to give you the idea." Eyes alight with amused anticipation, he flipped over a page. "Here," he began, "commences the tale of Sigmund and how he abode many years like a wolf in the wood and in the end begot a child on Signy, his sister, all to the purpose of slaying her husband, Siggeir, who had been the bane of Volsung, their father."

This time it wasn't necessary for Faustopheles to do anything. Precisely on the last word, the phantom behind the reader touched his shoulder. Promptly the man's alert and likely face became haggard with a mad desperation.

"Ask him if anything ails him," Faustopheles urged me.

Great as was his hold over me, I summoned strength to resist. "I won't! He might do something like the other one."

"If so, he'll only do it to himself and not to you. Don't be so squeamish." When I only shook my head dumbly, he snorted. "You'll have to get more seasoning before you're ripe for where you're going. I'll stir him up myself."

"We would like for you to go on," he said, picking up the volume which the young fellow had thrown to the floor. "I believe you left off at the word 'father.'"

"It's a word I shouldn't be able to—don't deserve to pronounce," the other said thickly. "There," he went on, pointing a shaky finger at the book, "is the story of a man who acted as a man should, letting nothing and no consideration stand in the way of the vengeance he owed his murdered parent. Sir," he said suddenly to me, "I do not question your legitimacy, but did you know your father?"

That was something it hadn't occurred to me to think about, but I tried to remember. "Pretty well, I guess. We got along all right when we didn't see each other too often."

"Ah? I knew mine well, and found him as much above all other men in qualities as in his royal rank. That man was murdered, sir—and do you know where your mother is?"

His disconnected questions made me think he was raving, but answering seemed simpler than trying to disregard him. "Yes," I replied, my mind picturing a certain rainy day in a cemetery.

"I know where mine is, too," he gritted.

"That's fine," I said. He looked ready to pursue the subject, so I thought I'd change it. "Have you any idea who committed the crime—killing your father, that is?"

"A most exact and certain one," he nodded.

"Has anything been done about it?"

"There has not been and will not be," he told me in a suddenly quiet voice. "He will not be brought to book, because I have knowledge only, not proof. And as for taking justice into my own hands—" he broke off to give a sickly smile. "Look at me, sir; I am an assembly of so many parts and cannot form a quorum to pass a resolution. I have an intellect to plan an action with any man in the land; I am as big as you, and stronger, I should say; I am accounted a soldier who does not shrink from the battlefield. And with all this, I cannot bring myself to go to the man who murdered my father and kill him where he lies sleeping beside my mother. Oh, Christ and my God!"

With that ejaculation, at once hopeless prayer and bitter oath, he became as impotent to speak as he claimed he was to act. For a second he was still and staring, then he whirled to stagger away as blindly as if he, too, had lost his sight.

It seemed to me that he was carrying away within him the whole burden of man's most grievous problem—that of holding brutality in check and taking the profit out of it without resorting to it; but Faustopheles nudged me in the ribs. "You can't please them. The first one was all upset because he had killed a father he didn't recognize and slept with a mother of whose existence he was unaware. All right; for the purposes of discussion we'll grant him reason. But where does that leave young Hamlet there? He didn't do either of those things, but he is wretched because somebody else did. Can you add that all up and get anything but foolishness?"

"Yes," I asserted, more because I loathed his

grinning face than because I had a viewpoint. "Sure, I can!"

"Proceed then, by all means."

I thought for a minute, determined to try to make a statement that would stand up before his ridicule. "In both cases," I at length blurted, "the real consideration is that a scheme of life was kicked out of shape and couldn't be fixed up. Whether you do it yourself or somebody else does it for you is a side issue. The result's the same, if you can't see your way to go ahead without making things worse."

"I see." His lips pursed mockingly. "You know, Silverlock, you have a better sense of humor than I at first thought, and that phrase, 'a scheme of life,' is the funniest thing you've said so far." He spat, and we both watched the little pool of saliva spread until it had found its limits on the unpolished granite floor. He spat again, and the result was different, though equally formless. "There's how much scheme a life is allotted. No more than for any other splatter in the dust and dirt and dung of the cosmos."

"Not for a man," I insisted.

"For a man," he nodded, "although, to be sure, in your case, it's probably different. Tell me about your scheme of life, won't you?"

I glared at him. "I haven't got one," I admitted, when I couldn't think any out, "but that doesn't mean that I couldn't have had. Men aren't just things that circumstance works on like a lathe. They do things to circumstance, right back at it; and create as much for themselves as was ever given to them. If a world was pulled together out of the Void, why they have built another right on top of it; and like all building it has foundations and a top, dimensions and measurements."

"My, how wonderful!" He clicked his tongue as though in admiration. "And has anybody ever caught sight of all this?"

His question snuffed out that flare of rebellion likewise. For when I paused to think of an answer, I had time to wonder if I believed what I was saying.

"It doesn't seem probable." My shoulders slumped in recognition of a new defeat. "I guess I was only talking to keep from having to listen to you all the time."

He snickered. "As long as you're tired of dangling from the nub of metaphysical rope, drop down, and we'll go on with our investigation of reality."

XXVIII

⚭ At the Bottom ⚭

STRANGELY, Faustopheles made no move to enter the dungeon at the next level. It was all one to me, but as we were about to proceed downward, we were stopped. The one who stepped from the cavern to intercept us was a soot-colored demon with yellow eyes.

"Bring the man right in, Faustopheles," he intoned in a barker's voice. "It is never too late or too early. The show goes on without a break every minute of e-ternity, and there's no such thing as a dull minute. Your time cheerfully re-funded, if there is not a laugh every split sec-ond."

"Keep your time for those who are short of it," my companion told him.

The other refused to get out of his way. "Now, now, Virgilio; I know you haven't been partial to our show recently, for some reason or other, but I can tell by the look in your charge's eye that he feels otherwise." In spite of the fact that he stood his ground, he spoke, I noticed, with a certain deference. He was more companionable when he turned to me. "I feel per-fectly sure, not to say positive," he chanted, tapping his brow, "that a man who gives so much outward ev-idence of inward horse sense is not going to be willing to pass up the best enter-tainment to be found from top to bot-tom of the A-byss."

"If it was important for him to go, I'd show him through myself," Faustopheles said. "Come on, Silverlock."

"He has the right to answer for himself," the other retorted. "How about it, friend?"

As I have said, it had been a matter of indiffer-ence to me. It ceased to be when I knew Faus-topheles opposed it.

"I'd like to look around," I answered.

"You'll have to do it some other day," my guide snapped.

I really hadn't expected to get my way, but the custodian of the ward spoke up again. "Visitors," he said, in the tones of an MP passing on a head-quarters directive to a colonel, "are not to be stopped or impeded from reaping the benefits of any of the amazing and profoundly educational demonstrations put on in these premises."

It was apparent that Faustopheles wasn't going to challenge that by-law. With a small glow of satisfaction I followed him as he stamped into the cavern. The custodian, all business, walked with me.

"In this level of the A-byss," he lectured, "we have those who betray themselves. We are lucky enough to have specimens of all the known var-ieties, but I rec-ommend to you as the most com-ic of all the ones who school themselves to believe in one code of conduct, and then de-vote their time to the course of action best calculated to give them a low o-pinion of themselves. Funny? Pal, I tell you—"

"We have to be here," Faustopheles interrupted him, "but we don't have to stay long, and we don't have to listen to you. Now where's that Anna what's-her-name I dropped by here not too long ago? We'll see her and get out."

"I'm not sure which one you have in mind," the custodian said, dropping the professional tinniness out of his voice. "What's her trouble, private and imaginary or social and illusory?"

"Oh, social complicated with the usual business of arguing with reality," Faustopheles said. "She claims to be a princess or a countess or some such stuff."

"I remember her now. She's right over there, but you'll have to wait around if you want to see the whole show. They're just finishing up with her."

"The tag end will be enough for us," my companion stated. Beckoning to me, he strode across the floor so fast that I had to stretch to keep up with him.

I had already observed that the torture here was in the hands of individuals who all more or less resembled the custodian in appearance, mannerisms, and voice. Each with a pointer in his hand, there was one standing beside each of the victims. Some stood at ease on their platforms, as if waiting for the proper moment to commence activities; but most were in the dramatic throes of barking, using their pointers to indicate their cringing victims. They were all in a measure successful, for they commanded the attention of small but intent audiences which followed their words with morbid relish.

The inmate called Anna was very pretty, with the bearing of a fashionable young matron. She had no pride in her status then, however. She was taking the publication of her private affairs hard, and shame pressed down on her so heavily that she could barely hold herself up. Her eyes showed that she was nearing the breaking point, either of the spirit or the mind or both.

The barker, on his part, was joyously reaching the climax of his spiel. "To sum up," he cried, touching his victim with the pointer, "this woman de-liberately yield-ed to the lusts of the flesh—temptations to which you and I are also subject, through, of course, we have the mor-al strength to resist them—and now she is astonished to find that her collaborator in vi-olating the sanc-tity of her marital tie is not himself a re-liable do-mestic char-acter."

He broke off to smile while a buzz of excited comment rose and died among his audience. "He has be-come bored with her, ladies and gentle-men, and now she is in a di-lemma. She can-not go back to her wronged spouse, nor can be assoc-iate on ac-ceptable terms with you, her former friends, who pre-fer the society of people with a stab-ler standard of eth-ics. What will she do?"

For a moment there was silence while Anna, considered the same problem, stood looking at something. What she saw I don't know, but she suddenly threw herself forward with a cry foretel-ling self-destruction. I thought she hoped to win a mortal hurt by hurling herself from the platform, but in mid-air something struck her. Bouncing terribly, like a man I had once seen hit by a speed-ing truck, she dropped lifeless.

As I turned numbly away, the barker was raising his voice above the tabloid-fan gasps of the spectators. "Stick around, folks, and watch Anna pay for her wan-ton indiscretion again. The next show will be pre-sented in ten minutes."

During the course of a business I had found so disturbing Faustopheles had got over his bad humor. "Just to be sure you don't miss it," he chuckled, as he fell in step with me, "let me point out the most amusing aspect of that farce."

He had overwhelmed me so often that it seemed useless to object to anything he told me, but I made a feeble effort. "There's nothing funny about reaching a point where life has to stop because it can't move a degree in any direction." I wouldn't look at the grin I knew to be on his face. In fact, I didn't even look where I was going; and he was so intent on arguing his thesis that for once he followed my lead.

"I was afraid you wouldn't get it. See here. To invent a spiritual passion to put a white collar around a physical urge is a commonplace folly, but Anna did better. She entered an alliance whose best feature is that it supports no burden and then decided to put all the weight of her welfare on it. Can you top that for absurdity?"

"There are two sides to anything anybody does," I muttered. I had to hesitate there, then a faint recollection of my mathematics gave me a boost. "On one there's the fact of the action. You can't change that; it's fixed. But on the other side is what it means, and that's a variable." Conscious that I was hampered by a lack of knowledge of the facts in this case, I was debating whether it was worthwhile to ask him, when I saw something that made me lose such interest in the discussion as I had.

"But it can't be!" I exclaimed, commencing to run.

"Stop!" Faustopheles cried. Ordinarily he could have caught me; but something had distracted him, too, and he didn't seem able to take his usual decisive line. "Don't go there, Silverlock! We've got to leave now!" he called after me. "Oh, all the devils, and I among them!"

By then I had arrived at my point of attraction and was pausing uncertainly. What had drawn me was the sight of a girl, another one of the inmates, standing with her barker before a queer assemblage of people. I noted no more about them because my attention was fixed with a disbelieving dismay on the young woman.

The baby she was holding did not hide the letter 'A' sewed on the front of her dress. In other ways, too, she was differently clad from when I had last seen her; but that didn't make the identification any less positive. It was Rosalette! Convinced, I began to push through the audience of queer-hatted men and over-dressed women. Meanwhile the barker was going on with his harangue.

"Now the re-markable thing about the scandalous conduct of this little lady is that she was not driv-en to it by any of the harsh nec-essities, a consid-eration for which makes us who have tender hearts con-done with if not par-don a har-lot's course of pro-cedure." He paused to smirk while his listeners exchanged knowing glances. "You will all excuse me, I am sure, if I do not choose to state what that course of pro-cedure is before a mixed au-dience."

By that time I had elbowed my way to the front rank of onlookers. There Faustopheles caught up with me. He was glowering evilly, but I recalled my rights as explained by the custodian.

"I want to see this girl," I said, shaking off his hand. While speaking, I looked again to be sure, at close range, that I actually did know her. Feature by feature it was the face I remembered, though the stony control that held them all together was something new.

"What do you think you're going to do?" Faustopheles demanded; but I moved too quickly to be stopped.

I didn't know what I expected to accomplish myself, as I vaulted up on the platform. I was simply obeying an impulse to stand between defilement and something I honored. Whatever I believed or did not believe about myself or other people, it had not yet crossed my mind to think ill of her. If she was in any trouble, it must be somebody else's fault; but in any case she must not stand up there any longer to be a buckshow.

She glanced at me as I rose to confront her. Yet it was a bitterly self-contained look, with no hint of recognition.

"It's Shandon, Shandon Silverlock," I told her. "What are you doing here? Where's Aucando? What's happened?"

"He asks what has happened," the barker said, pushing me aside and winking at the crowd. "I have not time at this junc-ture to teach him the en-tire al-phabet of so-phistication; but I'll go as far as 'ABC' before pro-ceeding to disclose the mor-al lep-rosy of Hester here." With three quick taps of his pointer he indicated the letter on her dress, the infant she was holding, and the girl herself. "A's for adultery, B's for bastard, and C's for chippie." Picking me up by the nape of the neck, he dropped me off the platform. "Take him away, Faustopheles, I abjure you. This show is wasted on that degree of naiveté."

Baffled by the fact that the barker had used a strange name for the girl, I let myself be led off. We had gone perhaps a dozen paces before an explanation came to me. I balked.

"That's it! She's taking a rap that belongs to somebody else. They're calling that girl Hester, when it's not her name at all."

Faustopheles was looking backward himself, so preoccupied that he once again let me call the turn. "Of course, it isn't her name," he mumbled.

In my excitement I didn't think it strange that he agreed with me. "But we can help her!" I cried. "They're bound to let her go if we just talk to them and back each other up that she's really Rosalette."

He whirled upon me so suddenly that I drew back. "You infernal nincompoop!" he hissed. "You idiot! How would that help Gretchen?"

While I stared back at him the barker, reaching the end of his spiel, asked: "And now what will Hester do?"

Remember what Anna had done when such a question was put, I was leaping toward the platform when the girl spoke. "I shall bear what I have to bear."

It wasn't simply because the words were a denial of any will toward suicide that I stopped in my tracks. The voice was not Rosalette's. The barker had known what he was talking about all along. Turning away in confusion, I observed that Faustopheles had kept pace with me in my lunge to the rescue. The voice, I saw by the fact that he, too, had halted, had convinced him of his mistake likewise.

He smoothed his expression so fast that I almost missed a glimpse of his agony. The relief I was experiencing kept me from realizing the implications on the instant. It was only on the second take that my mind discovered what I had seen. His house of scorn had a chink in it, and emotion had blown through it as readily as it had through the walls of despair in which I lived.

In my case I felt that it had blown for the last time. What had happened to me did not seem significant, now that it was over—stupid and humiliating rather. My mind had slipped its chain when I had let the recollection of dead feeling trample down the logic of actualities. Even if the girl had turned out to be Rosalette, that was no guarantee that she hadn't crawled into the wrong man's bed. I felt silly about the whole business and would have been sullen, if I had been the only victim of wrong identification. As things stood, I grinned at my guide.

"You had a bad moment there, didn't you?"

"Worse ones await me." He was perfectly composed, and I saw that it would be a waste of time to try to get a rise out of him. All the same, the minute we had shared passion and foolishness had an effect. The dominance he had won over me was watered by the knowledge that he was vulnerable.

It wasn't much of a dispensation. It amounted to no more than a vague feeling that it might help to find out what was behind the sign of weakness I had discovered. I didn't succeed. I not only failed to gain back any ground but lost more. Yet at a time when I had almost come to believe that to argue with him was to dispute against fiats, a corner of my mind was freed to hold a question.

Faustopheles on his part grew more and more confident the lower we descended. As we entered the last of a series of dungeons, he met my hostility with a smile of triumph.

"You have seen the comedies whose wellspring is violation of the illusion of man's moral worth. Now in this level, next above the Pit's fundament, you will see the comedy of martyrdom for a fancied nobility."

Looking around for the usual crowd of victims, I shrugged. "I don't see anybody," I reported.

"There's only one inmate, partly due to the scarcity of even fancied nobility and partly due to the size of the specimen in stock." He put one hand on my shoulder and pointed with the other. "The odd-looking formation sticking out from under that fold of rock is a clenched fist. Don't get too near. It sometimes twitches."

Under examination the object we were passing did resolve itself into a set of huge knuckles and hairy fingers. As we proceeded parallel to a forearm the size of a Douglas fir, it began to strain against the stone which pinned it down at the wrist. In conjunction with the groan which scarified my ears, this made me jump.

"Is there any chance of him getting loose?"

"Considering," Faustopheles said, "that he can't get a hand free to fend off the great bird now digging at his entrails like a hen scratching for worms, I doubt if he'll work up the energy just to take a slap at a midge like you."

"My God!" I breathed. The idea of being preyed on by something with the impersonal cruelty and hot voracity of a bird was peculiarly appalling. "Won't it kill him?"

"You know better by now," he responded. "Like everyone else, he'll be healed for a renewal of agony. Stop right here."

I obeyed. We had rounded the bulge of the shoulder, and I now had a clear view of the sweating, tortured face in profile. Thinking again of the bird's cold eye and darting beak, I grimaced.

"What could he have done to deserve anything like that?"

"Enough," my guide said, "for you to know him as your worst enemy."

"Mine?"

"Yours and every man's, as I will prove." He nodded for emphasis, then raised his voice. "Speak up, Prometheus, and say why you lie here, your wisdom useless and your skilled hands helpless to keep Zeus' eagle from fattening on your guts."

Slowly the face turned toward us. It took a while for my eyes to assemble an impression of the vast features; but the face reminded me of Lee on Stone Mountain.

"You know my story," the sufferer said hoarsely, when his eyes had focused on us.

"But this man with me does not," Faustopheles retorted. "He has the right to hear it from you, and don't fob him off with the one about bringing fire in a fennel stalk. Tell him your master stroke of evil."

Anger surged into the fellow's face. "That was no evil; it was the righting of evil!"

"The greater the crime, the more they like to justify it," Faustopheles sneered. "But tell it to one of your victims here, and let him be the judge."

The bird must have been digging in. I could feel the claws in my own vitals as the giant's lips pressed together, his eyes closed. After a little they opened again, alert eyes that gave no sign that the intelligence behind them had been dimmed by atrocity.

"He shall judge," Prometheus declared. Seeing my image in the huge pupils, I felt that I was being judged, too. Uneasily I concentrated on his words, as he continued. "When man became an item of creation, he was like a forge with no smith. All the mechanical properties for great doing were there—but not the spirit to aspire, the mind to conceive, and the will to direct. Men moved about the earth with the vacant eyes of sheep, driven by no compulsions other than those which urge worms through the ground or lead toads to hop from one spot to another."

He had been speaking calmly, but now a ring of pride came into his voice. "It was I who changed all that. Unwilling to see the fine craftsmanship which had gone into the making of humanity wasted, I gave men the powers to know, to do, and to care."

"You heard him, Silverlock!" Faustopheles gripped me and spun me to face him. "He's accused out of his own mouth!" Having been prepared for a totally different type of revelation, I was taken by surprise. "Is *that* what you meant?"

"Isn't it enough? Your ancestors must have been scanted when Prometheus was endowing mankind with brains, but try to follow me. What is the source of your own or any man's grief but the awareness of hopelessness, the wish to do something about it, and the knowledge there is nothing to be done?''

These were indeed my griefs. When I gazed back at him, speechless, he gave a victorious smile. "Why if a man had been left with no desires but to take in food and to get rid of his semen in season, he would have no troubles. There would be no crazed reaching for things without substance. There would be no invented morality to make a hard, barren lot harder and more barren. Better than that, no inkling of your silly fate could rouse you from the placidity of your stupor.''

Making me face Prometheus again, he pointed. "Those are the blessings you could have had if this fellow could have minded his own business. There, for all his protestations of self-righteousness, is the author not only of your sorrows but of your infinite capacity for living with them in foreknowledge and memory. Shall we walk around and cheer for the bird that implements his punishment?''

"That wasn't the bargain," the giant said. "He can observe the source of my pain if he wishes; and whether he does or does not, there will be neither easing nor aggravation of my torture. But the agreement was that he should judge me for the act you condemn. I want his verdict.''

"I know what it will be," Faustopheles said, "and so would you, if you had any gauge of values outside of experimental egotism.'' Because I was standing with my head down, pondering, he shook me. "Tell him, mannikin! Here's your one chance to throw a little of your forlorn bitterness back into the face of the alchemist who poisoned you."

In spite of him I was not to be hurried. On the one hand was all the footless wretchedness of which Faustopheles knew me to be possessed. It should have clinched the argument, but, having caught sight of something, my mind swung heavily to consider the other side. Suppose I was, indeed, born to a greater emptiness than I now felt? Suppose I was bare of sensibilities and had no longing to do more for myself than benevolent elements could provide? It was appalling to think of, and the concept of vacuity grew more appalling the longer I dwelt upon it. Raising my head, I saw myself once more, standing a little straighter, mirrored in Prometheus' eyes.

"It's better the way it is now," I said in answer to his questioning look.

"There's his answer and mine, too," the giant said. "Defeat—and I know its flavor as well as anyone—is better than sterility, Faustopheles." I was glad he had a chance to smile, for the next instant the bird must have gone to work on him once more. He groaned, and while he was still writhing Faustopheles hurried me away.

We were both silent as we left, my guide because he was disgusted with me, and I because I felt that I ought to have said more to a person punished for being my benefactor. "Is that really all he is being tortured for?" I finally asked.

"Madness should always be pegged down out of the way," he rasped.

"But they did that other thing to him! Besides, he isn't crazy."

"You think not? What would you say if I told you that he acted in the full knowledge that he would be apprehended and punished?"

"He couldn't have!" Yet as I said the words, I thought of Gawain throwing his helmet on the ground back at the green chapel. "It's possible," I corrected myself.

The tiny lift to my heart as I made that pronouncement must have been reflected on my face. In any case he sensed and resented it.

"Believe in the false face of nobility and the hypochondria of wrong doing if you will," he snarled, "but they come to the same end. The same ultimate desolation snuffs them both up without changing expression. Struggles do not help; prayers and *mea culpas* do not help; boasts and defiance do not help, any more than protestations of good intentions or claims to achievement. There is only one stone in the burial ground of Eternity, and its inscription reads: 'Nothing Matters.' "

He was trying to catch my eye, but I wouldn't give him the satisfaction of letting him see that I was down again. "That may be so," I said, as indifferently as I could manage.

"May be! I tell you that it is so, and I will show that it is so. Where we are going now there is no vent, chink, or floor draft to admit a breath of any other conviction."

The smoke thickened as we dropped lower; but it also became translucent to expose a sight of the conflagration which created it. When we reached that point I flinched.

"I'm not going any farther," I told him.

"Not afoot," Faustopheles agreed, springing to

catch me under the arms as I attempted to retreat. He laughed as I wasted my strength trying to get away from him, then he leaped out into space with me. Simultaneously there was a ripping sound, and, like a parachute bursting from its casing, giant bat wings came through slits in his jacket to spread and beat the air.

We had dropped sickeningly before they caught hold. Thinking we wouldn't make it, I shut my eyes; but when nothing happened to us, I worked up courage to look. Faustopheles was bearing me over what seemed to be a lake aflame. The smell of burning sulphur no less than the heat made me gasp so that I could not voice a protest.

Half-blinded also, I didn't see the cliff rising from the molten surface until we had all but reached it. I thought he intended to dash me against it, but at his cry doors yielded before us. These swiftly closed to seal us in a vestibule, where Faustopheles set me down.

When I had cleared my lungs of smoke and my eyes of tears, I found myself, to my surprise, in reassuring surroundings. The entire vestibule was skillfully, if ornately, decorated, including the double doors directly before me. I examined them, then stretched my neck to make sure.

"You're right," Faustopheles said. "They are of gold."

I looked at him quickly as an explanation occurred to me. "Are we through with the Pit and on the way out?"

"We are at the bottom of the Pit, and there is no way out," he answered. "Get in front of me and walk straight ahead."

XXIX

❧ A Brace of Courts ❧

I STOPPED when I was past the doors; but Faustopheles shoved me; so I walked on, half blinded. All I could see was that we were in an immense room with towering walls. They gleamed like hot wires in the brilliant light. The only refuge for my eyes was the richly carpeted floor.

"You'll get used to it in a few minutes," Faustopheles said. "Hold your present course."

I did so, taking only occasional glances at the decor. While it was too lavish for my taste, the workmanship was exquisite and the materials of breathtaking quality. Certainly nothing I saw gave me any cause for alarm. It was my nose rather which first furnished me with a warning. I walked a few more steps before I was able to recall why the smell suggested danger; and then I couldn't believe I had isolated the right memory. It has been a long time since my nostrils had been familiar with the musk peculiar to a nest, say, of rattlers. Yet the farther I advanced, the stronger grew both the odor and the conviction that it could be nothing else.

As Faustopheles had promised, my eyes were doing better. We were approaching a long conference table of polished jade. At the far end was a throne-like chair whose upholstery was studded with jewels. The framework of the lesser chairs flanking the table was of solid crystal veined with what I took to be white gold or platinum.

The reflected light thrown by these was so strong that I thought them empty. Then I stopped short, discerning the occupant of one after the other. Hovering on a sinuous stalk of body above each of them, the throne included, was the head of a huge cobra, its eyes fixed upon me.

It would have been a hard thing to look upon in any case, but against a background of such elegance it was revolting as well as frightening. With a yell I spun to flee, but Faustopheles intercepted me.

"We arrived at an awkward moment," he said in a tone that was meant to be soothing as well as amused. "Wait for it to pass."

"I don't want to!" I cried, struggling wildly. It was useless, and his own lack of panic made mine absurd. I quieted, and he released me.

"Look again," he directed.

As it was more upsetting to have the snakes behind my back than before my face, I complied. There was now a man's head to every chair, and while I stared the transformation was completed. Arms separated from serpentine trunks, which in turn took on human proportions. At the end handsome, richly clad persons were sitting at ease. Yet it was worse than before. Their distinguished bearing notwithstanding, they fixed upon me eyes that were still and exactly the eyes of poisonous snakes.

As I fidgeted, not knowing what to do or say, Faustopheles spoke up. "Great King and Emperor," he said, bowing to the mighty fellow lounging on the throne, "I have brought you a new subject, one Silverlock, to share the bounties of your reign—and those other things we must share."

"Does he belong here?" the emperor demanded in a hard, resonant voice.

"Not without some effort on my part, he does." Faustopheles bowed again. "Those in the higher levels of the Pit still owe allegiance to some creed, but I have so worked on him that he clings to nothing but a vague spirit of rebellion. Even that isn't out of place."

"No. What are his talents and capacities?"

"Being a man, not many or great," Faustopheles admitted. "But all we can capture or suborn serve our purpose." There was a general murmur of assent, and he continued. "My thought was that we should keep him here until we can determine by observation the use to which he can best be put."

I hadn't interrupted, because I hadn't been able to speak, but at that moment my voice came back to me. Not matter what happened afterward, I felt nothing could be as bad as this place.

"I'm not staying here," I announced.

Their reptilian eyes showed no emotion, though their mouths laughed. "But I'm going on to Hippocrene!" I cried, looking from them to Faustopheles. "You knew that all along."

He was regarding me with the sly malice I had

seen on his face at our original encounter, when he was disguised as a tattered cripple. Reading the expression, I knew myself trapped.

"But that was our bargain!" I protested.

"Our bargain was that I would take you as far as I could," he slipped it to me. "I have done so, for there is no farther than this. Of course, you are free to turn around and go back."

He drew a snicker with that from everybody but me. Thinking of the expanse of flames just outside the doors, I winced.

"No, it has to be forward," I said, my voice cracking a little. "It must be possible! You told me you wouldn't deviate a yard from the road to Hippocrene."

"You shouldn't believe everything you hear from strangers," he instructed me, "and not always from other people, either."

He was having fun with me, but I couldn't afford to get angry. "Look, Faustopheles," I pleaded with him, "I'm not asking you to take any more trouble yourself. Just show me the way, and I'll go alone."

"Go on to where? Do you want me to build an extension on finality for you?" He shook his head. "If you'll think back, I warned you when you entered that there is no way out."

"None," the emperor seconded him. "Even the pull of gravity can help you no farther, for you are now at the bottom, here to abide, as do all abide who join us."

Whereas I had thought myself at the end of my string before, it had not been so. The very act of moving from place to place is an anodyne, because suspended in it, in however weak solution,

is the hope of moving toward betterment. But
with that taken from me, I knew at last what
emptiness of being was like.

I was trembling all over as I gazed around me,
trying to think. In a moment I knew I would give
the scream signifying that the ligaments of control and with them all resistance to Faustopheles
had snapped; but I hadn't reached that point
yet.

They were watching as I sought distractedly for
something suggesting a means of escape. Finally,
having exhausted every other possibility, I stared
back at them. It was futile to look for sympathy
behind such faces; but I collected myself to try to
read in them what they actually knew.

They kept my mind from theirs; but even so I
suddenly knew something myself. The potency of
their assembled personalities enabled my instinct
to grasp what I had failed to sense in one of them
alone as represented by my guide. The fact that a
statement came from my mouth there was suffi-
cient grounds for discrediting it. That truth, or
what I hoped would prove a truth, stiffened me
with the will to make one more counterattack.

"I don't believe it!" I shouted. "I don't believe
there is nothing more than this!"

The grins which remained to taunt me after
their laughter did not last long. They got lost in
expressions of astonishment, for from somewhere
there came the sound of singing.

> I have known both joy and grief,
>   Neat or mixed together;
> Cold and heat I've known and found
>   Both good drinking weather;

Light and darkness I have known,
  Seldom doubting whether
Tammuz would return again
  When he'd slipped his tether.

It took a mighty voice to reach clearly through those walls. It was not just any voice, either. I strained toward it, intent to make sure.

I remember gaudy days
  When the year was springing:
Tammuz, Gilgamesh, and I
  Clinking cups and singing,
Till Innini sauntered by,
  Skimpy garment clinging
To her hips and things like that—
  Tammuz left us, winging.

So we welcomed Enkidu
  When he came to Erech;
He was rough as hickory bark,
  Nothing of a cleric;
But his taste in wine and ale,
  That was esoteric,
And he used a drinking cup
  Which would strain a derrick.

It was Golias, beyond doubting. He was on the far side of the wall behind the emperor, and the growing volume of his voice showed he was coming nearer. As far as effect was concerned, he had already made his presence felt. His tone was as carefree as the words, and the impact of his jauntiness drove a hole in doom to let me breathe again. The tension which had threatened to break me eased. Nor was I the only one affected. Recov-

ered from their astonishment, the others were
glowering. The shattering of gloom was an aggravation to them in proportion as it was balm to me.

I still couldn't locate anything that looked like a
door, but Golias was plainly moving right toward
us.

> Khumbaba then felt our strength
>   In the magic cedars,
> And we battled Anu's bull,
>   Pride of Heaven's breeders;
> Thrice we struck, and once it fell,
>   Drawing wolves for feeders,
> While we strode where drinking men
>   Called for expert leaders.
>
> Tammuz must have joined us there,
>   But he'd just got wedded,
> And Innini, blast the wench!
>   Hacked him as they bedded.
> Damn such honeymoons as that!
>   Just the sort I've dreaded;
> For a drinking man is spoiled
>   Once he is beheaded.

On the last word a panel in back of and to the
right of the emperor bounced open, and Golias
followed the foot that had kicked it into the room.
Cool beneath the baleful glares of the owners, he
finished his song while he appraised the situation.

> So we waked him with a will,
>   Ale and tear drops pooling,
> Then we drank to him for months
>   While the year was cooling;

But he came back with the grass:
    "Death was only fooling,"
Tammuz told us. "Fill my cup;
    I'm both dry and drooling."

Golias was always as polite as circumstances permitted. He ended his recital with a bow to the emperor. The latter, however, was not mollified.

"That's no song for this place," he grated.

"It fits the occasion, your majesty," Golias informed him.

"Precisely what," Faustopheles demanded, "do you mean by that?"

Golias did not answer him. Instead he glanced at me with a twist of a smile.

"Having some trouble, Shandon?"

"Hello, Golias." Remembering how cool I had been when I last saw him, I spoke diffidently. "They sort of won't let me go."

"If you hadn't made it this far, there would have been no chance of their doing so." Golias advanced from the doorway as he said that, and the way he did it showed me something. For all his surface casualness, he was tense and wary.

He was heading in my general direction when the emperor's voice stopped him. "Before you go a step farther, Orpheus, state your business."

Golias obeyed. He moistened his lips before he spoke, but when he did so his voice was steady.

"Great King and Emperor, I have come for this man, my friend."

Not until then had I been sure that he had come solely on my account. His presence had shaken my chrysalis of despair. This knowledge struck it like lightning and shivered it.

Yet the immediate effect on my mind was to stun it, so that I did not think of thanking Golias. I was still more conscious of Faustopheles than of anybody else, and my impulse was to see how he was reacting.

Recognizing the strength of this challenge to his domination, he scowled at Golias. "You may have come for him, but you won't get him," he said. "And you may think yourself lucky to get hence yourself."

I moaned as I saw that he was probably dealing in actuality. Unless Golias had brought along strong allies, the emperor's crew had the physical power to make us stay.

"He gave himself over to me," Faustopheles continued, "and signed it in his blood."

"Did you, Shandon?" From the anxious way Golias looked at me, I saw that this was an important point. I checked the facts before answering.

"Something was written in my blood, right enough. But I specified that he should lead me only along the way to Hippocrene. Then he lied and brought me here."

"No," Golias corrected me. "He lied to you if he said this was not en route. His imperial majesty's court is one of the great way-stops."

"It's no way-stop for him," Faustopheles declared. He looked at me as he spoke, and I felt my mind losing ground before the power of his eyes. "Oh, he squeaked and thrashed around like a muskrat being pulled under by a pike; but I dragged him down and down, and he knows there is nothing but hollowness, stupidity, and vileness."

It did, indeed, seem to me, as his brain bore

down on mine, that there was no sense in going farther even if it turned out to be possible. "You'd better get out if you can and think it's worthwhile, Golias," I said.

"When I'm ready. Is there anyone here," he suddenly shouted, "such a fool as to believe that because there is good, there is no evil?"

"There is evil," their triumphant voices called back.

"Then is anyone here," Golias took them up, "so reckless as to claim that because there is evil, there is no good?"

They snagged their breaths on that one. There was a silence which seemed to suck up the air. Then they all spoke, as if under an irresistible compulsion.

"There is good."

The phrase was a moan; and after it was stilled I heard a voice that could only have been that of the emperor. "I remember it," he whispered.

Yet it was not his concession which most influenced me. I had been watching Faustopheles, and his lips had formed the words: "There is good," too. At that moment I found myself with the power to look away from him.

Once again I was able to remember that Golias had come there for me, and all that fact stood for. Finding his eyes waiting, I spoke.

"I want to get out of here, and you can count on me now to work or fight for it. Is there a way?"

"None at all!" Faustopheles snarled. He sprang to confront Golias. "Do you think it really matters to us whether he knows there are better places? Does he think we came here from choice ourselves?" He paused for a grim laugh in which the others joined him. "But this is our place now. It contains us, blotting us up until we have no other identity. It is our only rightful condition, and will so assimilate him—no, both of you! That door by which you entered has shut forever behind you, Orpheus."

It sounded like our finish to me. I had a gagging vision of us two gazing into cobra eyes until our own were one with them. Golias must have had a similar notion, for his face tightened.

"Since when have you given orders here, Faustopheles? I'll prepare to remain only when I hear I must from your master." A second time he bowed to the mighty figure on the throne. "Great King and Emperor, I appeal for our rights."

Several guffawed at this. The emperor stared at him.

"You have none, unless you have more power than we can muster."

"By Delian Law we have one." Golias was deferential but firm. "As your all but omnipotence knows, we have the right—under certain circumstances—to ask for a trial before we can be detained in the Pit. In this case the circumstances warrant a trial, as I'll be glad to explain."

"And I won't be glad to hear. Delian Law, eh?" The emperor shurgged with the annoyance of greatness irritated at being reminded of a technicality which can't well be disregarded. For a while he considered, drumming his fingers on the arm of his throne. Then his face brightened with the look one who has found a way to adapt a technicality to his own service. "Your petition is granted."

"No! Let me beseech your mightiness to change

your mind," Faustopheles cried. "Orpheus has influence with the Delian Court. He'll go free."

"Quite probably." The emperor allowed himself a frosty smile. "But, knowing something of the fellow's proclivities and intractable nature, I don't want him around. I should be tempted to let him go anyhow; but it will look better if the court orders it. Meanwhile a proper decision will give us an unassailable claim to the other one. His case is something else again, and we shall insist upon—what's the word now?—justice." He raised his hand to point at his subordinate. "Handle the matter on our behalf."

When Golias turned to follow Faustopheles out, I saw that he had a small harp slung over his shoulder. Last man, I felt panicky at the idea the door might be shut before I could get clear. I crowded Golias going through the narrow opening, and he snapped a warning.

"Careful about those strings, boy! We're going to need that harp on the way back."

A path led away from the door into a blank, twilit region. Presumably this was Golias' means of approach, but it wasn't the way he returned. Faustopheles picked us both up, took to his wings, and soared.

It was not, therefore, until we were striding in his wake along a corridor leading to the courtroom that Golias had a chance to give me a whispered briefing. "There will be no jury, just three judges. Don't pay any attention to what Faustopheles said; they can't be bought or influenced by anybody. Don't say anything to them that you can't back up. They may look old enough for dotage, but they know the exact score. Let me do the talking first, but when your turn comes, speak up strongly and to the point."

"Right," I nodded nervously, wishing there was time for a more detailed discussion. Faustopheles, however, was already entering the court.

The case ahead of us gave me a minute or so to examine the place. Except for the desk at which the judges sat, the chamber was bare of furniture. It had, however, several doorways other than the one we had used. The man being sentenced when we came in, for example, was escorted down a passageway marked "Limbo" before we were beckoned forward by a faceless attendant.

The judges were as old as Golias had indicated, but as keen-eyed also. "Your honors," Faustopheles addressed them, as they silently looked us over, "I have brought two men who have appealed to the Master of the Pit for a hearing by you."

The judge in the center stirred. "If they have already been in the custody of the Master of the Pit, it doesn't sound like a proper case for this court."

"I don't think it is myself, Venerable Rhadamanthus," Faustopheles agreed. He was falling all over himself to be polite and bowed as he spoke. "However, his imperial majesty thought it best to leave the decision to the wisdoms of yourself and your equally sage colleagues."

"I see." If Rhadamanthus was moved by flattery, he didn't show it. "And how did they come into the emperor's hands?"

"I conducted this one to his capitol." Faustopheles here pointed at me. "The other undertook to attempt his rescue."

The three exchanged glances. This seemed to suffice for an agreement, for the presiding justice spoke with finality. "In the instance of the would-be rescuer we have jurisdiction. Following the instruction of precedent, we dismiss any case against him and declare him immune from either penalty or censure. The object of his zeal, having been brought to the Pit by one Faustopheles, in the natural course of his duties, must show cause why he should be allowed to appeal to this tribunal."

I looked anxiously at Golias, but he had already started to speak. "As one no longer under indictment, I ask the privilege of acting as advocate for Shandon Silverlock, the prisoner. He is rightfully here as a man anxious to continue his pilgrimage to Hippocrene in accordance with the direct instructions of the Delian."

"Ah." The judges again went into consultation simply by glancing at one another. "We have jurisdiction," the one on the right of Rhadamanthus said, "but I am moved to enquire why there is a case at all. If it is the will of the Delian that this man should proceed to Hippocrene, on what grounds does anyone take it upon himself to let, stay, or otherwise prohibit him from attaining his ordained goal?"

"Great and infallible Minos," Faustopheles answered him, "as you, who know all things, well know, the Delian never takes the success of a postulant for granted. The only thing implicit in his instructions is that the attempt must be made. Success, which is not commonly achieved, is something the individual must win for himself."

I saw by Golias' face that Faustopheles had foiled his effort to have the case against me dismissed also, even before Rhadamanthus nodded. "Yes." He nodded again, stroking his beard. "Yes. We will hear the case."

"There are many grounds on which I base my claim to the person of this Silverlock," Faustopheles began, "but in deference to the interests of this court, I will confine myself to stating why he should be prevented from faring nearer to Hippocrene. I ask for a judgment on that point solely, or rather what I request is a restraining injunction. My argument is built simply but indestructibly out of the fitness of things, itself a cardinal principle of Delian Law. A pity more people don't realize that."

After a malicious glance at Golias he went on. "A drink from Hippocrene is not something that can be purchased or handed over. It is not so much as on the gift list of luck. Please note that point. A fane protected by the rapine of chance was not meant to be found by dolts who somehow manage to lumber through, over, and around certain intervening obstacles. The Delian surely never intended that this should happen, or he would have taken steps to reverse the decision handed down in the famous cognate case relating to pilgrimages to Pieria. I offer it to the court as precedent.

"By 'drink deep or taste not,' the magistrate who handed down that important opinion plainly meant that only those capable of appreciating his worth should be permitted access to the facilities of the shrine in question. As appreciation in turn is a quality of experience, the issue must be found to devolve upon what the man has done to acquire this touchstone of values. Now I came to own the

mind of the prisoner to such an extent that I know,
among other things, his journeyings and doings
since reaching the Commonwealth. I can faith-
fully report that, in proportion to what might be
fairly expected of a postulant, the range of his
experience is pitifully inadequate. Why, he has
not striven among men on the banks of
Xanthus—enough in itself to make his pretensions contemptible. He has not been at the court of
King Noble, stood at Bazarov's grave, visited old
Goriot or Genji, or—"

"It seems to me," the third judge broke in, "that
the court would be better able to assess the worth
of the prisoner's experiences, if we knew where
he had been rather than where he had not. This, I
believe, we can learn better from him than from
anyone else."

"Assuredly, Venerable Aeacus," Faustopheles
agreed. "I am well content to have him voice his
own condemnation."

"Give a complete account but be terse," Golias
urged me. So, I began my defense. Before such
judges I avoided special pleading and any attempt
to magnify either the importance of my adven-
tures or my own part in them. Still, as I reviewed
my travels from the moment the *Naglfar* foundered, I gathered confidence. Lulled by my own
eloquence, I felt that they must surely be impressed with my accomplishment. I therefore
found the impassive silence which followed my
recital doubly disconcerting.

After a while Minos cleared his throat. "There
are, indeed, vast lacunae in the prisoner's experience, which makes me doubtful whether he is
qualified to continue. We must bear in mind the

fact, I need hardly say, that if he is permitted to reach middle earth again, he will find only one short and most pleasant leg of his pilgrimage awaiting him; so that a favorable decision is tantamount to granting him access to the fane in question. Also precedent, as Faustopheles has justly reminded us, makes a restraining injunction mandatory in unworthy or only partially worthy cases."

"May it please the court," Golias said, while my mind was floundering in vain search of something to add in my behalf, "the point brought up earlier by the most learned Aeacus could and should be extended to cover more angles of this debate. He said, in effect, that a man should be judged on his own positive accomplishments rather than on what others have done that he has not; and I hold this absolutely so. Surely the prisoner has not been to many places, and they some of the mightiest that the Commonwealth affords. You can add to the list begun by Faustopheles that he has not forced the door of Jason's house or lounged at Shandy Hall. No, and he hasn't hid out with Martin Fierro, hunted the Sampo, backed up Charudatta, and so on until I could grow hoarse from naming a tenth of them."

Golias dismissed them all with a gesture. "The fact is that, the Delian and yourselves excepted, nobody has been everywhere in the Commonwealth. Puck claims to have; but I think he's bragging, though I grant him a wider experience than the rest of us."

"Ah, yes, Puck," Rhadamanthus said. He didn't exactly smile, but his face relaxed an instant from its expression of inhuman nonpartisanship.

"H-m-m. Continue, pray."

"I will, sir. Now as complete coverage is not to be looked for, we can turn from that and consider what can reasonably be expected. This man has gone the three essential ways, those of chance, choice, and the oracle. If he did not follow certain routes, that is merely to say that he did follow others. If he has dallied in some lesser places, no road links the greatest ones only, although of these he has seen a fair share.

"I will conclude by urging one thing. It is, I submit, no part of the Delian's plan to have his lovely springs so fenced from seekers that they benefit nothing but the surrounding vegetation. A fane should be visited only by those fitted to honor it, true; yet it is also true that an unvisited fane ceases to be one."

The succeeding hush tore my nerves apart. If Golias looked confident, so, too, did Faustopheles. The judges could not be read. Minos folded his arms and gazed downward. Rhadamanthus pressed the tips of his fingers together and stared at them. Aeacus rested his chin on his right fist. Then they exchanged glances, and the aloof manner in which they did so made my stomach quiver. I felt that if they judged the case strictly on its merits, I was bound to lose.

At length Rhadamanthus let his fingers slide along each other and rested the hands thus clasped on the desk. "In the opinion of my brother Minos," he announced, "the prisoner, having failed to prove that he has earned the right to proceed, should be remanded to the custody of the Master of the Pit. I myself have some sympathy with this view."

I hardly heard Faustopheles' crow of victory. Vaguely I sensed that he reached for me; but he did not do so quickly enough to keep me erect. My knees gave way, yet the jolt with which I struck the floor had little to do with the fact that I lay still when I landed. Shock, moreover, had sealed my mind against taking anything further in.

In my state of semi-catalepsis it meant nothing to me that Rhadamanthus, after a pause, added: "Now, on the other hand, my colleague, Aeacus, inclines toward being persuaded by the argument of Orpheus, the learned counsel for the defense. I can see a degree of virtue in that argument likewise; and therefore, in the collective mind of this court, there is a reasonable doubt that we should be fulfilling our high function by interfering with the pilgrimage of the prisoner. It is our ruling, then, that he shall be released to proceed if he can, and for whatever it will bring him. The next case, please."

XXX

Good Company and Hippocrene

THE JUDGES paid no attention to Faustopheles' rage of protest, and neither did I. In point of fact I was still out of reach of any call on my emotions as Golias hurried me away.

The transition from joy to despair is often swift; but joy in its turn does not rush to fill the vacancy left by prolonged misery. Dulled by the pain of healing, I didn't try to talk on the way out from the lower world, and I may not have thought. I have only a hazy recollection of being ferried over a subterranean river by an old fellow sculling a scow. I don't recall much more of our encounter with a dog, nearly as big as Garm but with three heads, which went to sleep when Golias strummed his harp.

The turning point didn't come until we had emerged from a cave into a patch of woods. Not that I immediately realized that it actually had come. The temperature was comfortable, but it hadn't been oppressive in the region we had just left. The light was dim, but not more so than in most of the places below ground. The trees were leafless, but I had been too long in a place where nothing grew to expect anything else. It required a noise, or rather a joyous jumble of noises, to stir my balance wheel and set my gears in motion once more.

I absorbed the sounds, at once sweet and shrill, piercing and haunting, for some while before I identified them.

"It's the peepers," I whispered.

"Correct," Golias told me. "Woosh! I'm tired."

He seated himself on a small boulder, but I remained upright, sniffing and staring. Now I recognized that the air had a current of life running through it, that the gloom was due to honest twilight, and that the barren trees would soon be in leaf again. I shook my head unbelievingly.

"What happened to the winter?"

"You lost it in the Pit." He grinned and yawned. "Are you hungry?"

"Not yet," I said slowly, remembering that I hadn't eaten since my meeting with Faustopheles, "but I think I'm going to be."

"Well, stretch out and get your strength back from the earth, and in a few minutes I'll find out whether I did a good job of caching the emergency rations I left behind when I crashed the Gate to Orcus here."

He built our campfire on a ledge, not far from the cave, which overlooked a valley. While he cooked I was active in another fashion. One moment, propped on an elbow, I watched night settle in the lowlands west of us, bringing out lights from houses and towns strung along a river. At another I flopped over on my back to feel the wind run over my face and to watch stars brighten against the deepening sky. Best of all, I would roll over on my stomach and inhale a corps of lively, interlaced odors. And all the time the peepers sang of the wonderful beginning of things and of the even more marvelous possibilities stored by the future.

"I feel good," I suddenly announced.

"If you don't during Dione's Watch, you never will," Golias assured me. "Let's hope you can say the same thing after you tackle this grub."

"How did you know you'd find me with the Master of the Pit?" I asked, as I reached for my portion.

"I didn't; but I found you hadn't been sentenced. If you weren't there, you were no place I could reach you—I couldn't navigate the Tartarean Lake—so it was the only place to try. You see, when I thought it safe to come out of hiding after teaming up with Tyl, I looked up Tiresias, who told me you'd gone into the Pit but hadn't come out yet. Fortunately," here Golias bit into a corn dodger, and I could hardly hear him, "Glasgerion and Amphion aren't the only ones who can do things with a harp."

"They are not," I agreed, worrying the thick piece of bacon I held in my fist. Winning out, I swallowed a chunk. "What happens next?"

He waved his knife toward the lights in the valley. "We'll go on to Gandercleugh tomorrow and cut into the road to Riders' Shrine there. It's a good day's walk."

It was also a good day for walking under the soft, straying clouds and amidst the gay shrubbery blossoms which lined the road all the way to town. Gandercleugh was a pretty little village, but its best feature, as far as I was concerned, was the Red Lion Tavern. If my appetite had been only tentative the night before, the day of exercise had fully revived it.

It developed that one Ambrose, landlord of the hostelry, was an old friend of Golias'. "Mr. Shandon," he said, when we had been introduced, "we have excellent food here, and you'll get it in season—which is not so soon that the house can't make money out of you in other ways. Now you look like a man, and I say this in the mournful knowledge that not everyone has the soul and genius for it, capable of a craving for good liquor."

I hesitated. Wholeness was too new a thing for me to feel sure I was ready for any sort of celebrating.

"Why, I haven't been drinking lately."

"Poor fellow," he sympathized. "But you're willing to improve yourself, I'll wager."

If it was sales talk, it was better done than is usually the case, for he succeeded in looking as though he was generally interested and friendly. He pleased me, and I let him see it.

"I might try." It wasn't available everywhere in the Commonwealth, so I didn't put the question too hopefully. "Have you any whiskey?"

"Do you think I acquired bodily health, spiritual well-being, mental agility, philosophy, the knowledge and love of my fellow men, and the nine arts, of which the eighth is keeping a good house and the ninth is not going bankrupt while doing so—do you think I acquired all those faculties with the aid of nothing but hot chocolate and water?" He tapped me on the chest. "Sir," he said, dropping his voice reverently, "I don't merely have whiskey; I have Glenlivet."

The Glenlivet was worthy of reverence, being exactly what I needed. One slug of it eased the tension which was the last symptom of my recent bondage to woe. Refilling from the bottle which had been brought to our table, I leaned back with a sigh to listen to Golias and Ambrose.

The latter, it was manifest, prescribed nothing for his patrons that he didn't consider good for himself. "You're bound for Riders' Shrine, of course?" he queried when he had polished off a big hooker.

"I am," Golias nodded. "Naturally, I wouldn't miss the trip as long as I'm lucky enough to be in the vicinity. Shandon's bound for Hippocrene, though."

"Is that right?" The landlord looked at me with interest. "Well, he'll go most of the way with us anyhow. It ought to be a good journey. We've got a likely lot of pilgrims this year."

"I've been noticing." Golias sipped, peering over the top of his glass at the people stirring around the tap room. "There's old Falstaff, Dinadan, Alcestis—you two should get together and swap experiences, Shandon—Helias, Biron, and Maeve. Who else has checked in that I might know?"

"Oh, the incomparable Fiametta, of course, Tartarin, young Juan, Captain Suggs, Glycerium, Gisli, Mrs. Slipslop, and so on. I can't tick them all off at the moment, but we've got a full complement." Ambrose abruptly hauled himself to his feet. "Richard," he called out to an attendant, "bring Miss Watson over to our table, please."

We were all standing by the time the girl who had just entered the room joined us. She was lovely in a quiet fashion, but once you looked in her eyes you didn't care whether she was or not. While not eyes of great experience, they held the guarantee that they would know how to value experience when she met it.

"No, I've never previously met Miss Emma," Golias said, as he held a chair for her, "but I knew when I waked up this morning that something good was going to happen to me today."

"Besides the Glenlivet?" she wanted to know. "Not yet, thank you," she then said by way of answering the landlord's question, "I'll have the drink some time when I can't get flattery."

"There you go ruining my business," Ambrose upbraided Golias, "and I have only one night to shake these people down before they leave on their pilgrimage."

"You along with them," she reminded him. Next she looked from Golias to myself. "Are you two joining us?"

"I'll follow you anywhere," Golias swore, "but Shandon—a fickle fellow you'll do well not to trust—will desert you at the trail to Hippocrene."

I saw that he had deliberately led up to that in order to make a good impression on my behalf. He got results, for she gave me a grave consideration it warmed me to receive. I said nothing, being content to look at her. It occurred to me that we would get on well, given the chance; and the same idea must have crossed her mind, for she flushed.

"I think that's splendid," she said. "I've never met anybody who's made *that* pilgrimage."

"Yes, you have," I corrected her. "The fellow who just held your chair and lied to you about my character knows the place like a gold fish knows its bowl. If you can believe him," I added as an afterthought.

"And will you be as worthy of belief when you've been there?"

"I don't know," I said, enjoying the clean lines of her face, "but suppose on my return I told you that you were very sweet and beautiful?"

"I'd admire you for your forthright honesty. Mr. Ambrose, I'll take that drink now. A glass of sherry, if you please. I find this other stuff going to my head."

I smiled, partly at what she had said, partly at what I had said, and partly because she knew I meant it. Then, thinking of how it would have enraged Faustopheles to find me enjoying myself after such a fashion, I chuckled. It was my first attempt at open mirth since leaving the Pit, and it broke trail for laughter to follow. And when dinner was over, and Emma had left us to a fine stag evening at which we were joined by Dinadan and Gisli—two good gents—I was, if anything, in a gayer mood. Whether my meeting with her would ultimately mean much or little was of no consequence. What did count was that I was looking forward to seeing her the next day. The promise of new rewards made to me by the spring peepers during Dione's Watch had been kept.

It was well kept the following morning, too, when we set out, thirty strong in good fellowship, for Riders' Shrine. I had been leery of mounting

the nag they saddled for me, but needlessly so.
Nobody was in a hurry, so my progress was hardly
more dangerous or uncomfortable than sitting in a
traveling rocking chair.

Once assured I could be master of the situation,
I felt master of the day. Seeing that my horse was
bigger than that of the fellow called Juan, I made it
catch up and wedge beween his hay burner and
the one ridden by Emma. Golias was already on
the other side of her, and we rode thus from then
on. Emma smiled, and the sun shone from a sky as
clear as her eyes. Emma laughed, and a thousand
birds sang. Emma's hair blew in the breeze, and so
did myriads of apple, cherry, and plum blossoms.
Nor were those the only pleasures of the road.

"As marshal of this pilgrimage," Ambrose announced, when we had well settled down to our
pace, "I call it to order."

The gabble of a dozen conversations slowly
died. "What is the will of the marshal?" the handsome muscle man named Helias demanded. He
spoke with courteous interest, but as if he knew
the answer.

"It is my will that each of you in turn shall tell a
tale according to the best powers of your wit and
eloquence," the landlord responded. "Herein fail
not upon pain of my official displeasure."

"Does that mean you might withhold credit?"
Old Falstaff, the one who asked that question, was
a veteran lush or I don't know the signs. "If so I
yield."

"We all yield under them circumstances," Captain Suggs drawled. He milked his quid and spat.
"Get one of the girls to start it up."

"The fair Fiametta will begin," Ambrose declared, bowing to the woman on the horse next to his own, "if she will so favor us."

She did in a voice that had something of the exotic quality of her beauty. It was unthinkable that a woman who looked as she did should tell anything but a love story, and she ran true to form.

> In far Chang-an, his capital, Ming Huang
> Once loved and lost to death the Lady Yang—

she began; and went on to a dramatic if unusual ending. It was a good yarn, and so were those that followed, though some of them would have been barred from the chaste wave-lengths of radio. They made the morning pass quickly, and following a leisurely luncheon they resumed to demolish the hours of the afternoon.

Entertained alike by the stories and the intervening conversations with Emma and Golias, I largely forgot about my own pilgrimage until the latter signaled me to lag behind. "What's on your mind?" I asked, made impatient by the notion that somebody might usurp my place beside the girl.

"We're coming to the turn off for Hippocrene soon, Shandon."

"Oh." That was one thing I had learned not to try to buck. "How do I recognize it?"

"I'll show you. As a matter of fact, I'd planned to go with you a little of the way, but my turn's coming up."

Knowing that he had been itching to sound off ever since the story telling had begun, I grinned. "I wouldn't have you miss it and explode. Just tell me what I have to do."

"Around the next bend we'll come to an alder

thicket on the left side of the road. It hasn't been penetrated often enough for there to be a path, but bull your way through until you come to a cliff."

I frowned. "I don't have to go into another cave, do I? I've had enough of that."

"It's not a cave you'll be looking for; just a crevice that'll let you through to a little valley. Work your way up the trough of it and drink at the second spring you come to. The second," he emphasized, "and no other. And don't forget you're to take three drinks, if you can hold them."

"After the Glenlivet that shouldn't be hard. What about this gee-gee?"

"You'll have to go afoot. Don't worry about your nag when you dismount. He'll follow his stable-mates."

"So will I as soon as I've finished my chore," I promised. "If I don't catch up sooner, I'll see you at the inn tonight."

"I hope it'll break that way, Shandon."

"What do you mean you—" I was asking when the voice of Ambrose interrupted me. "Where's Golias?"

"Right here," my companion eagerly called back. "I'll give you the signal with my thumb," he murmured before he raised his voice again. "What is your will, good marshal?"

"I demand a tale of you."

"You shall have it forthwith," Golias promised.

At Angel's Camp in Calevaras County
There lived a man who sought to win a
    bounty
On every fact, or action, or event;
He'd back a hunch with his last buck or cent,

> Or let you pick your side; he didn't care
> Which way he bet, just so the bet was there.
> He'd bet you where a pup would hide a bone,
> Or if a bug was underneath a stone,
> Or just whose plate a fly would try to savor,
> Or which of fifty cows a bull would favor;
> And luck or genius so befriended him,
> This Smiley, not Leonidas, but Jim—

As he pronounced the name, Golias jerked his thumb in the direction of the clump of bushes we were passing. Reining in, I dismounted. Emma waved back at me and smiled encouragement. Dinadan winked in passing by way of wishing me well. After peering around at me in surprise, the nag, as advertised, ambled after its mates.

Determined to rejoin the procession as quickly as possible, I didn't waste much time. The alders were so thick that I decided crawling would be the most comfortable method of entry. Stooping to begin, I could hear Golias continuing.

> After the loss of such a gifted dog,
> He found much consolation in a frog
> He tutored daily, to improve its skill
> At jumping and at—

The combination of the bushes and the growing distance between us cut off the rest of it. Doggedly I proceeded on the last lap to Hippocrene.

After a few minutes of painful scrambling, I found the cliff and in due course the crevice. I first doubted if the latter was passable for one of my bulk, but once I had squeezed through for a few yards I had easier going for the half mile or so to the ravine of which Golias had spoken. Seeking the point where the two slopes which formed it met, I began climbing.

The white pine woods through which I was walking soon yielded at the core to allow me a view. The crest of the ridge topping the ravine was not far away, so presumably my goal was close. I stopped for a careful look around.

The little meadow was broken only by some wild cherry trees alight with blossoms, and a group of silver birch. From amidst the latter water shone. This proved to be a sizeable spring, but it was the only one there. Accordingly I proceeded toward the line of blue spruce hedging the uphill side of the clearing.

Beyond was a much smaller opening in the woods. In it were three redbud trees and a huge oak. A white stallion was cropping the little blossoms with which a hollow beneath the oak was floored. Scenting me, he gave a startled stamp and trotted a few yards before he commenced browsing again.

Somehow his hoof must have tapped a main in the water table, for from the spot where he had stamped a spring gushed forth. I watched it fill the hollow before I doubtfully approached. For all the novelty of its origin, here was unquestionably the second spring I had found; and Golias' instructions had been explicit.

Doubt vanished when I stood on its rim, however. Throughout the pilgrimage on which I had first been driven, and which I had latterly come to accept as inevitable, I had been unable to imagine the nature of the spring. Now I wondered why I hadn't guessed. Looking at that water—so clear that the faint flush on every petal in its chalice of arbutus blossoms was visible—was the match of smelling the April air around me. With a convulsive surrender of the spirit I threw myself down to drink.

The water bit my throat so that I could only take one gulp without pausing. I could say it reminded me of wood smoke, the taste of snow, a deep kiss, good whiskey, blood, and the smell of earth after rain; but no list of elements would suffice to give the flavor. In any case it took possession of me in a rush. It rocked me, yet I was avid for more and put my mouth to it again. Following the second round I got giddily to my feet.

Vaguely I knew that I was supposed to taste a third time. I could not wait around to do so. My mind was seething with a swarm of wonderful ideas. None of them had quite taken form; but I knew they would in a minute, and I had to be able to tell somebody about them. I had to catch up with Golias and Emma before eloquence burst out of me for the dazzlement of trees and the sparrows only. Yes, and I had something for the others, too. I had been forced to beg off when Ambrose had asked me for a story; but now it was different. I hadn't precisely grasped the substance of the one in my mind, but I had glimpsed the marvelous shadow it cast. It seemed to me that all I had to do in order to trap and hold the reality was to concentrate when the time came. And that also was too good to keep.

Unfortunately the riding pilgrims had gained a mile or more on me and would double that lead before I could get back to the road. Turning to run for it, I caught sight of the white stallion, nibbling redbud petals. He was the answer to my need, and I bounded toward him.

It was immaterial that I was without skill as a rider. That the nag was without a saddle meant no more to me, nor the fact that it would be impossible for a horse to negotiate the crevice. I was a man of inspiration in a hurry.

A factor which aided me was that the stallion, now that I was in a position to see him better, had a feathered appendage folded along his flank. The bone supporting it offered a good handhold when I scrambled astride.

The horse hadn't been able to evade me, because the redbud tree cut off his retreat. I had hardly thrown a leg over him, however, before he was in motion. He wasn't fooling around, either. He cleared the blue spruce in one leap, and he didn't come down. While I hung on by the base of his pinions, he soared and then spiraled. Apparently this was to gain his bearings, for in a minute his wings were sweeping us toward the afternoon sun.

My state of exhilaration prevented me from being alarmed at the flight. At the outset, moreover, I seemed to be doing exactly what I wished, heading right for the procession of pilgrims. It was only when the stallion failed to descend in spite of my commands, entreaties, and gymnastics that I realized I had overreached myself by mounting him.

The perception snapped me out of wildness on the instant. My cleared head knew that I should have obeyed the injunction of the Delian by taking that third drink of Hippocrene. But the same clarity made me see that I would probably not have been able to rejoin Golias, Emma, and the rest anyhow. I had drunk of Hippocrene and something different was in order. It had to be so. I had been to Hippocrene, and it was too great a thing to be merely an incident on even so pleasant a journey as that to Riders' Shrine. I had won my passport to the Commonwealth and must expect to take all the chances, for good and bad, that befall an independent operative.

For if I glimpsed what I had failed to gain by not drinking all I should have, I saw what the two draughts I actually had downed had done for me. They say the events of his life slide through a drowning man's mind. Similarly all the things I had seen and done since reaching the Commonwealth had returned to me during the first upward surge of my flight. They had returned to fix themselves in my consciousness in order and proportion, a portable spectrum of values, graded for all occasions. To one so equipped new places would never be too strange, nor would old ones lack the luster of novelty.

Peering backward and downward at the procession, I could see one of the tiny figures—possibly my old friend, still recounting the exploits of Jim Smiley, the frog trainer—throw out his arm in a storyteller's gesture. I threw out my own arm in a salute of farewell, meant partly for Emma and the rest but mostly for Golias.

After that I turned to see if I could find out where the stallion was taking me. This was more difficult to determine, because low clouds were banking to westward. In another hour we were flying over them, and so continued until the sun had dropped through them to give its final rays to the world below.

Made drowsy by the wind in my face, I had been nodding when the bottom fell out. I grabbed for my mount's mane, but that didn't help the hollow feeling in my stomach. The nag had peaked his wings like a striking hawk, and gravity had given him the green light.

Once I had accepted the fact that the horse was ready to make a landing, I felt better. I did while I still expected to see land, that is. When we were through the clouds, I found we were plummeting towards either a vast inland lake or the ocean.

The only refuge from water in sight was a large passenger ship almost directly below us. I had time to observe that its decks were deserted, as was to be expected at an hour dedicated to the bar, the dining saloon, and the coffee lounge. I also had time to wonder what my mount was going to do when it neared the high waves. My question was soon answered. He suddenly put his head down and bucked.

Off I went, hitting the water at an angle that made for a deep dive. The stallion had almost reached the clouds again as I surfaced; but I didn't bother to swear at him. My thoughts were for the ship in whose wake I was tossing. By the fading light I could just make out it was the *Western Star* out of San Francisco; and it wasn't getting any nearer. I raised my voice in a healthy bellow.

"Help! Man overboard!"

I thought my cry wasn't going to reach the two sailors lounging at the stern rail; but after several repititions one started running toward the bridge, while the other stayed to keep an eye on me. Waving in response to his shout of encouragement, I trod water, waiting to get my breath back.

A ship that size couldn't stop or turn around in less than a mile or so, and the life boats would need additional time to locate me at dusk in a rough sea. Yet I knew they would find me if I managed to keep afloat. A wave swept over me, but I shook the white belt of hair out of my eyes and started swimming strongly. Until the body melts and the brain ceases to gel, a man who has come out whole after having been put through his paces by the Delian has a heart for living.

AFTERWORD

The Songs of *Silverlock*

by

Karen Anderson

To me, the great delight of *Silverlock* is the songs. They positively demand to be sung. Some twenty years ago I set one of them to a tune borrowed from Gordy Dickson, and the next time I went to a science fiction convention, I sang it at a party. I am no singer; I can just about carry a tune if I hold on with both hands, but the song was a success. It was "Tammuz"—the song with which Golias sings his way to the Throne of Hell. Everyone at the party wanted to know where it was from, and were there more like it? Lots more! Various people, including Bruce Pelz and David

McDaniel, found the book and set more to music. The mildly raunchy "Old Man Zeus" is broken off unfinished in the text because a woman has just appeared on the scene; Ruth Berman felt this wouldn't do, and wrote an ending for it.

What kind of songs are there? Every kind: joyful, rowdy, tender, melancholy, angry: as diverse as human experience. There are drinking songs—"Tammuz" is one of them. Songs for a campfire circle—notably "Green Leaves." Not that there's a sole best use for any of them. Brodir's vikings take their oar-stroke from "East of Agamemnon," but it's fine for walking, sawing wood, or mopping the floor; and not bad for drinking, either.

You don't have to know the story to appreciate them; they're complete in themselves. At the same time, they point up the places and people and events, highlighting, contrasting, and adding depth. Floating down the Long River on Huck Finn's raft, we meet Izaak Walton; as Golias' song then relates, this same river is also the one that flows through Ferdiad's ford and under the windows of Shalott.

You won't find the tunes we've devised here. No matter. You can make (or borrow) your own, or simply chant the lines. It isn't for the tune that people still ask me to sing "Tammuz." The magic is in the words, lively, witty, and immediately understandable, however dusty with history the topic is. Clearly, Myers has taken his three drinks of the Hippocrene.

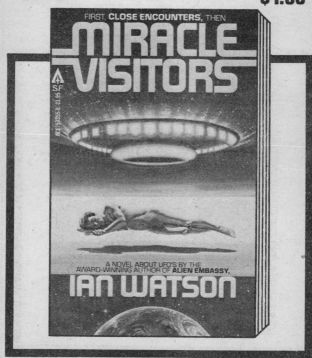

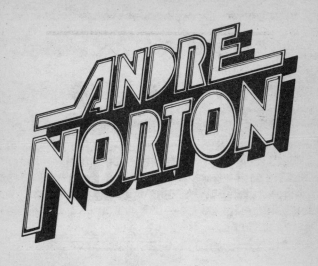

ANDRE NORTON

89705	**Witch World**	$1.95
87875	**Web of the Witch World**	$1.95
80805	**Three Against the Witch World**	$1.95
87323	**Warlock of the Witch World**	$1.95
77555	**Sorceress of the Witch World**	$1.95
94254	**Year of the Unicorn**	$1.95
82356	**Trey of Swords**	$1.95
95490	**Zarsthor's Bane** (Illustrated)	$1.95

Available wherever paperbacks are sold or use this coupon.

Ace Science Fiction, Book Mailing Service,
Box 690, Rockville Centre, N.Y. 11571

Please send me titles checked above.

I enclose $ . . . . Add 50¢ handling fee per copy.

Name . . . .

Address . . . .

City . . . . State . . . . Zip . . . .

Ursula K. Le Guin

10704	**City of Illusion**	$1.95
47805	**Left Hand of Darkness**	$1.95
66956	**Planet of Exile**	$1.95
73294	**Rocannon's World**	$1.95

Available wherever paperbacks are sold or use this coupon.

Ace Science Fiction, Book Mailing Service,
Box 690, Rockville Centre, N.Y. 11571

Please send me titles checked above.

I enclose $ . . . . Add 50¢ handling fee per copy.

Name . . . .

Address . . . .

City . . . . State . . . . Zip . . . .

POUL ANDERSON

48923	**The Long Way Home**	$1.95
51904	**The Man Who Counts**	$1.95
57451	**The Night Face**	$1.95
65954	**The Peregrine**	$1.95
69770	**Question and Answer**	$1.50
91706	**World Without Stars**	$1.50
91056	**The Worlds of Poul Anderson**	$1.95
	THE SAGA OF DOMINIC FLANDRY	
20724	**Ensign Flandry**	$1.95
24071	**Flandry of Terra**	$1.95